Advance Praise for *The Firelight Girls*

"In Kaya McLaren's *The Firelight Girls*, five women in different phases of life return to their beloved summer camp in Washington State when they learn it has fallen on hard times. All they set out to do is help the aging camp director close the camp's doors for the last time but instead they rediscover the nurturing, playful spirit of their younger selves. For these women, summer camp is a place their hearts never left.

"Touching, brilliantly insightful, and deeply compassionate, McLaren's novel tackles love, loss, grief, aging, regret, hope, and forgiveness in a narrative voice that is both gentle and honest. *The Firelight Girls* is a story of the places we love and how we never outgrow them, and a sweet reminder that sometimes we have to go back before we can move forward."

—Amy Hill Hearth, *New York Times* bestselling author of *Having Our Say: The Delany Sisters' First 100 Years* and the national bestseller *Miss Dreamsville and the Collier County Women's Literary Society*

Praise for *How I Came to Sparkle Again*

"This warmhearted and funny novel transports the reader to the small ski town of Sparkle, Colorado, where one snowy winter works its magic on several residents. Quick with the quips and repartee, the dialogue is a pleasure to read, as McLaren shows her readers how even the broken-hearted can get their sparkle back." —*Seattle Times*

"McLaren's intimate portrait of a seasonal town and its colorful characters makes for an entertaining ride."

—*Publishers Weekly*

"*How I Came to Sparkle Again* is a gem of a novel. I loved the fresh setting and quirky, endearing cast of characters. This novel is like a perfect run down a black diamond slope—fun and fast-moving and invigorating."

—Kristin Hannah, author of *Home Front* and *Fly Away*

"*How I Came to Sparkle Again* is a delightful novel of life, lessons, and growth for a plethora of characters. Lisa wants to love someone; Jill is trying to pick up the pieces of a shattered life; and Cassie and Mike are struggling with grief. Jill quickly moves off of Lisa's sofa (which is the only space available while Lisa remodels her house) and into 'the Kennel,' a ramshackle trailer that's home to the Cat Crew—Hans, Eric, and Tom. They groom the slopes every night, smoothing out the snow and getting ready for the next day of skiing. Jill moves into an empty bedroom, takes a job as a nurse in the emergency clinic, and babysits Cassie in her off hours while Mike is working. *How I Came to Sparkle Again* is a soul-satisfying treat for these long winter months!"

—*Romance Reviews Today*

"Kaya McLaren's *How I Came to Sparkle Again* is sad and funny and so much fun to read! Jill, Lisa, and Cassie are wonderful. *Sparkle* is both entertaining and wise!"

—Nancy Thayer, author of *Summer Breeze*

"*How I Came to Sparkle Again* weaves together the stories of two women and a young girl grappling with love and loss. Set in a ski town and featuring a cast of surprisingly hilarious supporting characters, this warm, satisfying novel is a treat."

—Sarah Pekkanen, author of *Skipping a Beat* and *The Best of Us*

"This novel is filled with all of my favorite things: characters who are so real you want to reach out and give them a hug; a magical setting; enough surprises to keep the pages turning; heartbreak, laughter, crying, and sighing. Not to be missed!"

—Susan Wiggs, author of *The Beekeeper's Ball*

"In a small Colorado ski town called Sparkle, second chances come with the winter's fresh snow. And it's here that McLaren weaves a wonderfully tender story of three lives in search of love and healing that will leave you crying, laughing, and wanting for more. A true page-turner, *How I Came to Sparkle Again* reads as fast as a run down the slopes!"   —Susan Gregg Gilmore, author of
Looking for Salvation at the Dairy Queen

"*How I Came to Sparkle Again* is a generous and endearing novel of loss and reconnection, of friendship and love and finding your way home to a small town called Sparkle, where the ski bums have big hearts and name their dogs after beer, and just the right number of people grow up into adults."

—Erica Bauermeister, author of *The School of
Essential Ingredients* and *Joy for Beginners*

the firelight girls

Kaya McLaren

St. Martin's Paperbacks

This is a work of fiction. All of the characters, organizations, and events portrayed in this novel are either products of the author's imagination or are used fictitiously.

THE FIRELIGHT GIRLS

Copyright © 2014 by Kaya McLaren.
Excerpt from *The Road to Enchantment* copyright © 2016 by Kaya McLaren.

For information address St. Martin's Press, 175 Fifth Avenue, New York, NY 10010.

ISBN: 978-1-250-10502-8

Our books may be purchased in bulk for promotional, educational, or business use. Please contact your local bookseller or the Macmillan Corporate and Premium Sales Department at 1-800-221-7945, ext. 5442, or by e-mail at MacmillanSpecialMarkets@macmillan.com.

Printed in the United States of America

St. Martin's Griffin edition / October 2014
St. Martin's Paperbacks edition / December 2016

St. Martin's Paperbacks are published by St. Martin's Press, 175 Fifth Avenue, New York, NY 10010.

10 9 8 7 6 5 4 3 2 1

To all my Camp Zanika friends,
but especially Sasha "Madison" Hull Ormand,
Sue "Tate" Hart, Mike "Alvin" Rolfs,
Dawn "Crackle" O'Brien-Haynes,
Lola "Sage" Rogers, Ramiro "Spectre" Espinoza,
Lisa "Gong" Stevenson, Rodie "Rodie" Burd,
John "Audubon" Flack, Joe "Shaggy" Dunkley,
Colleen "Cole" Meadows, Lisa "PouPou" Waldo,
Marc "Scout" Turnbull, Susan "Buzzy" McCutchen,
and my fearless camp director,
Rhonda "Hutt" Hutton. I WO-HE-LOve you all.

And in Memory of Mara "Gypsy" Rogers.

prologue

ETHEL 2012

October 7, 2012

Dear Camp Firelight Alumni,

    I regret to inform you that Camp Firelight will be put on the market at the end of this month. For the second time in the last four years, the well has gone dry. The Firelight Girls used reserves to frack the well then, and do not have the tens of thousands of dollars it would take to drill a new well. You are cordially invited to come out next week, say your farewells to the place we loved, and help me clean it in preparation for its sale. Please bring a few gallons of water with you, if you can.

Yours truly,
Ethel Gossman
Former Camp Director and Current Member of the Board of Directors

monday

ETHEL 2012

Ethel sat across the small table, eating cornflakes and talking to Haddie's urn, which now sat where Haddie's food used to. A few months ago, Ethel had found the urn to be a bit impersonal, and so she had drawn a face on it with a Sharpie marker and tied several lengths of black yarn to the lid as a makeshift wig. Recently, she had acquired a hand-knitted wine bottle cozy that she fashioned into a stocking cap for the urn. After all, it was beginning to get cold outside.

"Are you ready to go to camp today?" she asked the urn.

Adjusting to Haddie's absence after sixty years had been unfathomable—so unfathomable, in fact, that Ethel hadn't adjusted to it.

There had been several traumatizing moments associated with the passing of Haddie: the moment Ethel realized what was happening and that she could lose her, the moment she had to tear herself away from Haddie's pleading eyes and tight grasp to make the phone call Ethel had hoped would save Haddie's life, then returning to Haddie's lifeless body after the call, knowing she had abandoned her best friend and companion during her final moments of life. And then there had been that moment Ethel had picked up Haddie's urn from the funeral parlor.

"I can do this, I can do this. She's not in here, she's not in here, she's not in here, she's not in here . . . ," Ethel had quietly whispered to herself as she walked into the funeral parlor. She had settled the final bill and then was handed this urn. It was much heavier than she had expected, and although that caught her off guard, it seemed appropriate that the weight of her loss should be so great.

In the days prior to picking up the urn she had imagined Haddie in heaven, but after Ethel held what remained of Haddie in her hands, the physicality of ashes began to seem more and more real than spirit. It wasn't instant. As she walked out of the funeral parlor on that day, she was still repeating, "This isn't her, this isn't her, this isn't her, this isn't her."

Ethel had paused on the sidewalk for a moment and looked at the world around her, this world that had never understood the love Haddie and she had shared, this world that had at times been so unkind. Was she really supposed to plan a memorial service and invite to it people like Haddie's religious family—people who had no idea who Haddie really was? People who would have called her a sinner and banished her if they had? A feeling washed over Ethel, something she hadn't felt with that intensity since they were young—that feeling like it was Haddie and she against the world. She gripped the urn tighter and slipped into the safety of her car, where she placed the urn gently on the passenger seat.

As she drove down the road, she found her hand resting on the urn as if it were Haddie's leg, only significantly colder and harder. Maybe that had been the turning point in Ethel's attachment to the urn—that moment that had simply allowed Ethel the comfort of habit.

Now, almost a year later, Ethel chatted at the urn across the table from her while she ate her cereal and made a list of things to remember. "Oh yes, good thinking," she said to the urn when a new idea popped into her head. She continued to talk to the urn while she washed her dishes and while she packed her things, and then she tucked it into her coat and headed out the back door.

Crunchy vine maple leaves littered the brick stairs from the cabin down to the lake. As Ethel descended the steps, she dragged her old green army surplus duffel bag behind her. Everything she could possibly need fit into it. A couple of times, it picked up speed, so that she had to step aside and let it go. After it hit a tree and stopped, Ethel resumed dragging it down to the dock. On her hands and knees, she rolled the duffel bag into the canoe and set Haddie's urn comfortably on top. Then Ethel made four more trips back up for jugs of water.

Ethel loved this charming cabin Haddie and she had shared since they had retired. It was just two miles down the south shore from Camp Firelight, which had been their home for over forty years. Although significantly quieter, it had still felt like home. Almost every morning they had kayaked past camp as if they were its guardians, which was exactly how they had felt.

On this day, since she had such a large load, Ethel took the canoe instead of her kayak. She sat on the dock and gently eased herself onto the seat. It was the first time she could remember taking the canoe out all by herself. It felt so empty without Haddie in it.

As Ethel paddled down the south shore, she wondered if anyone would show up at all. She'd always thought camp was important to many people, but maybe she was wrong. After all, had it really been that important, it wouldn't be going defunct. Maybe she would be all by herself out there this week. Sometimes she liked having camp all to herself, but under these circumstances it would be like having a funeral for someone she cherished and having no one else come. She looked at the urn. Yes, it would be just like that. There was comfort in being in the presence of others who knew what was lost. She couldn't bear to go through another loss without that.

When she paddled around a little point, she saw her neighbor, Walt, floating in a cove in his rowboat. It was hard to miss his red plaid wool coat and matching cap with earflaps. He was around her age and had lost his wife about a year before she had lost Haddie, and something about just seeing him was a comfort to Ethel—perhaps that he was proof a person could somehow endure this heartbreak, or perhaps that he was proof she wasn't as alone as she felt most of the time. She saw him fishing on every calm day like this one. On most days the lake was windy chop and on those days he often didn't bother, but these calm days were not to be taken for granted. He missed not a one.

She paddled right up to him. "Good morning, Walt. Any luck?"

He held up two perch. "Dinner is served."

"Well done, sir," she replied.

"You look like you and Haddie are going somewhere." He was the only person who knew about Ethel's attachment to the urn. The first time he saw it, she knew it needed explanation and, since he had recently gone through the same thing, she knew he would understand rather than judge her.

"We're off to close up camp. They're shutting it down for good."

"No," Walt said.

"I know. I can't believe it either."

"It seems like just yesterday I was twelve and getting pelted by the mud balls you Firelight Girls threw at us whenever we'd sneak out of the Boy Scouts camp and try to raid."

Ethel smiled as she remembered making mud balls.

For a moment, both of them were silent. Then he asked, "How long will you be there?"

"A week."

"I'll bring you some fish."

"Why, I would appreciate that, Walt. I'm hoping some old friends will show up and help."

"Then I'll bring plenty of fish."

"All right, then. I'll leave you to it. Always a pleasure, Walt," and with that she pushed off from his boat and paddled away.

"Good luck, Ethel. I'm so sorry," he said as she left.

The north shore of Lake Wenatchee had changed so much in recent years because people in the software industry had bought up the charming cabins, leveled them, and built giant dwellings they rarely visited. But the south shore, where she lived and where camp was, was in the shadow of Nason Ridge and didn't get the sun that the north shore did, so it wasn't as appealing. Therefore, it had been mostly spared.

Elks Beach was closer to the Lodge than the main waterfront area, so Ethel glided in there, stepped out in her tall rubber boots, and pulled her boat in. Oh, this place. Of all the places in camp, this place was her favorite. She held Haddie's urn to her chest and breathed in deeply. "It's our place, Haddie. We're here." Ethel put the urn down and lay next to it, then reached over and placed her hand on it. It was nothing like Haddie's hand—nothing like it. But having something to touch had come to feel comforting anyway. It was better than having nothing at all.

When the moment passed and she was ready to get up, Ethel wrestled her duffel bag out of the canoe and dragged it up the pebble beach, up the bank of tangled roots, and up to the main trail that took her to the Lodge. Although the Firelight House had been their home for forty years, Ethel wanted to sleep upstairs in the Lodge, where it all began. She didn't know how to say good-bye to a place that was at the core of who she was, but she figured maybe a person just started at the beginning.

The Lodge was the oldest of all the structures at camp, made of long, straight, old-growth cedar logs. Unfortunately, paint was invented before stain and so it had been painted brown at some point. It always struck Ethel as tragic to cover up the character of the wood.

Above the huge picture window Ethel reached up and found the key she had hidden so long ago. Yes, it was still there. She unlocked the padlock on the giant door and, with a great heave, pushed it open.

The Lodge had always been the heart of camp. It had a kitchen in one end and a mammoth stone fireplace in the other. On the wall hung an old black-and-white photograph of it being constructed in 1933, one log at a time. She breathed in deeply and tried to pick apart the smell like wine connoisseurs did with a fine Pinot. Cedar. Fireplace. Dirt. Subtle hints of paste and tempura paint. Memories. Yes, mostly it just smelled like memories.

Just before the kitchen door was a staircase leading to the dorm room above the kitchen where the cook and her helpers used to stay. Gripping the handrail, Ethel slowly ascended the stairs and entered the quarters she and Haddie had shared with Cookie their first year when they were kitchen staff instead of campers. After pausing in the doorway to take it all in, Ethel put Haddie's urn on her old bunk and then unrolled her sleeping bag on the bunk that had been hers. Overwhelmed with the heaviness in her heart, she lay down. *Oh, Haddie.* What Ethel would give to see her in this room again for even just one minute. Ethel rolled over onto her side and stared at the urn on the bunk across the little room.

AMBER 2012

Amber Hill woke up in the middle of the night needing the bathroom. After she used it, she detoured through the living room looking for her mother's purse to see if she had made it home from the bar where she worked nights. There it was, sitting on the end of the counter. When Amber turned around, there was a dark-haired man standing in the hallway, his eyes hollow and vacant and devoid of conscience. She could see that right away.

He stared at her fifteen-year-old body. "You're even hotter than your mother," he said.

It was one of those moments when time slowed down and Amber suddenly had a very keen awareness of everything. She was aware, for instance, that the fireplace poker sat in the stand just two steps from her. She was aware of a chair that was within arm's reach. She was aware of a picture that hung on the wall in a glass frame. She was aware of his size in comparison to hers and aware that if she locked into battle with him—even with a fireplace poker or a shard of broken glass from the frame—she'd likely not win.

"Hey, Mom," she said, as if her mother was standing right behind him, and when he turned around Amber tipped the chair over in his path and bolted out the door and into the woods. She heard him stumble out of the trailer behind her, so she kept going.

Her impulse was to continue running, but she had to be careful, so despite her panic, she slowed her pace. After all, sticks could pierce through her foot and branches could stab her in the eye. She could not afford to fall. And she had to be wary of the noise she made.

After a little while, she stopped and listened but couldn't hear anything over her own heartbeat. She waited for the loud beating to slow and listened again. Although she heard nothing, she walked farther away still. A broken branch on a downed tree reached out and snagged her flannel pajama bottoms, tearing a breezy hole in the pant leg. Almost immediately after that, she walked too close to some devil's club and it scratched her arm.

She realized it was probably safer to stop than to continue, so she sat down at the base of a large tree and leaned back against it. Hearing a semitruck pass on Highway 2 nearby gave her confidence that she could find her way out of the woods when light returned. But would she make it through the October night? It was cold and she was in nothing but her pajamas. She put her arms inside her short-sleeved T-shirt like folded wings. She wished they were real wings, wings that could take her far, far from her life here.

There, at the base of the tree, she weighed her options. She could walk to a neighbors' house, knock on the door, and hope they didn't mistake her for a threat and shoot her in the middle of the night. In these parts, that was a big gamble. What else could she do? She could walk to the highway and hide behind a tree until she saw a state patrol car. But if she asked for help from anyone, she would end up in foster care, potentially living with a man every bit as creepy and dangerous as the one in her house right now. That was not an option. If she entered the foster-care system, she'd probably have to change schools—maybe even several times. She'd never be able to keep her grades up if she had to change schools, so seeking help was also not an option. After all, right now she had straight A's. Grades meant scholarships, and scholarships meant a ticket to a better life. It was the only ticket she had, and one she could not afford to lose.

But another night like this was not an option either. In winter, a night like this would be deadly. In addition, if she had been sick or injured and hadn't been able to move as fast she might have been raped by that man. No, this could not happen again.

From day one of Amber's life, her mother had been on her own. It had been a hard life, but it hadn't always been as bad as this. For a few years, Amber's mother had wait-ressed at the Diner and had been home at night with Amber. But nine years ago, that all changed. When the opportunity arose to work at the bar, the hourly wage was better and so were the tips, so her mother took it. She had assured Amber that life was going to get easier. Maybe it had for her mother, but it sure hadn't for Amber. Since her mother changed jobs, Amber only saw her for about ten minutes after school and spent the rest of the night alone—that is, until her mother came home around 2:30 a.m., often with a stranger. Amber forgave her and hated her at the same time. She had only been seventeen when she'd had Amber and dropped out of school. What a hard road. Amber really couldn't imagine how her mother had done it as well as she had. But sometimes . . . well, sometimes like now, Amber just hated her for being so stupid and so neglectful. Amber hated her for being unable to do better.

Eventually, the sky began to brighten, barely enough to be noticed by eyes that weren't desperately searching for a sign that night was ending. But even when the sun rose, it wouldn't mean that it would be safe to return home. Who knew how long it would take for that guy to leave?

Amber was cold to the bone and seriously wondered whether she'd outlast him or freeze to death before he left.

She slowly picked her way back through the forest. His sparkly blue Plymouth Satellite still sat in their driveway, so she wandered back deeper into the woods to wait a little longer. Surely she would hear it when he fired that beast up and took off. Tired and shivering, she curled up in a little ball at the base of another tree. *Never,* she vowed. She would *never* be at the mercy of her inept mother like this again.

The sun rose completely, and still Amber did not hear the engine of his car. A small patch of sun filtered through the forest and she moved into it to let it offer what warmth it could. If the man didn't leave soon, she wasn't going to make it to the school bus on time. But then, what was the point? She was so sleepy, she'd never be able to stay awake anyway.

She dozed a little until a loud noise woke her. Sure enough, when her mother's lover turned the ignition of his souped-up V-8 the whole neighborhood heard it. Amber shook uncontrollably and wondered if she'd ever be warm again. As she walked home through the woods, she made a mental checklist of all the things she would need: Her book bag. Every pencil in the house. Any money she could find. A sleeping bag. Enough clothes to get her through a school week without looking odd. A winter coat and boots. Tampons. Toiletries. Toilet paper. Flashlight and batteries. That might be wishing for too much. A knife. Matches. Lots of matches. Some kind of shelter. They never went camping and didn't have a tent, but there was a tarp on the woodpile. That would have to do. Food. Any food she took wouldn't last long. She needed a sustainable plan. She needed a job.

Once she was back to the clearing around her mobile home, she stopped at the woodpile and folded up the tarp carefully and put it under her bedroom window. Next to the woodpile sat her bike. That would help. People were less likely to pull over and ask her questions if she was on a bike.

Then she opened the door and walked in. Her mother was not only awake but also vacuuming the same spot over and over. Amber stood in the doorway, assessing the situation, and knew deep down that something was very wrong. Her mom was on something bad.

"Where have you been?" Amber's mother asked, agitated.

"I thought your boyfriend was going to rape me, so I left," she replied.

"What a stupid thing to think," her mother said. She was definitely not acting like herself.

"Yeah, you may be right," Amber said in order to diffuse things.

"I *am* right." Amber's mother didn't take her eyes off the spot on the floor.

"Okay," Amber said. As she walked away, it struck her that this might be the last time she saw her mother. It was unlikely, but it was possible.

Once inside the bathroom, Amber locked the door and turned on the shower. While she waited for the water to warm up, she gathered the things she would need that were in the cupboard under the sink, wrapped them in a towel, and set them by the door.

The hot water felt heavenly and brought her back to life. From now on, it would just be school showers. How would that work? Most girls were in and out, keeping their hair dry. She'd need to wash her hair and shave her legs. The other girls would notice that she was doing something abnormal. Would she be able to make it to her next class on time? How was she going to do laundry? She'd have to figure that out later.

Picking up her towel with her things wrapped in it, she went to her room, shut the door, and locked it. Her heart raced from fear she would get caught, fear of being on the receiving end of her mother's anger in the state she was in, fear the man would come back. She frantically pulled things out of her closet and made piles on her bed. In the first pile, she placed the things she'd need just to get through the next two days. Then, in the second pile, the things she'd need to get through a little longer. And finally, in the third pile, things she'd need to get through the winter. Those winter things were bulky, so instead of packing them, she put them on. As for a knife, matches, and food, she would have to figure out another place and another way to get them, and she'd have to forget about a flashlight and batteries altogether. She put as many things as she could into her little school backpack and stuffed the rest of the things she would need in two pillowcases.

It was stupid, she knew, but she looked at Woof Woof, her favorite stuffed animal from when she was little—a grungy little yellow dog with absolutely no fuzz on his back after the years of being handled by her. Logically, she knew the stuffed dog was just some fake fur, stuffing, and thread, but for some reason she just couldn't stand leaving him behind. She took two T-shirts out of one of the bags and packed Woof Woof instead.

Then she opened her window, threw everything out, and hopped out herself. Slipping her book bag over her head and across her body, she shoved the tarp in it, and then put her backpack on after that. With a pillowcase in each hand and each hand on the handlebars of her bicycle, she rode off.

Now she was just a girl on a bike, her pedals like the wings she had wished for. Wings that could take her far enough.

* * *

The pillowcases bumped awkwardly into her front bike tire every time she corrected or counter-corrected as she pedaled as fast as she could down the Lake Wenatchee Highway. She hoped she looked like a homeschooled kid returning from an overnight and not a runaway. The fact that it was mid-morning on a school day and she wasn't in school made her nervous. Traffic was light, but that didn't mean a sheriff wouldn't drive by. She pedaled even harder.

It took perhaps three miles before pure panic worked itself out and Amber realized she really had no plan beyond *escape*. Now that escaping was accomplished, she had things to figure out, like what she was going to do for shelter and where she was going to catch the school bus.

Clouds had begun to drift in—not many, but enough to get Amber thinking. All she had was a sleeping bag and a tarp. If her sleeping bag got rained on, it could take days to dry. That was a mistake she could not afford to make this time of year.

At the junction of the Lake Wenatchee Highway and the South Shore Road, she turned into the state park and campground. It would be nice to stay there. The campground had toilets with toilet paper. That was huge. But she couldn't afford the camping fee for even one night. Getting off the main drag felt safer, so she continued up the South Shore Road past many cabins—two-thirds of which appeared to be empty. Should she break into one? She weighed the pros and cons and decided that making any choice that might land her in juvie hall was not an option.

At once, she began to panic about what she was going to do when it snowed. One tarp certainly wasn't going to do it then. She supposed she could steal some tarps off other people's woodpiles pretty easily, but even then . . .

Along the road she continued, one mile, two miles, then three, wondering if staying in her home would have been the safest of all choices, wondering if she had made a mistake that would make every night just as miserable as her last one had been. Then she saw it. The answer to her prayers. A sign welcoming her to Camp Firelight. No one would be in a summer camp in October or for the rest of the off-season. How hard could one of those cabins be to break into? The likelihood of getting caught seemed almost nil. A real roof and almost no risk. *Thank you, God.*

She walked her bike around the gate and partway down the steep hill until she noticed four small cabins to her left. One of these would be best, she decided, for when the snow came it would be easier to be near the road.

The only windows she could reach on the first two cabins were the back ones, and both were locked. She walked on to the third cabin. All of its windows were locked, too, but low enough that she could get the leverage she'd need to force one open if it came to that. But she walked on to the fourth cabin, leaned her bicycle against the back, and tried the first of the two windows that she could reach. As she jiggled it, she watched through the glass as the lock rose up from the loose screw that held it in. The wood was old, and after she rammed it a few more times it finally gave.

There was no fireplace or woodstove inside. There was no place to prepare or cook food. It was nothing but four bunk beds and a larger cot, presumably for the counselor. How this was going to work this winter in deep snow Amber did not know. More blankets would be needed—that was for sure.

She picked a top bunk in a corner that seemed least likely to be seen from the windows most likely to be looked in, crawled up the ladder with her sleeping bag and alarm clock, and gratefully surrendered to the sleep she hadn't gotten the night before.

SHANNON 2012

As Shannon Myers walked up the sidewalk toward the front door of the school, dread filled the spaces where she used to have pride. Teaching was such a different beast now. The heavy bag she carried weighed her down in more ways than one.

Mr. Karwacki, her principal, caught her on the way in and pulled her aside. He was two years from retirement and as fed up as Shannon was. "She's here."

Shannon didn't have to ask. She knew who he was talking about. Ms. Trujillo from the Educational Service District, funded by the state to help teachers raise their test scores.

"I'm sorry you have to jump through this flaming hoop of bullshit. Just be like one of those bobblehead toys today." He demonstrated by nodding emphatically. "Whatever she says, you just smile and nod, and say, 'Great idea! I'll try that!' like she just invented the wheel. If we fight them, they'll fight back. If we act like we're on board and have learned so much from them, they will feel successful and go away."

Mr. Karwacki was like a father to Shannon, and just about the only thing that kept her sane in today's education climate. She nodded obediently, and as she turned to go down the hall he patted her on the shoulder.

When she got to her classroom, Ms. Trujillo was already

waiting for her. Her short black hair was as impeccably styled and sleek as her tailored suit. "Good morning, Shannon," she said with a forced smile. She had about ten years on Shannon, so the absence of genuine smile lines was noticeable.

"Good morning," Shannon replied, and shook her hand. "I made a big dent in this," she said, taking out a binder and opening it to show her. Ms. Trujillo had wanted Shannon to write four or five learning targets for the twenty new national reading standards for each of the six grades of English she taught and then look through her curriculum to find the places where she would or did teach those six hundred targets. It was an impossibly large task, and when it was over they would do the same thing for the communication standards, since writing was a big part of those. It never ended. Somehow, she was supposed to do that and keep up with all of the grading she had to do and the lesson plans she needed to write. There weren't enough hours in the day, and it left her with a perpetual sense of failure.

Even if she did hit every single one of those targets, it didn't mean her students were going to do their part to learn them. Many would. Others felt entitled to an education they didn't earn and had nothing invested in their state test scores. Some knew they would inherit their family farms or ranches one day and had flat out told her they would never need the skills she tried to teach them. Still others were born with Fetal Alcohol Syndrome that made learning difficult, or dyslexia, or were on the autism spectrum and preferred to use the dots on the answer sheet to make interesting designs. She could do her part, but she couldn't do theirs, and yet it all came down on her.

She looked at Ms. Trujillo's face, hoping for any trace of approval or at least recognition of how hard Shannon had worked, but Ms. Trujillo simply nodded and said,

"Some of these need work, but you're off to a strong start."

It was never enough. This sense of failure was bringing her to her knees.

"Let's take a look at your lesson plans," Ms. Trujillo said.

Shannon obediently opened her plan book. It had her poem of the day and "learning to write a persuasive essay in five paragraphs" listed as what they were going to do.

"I don't see your learning targets for today. What is it that you want your students to be able to do after you're done teaching today's lesson?" asked Ms. Trujillo.

"Well, it varies from student to student," Shannon answered. "By the end of the week, I want each student to be able to write a persuasive paper using the five-paragraph essay structure, but those aren't things a student learns in a day."

"Shannon, I meant it when I said that each day you need to write the one or two targets that you're teaching to on your board so all the kids know what they are accountable for learning." Shannon inhaled deeply as she was being scolded, so Ms. Trujillo changed her tone. "You really will be surprised how much better kids will focus and how much more they will do when they know what their targets are."

Shannon nodded, doing her best to force an expression that would look like she was on board even though her bullshit tolerance was being greatly exceeded.

"Well, then today, perhaps your learning targets should simply be 'Identify the components to a five-paragraph essay structure' and 'Select a topic for a persuasive essay.'"

"Those are great. Thank you," said Shannon, going to the board to write them down before she forgot them. It was utterly stunning—the waste all of this bullshit

created. With Ms. Trujillo's salary the school could buy
much-needed computers. Were these sentences on Shannon's board and a binder full of documentation of things
she was already doing really worth more than computers?
And if she weren't so overworked and disheartened,
wouldn't she bring a different level of enthusiasm to her
teaching that might engage more students?

Ms. Trujillo looked back through Shannon's plan book.
"It looks like you spend a lot of time on poetry. What do
students do when they first come into your room?"

"I take attendance first, and then read the poem of the
day. I realized a few years ago that I was expecting them
to use descriptive language in their writing when they
really hadn't developed a descriptive vocabulary, so I
began reading them a poem a day. It only takes a couple
minutes, and usually it exposes them to at least one new
word. We talk about what the word means, and then discuss the meaning or the relevance of the poem for a couple
minutes afterward. It's a nice moment when I check in
with everyone and see how they're all doing. Sometimes
a student has written a poem that they want to share. It's
really nice to showcase their new descriptive vocabulary
and celebrate their creativity."

Ms. Trujillo was not impressed. She nodded, trying to
appear as though she were considering Shannon's way of
doing things even though she had already made up her
mind. "Your students need an entry task when they come
in so that they're working every single minute of class.
Some teachers write a sentence on the board with lots of
mistakes and the students have to find all of them and rewrite the sentence correctly on their paper. Or other
teachers write a sentence on the board for the students to
diagram. After you do one, do the other. Save the poetry
for a unit. Your first priority is to teach kids to write well.

Let me help you by writing two sentences for today so that you don't have to think of any off the top of your head. Next week I'll leave a book in your mailbox with sentences for every day to help you with the rest of the year. You'll be surprised and impressed with what a difference that alone will make in your test scores. We're going to bring your performance up to snuff in no time."

Shannon bristled. *Bring your performance up to snuff.* Oh, how she hated the constant nitpicking and these endless messages of failure. But she thought of Mr. Karwacki, whom she'd do just about anything for, and so she nodded her head and said, "Great idea. I'll try that," even though inside she was steaming.

Just then, the bell rang and as the kids rushed in she heard Brian call Luke a motherfucker and looked up just in time to see Brian give Luke a big shove from behind. Luke turned around and punched Brian in the face. And that was when Brian grabbed Luke's throat and wouldn't let go. "Stay away from my girlfriend," Brian seethed.

"Quick, go get Mr. Marshall and Mr. Hawk," Shannon said to the student closest to her. She dialed the office on her phone and dropped the receiver on the desk. "Tell them I need help," she said to Ms. Trujillo.

Then Shannon hustled over to the boys. Luke was turning purple. Shannon felt panic rise in her throat but fought it and said, "Brian, let go." He didn't flinch. "Let go!" she ordered again.

Meanwhile, students from other classes were rushing in to see the show. Brian didn't loosen his grip but glanced over at her.

"Let go," she said firmly.

To her relief, he finally did.

Mr. Hawk, Mr. Marshall, and Mr. Karwacki pushed

their way through the crowd and escorted Brian and Luke away just as the final bell rang.

"I notice you don't have any classroom rules posted," said Ms. Trujillo. "We'll work on your classroom management, too."

And that's when Shannon reached her boiling point. Before her students dispersed and sat down, she shouted, "Does anyone here think Brian and Luke's fight could have been prevented if I had only posted 'No fighting' on the wall?"

The class of juniors laughed.

"Kids, you remember Ms. Trujillo. She's going to be your teacher today, since apparently I don't know my ass from a hole in the ground."

On her way out, Shannon picked up the fat red three-ring binder full of her national Common Core standards alignment documents and threw it against the back wall. It snapped open and showered papers everywhere. She looked at Ms. Trujillo and said, "I cannot endure one more ounce of your bullshit."

As Shannon walked down the hallway, her righteous anger quickly gave way to regret. What had she just modeled for her students? That throwing things and swearing was how to solve problems? *Super. Great job, Shannon,* she thought sarcastically. As she approached the office she decided that it was only prudent to tell Mr. Karwacki first.

Through his window, she could see him talking to Luke. Brian sat in a chair outside. Gently she tapped on the glass, and Mr. Karwacki waved her in.

"Are you okay?" she asked Luke sympathetically.

He nodded and said, "Yeah," but she could tell he was still shook up.

She put a hand on his shoulder and said, "Luke, I have to talk to Mr. Karwacki, so cover your ears." She cracked a smile when he actually did. To Mr. Karwacki she said, "I snapped."

He shut his eyes for a moment. "Uh-oh."

As Shannon gave him the rundown, Luke struggled to keep a straight face. Shannon pointed at him and said, "Your ears are supposed to be covered," even though really she didn't care. He wasn't hearing anything her whole class hadn't already heard.

"Well, obviously I have to take some kind of disciplinary action. Do you want a union rep in here for this discussion?"

She shook her head. "You know, I'm not sure I care what happens to me," she said, surprised to hear herself say it. "Lately, I've just been thinking there's got to be more to life than this. Everything seems like bullshit. I spent nine hours of my weekend making a dent in aligning my curriculum to the new standards and another six hours grading papers. That's fifteen hours of my whole weekend. I work all day, I grade papers all night, and I spend my weekends doing lesson plans and bullshit. I have no life. I totally missed the boat on life. And then I come back here—to the one basket I've put all my eggs in—and get criticized by that lady no matter what I do. I used to love my job. I used to feel proud of the work I did. I hate my job now. In fact, I hate my whole fucking life."

For a moment, she had forgotten Luke was in the room. She looked over at him, and this time there was only concern on his face where a smile had been just moments ago. He stared at the floor, his hands still over his ears.

Mr. Karwacki didn't seem mad at all—quite the opposite. He seemed downright understanding as he said, "Well, how about you take some time off to think about whatever it is you're thinking about, and I'll tell people you're on disciplinary leave so I look like I'm doing my job. Come back in a week or two and we'll talk. But if you decide you want to return and continue to teach, you'll need to apologize to Ms. Trujillo. You know that, right?"

She nodded. She knew it. Although she was not sorry for speaking the truth, she was sorry for losing her composure in front of the kids. There was not a lot of dignity in that, and in that moment she had not been a good example at all. Yes, she could honestly apologize for that.

So she simply said, "Thank you, Mr. Karwacki. I'll be in touch," before she walked out of his office and out of the building.

As she walked home, Shannon knew she should be feeling the pressure of her life collapsing in on itself like a white dwarf sun, but instead she felt what she could only describe as "opening." It was as if her life had just squeezed her out the way a mother's body squeezes out a baby. Being born probably seemed like the end of safety and security at the time, too. It happened. People grew and no longer fit inside their old lives anymore.

Even though she knew she should worry about making her house payment, all she felt was relief. Now the worst-case scenario would be that her house would be repossessed, but an hour ago her worst-case scenario was that she would spend the rest of her lonely life living in it. Her new worst-case scenario didn't seem that bad compared to the old one. Yes, this morning when she looked at her life ahead of her she had felt sentenced and now, it turned out, there was an open window she could crawl out of. It would only be open for a week or two, and then it would shut. If she lost her nerve, she would again find herself sentenced to this lonely small-town life working tirelessly in a profession that had become no different from being married to someone who told her daily that she was ugly and stupid no matter what she did or how hard she tried. That's exactly what teaching had become.

She looked up at the leaves and thought about all the times she had wanted to see New England in the fall but could never get away from work. This was her big chance.

But when she reached home and rifled through her mail, she found a postcard from her old camp director, Ethel, that changed everything. First Shannon called her old best friend, Laura, to whom she hadn't spoken in years, and left a message. Then she packed some things, locked the door behind her, and let her tires spin out just a little bit as she drove out of North Prairie.

ETHEL 1950

Elks Beach was where Ethel had first fallen in love. Haddie and she were just fifteen, both counselors in training that year, in cabins next to each other. Both groups of kids from those cabins had just returned from a hike they had taken together, and the counselors had taken them to archery or arts and crafts upon return. Ethel felt grimy and was going to sneak off to the shower when suddenly the skies opened up and rain began to thunder on the tin roof. She looked out the window, and there was Haddie in her red bathing suit, sudsing up, showering right there in the rain. The heavy rains tried to pull the curl out of Haddie's dark hair, but still it hung to her ivory shoulders in waves.

Immediately Ethel put on her bathing suit, ran out the door, down the stairs, and joined her.

What Ethel remembered most was a feeling of awakening. She had never been so aware of her own skin, every little drop, every little breeze, the soft earth under her feet, how laughter released energy and cultivated it at the same time.

"Let's swim!" Haddie proposed mischievously. Swimming was only allowed in the designated main beach area where there were lifeguards, but although Ethel was worried about breaking the rules, Elks Beach was set back and hidden. There was reason to believe no one would ever know.

Haddie's smile had a hold on her, and in that moment Ethel knew she'd likely follow her anywhere.

"Cold" did not begin to describe Lake Wenatchee. Near as Ethel could figure, the water had been snow about five minutes ago. It was *painfully* cold. But she followed Haddie to the beach and into the water. There was no getting in slowly. It was all or nothing. They ran in up to their knees and dove in.

Above, lightning flashed across the sky, and thunder boomed. Electricity was literally in the air. They treaded water near each other, laughing. Ethel looked in Haddie's eyes and thought she saw the same thing she suspected was in her own. Love. Joy. Magnetism. But it couldn't be. Ethel was sure she was the only girl in the world who had feelings like these.

Another bolt of lightning arced over the lake, thunder cracking right behind it.

"We should get out," Ethel said.

"We should," Haddie agreed, but she made no move to do so. She glanced down at Ethel's lips.

Ethel's impulse to kiss her at that moment was so strong, but she didn't dare. What did one glance mean? Probably nothing. She imagined the explosive reaction and irreparable consequences if she had read the situation wrong and acted on her impulse. Not only would she lose Haddie's friendship; she'd likely get kicked out of camp, and her parents most certainly would shun her. The stakes were far too high.

"Come on," Ethel said, swimming back to shore. Her feet hit the smooth gravel, and she ran for her towel, wrapping it around her, and turned just in time to see Haddie emerge from the lake, water dripping off her face, her hair, her chest and arms, cascading off her hips. Haddie walked up onto the beach in no particular hurry, undaunted by the cold, undaunted by the lightning. It was if Haddie were some mythological water goddess, fearless in her own element, Ethel thought.

After they dressed in their respective cabins, the rain subsided. Haddie built a fire in the ring of rocks out front. Ethel and she sat just close enough to the flames to offer their hair a chance to dry. They exchanged glances across the fire—Haddie's direct and daring and Ethel's awkward and timid. It just seemed implausible that Haddie, or any girl in the world for that matter, was thinking and feeling what Ethel was. Haddie's father was a preacher, for God's sake. There was no way Haddie could be thinking and feeling what Ethel was. This thought embarrassed Ethel, but then she looked up and read Haddie's face. It seemed to be saying, *Are you feeling this? Aren't you thinking this? Then don't make this complicated. It's simple.*

Ethel was still shivering from swimming in the cold water, and yet in her heart she'd never been warmer. She looked up again. Haddie gave her a little smile as if she could read her mind, and this time Ethel bravely held her gaze and smiled back.

But then, just as Haddie started to say something, the girls in their cabins came running back. And the spell was broken.

SHANNON 1980

Few things were more miserable than being in a cast in the summer, but loneliness was one, and Shannon was both. Normally, she did two things: go to school and practice ballet. Since she had spent all of her free time practicing for an important recital, she really didn't have any friends outside of her ballet school. And since ballet was so competitive, she didn't really consider any of her ballet friends to be true friends. Even if she was wrong about them, they spent all of their spare time practicing, too, and so now that Shannon was recovering from breaking her ankle during the most important performance of her life they didn't have time to be her friends anyway. Shannon's parents grew weary of watching her mope around the house, so despite her broken ankle they signed her up for camp. Unbeknownst to them, this terrified Shannon.

First, she didn't know anything about making friends. Second, she had no idea how to be excellent at camp. Her stomach burned and cramped the whole drive there. Even the worst of her pre-performance jitters had never been this bad.

"This will be good for you," her mother had said as they walked from their car to the Lodge slowly so that Shannon could keep up on her crutches. "You can do all the things you've never had time to do."

Shannon didn't even really know what those things were, but she couldn't imagine anything fun that she could do with her stupid cast.

While her parents stood in line for check-in, she sat on a bench in the Lodge, elevating her leg while she watched all the other kids. In front of her parents, a couple girls squealed and hugged each other. They were old friends,

Shannon could tell. She wasn't sure why she hadn't considered the possibility that some of the kids up here would already know one another. Her spirits sank even more, as she knew she was going to be even lonelier than she had been by herself.

Behind her parents was a girl who looked like she might be the same age. Her long brown ponytail reached her low back. Shannon tried to imagine how huge the bun on top of her head would be if she was a ballet dancer. It would be way too big and heavy. Then the girl turned to look behind her and Shannon saw her face. She was nervous, too, and this filled Shannon with hope, hope that someone in this camp felt the same way. But then another girl ran over to this girl with the too-long ponytail and hugged her. Shannon's hopes were dashed. The girl wasn't as alone as Shannon was. She already had at least one friend. So why did she look so nervous? What could she possibly be worried about?

Shannon watched as the girl's dad began to mutter loudly about what was taking so long, and as the girl's mother tried to pacify him the girl turned her head and squeezed her eyes shut tight, almost like a wince, but longer. *That's* what she was nervous about.

After Shannon's parents had their turn, Shannon watched the camp director gesture for them to wait for a moment while the girl behind them checked in, and then, after the girl kissed her parents good-bye, she and Shannon's parents walked over to Shannon together.

"Shannon, this is Laura," Shannon's mom said. "She's going to be in the same cabin as you, and since she's been here before, she's going to show us the way."

"Hi," Shannon said awkwardly, and stood up on her crutches.

"Hi," Laura replied. She picked up her giant duffel bag and led the way.

Shannon followed, with her parents behind her carrying her things. Her mom attempted to make small talk with Laura and from time to time Laura would turn around to answer a question, but she didn't elaborate. She wasn't particularly talkative. Shannon's hope for a friend diminished even further.

As she followed Laura up the two steps and into the door of the cabin, the other girls who had arrived already paused their conversations to see who was there and size her up. One murmured, "Bummer," which Shannon first took personally before realizing that the girl was talking about her cast and not her.

From the corner of her cabin, her counselor, Janet, stepped forward and extended her hand. "Shannon, hi! We've been anxiously awaiting your arrival and we're so glad you made it!" She looked down at Shannon's cast and said, "Ugh! That's rough. But there will still be plenty of fun things to do here with us. You're going to have a great time." As Shannon said hello and answered questions about where she lived, she still could not figure out what the rules were here and how to be the best. It was not obvious.

Janet pointed her to an empty bottom bunk, where her parents put her things. "I promise to take excellent care of her," Janet told them.

Then Shannon's parents kissed her good-bye and left her there. Looking out the window and watching them walk down the path without her, she was filled with anxiety and dread.

Laura greeted Janet and then a couple more old friends who were settling into their bunks. There were seven other girls altogether, all of whom Shannon was sure were going to reject her, because as she looked around what she suddenly realized was that she not only knew nothing about how to make friends; she also knew nothing about how to be a friend. Nothing. This was going to be a problem.

An hour later, Shannon sat on a log overlooking the little sand and gravel beach while the rest of her cabin shivered on the shore waiting their turn to take their swim tests. She never thought she'd actually be grateful for her cast, but judging by the shrieks, the water was extremely cold, and since the sun wasn't out, swimming in water like that was unthinkable. Her cast had actually saved her this time.

Ethel, the camp director, sat next to her on the log for a moment. "How'd you hurt your leg?" she asked.

"Ballet," Shannon replied, and added, "I used to be great."

Ethel paused thoughtfully and then said, "That's what I love about camp. You don't have to be great. You can just be a kid." And then, as she stood, she said, "Explore, try new things, imagine, make new friends. That's all kids need to do," as if those were the simplest things in the world.

SHANNON 2012

Something about driving up the South Shore Road after all these years still filled her heart with excitement and joy. She slipped U2's *Joshua Tree* CD into her car stereo and turned it up loud, just like she had when she was eighteen, nineteen, and twenty, and she let the music and the scenery take her back.

When she came around a turn much too fast, she saw an animal in the middle of the road and hit her brakes.

Startled, the long, lean creature ran gracefully off and down toward the lake, and only when it moved did she realize what it was—a cougar. A cougar! She had never seen one in real life before. Wow, a cougar! She couldn't wait to tell Ethel.

Shannon drove another quarter mile before seeing the sign welcoming her to Camp Firelight and continued just a little beyond that to the parking lot. After she put on her large backpack that she hadn't used since the mid-1990s, she ran down the steep trail into camp.

"Hello!" she called out, but no one answered.

The door to the Lodge was unlocked, so Ethel was clearly up there somewhere. Shannon dumped her backpack there and then continued to run. How good it felt to be back! Across the bridge and the small playfield she ran, and down the steep little hill to the waterfront. Before she continued her search, she paused to walk out onto the long floating dock, look across the lake at Mt. Dirtyface, and just sit for a moment. *I'm here!* she thought. *I'm here!* Even though the camp was going to be sold, it felt wonderful simply to be back, and to be back in this pivotal moment in her life when she needed to reboot her soul. She hoped so much that Laura would come. How great it would be to be together here again.

With that thought, Shannon stood and began walking down the water's edge. In a patch of sand among the pebbles that covered most of the beach was a large print, similar in size to that of a bear but rounder and with no claws—cougar! Two cougar things to share with Ethel! Ethel would love it! It had been an unusually dry summer and fall, so perhaps many creeks had dried up, driving wildlife down from the mountaintops to the lake.

She checked the Lodge again, but Ethel still hadn't returned, so Shannon walked the quarter-mile trail out to Moose Beach. As she neared, she saw Ethel through the trees sitting on a log and talking to herself. Shannon paused for a moment to watch. If Ethel was praying, it seemed like she should be done relatively soon, but as the moments ticked on Shannon realized it was more likely that Ethel was simply talking to someone who wasn't there. *Could she be in the early stages of dementia?* Shannon wondered, suddenly fearful. Regardless of whether Ethel had lost her mind or was simply talking to a ghost, Shannon didn't want to cause her alarm or embarrassment, so she simply walked back to the main part of camp and through it and continued on down the one-mile trail to Windy Point.

There she simply sat on the wooden bench perched on a rock outcrop and waited—waited for answers about the next step in her life, waited for the right moment to return to camp, waited for the osprey in a nearby tree to launch and dive for a fish, waited.

RUBY 1940

Things Ruby did not like included but were not limited to: shoes, socks, tights, lace (it itched and scratched), having her hair combed, having her hair cut, scrubbing her nails before a meal, pretty much anything having to do with hygiene or personal upkeep, coming inside, sitting down, sitting still, sitting quietly, and absolutely everything that fell under the umbrella of "acting like a lady . . ."

. . . which was why she now believed Camp Firelight was the greatest place in the world. Sure, just an hour ago she was crying as her parents drove away, calling after them desperately and then sobbing into Miss Mildred's leg. Ruby was only six after all. But now that moment had passed and this new moment was proving to be just about the most fun a girl could have.

Rain fell hard from the sky, but her counselor didn't make them come inside as Ruby's mom would have, while telling her stories of kids who had died from catching a cold. No, Ruby's counselor took them to the little beach, where they kicked their shoes off and ran around in the rain, splashing in the shallow water, singing. A little girl named Ethel hooked her elbow in Ruby's and ran in a circle as if they were square-dancing on the edge of the lake. They sang happily, jumping, splashing, and running until they were soaked and cold.

And after, because she was cold and the water was hot, she didn't mind taking a shower. Plus, there were frogs in there, which made it considerably more fun.

As she stood in the warm stream of water singing, she vowed she'd never succumb to becoming a lady. She had every intention of feeling this wild and free forever.

RUBY 2012

It was the first time Ruby had ever been at camp without her sister, Opal, and it felt wrong. The old gang was gone. Opal was gone. Haddie was gone. And Ethel . . . well, Ethel was gone in another way, but that was all Ruby's fault.

Walking across those pebbles on the beach brought it all back—what she had lost when she lost Ethel. All that joy. Ruby could still see six-year-old Ethel singing on the shore and still feel the sweetness of her arm in hers. She took one last look at the beach before climbing the little hill back up to the playfield.

She had missed out on so much in the decades since her big mistake. It made her sick and weak to think about it. She leaned on her walking stick for a moment and then, feeling like she was about to pass out, sat down on a bench near the playfield and put her head between her legs.

She listened to the birds sing song after song until finally someone walked up to her rather briskly. "Are you okay?" It was Ethel. Ruby still recognized her voice.

What should she say? "Ethel . . . ," she began, but choked up.

"Yes, it's me: Ethel. What's going on? Do you need an ambulance? The phone here is disconnected and I don't have a car, so I'd need to paddle to a neighbor's house to call, I'm afraid."

"No. No ambulance. It's just . . ." Ruby sat up so Ethel could see her face and noticed how Ethel's had changed. Age softens some and makes others appear more severe. Age had softened Ethel. As she looked at her friend's silver hair and the many lines in her face, it hit Ruby even harder how much time had passed. "I came here to apologize and I just . . . I don't know . . . I just . . . I think I'm having an anxiety attack."

Ethel studied her closely. "Ruby?"

"Ethel, if I could change just one moment in my whole long life, it would be that one. I would give anything to go back and do it differently . . . to do anything but what I did. I know 'sorry' is too small a word for that and for decades of silence."

"It was a different time," Ethel said, but it seemed forced and cold.

Ruby reached into her pocket for the sympathy card that she had bought last year after she'd heard about

Haddie's passing. "It seemed too audacious to send this last year and so I didn't, but I wanted you to know how sorry I was about Haddie. . . ." She held it out for Ethel.

Ethel held her hand up as if to stop the card from coming near her. She didn't want it. "Do you need help getting to the Lodge?"

Ruby paused for a moment to feel the level of panic coursing through her veins, to feel how hard her heart was beating, to feel the ease with which the air now filled her lungs. It was improving. "No, I think I'm okay now," she said. And she realized that even though she knew it wasn't reasonable for Ethel to forgive her for a lifetime of banishment, even though she hadn't expected it, somewhere deep inside she had dared to hope for a miracle. And it wasn't going to happen. Ethel's indifference stung worse than anger or even hatred. And Ruby knew she deserved every bit of it.

"Okay. Well . . . Listen, I have someplace I have to go, but I don't feel all right just leaving you here."

So Ruby let Ethel walk her to the Lodge and guide her to a chair near the fireplace, where a fire still burned.

"Excuse me for just a moment," Ethel said, disappearing into the kitchen and returning with a cup of water for Ruby.

It didn't feel to Ruby so much as an act of caring as it was an act of duty, but still common decency counted and so she said, "Thank you."

"You're welcome. See you at dinner." And with that, Ethel left.

Ruby tried to digest what had just happened. Ethel hadn't engaged. And it left Ruby looking at all of her regrets, her sorrows, her shame. Ethel hadn't lightened any of that burden for her, and why would she? Ruby stared at the floor in front of her, as if she could actually see her regrets, her sorrows, and her shame—as if those things were boxes of junk before her—and she realized if she was ever going to get rid of it, she was going to have to forgive herself. No one was going to do it for her—certainly not Ethel.

What would that even look or sound like? Ruby wondered. *Forgive myself.* It sounded so easy. She attempted to do it every day. She really did. *Forgive myself,* she told herself, but that was about as far as it went. The voice in her head was sharp and impatient. It had no compassion, no mercy for her. It was mean. Even if she could say to herself, "I forgive myself," the tone somehow insinuated that she wasn't worthy of good friends or true love.

Forgive myself, she tried again, but she couldn't let it go, couldn't redeem herself, and couldn't feel compassion for her twenty-one-year-old self who had made a mistake.

RUBY 1955

Shortly after Ruby turned twenty-one, she and Gil exchanged vows in the large backyard of her parents' house in Wenatchee. It was a small gathering. Gil's only guest was his younger brother, Andy. His parents lived in Missouri, so Washington State was too far to come, especially during summer when they couldn't leave their soybean farm.

Ruby's mother worked in the kitchen, making a special dish that she had read about in the *Ladies' Home Journal.* She had made a beautiful cake, too, frosted delicately with real cream frosting.

Ruby had met Gil at the Apple Blossom parade the previous year when he was one of the elite forest-fire fighters based out of Entiat. When summer was over, he was hired by the Portland Fire Department, and so for a year they had simply exchanged letters while she wrapped up her second year at secretary school. Suddenly she realized that it had been a mistake to think letters had been enough to really get to know Gil. It clearly had been too easy to fill the void in a long-distance relationship with her own fantasies. She had imagined her wedding many times, and not once had it looked like this.

While the rest of the party mingled in the backyard, drinking punch and waiting for the cake to be cut, Gil and Andy had wandered into the house and were listening to a baseball game on the radio. Gil had actually lain on the couch with his feet up.

"Hi, Ruby. I hope you don't mind. I've just been working really hard lately, and it's been a long time since I've seen my brother."

In that moment, Ruby saw everything she needed to know about her future. She was going to be Gil's servant. If he loved her, she could have called herself his wife, but a man who loved his wife did not lie on a couch at his own wedding reception and listen to a baseball game as if it were any other day. A man who wanted a servant did that. Ruby was surprised Gil did not ask her to bring him anything.

In a few moments, they would cut the cake and then she would sit in the passenger seat of Gil's car. People would throw rice at them. And then he would drive away, taking her to a new place where she had no friends or family and no way out. Along the way, he would stop at a motel somewhere and take her virginity.

Ethel, Haddie, and Ruby's sister, Opal, had wandered in just in time to see reality wash over Ruby's face as she looked at her new husband on her parents' couch. Ethel grabbed Ruby's arm and pulled her into the bathroom.

Ruby looked at them with wide, horrified eyes. "Oh my God. A mistake has been made," she said simply.

"As long as you don't consummate the marriage tonight, it can be annulled, as if it never happened," Haddie told her. "Say the word, and we'll make a run for it. We'll go back to camp and make sure no one can find you until this mistake is undone."

Ruby paused and then gave one decisive nod.

"Out front in ninety seconds," said Opal.

"Should I tell Mom?" Ruby asked Opal.

"Only if you want her to try to fix it by getting Gil off the couch so he can either change your mind or chase you," Opal replied, sticking a toothbrush down the front of her dress.

"What are you doing?" Ruby asked.

"This is all we really need until we get your annulment Monday. Running away is no excuse for bad breath and tooth decay," replied Opal.

"Good idea," Ruby said, and stuck a toothbrush down the front of her dress as well, her dress that had been her grandmother's and then her mother's, who had altered it lovingly for her.

Before she left, Ruby stopped in the kitchen and put her arms around her mother. "I want to thank you for everything you've done to make this day special for me," she said. "I am so lucky to be so loved."

What she was about to do was possibly going to cause her parents great embarrassment. The wedding certainly had put them out a fair amount of money. Such a waste. If only she hadn't been living in a fantasy world, fed by nothing but empty words. If only Henry had come home from Korea three years ago. If Henry had come home, she never would have met Gil in the first place.

"You *are* so loved," her mother replied.

"I love you so much, too, Mom." Ruby kissed her

cheek, squeezed her hand, and stepped away. She looked out the window at her guests in the backyard—close friends and cousins mostly, and her older brother, John, among them.

And then she slipped out the front door into the passenger seat of Opal's car. Ethel and Haddie sat in the back. "Don't peel out," Ruby said to Opal.

"I'm not stupid," Opal replied, and turned the wheel toward camp.

That year, Ethel was the assistant camp director and Haddie was a lifeguard. Ruby envied them. They were living the dream. No one seemed to expect them to be teachers, nurses, or secretaries. No one seemed to expect them to get married. At least not yet. How had they escaped all these expectations? They appeared to be so free, while Ruby felt so trapped.

"I'll ruin this dress," Ruby fretted.

"We'll loan you clothes," Ethel assured her. "You don't even have to take this dress out of the car. When we get to camp, we'll bring clothes up to you."

Haddie said, "Maybe you and Opal should backpack up to Hidden Lake just in case anyone thinks to come looking for you at camp. They'll never find you there."

"Good idea," Opal said. "Then on Monday, we'll go to the courthouse and get a judge to make this whole thing go away." She turned to Ruby. "It's okay. You're okay now. Everything's going to be okay."

As it turned out, Ruby's parents had come to camp looking for her, while she and Opal were hiding at Hidden Lake, and while she never did find out the whole story of what went on at camp in her absence, she was able to piece together a few things. First, a discussion about her whereabouts and motivation quickly escalated into her father shouting something about how his daughters weren't going to turn into old hermit spinsters like Ethel and

Haddie surely were going to. Threats were made. And after he stormed away, Ruby's mother followed him for a bit but then came back to apologize for his brashness, and when she did what she saw was Haddie comforting Ethel, brushing the hair out of her face and kissing her on the lips. To her credit, Ruby's mom didn't blab it all over town, but she did call up Ethel's mom and tell her. Ruby didn't know the details of that fallout either but did know Ethel and her mom hadn't spoken since that unfortunate incident.

How do you apologize for something like that? How do you apologize for causing someone and her mother to become estranged? If only Ruby had never gotten engaged to Gil. If only Ethel had never been put in that position by helping her.

It got worse. The following Monday, a judge did eventually grant Ruby an annulment, but not before an uncomfortable series of questions about whether she just had wedding night jitters. When she did return home, she was a single woman again. The moment she walked into the house, she had to face her father's wrath and her mother's questions, like, "Do you kiss other women or allow other women to kiss you in a way that is normally reserved for men?"

After that, it was . . . uncomfortable to be friends with Ethel and Haddie. Ruby's parents were scrutinizing every move she made. *Run out on your wedding day because your feelings were hurt?* That made no sense at all to them. After all, her mother reasoned, a married woman's feelings were hurt much of the time. It was part of marriage.

So, when Ethel called one evening to check on her, Ruby had asked her to please not phone her house anymore.

Ethel was silent. Ruby's insides felt as if they were

being wrung out like wet laundry, twisted. It was wrong. And it was what she felt she had to do in order to survive.

In all these years, she'd never made it right. How could a person make something as big as that right? Ruby couldn't.

ETHEL 1955

Stunned, Ethel hung up the phone and looked at Haddie. "Ruby doesn't want me to call her anymore."

Haddie's face immediately reflected the wounds Ethel would come to feel as her disbelief wore away. At first, Ethel was more uncertain and confused than anything else. After all, how does someone tell another to simply stop being a friend after fifteen years? How does she just forget all the good times? It made no sense.

And still there was this other part of her, a part deep inside that wasn't rational—the part that simply memorized everything she'd been taught, all the subtleties of "normal"—and that part of her wondered whether she had done something wrong and didn't deserve friendship or acceptance.

For the first week, she kept hoping Ruby would sneak away from her house and call them and tell them her mom had made her say that, but she didn't mean it. As the first week gave way to the second week, Ethel lost more and more hope, until, a month later, she had none.

One evening while Haddie built a fire in the fireplace, Ethel stopped and studied the framed picture of the three of them and a few others on the dock back in 1953. She looked at Ruby's eyes, which, like always, held the promise of harmless mischief. They held no malice, no sign that one day she would inflict this much pain upon Ethel. It heightened Ethel's sense of betrayal. She had expected to be rejected by society for loving Haddie but hadn't expected to be rejected by Ruby, and that spurred Ethel to take the picture off the wall and throw it on the floor, smashing it.

Haddie jumped and then paused for a moment before she reacted. She took two steps toward Ethel and put an arm around her. "We're in that picture, too, you know."

It was true. That was the thing about bad intentions. They couldn't be done to another without being done to oneself as well. And as she looked at the broken glass on top of the image of Haddie, Ethel's heart filled with regret and her bottom lip began to tremble.

"Come here," Haddie said, putting her arms around her.

Ethel sobbed as if she'd just found out Ruby had died, because in a way she had. "How could she ruin everything?" she asked Haddie.

"I don't know," Haddie answered simply.

"We were good friends to her! We were good friends!"

"Let it go. If you can, Ethel, just let it go."

"But I don't understand!"

"We don't have to."

Ethel pulled away and looked at Haddie's face.

"We don't have to understand," Haddie said. "And really, we can't. No one can ever really know what it's like to be someone else. We just have to know that in her heart, she really does love us. She just doesn't know what else to do."

Ethel shook her head defiantly, then slowed and softened until she barely whispered, "Will everyone we love desert us?"

Haddie shrugged apologetically. "Maybe. But we've

got each other. That's more than a lot of people will ever have."

Looking at the floor again, Ethel said, "I'm sorry I broke the picture of us."

"I know," Haddie replied. She bent down and began to help Ethel pick up the jagged shards of glass that had scattered everywhere.

ETHEL 2012

A card? Ruby shows up after fifty-seven years and she wants to give me a card? She dismissed Haddie and me like we were worthless and completely missed the rest of Haddie's life, and now she shows up and hands me a card like Haddie was even worth two dollars and fifty cents to her? Ethel was fuming. She didn't want to be, and she hoped she hid it well, because there was nothing dignified about a fifty-seven-year grudge and she didn't want Ruby to think she had any power over her at all. She wanted her to think she was completely unaffected, that her life had been good, which it had, and that it was Ruby's loss, which it was. But Ethel also knew that it had been her loss as well. It wasn't as if she and Haddie had just been able to go out and replace Ruby. Ruby couldn't be replaced, and her absence had been felt—especially at first.

Ethel had lied when she told Ruby she had somewhere to go, saying that only because she needed to step away. Now, outside the Lodge, she looked around for something to do. Up the hill sat the "Holiday House," the nurse's cabin. Surely there were tons of first-aid supplies that needed organizing, so Ethel took the master key off the ledge of the window once more, walked up the hill, and let herself in.

Opening drawers and cupboards, she discovered that everything was already packed away nicely. The Holiday House was in good shape.

She sat on a cot for a moment as it sank in that she'd have to share her last week here in her old home, the home where she and Haddie had shared so much life and love, with someone she had spent the last fifty-seven years being angry at. As the weight of it hit her, she lay back on the cot, stared at the ceiling, and said, "Oh, Haddie. You were always my source of grace. I sure wish you were here with me now."

And it may have been Ethel's imagination, but she thought she heard Haddie's voice reply, *Well, what are you going to do, Ethel—throw mud balls at her? Chase her with a broom? Come on, don't make it hard. Just forgive and go on.*

LAURA 2012

"Hey, Steve," Laura said as he walked in the door at the end of the workday. He gave her a little hug and kissed her cheek. He always smelled so good when he came home from the lumber store, like pine and cedar. She rested her head on his chest and squeezed him back. That was the thing. They were still affectionate like that. And it felt genuine. She wondered what was so wrong with her that she couldn't jump from this affectionate place to a place that sizzled like the fajitas she was making.

She reached over and stirred the meat and vegetables in the skillet before they burned.

"My old camp director, Ethel, contacted a bunch of us last week to say camp is closing for good, and she invited us to come out this week and help her clean it one last time and close it up."

"Hm," Steve said as he carried food from the kitchen to the dining room table.

It wasn't the first meal they'd had alone. There had been plenty of times when Alison was out with friends or involved in some activity and Laura and Steve had eaten by themselves. She wasn't sure why it felt so different now that Alison had just left for college. Perhaps because this was going to be the new norm and it didn't feel normal at all. It felt empty and unsure.

"Shannon left a message to say she is coming, but I can't believe she can really miss that much school, so I don't know how long she'll be there. And I don't know who else, if anyone, will be able to help on such short notice. I feel uneasy about Ethel being out there by herself. She's well into her seventies now and could trip on a root and break a hip. The phone is shut off up there, which means she'd have to go back to her own house to call herself an ambulance. I don't like that at all."

Steve nodded. "Seems like a bad idea."

"I was wondering how you'd feel about me spending the week out there."

Steve paused and looked at her. She thought she saw just the tiniest glimmer of fear pass through his eyes. Maybe it was sadness. Maybe it was nothing at all, nothing but her imagination.

He shrugged. "Gotta do what you gotta do," he said, and spooned some meat and vegetables onto a tortilla.

"I don't have to go," she said. "I can stay here with you. I mean, I know there have been some profound changes in our home just this weekend, and I don't want you to feel lonely."

His expression softened. "No," he said. "Go. I'll be all right."

She looked across the table at him, grateful. Steve was handsome. His eyes were warm and green, his jaw strong and well-defined, and his scruffy whiskers were sexy, albeit abrasive. He was due for a haircut. The reddish-brown tips of his hair were long enough to begin to curl. They touched the collar of his flannel shirt and lay against his thick, manly neck. She loved that neck.

He caught her staring at him and looked at her curiously. "What?" he asked.

She smiled self-consciously. "I was just noticing how handsome and sexy you are."

He shook his head. An expression washed over his face as if to ask her if she thought he was stupid. As she was taken back, her eyes welled up.

She reached across the table and put her hand on his, the one that held his fork, and he looked up at her again and took in her expression. He put his fork down, turned his hand over, and held hers.

"I meant it," she said. "I was telling the truth."

He nodded. "Okay. I'm sorry."

"You don't have anything to be sorry for." She tried to find the right words.

He reached across the table and smoothed her hair out of her eyes, and that gentle, loving gesture made her feel even worse. "What?" he asked softly. "What's going on inside you?"

"I know there's something wrong with me. That there has been for a long time. And when you couldn't believe that I thought you were handsome and sexy, I just . . . I just saw how damaging . . . my problem has been."

He lowered his head and nodded.

"I want to fix it," she said.

He kept his eyes low and continued to nod and finally looked up with an expression that said both, *Thank you,* and, *I'm afraid it's too late.*

As they finished their dinner in silence, the image Laura had was of herself sitting in the middle of a vast pile of rubble—her home, her wreckage, her doing. In it, Steve was caught and pinned. Her fajitas tasted like guilt—metallic and bitter—but she choked them down anyway. Finally, the tension was too much, so she excused herself and then rushed off to pack her things.

And an hour later, she approached Steve slowly and awkwardly. She kissed him on the cheek, told him she loved him, and lingered for a moment.

He didn't say it back. Instead, he simply said, "Have fun at camp. See you later."

"Thanks," she said, and listened to the empty sound of her footsteps echoing in the house as she walked out the door and shut it behind her.

Oh yes, Laura thought as she walked down the trail from the parking lot by the light of her flashlight. There was something profoundly comforting about places a person knew in the dark, these trails like old friends she hadn't forgotten. The young trees had grown. They looked different. But it felt the same. Well, the same, but emptier.

In the beam of her flashlight she could see crimson vine maple leaves that had fallen. They littered the trail like rose petals in a wedding. In the distance, she heard a great horned owl. Her senses felt so heightened here. She had forgotten this feeling. It felt like being much more alive than she had felt in a long time. Each footstep left her with a greater and greater sense of connection with all living things.

As she passed the cabins on the hill, she could smell a fire burning . . . oh, how she loved that campfire smell. Then, from the Holiday House, she could see the lights on in the Lodge, exactly where she expected to find Ethel and anyone else who might be there. Laura pushed the big old door open and peeked her head around it, spotted Ethel by the fireplace with two other ladies, and did her best owl call. "Hoo, hoo-hoo-hoo, hoo-hoo-hoo!" she called, and then smiled.

As Ethel answered Laura's owl call, Shannon jumped up and ran over to her. "Laura!" she called out joyfully as she hugged her and rocked back and forth in a silly dance.

At one time, they had been almost inseparable. And then life happened. Life and kids and family. Yes, life happened until Laura barely remembered who she once was, until she barely remembered those precious few years when anything seemed possible.

"Aw, man, is it good to be here!" Laura said. "God, it's good to see you again!"

"Together again!" Shannon exclaimed.

Then Ethel walked up and said, "I'm so glad you could make it, my little naturalist. Did you hear that big owl singing out there tonight?"

"I did," Laura answered, hugging her. Ethel, the mom Laura would have preferred to have had. Ethel seemed much more delicate now. How precious she was.

"Did you see him?" asked Ethel. "He's a big guy!"

"No, I didn't get to see him." Although Laura talked about the owl, a flood of memories rushed back to her, memories of being on nature walks with Ethel. "What a blessing to be back here together again," Laura said, looking into Ethel's twinkling eyes.

Then Ethel, remembering her manners, said, "Laura, I'd like you to meet Ruby, who was my friend during my early Camp Firelight years." There was unmistakable tension that Laura couldn't put her finger on, but it was real. Growing up with her raging alcoholic dad had taught her to accurately tune into and assess the energy in a room when she entered, and she hadn't lost that ability.

"Ruby. Pleasure to meet you," Laura said, shaking her hand.

"Likewise," Ruby replied, and sat back down again in her chair by the fireplace.

For the next hour, they all chitchatted, which was different from talking. It was edited. Instead of saying, *My youngest just left for college and I'm sad and lost and thinking of leaving my husband,* Laura told the edited version of her life where it sounded idyllic. The others did the same. She noticed Shannon used euphemisms such as "transition time" and "exploring what I want to do in the next era of my life." *Is she going through a divorce?* wondered Laura. She didn't recall Shannon getting married. And Ethel and Ruby were sugarcoating the loss of the camp, pretending to feel more acceptance than they did. They may have been even been pretending to like each other, too. Laura still couldn't quite decipher what was going on there.

When the evening began to wind down to a close, Shannon asked, "Ethel, can Laura and I stay out in Moose?"

"Better make it Elks," Laura said. "Moose is too far to the bathroom."

"When you're my age," Ruby said, "every place is too far to the bathroom."

"Amen," Ethel agreed, and handed Laura the key.

"I just peed on a spider and two moths," Shannon announced as she walked out of a stall in the bathroom.

"I forgot about that," Laura said. "There were always moths in the toilet. I wonder why. And this smell. What is this smell? I missed this smell."

Shannon breathed in deeply. "I'm going to go with Pine-Sol with a twist of mold."

"It makes me really happy."

They poured themselves paper cups of water from the plastic jug Ethel had left on the windowsill, brushed their teeth over the giant metal trough that served as a sink, and spit. "Listen to this," Laura said as she poured a little water from her cup over her toothbrush. "I love the sound it makes. It's the sound of the beginning and the end of a happy day."

"We tie-dyed a whole lot of underwear in this sink."

"Ah, yes. We did," said Laura as she remembered.

"We should do it again." Shannon proposed. "Wait. All mine are black."

"We should raid Ethel's and tie-dye them," Laura said with a mischievous smile.

"You did not just say that! You? Ethel's pet? I'm shocked! When did you get this sinister streak?"

"When I had teenagers."

"Of course." Shannon smiled.

As they walked from the bathroom to their cabin, Shannon's words sank in. *Ethel's pet.* It was true. She always was Ethel's favorite. Laura wasn't sure why, exactly, but she and Ethel just seemed to fit. "Do you think she's okay?"

"Ethel?" Shannon thought for a moment and then shook her head. "I can't tell." After a pause, she added, "Maybe we shouldn't tie-dye her underwear until we know."

Laura laughed and said, "That's probably a good idea."

As they passed by the fire ring outside their cabin,

Laura said, "I think I might build a little fire tonight. I'm not quite ready for bed."

"I wish I could say that," Shannon replied, climbing the stairs. "My heart wants to sit by a fire all night, but my body's not going to go along with that. I'm going to be asleep in about ten minutes whether I want to or not. I've had a long, strange day."

"Yeah?" Laura asked, hoping Shannon would say more.

"It's possible I snapped and walked out of work today, but not before saying a few choice words."

"It's possible?" Laura asked, like a parent.

"Yeah . . . ," Shannon said slowly. "It's possible my teaching career is over."

"Oh no!" said Laura sympathetically.

"You know, it's surprisingly okay with me. I could get my job back if I wanted it, but I don't think I do. I don't know. It feels like time for something else . . . something happier. So, yeah, as much as the seventeen-year-old in me wants to stay up all night catching up with you, the forty-three-year-old in me isn't capable."

Laura laughed. "I understand."

"Enjoy your fire, though. And we'll catch up more tomorrow."

In the dark, it could have been 1987. Shannon's voice sounded the same. The earth under Laura's feet felt the same. Everything smelled the same. Yes, the darkness hid everything that had changed, it seemed to Laura. It hid wrinkles and bodies that had thickened. It made her regular life seem far, far away.

"Sleep tight," Laura said.

"You too."

As her fire died down to coals, Laura closed her eyes for a moment and listened to the sound of peace. How nice it was to have this space completely free of expectations—or, rather, disappointments. She didn't have to hear the sound of the hallway creaking, her husband still up after she'd gone to bed—or listen to him creep in after he thought she was asleep and slide under the covers next to her as quietly as he could. How she loathed the sound of him not rocking the boat. Tonight, she didn't have to listen to the *I love you* that was not said. No, here it was all just neutral.

Space felt so good. It had been so long since she'd had enough space to realize where she stopped and other people began. Even now, all alone on the porch, it still wasn't clear. Inside herself she pictured a knot with many different kinds and colors of rope—only one of which was hers. The other ropes were her family members and their stuff. As she held the image of the knot in her mind's eye, she saw the knot beginning to loosen. It was a start.

From time to time, she heard autumn leaves rustle, a chipmunk's claws scratch the trunk of a tree while it climbed, and, from under the porch, a frog croaked very slowly. But she did not hear judgment, resentment, anger, or abandonment—only peace.

And suddenly she wished she had not told Steve she wanted to change. This solitude suited her perfectly. Neutral contentment. Peace. How would she break it to him?

Her thoughts were interrupted by the song of a great horned owl: *Who, who-who-who, who-who-who.* Other people thought its call sounded like, "Who cooks for you? Who cooks for you?" but to Laura, it sounded like, "Here comes the bride, comes the bride." She lifted her hands to her mouth and answered. Back and forth, back and forth they sang until the owl swept down low and landed in a branch where it could see her. It sang one more time, *Here comes the bride, comes the bride.*

Her mind drifted back to her own wedding. If she had

it do over again, would she? Yes. But if marriage was something that had to be renewed annually like a magazine subscription, would she renew? No. So when the owl called out the wedding march to her again, Laura answered in English: "No."

tuesday

AMBER 2012

Amber woke up with Woof Woof held tightly against her chest. The wind had blown last night, causing a branch to scrape against her window. She felt a bit embarrassed about regressing from fifteen to five when it scared her in the middle of the night, crawling down the ladder, and searching in the dark through all her belongings until she found Woof Woof. But no one was here to see. She had forgotten what a comfort this stuffed dog could be and kissed his head. Even though she knew, of course, that he had no feelings, she felt funny about leaving him alone in the cabin, but she couldn't take him to school, so she placed his body inside her sleeping bag with his head poking out.

Today was going to be a challenge.

First, she had to catch the bus, and that required bicycling to the nearest stop—three and a half miles down the South Shore Road to the junction of the Lake Wenatchee Highway, right next to the state park. The ranger's kid was picked up there. Amber would need a forged note to get on and off the bus at a new location, so she opened up her binder and practiced her mother's script before finally writing: "Please allow Amber to get on and off the school bus near the state park. Now that I am working night shifts, I'm having her stay with a friend near there."

Then, anticipating her arrival at school, she wrote another: "Please excuse Amber for her absence yesterday. We had a family emergency." Had anyone ever gone to juvie hall for forgery?

Her stomach was turning inside out. She had not eaten in a day and a half and hoped the school cook was feeling generous this morning, because she was Amber's only hope. She would surely pass out in second-period P.E. if she didn't eat.

After crawling out the window and shutting it behind her, she checked her alarm clock and slid it into her messenger bag so she could see exactly how long it took to ride her bike to the bus stop.

Nineteen minutes. Walking her bike up to the road added four minutes to the fifteen it took to ride. But what was she going to do once the snow fell? Her mountain bike tires would grip on some days, but other days it would be pure ice. What if she fell and broke her arm? Who would help her? Who would take her to the doctor? And how would she get out without someone calling her mom or Child Protective Services? This new situation was a house of cards. There was no room for error. None.

She hid her bike in the forest near the end of the road and walked the rest of the way to the bus stop. The ranger's son was already waiting there, so when she joined him she told him the story she had just made up. He was only in junior high and too shy to make conversation, so, to her relief, they just waited for the bus in silence after that.

On the bus, she found a seat near the front to minimize the attention the other kids gave her. She sat, took out her binder, and made a to-do list, anticipating as many problems that might arise as she could.

At school, the secretary merely asked her if everything was okay and Amber said that yes, they were okay, but that her mother's salary had dropped and now she needed a form for free and reduced lunches. No problem.

"A lot of families are going through a rough time right now," the secretary said sympathetically.

Next, Amber went to the school cafeteria and told the lunch lady about how her mom recently had a change in her employment and hadn't been able to go to the grocery store. Amber showed the lunch lady the form she had picked up in the office and promised to bring it back tomorrow. To Amber's relief, the cook handed her a waffle and some orange slices and told her not to worry about it today. In her whole life, she had never been so grateful for food. She must have wolfed it down too fast, because the cook waved her over and handed her a plastic bag with extra orange slices in it for the road.

There were some angelic people in this world. Maybe this was how it was going to be. Maybe kind people were going to come along just when she needed help most. She really hoped she could pull this off.

At her locker, she smiled at the group of girls she called her friends. That was the thing about having her mother as a mother—it didn't lend itself to having friends over, and that was an important bonding rite. Any one of those girls would help Amber, she was sure, but she was equally sure not a single one would keep her secret. She would surely end up in a foster home if they began to suspect something was not right.

She had missed a math test yesterday and needed to ask Mr. Morris if he would let her make it up. He was pretty strict, and she could not produce a doctor's note. That was his policy: If you missed a test and wanted to make it up, you had to have a doctor's note. She peered in his room and then walked in with great trepidation. He sat at his desk peering down at papers through his glasses, a cross look on his face, marking problems wrong, and writing a score on the top.

"Mr. Morris," she began. "I know what your policy is about missing tests, but I'd greatly appreciate it if you'd make an exception. Yesterday we had a private family emergency, and although I wanted to come to school, it was not my choice."

"My policy is clear," he said. "So you'll have to take that up with your parents."

Amber panicked and pleaded, "My mom doesn't care about my grades like I do. If you deny me the chance to make up this test in order to send a message to my mom about the importance of me being here on test days, it won't do any good. She doesn't care. Only I do. Please don't punish me for my mom's problems. School is my way out." It was that last sentence that got his attention. Had she said too much? Oh God, she had. She hadn't said anything that he could call CPS over, but she had said enough to put herself on his radar.

He studied her for a moment. She must have looked desperate. "Don't let it get out that I made an exception," he said, reaching into a folder and handing her a test. "You can start it now and finish it at lunch."

"Thank you," she said with a big sigh of relief.

He gave her a little nod, her cue to walk away. But as she slid into her desk she looked up and saw him looking at her with a very concerned expression on his face. *Oh no,* she thought. She was without question on his radar now. No more slipups in here. She had to make it look like yesterday was an anomaly—just a temporary problem. It was going to be hard. Of all her teachers, he gave the most homework by far, and as the days got shorter she'd have almost no time to finish it. If her grades slipped, he would notice and he would know something was very wrong.

Suddenly two and a half years seemed an impossible amount of time to keep up appearances. How was she ever going to pull this off?

After P.E., Amber took off her sweaty clothes and put them in her gym locker. Her shirt was going to stink tomorrow. Although she had packed two extra T-shirts, she had taken them out to make room for Woof Woof. How was she going to do laundry? Going to the Laundromat would mean missing the school bus back to Lake Wenatchee. Was there any place up there with coin-operated laundry machines? She didn't think so. Maybe at a private campground, but they were all closed now. Maybe she'd have to wash her clothes in the sink here. The other girls were sure to notice that. They were also sure to notice if she started to smell. One of her choices was less offensive than the other.

She walked to the shower after most of the others had done their obligatory five-second rinse, clutching her towel around her like they all did. There was a ten-minute break between second and third period that gave her a little extra time, for which she was thankful. She showered as quickly as possible and washed her hair with the soap from the soap dispenser. She looked at the clock, pleased that she'd have time to stick her head under the hand dryer.

As she walked back to her locker, she passed a group of popular girls who had lingered to perfect their makeup in front of the large mirror. They looked at her with disdain, and Stephani Adams said, "How come you took a shower here instead of home? Do you like people watching you wash yourself?" The others laughed.

If Amber were still living at home, there would be only one right answer, and that would have been a solid punch to Stephani's immaculately made-up face—preferably something that would leave a bruise to let everyone else in the school know that there was a price for choosing her to pick on—but since she could not get into trouble there was no right answer. It seemed like she'd be made fun of less for being poor than being an exhibitionist, so she said, "Our hot-water heater is broken." She wanted to add "bitch" but knew that could easily escalate to a fight, which would land her in the principal's office with a phone call to her mother.

Amber walked on by, waiting to see if the ridicule would continue or if Stephani would back down. "Bummer," Stephani said. "I guess that explains why you looked the way you did this morning," implying that Amber had looked bad.

"Yep," Amber said, getting dressed quickly. She thought of at least five great insults she could deliver back. It would feel so good to shut Stephani up.

But it didn't work like that. It would inflame the situation, so Amber merely walked over to where the hand dryers were mounted on the wall and stuck her head under one.

Stephani and her friends looked at Amber and laughed hard. "Nice," Stephani said sarcastically.

Amber shut her eyes. How badly she wanted to punch Stephani and put her in her place. Her mind raced with all the things that were bringing her mighty close to her breaking point—her mom vacuuming the same spot for God knows how long, her creepy lover or dealer or whatever he was, spending a night freezing in the woods, bicycling down the road with two pillowcases knocking into her tire, riding her bike three and a half miles to the bus stop, and trying to look normal here at school when nothing, *nothing,* was normal. She could freaking snap. Oh yes, she was dangerously close to her breaking point.

Was this how it was going to be every day when she

took her shower? If so, she was going to end up in foster care for sure.

With her eyes still shut, she remembered a time long, long ago when she was very little and her mom dried her hair with a towel. When her hair no longer dripped, her mom helped Amber into fuzzy pajamas with feet and snapped up the front. After her mom rubbed Amber's head with the towel a little longer, she collected her up in her arms and carried her out by the fireplace, where they sat in its warmth and her mom combed out the tangles in her hair.

What Amber would give for a wonderfully normal moment like that now.

ETHEL 2012

Ethel woke as the first morning light illuminated the room. Ruby had taken the bunk that had been Haddie's and was snoring loudly. Since Ethel could not get back to sleep, she rose, dressed, and then reached into her big green duffel bag and pulled out Haddie's ashes. Tucking them under her arm, she tiptoed out as quietly as she could.

The crisp morning air bit her nose, but still, how wonderful it felt to wake up at home—her true home, even if it was just for a few more days. Things didn't last. The urn in her hands was evidence of that. And who was to say that things that lasted were more successful than things that didn't last?

The Firelight Girls were undeniably antiquated. Their pledge echoed in her memory. She lifted her hand and said the words out loud: "I promise to keep the fire in my heart, my hearth, and my life's work burning so that it casts its glow on everyone and everything around me. May the world be a better place in the glow of my firelight."

As Ethel walked along, she adjusted the urn so that the face she had drawn looked out at the camp. "The world sure was a better place in the glow of your firelight, Haddie. That is the truth. The Firelight Pledge. Can you believe I can still remember that? I can barely remember my own phone number, but the Firelight Pledge is etched in my brain. You've got to love it." She sighed. "My, how things have changed since we were first campers here. People don't take oaths or make pledges anymore. Have you noticed that? When did that became unfashionable?" She laughed. "You're right; it probably did go out of style along with citizenship. Yes, it was another time. I don't know if it was entirely better or entirely worse. Maybe there were simply trade-offs."

She stopped in the bathroom and set Haddie's urn on the windowsill above the sink next to the jug of drinking water for tooth brushing and face washing. Shannon had hauled two buckets of water up the previous day and put one in each stall, so there was water to flush with. Ethel turned on the sink faucet just to see what would happen. All she heard was a hollow noise.

How had it come to this? Ethel never thought she would see this day—not in her lifetime. But here it was, happening before her eyes . . . the end of camp.

When she retired from being the camp director of Camp Firelight back in 1999, she thought sitting on the board of directors of North Central Washington Firelight Girls would be a way she could still contribute to the place she loved. Never did she think she would be part of its undoing, but at the last meeting she and the other board members had looked at the cost analysis budget sheets before them. The numbers were beyond bleak. They were hopeless. The whole situation was hopeless. Enrollment in the Firelight Girls was down, so cookie sales were down. The result was that the cost of camp went up. When it became less affordable, enrollment dropped. And then last summer the situation had gotten even worse.

Four years prior, the water well had almost stopped producing and the board had been faced with a tough decision about what to do about it. They were told that for eight to nine thousand dollars they could have it fracked and that might get things going or they could drill a new well for ten to fifteen thousand dollars and maybe find water on their first try. The problem was, given the rock outcrop they were sitting on, it could take three tries. In that case, a new well could potentially cost forty-five thousand dollars that they didn't have and were unlikely to get. So, four years ago they scraped and scraped and played with numbers, wrote a grant, and somehow raised the money to frack the well. And for two years it seemed the problem had been solved.

On the third year, though, they noticed changes in the quantity of water it was producing, and then by the beginning of last summer there had been only a trickle. They barely had enough water to do dishes at all—definitely not up to health standards—so they certainly didn't have water for showers or toilets. Kids had to swim in the frigid lake to get clean, and they had to haul water up the hill in buckets for the toilets. It was not good.

The Health Department came out the day the well ran completely dry and shut them down. And then the American Camp Association came out two days later and suspended their certification until they fixed the problem.

The camp director had to call parents and send kids home early and cancel the last two sessions of camp, ruining the camp's reputation and devastating the Firelight

Girls' financial situation. Now there was food, electricity, and garbage service they couldn't pay for, and on top of that they needed ten to fifteen thousand additional dollars for a new well—and that was if they hit water on the first try, and they already knew there was a very real chance they'd have to try two or three times before hitting water. Their debt combined with the cost of drilling two or three times could easily top fifty thousand dollars.

The executive director had stood before them and choked out the death sentence for camp. "So, you see, we're in too big of a hole to ever dig ourselves out. We can't pay our debts. We have no choice but to file bankruptcy and close our doors."

Now Ethel turned the faucet back to the off position and shook her head in disbelief. "Oh, Haddie, how could things have gone so wrong in just thirteen years? As much as I like to think this never would have happened if we hadn't left, I don't think it's true. I think—"

Just then Ruby walked into the bathroom. "Good morning," she said, and looked around to see to whom Ethel was talking. Ethel saw Ruby's eyes land on Haddie's urn, and suddenly she felt ridiculous. A moment ago the urn had been Haddie, and now it was simply a metal vessel with a face drawn on it and some yarn tied around the top. "Good morning," Ethel replied, and then she turned her back on Ruby and rinsed her toothbrush.

Ruby was polite enough not to say anything about the urn or the talking. She slipped into a stall, and Ethel jumped on her opportunity to escape.

Again she slid the urn into her coat, hoping the magic would return. How odd it struck her that something that was so comforting one moment could be the source of so much shame the next. With long strides, she walked down the hill toward their favorite place—Elks Beach—and once there she took the urn out of her coat and set it next to her. But this time, when she talked to it, it wasn't the same. It was as if Haddie's spirit had left the urn. And for the first time in a very long time, Ethel dared to ask herself, "Have I lost my mind?"

ETHEL 1951

When Ethel had finally returned to camp the year after she and Haddie had swum in the rainstorm, she ran to Elks Beach, her anticipation high. All year, they had written letters. Ethel's heart always skipped when Haddie wrote about missing her and missing camp, about how fun that day was when they showered in the rain and swam in the lightning, and her heart sank when Haddie wrote that she was going to prom, even though she also wrote that the boy who was her date was just a friend. It seemed inevitable to Ethel that one or both of them would succumb to societal pressures to marry a man, have children, and play the part. Once one of them did, it would be gone forever. It would be a place neither would be able to find her way back to. The magic would be over.

When Ethel reached the beach, it was as if everything inside her just opened up and smiled. Haddie was there, waiting for her. Ethel ran into her arms, and they laughed with joy.

"Can you believe it? We're staff now!" Ethel said. They had both been chosen to work in the kitchen. The pay was nice, but what Ethel really wanted was time off with Haddie when they were accountable to no one, when they could find sunny spots on the lakeshore and simply be together.

"I've been thinking," Haddie said, "that one of us should be camp director one day and the other should be assistant camp director, and we could just live here together until we're really old women."

It was to Ethel what marriage proposals were to other young women.

That summer, Elks Beach was more or less theirs. Although kitchen staff generally lived above the kitchen, those quarters became insufferably hot, so no one minded or thought anything of it when Ethel and Haddie dragged their mattresses and sleeping bags down to the shore and slept under the stars on all the nights it that didn't rain. Under the pretense of being cold they had pushed their mattresses together on a night when the temperatures got down into the low forties, and somehow the mattresses just stayed that way. The mosquitoes were fierce and so the girls always slept with their arms in their sleeping bags, but they always woke up nestled next to each other.

RUBY 1946

Ruby's favorite thing about camp when she was twelve was not doing dishes. As the campers finished eating, they sang songs while they scraped their plates into a coffee can and then stacked them. And that's when Ruby's favorite part of the day came—when one person took the pile of plates to the little window of the dishwashers' station and that was it. Poof. Gone.

Just two days ago, Ruby stood at the sink, elbows deep in suds, scrubbing a particularly difficult cheese-coated casserole dish. "Why do I have to wash all the dishes all the time and John never does?" She glanced over at her brother, who was leafing through the Sears catalog, looking at BB guns.

"Because your brother mows the lawn and chops wood," her mother answered.

"He doesn't do either of those things three times a day—or even year-round," muttered Ruby.

"You can stop that attitude right now," her mother said firmly.

The discussion was over. Ruby's place as a girl was reaffirmed—she was destined to be a servant or, at the very most, a second-class citizen. At school, John and the other boys got to have P.E. in the shiny new gym with the nice floor while they, the girls, had P.E. in the old gym with the warped floor. And afterward John and the other boys had a towel service, but the girls had to bring their own towels. After school, boys had the opportunity to participate in sports, but if you were a girl, your only opportunity was to cheer for the boys. "It's just the way it is," her mom had explained, but nonetheless, the injustice of it infuriated Ruby.

But not this summer. No, not this summer at camp. Here at camp, she was a second-class citizen to no one. Here at camp, she was no one's servant. Sure, there were chores they did after breakfast and flag ceremony, but these chores didn't bother her because everyone made the mess and everyone helped clean it up. It wasn't like everyone made the mess and only the girls cleaned it up. How she loved her two months a year of equality.

She scraped her lunch plate, set it in the pile, and watched the pile get carried away to a land where it was not her problem.

And when lunch was all over—songs, announcements, and rest hour—Ruby and Ethel went to the archery range to practice. Ruby took her mark, pulled back her bow, and shot the arrow straight into the center of the target. Bull's-eye. It made her feel powerful and just a little bit dangerous. Yes, she was every bit as good as a boy—at least here, and at this.

RUBY 2012

How things change. Years ago chores were a burden, but after a lifetime of living alone they felt like an honor. What Ruby realized at some point along the way was that cooking and dishes, laundry and sweeping, all of these little tasks could be acts of love. They weren't always. She sure hadn't done them in that spirit when she was a kid, but now, after decades of sharing meals with no one, of sharing a home with no one and sharing a life with no one, Ruby rather enjoyed the simple act of scrambling eggs for people other than herself. These were the rituals, she'd come to realize, that connected people.

Shannon and Laura entered the kitchen with bright smiles. "I swear, there are certain smiles people only smile at camp—no matter how old we are," Ruby said, looking at them.

"It's so bittersweet, though," Laura replied. "I mean, how great to be back, but how hard to say good-bye to this place."

"I never thought I'd be back," said Ruby.

"Can I help?" Shannon asked.

Ruby saw something in Shannon's eyes that reminded her of herself and noticed she also wore no wedding ring. "That would be great," Ruby said. "Will you shred potatoes for hash browns? I can't be trusted with any kind of grater."

"I think the last time anyone made breakfast for me was Mother's Day 1998," said Laura.

"I went out to brunch for Easter with my parents last year. Someone made me breakfast then," said Shannon.

"Oh, does that count?" Laura asked. "Then I guess it has been more recent. But wait, should it count if you pay them? I don't think it should count if you pay them."

"I'm normally not a big breakfast eater," Ruby said, unable to remember the last time she shared breakfast with anyone. It hadn't seemed like a big loss. Breakfast had never been her favorite meal.

"Yeah, I'm a cereal girl. It's like dog food for people," Shannon said.

Ruby laughed with Laura and said, "I suppose it is."

"Yep, you just open the box or bag and pour, and voilà, the meal is served," said Shannon. She piled her grated potatoes on the cutting board and asked, "Should I go ahead and fry these up?"

"I think so. I don't know where Ethel disappeared to. I saw her in the restroom this morning." She stopped herself before she told them about the strange doll that Ethel was talking to. On one hand, Ruby wanted other people who cared about Ethel to know, but on the other hand, it seemed wrong to make assumptions. "Laura, would you mind ringing the bell for her?"

"I get to ring the bell!" said Laura excitedly. "Wasn't that the best thing about kitchen duty? That illustrious chance you'd get to ring the bell? Oh, I just loved to ring the bell."

"You should get a bell for your house," Shannon told her. "You could ring it before every meal!"

"I bet my husband would love that!" Laura replied as she walked out the door.

Ruby found a skillet and began to scramble eggs on the stove next to Shannon and her hash browns.

"So you and Ethel go back quite a ways," Shannon said.

"Nineteen forty," Ruby replied. "We were six."

"Wow. That's a long time to know somebody."

Ruby wasn't sure how to respond to that. She hadn't known Ethel for decades.

After a little pause, Shannon asked, "Can you tell if she's doing okay? I can't tell. I mean this has got to be really hard for her."

Ruby, unsure of the best way to answer, avoided the question altogether. "I can't even imagine."

Laura returned and set the table. Ruby loved the ritual of table setting, the preparation of this place where they would come together. It had something to do with taking an ordinary thing and making it special.

A few minutes later, Ethel walked in and apologized for holding up the show—she had gone for a walk, she explained. Ruby and Shannon put their food in large serving bowls and set them on the table. And as Ethel led grace—"Back of the Bread," a short one, thank goodness—Ruby hoped that the love with which she had made the eggs would infuse them and nourish her old friend.

SHANNON 2012

There had been noticeable tension at the breakfast table. As Ethel lined out a plan with all of them for systematically cleaning out cupboards and closets, it was clear she was off. It was understandable, given the circumstances, but to Shannon it seemed like there was more to it. Ruby and Ethel didn't act like old friends the way Shannon and

Laura did. There was no ease, and Shannon noticed that Ethel rarely looked at Ruby.

But as Shannon and Laura began cleaning up they reminisced about their favorite camp songs, and as they washed and dried dishes they sang them—all the old silly ones that they sang after meals: the one about the boy and the girl in the little canoe, the one about the woman who rides the crocodile down the Nile until he eats her, the one they sang in the fake German accent as they pointed to different body parts and gave them ridiculous names, the one about swimming in the swimming pool, and the one about being good friends with a dinosaur. And when they sang, Ethel and Ruby puttered about and joined in.

Songs. There was something about songs that made everyone feel like they belonged. It was songs that eventually had pulled Shannon into the group her first year here. She had tried to resist them but just couldn't. Songs were contagious.

And now as they sang, it seemed things were lighter. Ethel even glanced Ruby's way.

In between songs, Ethel said, "You know, I do believe the last time I saw you two doing dishes together here, you were planning a big backpacking trip from here to Stehekin following the last session of camp. I remember because I was very concerned because you all thought that you didn't need tents."

Shannon and Laura looked at each other and started laughing.

"Oh my God, that trip was a disaster!" said Shannon.

"It snowed," Laura told Ethel. "Fortunately, Mary's dad made her take a tent. But it was me, Shannon, Mary, Michelle, Jen, and Teresa. So the six of us crawled into that two-man tent—" Laura began to cry from laughing so hard.

"—and we had to sleep the short way, all on our sides spooning one another." Shannon was laughing hard, too. "In the middle of the night one of us would wake up and call out, 'I've got to turn over!' and then we'd all have to turn over together!"

Ethel and Ruby laughed and Ethel said, "Ah, to be young again."

"You never think anything bad is ever going to happen to you," added Ruby.

Laura wiped the tears from her eyes and said to Shannon, "Remember how Michelle was in charge of the toilet paper and she only brought one roll for all six of us for the whole week, so she rationed it and only gave us two squares each time we needed some?"

"How could I forget?" Shannon laughed. "I'd use leaves or a rock or moss or whatever I could find for the first wipe and use the toilet paper for polishing."

"Polishing?" Laura howled. "Polishing? I'm picturing you—" She put her hand in the air and moved it in vigorous circles as if she were washing a window.

Shannon laughed and shook her head. "No, it wasn't like that."

"Speaking of polishing," Ethel said. "There's Windex and paper towels on a bench by the big picture window." She pointed to the main part of the Lodge.

Laura put away the last dish and followed Shannon to the job they had just been assigned. "I'm not going to be able to do this without thinking of you polishing your butt now." She held her stomach. "It hurts! Laughing this hard hurts!"

"I know," said Shannon. "A person needs to train to prepare for this level of laughing."

"Remember how hard we'd laugh at night when we were all supposed to sleep? Janet would try to get mad at us, but then she'd start laughing, too—"

"Oh, Janet. She was the best," said Shannon.

Laura scratched her head and asked, "Do you remember what was so funny? Because I can't for the life of me remember what was so funny."

Shannon thought for a moment and said, "No. I think maybe we were all just really tired and punchy."

But Laura's eyes lit up and she said, "No, wait. Remember that time Michelle farted while climbing the ladder up to the top bunk? That's what got us going that one time."

Shannon did remember. "I had never laughed so hard in my life." She hadn't. She had been such a serious and competitive child, but in that moment she suddenly realized that there was so much more to life than ballet and that she had been missing out on it.

Shannon rested her hand on a log in the wall as if it were a trusty horse and said, "You know, sometimes it just hits me so hard—this question of who I would be today if my parents hadn't brought me here to camp that first year. It just set me on such a different path. The things that had seemed so important to me before I came just didn't seem as important to me after spending the summer with you guys."

"Yeah, if it hadn't been for us, you'd probably have gone on to dance in the New York City Ballet. It's a good thing we came along," Laura joked.

"No, seriously," Shannon said. "I would have had an eating disorder, and then when I could no longer perform at that level I would have had an identity crisis. . . ." She thought for a moment. "Wait a minute. That's more or less what's happening now only without the eating disorder." She started laughing again.

"Aren't we all?" asked Laura.

"I wonder what I'm going to do next. Oh God, what if I end up working at Taco Bell?"

"You won't," Laura said.

"I could learn to drive a wheat combine," said Shannon. "And all day long, I'd just drive that tractor and listen to Blake Shelton. I wouldn't have to talk to a single soul."

"Good idea, but the next wheat harvest is almost a year away," said Laura. "Don't worry. We'll think of something." Then, she sprayed Windex on the window and began scrubbing with a paper towel. "Polishing!" she said, and started laughing all over again.

Looking as the tears began to stream down Laura's face once more, Shannon couldn't help but laugh again, too, and then neither of them could stop. It was that kind of laughter that morphs into something having very little to do with its origin, that kind that becomes a catharsis where every emotion a person had held back for the last decade finally escapes. Shannon wondered if Laura could also see it for what it was—the full spectrum of bottled-up feelings. When she turned to look at Laura, she could see that yes, in fact, it was easy to see through cathartic laughter. Laura was actually crying tears and tears and more tears.

SHANNON 1980

Shannon could recall the exact day she became a kid. She couldn't tell you the reason why that was that day or that moment—only that it happened, that something washed over her, something as joyful as sprinkles on a cookie or a sundae.

Nothing had felt particularly unusual when she woke up that morning, although she did not look around her cabin with negative thoughts for anyone or for the experience itself. Nor did she have any thoughts of superiority. In retrospect, that was unusual. At breakfast, she found a seat at her counselor's table and sat right next to Janet.

When breakfast was over and people began to sing, Shannon felt different somehow. To her left, Janet sang her heart out even though she could not carry a tune—not even close. Shannon studied her for a moment. How could someone enjoy doing something so much when she was clearly so bad at it? It was revolutionary to Shannon. All this time she had thought happiness came from excellence, but here was Janet completely happy and not remotely excellent. It forced Shannon to construct an entirely new set of beliefs.

She began by singing with Janet when the group started singing the song about the little rabbit in the woods who was protected from the hunter by a kind old man. Shannon sang along, and when it was time for the second verse—the rock-and-roll verse—she played her air guitar and sang its riffs with more gusto than anyone else. Yes, it was undignified and unsophisticated, but as it turned out, it was also silly and fun.

That feeling of silliness was what Shannon remembered most—how it bubbled up inside her belly and then all the way up to her chest as if she were carbonated like human soda pop. It was light and airy and almost tickled.

So this is what it feels like to be a kid, she thought.

ETHEL 1940

Ethel was only six on her first night at camp. She pulled a tiny nightgown out of her duffel bag and laid it on her bed upside down. Early July nights were still something close to frigid, so when she took off her shirt and pants her tender skin puckered in protest. Slipping her arms into the bottom, she sort of dove into her nightgown where it lay on her bunk. Then she crawled into her bedroll. It was every bit as cold as she was.

Her counselor told a bedtime story about magical animals that visited the little girls of Camp Firelight, but even though the animals were friendly in the story, they got Ethel thinking about the real ones—the ones that weren't magical or friendly. What if she had to go to the bathroom in the middle of the night? Would a bear eat her counselor and her? She wanted to go home to her house, where she didn't have to go outside to go to the bathroom at night.

The fact that her sleeping bag was so cold only made her emotional state worse, and she longed to walk down the hall of her house and crawl into bed with her sleeping parents, all warm and cozy. Sure, at some point her mom would wake and bring her back to her own bed, but if she pretended she was asleep sometimes her mom still carried her, and Ethel loved those indulgent thirty seconds of getting to be a baby again.

What if her parents were missing her right now, too? What if they were sad and felt like crying because she was away? What if they died while she was at camp and she never saw them again? She imagined living all alone in their house, and it was this thought that finally sent her over the edge.

She began to cry, thinking of how badly she wanted to be in her mother's arms again, of how badly she wanted to cling to her dad and feel the scratchy wool of his sweater on her cheek. Sometimes he sneaked down to the basement to smoke a cigar and the scent of it mixed with the wool and lingered. Her mom, however, smelled like things in the kitchen: dish soap, apples, and bread, but with seasonal twists—a hint of cinnamon in the autumn, lemons and sugar in the summer. When Ethel's parents' skin was warmed in their bed, their smell collected under the covers and then escaped in wafts of fragrant wind when they shifted. How she ached to feel those warm whooshes of air on her face and smell her parents.

She tried to silence herself, not wanting to be the big baby in the cabin, but the grief was building and building inside her like a volcano threatening to erupt. She sniffed as quietly as she could.

And that was when a little hand reached out to her from the next bunk over. It belonged to Ruby, the little red-haired girl. Ruby's little hand found Ethel's and held it.

The counselor continued her story, and Ruby continued to hold her hand until Ethel finally surrendered to much-needed sleep.

ETHEL 2012

That night, as Ethel chopped chicken, carrots, onions, and the potatoes that Ruby peeled, she thought of something Haddie had once said about trust—that there were no shortcuts, no substitute, for "time spent and space shared." Ruby and Ethel worked in silence for the most part, and although it was terribly awkward, Ethel tried to appreciate it for what it was—time spent and space shared. Considering the last fifty-seven years, it was actually a huge step.

Ruby kneaded bread while Ethel threw the soup together and wrestled with her own resentment and bitterness. She didn't want to feel like this. And the worst part was that Ruby hadn't done anything that Ethel hadn't. She hated to think of it. She tried her best to block out that memory, but it bubbled up. Truth did that. It bubbled up to the surface like a geyser, and this particular story was going to be like Old Faithful.

"I did the same thing," Ethel blurted out. "I turned my back on two of my all-time favorite staff members because of pressure from the board. And I'm thinking that maybe it's because I could never forgive myself for that, that I'm having trouble forgiving you."

Ruby simply looked at Ethel and waited for more.

Ethel looked at Ruby apologetically. "I don't know why I said that. I don't know what I'm hoping to accomplish. I mean, neither of us can change what we did, or undo decades of damage. The past is like concrete that hardened or a broken bone that healed wrong."

The look on Ruby's face was one of pure compassion. "I've spent the last fifty-seven years thinking about forgiveness from every angle, and I've figured out a couple things. The first is that everyone has made big mistakes. Everyone has regrets. When one person apologizes, the other person feels less alone in her own regrets. Shame is a lonely thing. Thank you. Thank you for making me feel less alone."

Ethel said awkwardly, "You're welcome."

Ruby was quiet for a moment, and then she said, "I've come to realize that forgiveness is a practice, like cleaning my bathroom regularly. Doing it once isn't good enough. There's not this moment when I finally do it right and then I'm done for the rest of my life. It has to be done daily, or at least weekly. It's like this. We're human. We poop. We're going to continue to poop. So we're going to have to continue to clean our toilets. And we're also going to continue to make mistakes. It's part of being human. So along with trying to fix our mistakes, we're going to have to keep forgiving ourselves for those mistakes, as difficult as that may be. Whenever I clean my toilet, I think about it. I'm going to continue to poop and I'm going to continue to screw up. The best I can do is clean up after myself and forgive myself the best I can and get on with my day."

Ethel laughed. "Classic Ruby. Classic." She reached out for Ruby's hand. "I really have missed you. There's just not another Ruby in this whole world."

Ruby gave Ethel a tearful hug.

Then, even though Ruby hadn't asked, Ethel told her the story of the thing she regretted most. When her confession was done, she felt different somehow—no less regretful or ashamed, but braver, perhaps. And understood. Almost forgiven. Almost.

ETHEL 1981

Ethel had been going over the food budget for the next year when she got the call from Mary Hallstrom out in Ephrata.

"Ethel, I'm afraid I have some alarming news. It seems that two of your counselors last year were *lesbians*. I just got a call from Barb Nelson, Janet Nelson's mother. It seems Janet brought Sue Mayer home for the weekend, and Barb sensed something was wrong, so after Sue left, she asked Janet about it, and Janet told her that yes, she was a *lesbian,* and yes, she and Sue were involved. Can you imagine how horrified Barb was? Well, she disowned her immediately and then she called Shirley and me right away to tell me to make sure they weren't hired back again next year."

What could Ethel say in response to that? If she weren't careful, she and Haddie would be next. Imagine, not living and working at camp. Imagine being forty-four and having to find an entirely new profession. What else would she do? What else would Haddie do? Ethel couldn't imagine anything else. And so, scared, she simply said, "Okay."

Okay. With that one word, she blackballed Janet from camp. Janet, who had been coming to camp since she was seven. Janet, who sometimes cried on the day she returned at the beginning of each summer because she was so glad to be back in her favorite place, in the place she belonged. Janet said something just that last summer that haunted Ethel now: *We all have the families we are born into, but camp is our family of choice.* Janet had always been one of Ethel's favorite kids because she embodied so much joy. She sang songs with great enthusiasm at meals, and at bedtime when Ethel strolled around the camp she often heard Janet singing the little ones to sleep tenderly.

Lesbian. Mary had said it as if it were synonymous with "devil." As if it were the Plague—contagious like that. Janet was no devil. Not even close. And love was no plague.

And Ethel's silence had been an act of agreement with something she knew was not truth.

When Ethel was growing up, her parents had often talked about all the people in Germany who let Hitler take over their country—how important it was to heed the lesson of that and stand up for what was right. But as she hung up the phone after listening to Mary, Ethel understood how the Holocaust had happened. There came a point when the enemy was so much bigger than just one person and when it seemed being one more person persecuted wouldn't make one bit of difference in the outcome. Still, she hated herself for what she had done.

Three months later, Janet had come to visit her at the office. After all, Ethel had been the matriarch of Janet's *family of choice.*

"Hi, Ethel!" Janet had said, bubbling over with happiness.

Instead of happiness, Ethel felt fear. Janet didn't know about her mother's call to Mary and didn't know she'd been blackballed. And Ethel couldn't bring herself to tell her. "Hi, Janet," she said in a way that was forced and noticeably not warm.

Janet paused for just a second and then decided not to let that deter her. "I'm having a great time in college! I took this women's studies class that was so interesting, but I'm also studying economics because I want to help third-world women get more economic power. I was thinking about trying to get a job with US Aid after I graduate. I just feel so inspired, you know? Like anything is possible!"

Ethel smiled sadly.

Janet paused again, her expression confused, and then she tried once more to engage Ethel. "Well, I sure am excited about camp next year."

Ethel looked down at her desk and nodded. What if a board member walked into the office right then? What would happen? Any association with Janet could sink her. *It's a job,* Ethel told herself. *It's a job and I have to do what my boss asks. This isn't my fault. I'm just following my boss's orders.* Maybe Janet would find a job at another camp. Firelight wasn't the only camp in the world. But Ethel felt sick even thinking it, because she knew that for Janet, it was.

After an awkward pause, Ethel said, "Well, thanks for

stopping by," in a way that didn't really mean "thank you" at all but, rather, "you are excused now."

"Well, I can see I caught you at a busy moment. But I wanted to say hi. So, hi!"

"Hi," Ethel said, starting to melt. Janet had one of those pure hearts filled with nothing but good intentions. She was a good soul and she didn't deserve this at all.

As Janet turned and walked out the door, she said, "I love you, Ethel."

That just about destroyed Ethel. It did. And she couldn't lie by saying nothing to this child she had watched grow up over eleven summers. "I love you, too, Janet." But the moment it passed her lips, she wondered if that was the truth either, because maybe love didn't count unless it was bigger than one's fear for oneself.

She rested her head in her hands and wished with every fiber of her being that the world was different.

LAURA 1980

Laura had watched her mother apply thick makeup to the tender skin under her eye until the color no longer jumped out. Still, the swelling could not be hidden. But in the summer, Laura's mother told people she had gotten an insect bite or bee sting there and that seemed to satisfy the curiosity of those who expressed concern.

As her parents and she stood in line for check-in at camp, Laura looked nervously around. Would anyone be able to tell? To her relief, her old friends ran up and hugged her and then ran off to hug someone else, without ever really looking closely at her mother.

"What's taking so long?" Her father began to grumble, much to Laura's horror. She wasn't sure what she would do if he was rude to Ethel. Laura turned away so he wouldn't see her shut her eyes and silently pray that he would stop and just be patient, check her in, and go far away.

When she opened them, Ethel caught her eye in a way that seemed to ask whether she was okay. Laura gave her two very subtle nods, but the fear in her eyes still showed.

Then at last the wait was over. She kissed her mother good-bye. Laura's father tousled her hair and said, "Give your dad a hug and a kiss." *So he was playing the part of the caring father now,* she thought. *Okay.* She knew how to play along to keep him pacified. And afterward, much to her relief, they left.

Ethel asked her to show a new girl to their cabin—Shannon—and that was fine with Laura. She led the way out the little path toward the cabin, a path she loved so much it almost took on magical qualities. It was as if all the love so many kids had for camp had soaked into the ground and made everything seem enchanted. As she walked, her burdens seemed to fall away on the side of the trail—the tension her body chronically held from being on alert . . . the negative words and harsh tones of voice she had overheard through walls . . . the secrets she kept about what was under her mother's makeup. . . . Laura just let all of those burdens fall off of her. The earth, she thought, could handle it. After all, the earth had a wonderful way of turning manure into compost.

Shannon's mother tried to engage her in conversation, but Laura couldn't really take it in. There was no room for anything to come in—only out, like express lanes leaving the city. By the time she reached the cabin, she felt noticeably lighter.

She put her hand on the weathered doorknob like the

touchstone it was, opened the door, inhaled the musty cabin smell, and smiled. Her friends called out greetings that filled the places inside her that she had just cleared. Funny how a place a person only visited for one season a year could be her true home.

LAURA 2012

When she heard the dinner bell Laura hustled down the trail to the Lodge. On her way out, the trail had seemed shorter than she had remembered, but now that she was in a hurry it seemed significantly longer. Along the way, she spotted a pileated woodpecker, some deer tracks, a dung beetle crossing the trail, and some ruby-colored mushrooms. The tops of the mushrooms were concave and held little pools of water, like magic worlds all unto themselves. She'd never seen these particular mushrooms before, and something about this new discovery gave her joy.

My true home, she remembered thinking as she walked this path as a kid. *My true home.* Was that still true? Maybe a person didn't have just one. Certainly the house where she had rocked her babies to sleep at night, where she'd spent many Christmases with her family, where all the defining moments of the last twenty years had taken place, had to be considered her true home. *We are our choices,* she'd once heard, and considered those words again. It was true. And the home she shared with Steve housed that part of her—the part she had fostered with her choices. But this place . . . this place housed her essence. There was something very pure about it. It made her feel more like herself than she'd felt in a long time—

not the self that was fenced in by a lifetime of choices, but the self that once dwelled in infinite possibilities.

The Lodge smelled like chicken and bread. And when she opened the door, she didn't feel the same level of tension as she'd felt last night or even this morning. The chitchat reminded her of happy birdsongs now. She took the last remaining place at the table and bowed her head when Ethel began to sing "'Neath These Tall Green Trees," the grace Laura suspected for years was the one that Ethel picked when she was hungry because it was short.

Although the chitchat was happy, Laura didn't think she could stay on that level much longer. Pretending everything was okay exhausted her. She'd been doing it for far too many years. They were all in the process of experiencing a big loss, and if they had come here to say goodbye to this place together it needed to be spoken. "I was thinking about homes," she shared with the others after they sat down and had begun to serve themselves up. "About how different places house different parts of us, and how no other place in the world could house the part of me this place does. *Where will it go now?* I've been asking myself. *Where will that part of me live?*"

"Almost all of me lives here," Ethel said, and Laura was relieved to see the sadness in her eyes. Truth. How good the truth felt, even when it was so heartbreaking. Ethel continued, slowly and deliberately choosing her words. "So, I've been asking myself the very same thing. I think, perhaps, those parts of us will always live here no matter what becomes of this place."

Laura looked into Ethel's eyes and nodded. Yes, she could accept that answer. In fact, there was something rather reassuring about it.

"I've been thinking," Ethel went on, "that maybe those parts of us continue to live here long after we leave the bodies we inhabit and leave this earth."

AMBER 2012

When the school bus dropped her off, Amber walked up the road, found her bike in the forest, and carried it back to the pavement, still undecided about where to go first. She needed a job. That was the only way. And since she needed the school bus to get the twenty miles back up here to the lake, her job had to be up here. There were only three businesses in the area: the bar where her mother worked, the small grocery store across the street from the bar, and the Diner five miles away at the intersection of the Lake Wenatchee Highway and Stevens Pass.

Being hidden in a kitchen doing dishes seemed like the most invisible job, and therefore the best one, so she pedaled down the highway and past the trailer to inquire at the Diner.

When she opened the door, warm air heavy with the smells of food smacked her in the face and made her stomach growl even louder. She breathed it in deeply. Fish-and-chips, chicken and mashed potatoes with gravy, cheeseburgers. Her mouth watered. Oh, if she could just wash dishes here, she could eat leftover food when no one was looking. A week ago that would have sounded disgusting to her, but now it sounded like heaven. She looked around at the patrons. A trucker cut his chicken, sliding it into the mashed potatoes and green beans next to it. In the next booth, a little boy had eaten four bites of his toasted cheese sandwich and left the rest there, along with a big handful of fries. A whole half of toasted cheese sandwich just sat there, untouched. He was whining about wanting to go. Maybe if she stalled long enough, she could slip that half of sandwich into her pocket before she left. She eyed the restroom and wondered about stalling there, but before she could, the waitress came over with a warm smile and said, "Hi, sugar," as she grabbed a menu.

"No. I'm s-s-sorry," Amber stammered. "I'm looking for a job. Do you need a dishwasher?"

"Well, not very often, but sometimes we do need a substitute," the waitress said, and handed Amber an application. "You can take this with you or fill it out here. Then we can give you a call on those nights we need someone."

A call? Problem number one: Amber didn't have a phone. And then as she looked at the application, problems number two and three jumped out at her. She would need her Social Security number, which she didn't know, and the card itself to prove her citizenship. Problem number three? She would also need proof that she was sixteen, which she wasn't. The situation seemed so insurmountable, and she felt so desperate.

"Uhh, thank you," Amber said. "I'll take it with me."

How could she get by without a job and with nothing but fourteen dollars to live on for the next year? It would be impossible. She had no choice—she needed to stop at her house and find her Social Security card and birth certificate. It was the only way she'd ever have a shot at independence. Perhaps she could change her birthday on it, or perhaps she could make a copy and change the date on that and just submit that with her application. Resolved, she got on her bike again and rode back to her old home.

Outside the trailer, she hid her bike in the woods and then carefully approached the front door. It was after five and her mother's car was gone, so Amber found the key hidden under the stairs, unlocked the door, and locked it behind her.

The house had a strange smell, sort of like cat urine . . . sharp like that. What was it? It sure wasn't right.

Where would her mother have put these documents? On the kitchen counter was a pile of bills from the last two months, mostly unopened. Amber checked the cupboard where they kept the phone book, but it wasn't there either. However, she did take the opportunity to put two books of matches and a knife in her pocket. And while she was in the kitchen, she opened the cupboards and fridge to look for anything to eat. They were for the most part empty. In the cupboard was salt, pepper, onion powder, a can of mushrooms, and a can of Spam. Spam? Her mom must have picked it up on a particularly desperate day at the food bank. Amber wasn't desperate enough to take the mushrooms or the Spam. In the fridge there was mustard, ketchup, pickles, a little bit of ranch salad dressing, and one egg in a carton marked with an expiration date back in August. Amber wondered how it was that she had lived this long with such an incompetent mother. It was a miracle she was still alive. It really was.

As she scanned the whole trailer, her heart raced faster and faster as she opened cupboards, drawers, and closet doors frantically. She found a flashlight—score—but nothing else.

Reluctantly, she walked into her mother's room and rifled through the boxes in the bottom of her closet, hoping one might hold important documents. Amber found three boxes with shoes in them, one with pictures, and one with a syringe and burnt spoon. She wished it surprised her, but it didn't. She put the lid back on and kept on task.

Under the bottom box, something pink caught her eye—her baby book. She picked it up and opened it. There were her tiny footprints in black ink, notes her mother had made about how big Amber was when she was born, and a picture of her taken at the hospital. There was a picture of her getting a bath in the sink, a picture of her holding on to the edge of the coffee table when she learned to stand, a lock of hair from her first haircut, a photo taken on her first birthday where her hands and face were covered in icing, and a picture Amber had drawn of her mother and her. They were smiley faces, one large and one small, with little lines for arms and legs sticking out of each one. Amber smiled, imagining her mom with arms sticking out of her ears and legs sticking out of the bottom of her face. There was a page with a date entered in for when Amber took her first steps and a page with her first words: "Mom," "bottle," and "more." These were the things her mom found worth keeping.

When Amber turned the page, a paper fell out. Her birth certificate! *Jackpot!* She folded it up and put it in her pocket. *Thank you, God.* She put the book down and made one last attempt to find her Social Security card in her mother's dresser drawers and nightstand drawer, but no luck. Maybe her mother had sold it for drugs.

When Amber walked into her old room, her heart ached for her old things, for warmth and familiarity. It was exactly as she had left it. She quickly took a blanket out from under her comforter and reassembled the bed, hoping she was leaving no trace. She took the two extra T-shirts—the ones she had left behind—and rolled them up in the blanket.

Then, heart still racing, she left the house, locked the door behind her, replaced the key, and sprinted to her bike. It was nearly six o'clock and only the tail end of twilight lingered in the sky. Carefully, she pedaled on the outside of the white line, since she had no lights on her bike. In fact, she didn't even have a rear reflector. It had broken off one time when she had crashed.

In the light of intermittent oncoming traffic, she could see her own breath. The seasons were definitely turning. Only two cars had passed her from behind, each, it seemed, uncomfortably close. Within a couple miles, twilight surrendered to night.

She heard another car approaching from behind and got over as far as she could. Maybe she should pull way off the road when cars came from behind, she thought. Or maybe she should turn on her flashlight. But before she could decide what to do, the car's rearview mirror grazed her and she fell over into the shallow ditch on the side of the road.

The car skidded to a stop and a man jumped out and ran to her. "Oh my God! I didn't see you! Are you all right?"

Amber lay there for a second before she peeled her face out of the dirt, untangled herself from her bike, and sat. She was shaken, for sure.

"Hey! I'm so sorry! I never saw you. I heard something and thought maybe I hit a deer, but when I looked back, I saw you! Are you okay?"

Was she okay? She wasn't sure. "I think so," Amber said, uncertain.

"Well, let's take you to the hospital and have them check you out," he said. He was wearing a sport coat and tie, and his leather shoes shone. Amber noticed he was clean shaven and had a neat haircut, so he did not appear to be from around here. She looked over at his car, a shiny black Mercedes.

"No," Amber said emphatically.

"I really think we ought to make sure you're okay," he said. "I'll pay for it. Don't worry about that."

"No," Amber said. "No hospital."

He paused for a moment, uncomfortable and unsure. "Well, let me at least take you home. At the very least you're bruised up, and this isn't safe, riding in the dark." He picked up her bike and put it in his trunk.

"No, really," Amber said. "I'm fine. I really am."

"I can't ethically leave you out here after hitting you with my car. Let's get you home safely. Besides, someone else might run into you and kill you if you try riding home this time of night." He helped her up.

She didn't know what to do. He was a stranger, but he was right. The side of the road was not a safe place to be. And her right knee and her arm throbbed. Her head felt a little funny, too. So she picked up her blanket and got in his plush, immaculately clean car and gave him directions.

The three windy miles seemed like forever. She was so relieved when the Camp Firelight sign came into view. "You can drop me off here. I don't have a key to the gate," she said.

"I really would feel better if I turned you over to your parents," he replied, getting out and taking her bike out of the trunk. Would he give it to her or insist on walking it to her house?

"Oh, um, my mom works a weird shift, so she's not available right now. It's okay. I'll get cleaned up and be fine. Really, you've done more than enough. I'm sorry for the inconvenience. I should have had lights on my bike."

He looked concerned but let go of the handlebars when she took them from him. He reached into his wallet and took out a card. "If you decide to go to a doctor later, here's how to reach me. What's your name?"

"Amber," she replied, and then, as she turned to go, she added, "Thanks for the lift. Again, I'm very sorry for the inconvenience."

"Okay," he replied uneasily.

She didn't turn back around but heard him drive away as she walked around the gate and followed the dirt road into camp.

On her way back down the hill toward her cabin, she noticed the porch light on outside the bathroom. She hadn't noticed it the night before, but then she hadn't been wandering around after dark the night before. That's when one more glorious thing caught her eye. The door was unlocked. The padlock was locked on the doorjamb, but the part that was attached to the door had not been folded over the little U first. She felt like a game show winner as she opened the door and went inside. *Glory be!* There were six toilets and two gigantic metal sinks. She would totally be able to wash her clothes by hand in them. Who knew how long it would take them to dry, but regardless, she would be able to wash them.

She turned on the bathroom light so she could take inventory of her injuries—a light! She'd have a place to do homework after dark now! When she turned on the faucet, though, no water came out, no matter how much she cranked it. Weird. But a gallon of water sat on a shelf near the sink, and with that she wet a paper towel and washed up her scrapes.

Then, she gingerly lowered herself down to the cold concrete floor and unpacked her book bag, laying her math book and notebook out before her. It wasn't comfortable, but it was doable. Fortunately, she had completed most of her homework in class and on the bus, so there wasn't a lot that she needed to finish up—just six lengthy problems.

When her math was done, she made up fictitious income information and forged her mother's signature on the free and reduced lunch form and wondered what would be for breakfast the next day. She hoped it was something like eggs and sausage—something heavy that would hold her over instead of waffles and syrup that would leave her hungry after just an hour. When she packed everything back up and stood, she held on to the sink because her legs had fallen asleep and she needed to wait a couple painful minutes for the feeling to come back before she could walk.

Her stomach growled and burned. She needed to pocket more food at breakfast and lunch, but how could she do that and be discreet? If only she had been able to snag that toasted cheese sandwich at the Diner this afternoon. God, it had looked so good.

It was cold now and it was only October. She had seen no chimneys in any of the cabins she had walked by, so she knew none had fireplaces or woodstoves. She would have to explore more. Somewhere in this camp, there had to be a building with a fireplace in it. She'd break in somehow. Or maybe she needed to figure out how to move to town.

But tonight's discovery of the unlocked bathroom solved a couple of her immediate problems, and so for now it was enough to make her happy. She walked her bike back to the little cabin, crawled through the window in the dark, and felt around for her pajamas, for the ladder, and for Woof Woof. Her flashlight she would save for emergencies.

ETHEL 1952

Ethel and Haddie had helplessly watched the sky darken through the kitchen windows as they washed a seemingly insurmountable pile of breakfast dishes. They were eager to collect their mattresses and sleeping bags on the beach before the rain came. In the end, they got them just in time.

Since the mattresses were made of heavy cotton tick, hauling them up the stairs had been no small achievement. It required teamwork. Just as they unloaded the last one on their bunks, rain began to pelt the roof and the window.

"We did it," Ethel said breathlessly, collapsing onto her bunk, arms spread open wide.

"We did it," Haddie repeated, and collapsed onto Ethel's bunk next to her, her head nestled on Ethel's arm.

At first, Ethel froze, terrified. She was in uncharted waters without a map and didn't know how to read the situation or what to do. They lay like that for a couple of minutes before Ethel broke the tension by saying, "Tonight we have to listen to Cookie snore." Cookie, the cook, sounded like a tractor. At the moment, they could hear her clattering around in the kitchen below them, in the early preparation stage of lunch.

Haddie got up, and as she held out a hand and helped Ethel up she said, "The worst thing won't be Cookie's snoring. The worst thing will be sleeping on the other side of the room from you." And before Ethel could really absorb it all, Haddie kissed her.

ETHEL 2012

Right before breakfast that morning, Ethel had hidden Haddie's urn safely in her duffel bag but now that it was nighttime, she wished she could take it out and look at it. It gave her a new level of sympathy for all of the little kids who had come to camp for so many years with a favorite toy or perhaps a blanket hidden in the depths of their suitcase, hoping no one would discover it but risking being found out because they had been unable to think of coping in its absence. She felt the same way. *These things we love so much and are so afraid others will find,* Ethel mused. *They represent our vulnerable places.*

Ruby had stopped in the kitchen for a glass of water, affording Ethel a moment of looking across the room at the bunk where Haddie belonged before she returned and took up that space. It was funny, really, to think of all the young women who had slept in that very bunk in the sixty years or so since Haddie had and yet it was still Haddie who belonged there.

Ethel heard Ruby's footsteps coming up the stairs and turned her eyes to watch her enter.

"I miss Opal," Ruby said plainly. Opal had been Ruby's sister. Yes, the four of them—Ruby, Opal, Ethel, and Haddie—had been quite the group. "I miss Haddie, too. The four of us sure had some good times."

"Maybe they're watching from above," said Ethel.

"Well, if they are, I hope they respect my privacy in the bathroom. That's all I ask."

Ethel laughed. It was impossible to stay mad at Ruby. It just was.

"I think if they are watching," Ruby began as she changed into her nightgown, "that they would really like to see us raid Shannon and Laura's cabin."

Ethel laughed again. "Really, Ruby? You're going to play that card? You can't pass that off on them. It was always you that loved raiding the most."

Unfazed, Ruby said, "But I think we need to put some thought into it so that they blame each other and never suspect that a couple little old ladies were indeed the masterminds."

Ethel watched Ruby carefully fold up the fishing vest she had worn all day. "Is that Henry's?"

Ruby ran her hand over it. "Yes. I miss him, too."

Ethel knew all about missing. "He was nice."

"He sure was," said Ruby, crawling into bed. "That day

after I got his last letter . . . you know, when you brought me out here and took me out in a canoe? That meant a lot to me. You were such a good friend." The rest was left unsaid, but Ethel knew it was another apology.

"Good night, Ruby," Ethel said in the same way she would have said, *It's all right*.

"Good night, Ethel," Ruby said in the same way she would have said, *Thank you*.

Time spent and space shared. It was starting to work.

LAURA 1981

Words are no different than punches, thought Laura as she listened to her parents fight. It hurt her just to hear it. The whole house shook when a door slammed or when one of them stomped. She knew the little earthquakes would pass. They always did. But boy, when they were happening it was difficult to believe stillness would ever grace the house again.

She slid out of bed and slipped her hand between her mattress and box spring just as far back as her arm would reach. With her fingertips, she searched until at last she found it—a one-gallon ziplock plastic bag with her camp T-shirt inside. Carefully, she pulled it out so that she didn't tear the plastic, and then, as if she were hyperventilating and her very life depended on bringing this bag to her face quickly, she opened it and breathed in the smell of campfire smoke still steeped in the fabric. She closed her eyes and did it again.

In her mind, she was back around the campfire on the beach, roasting s'mores and laughing with friends. And as the sun began to set, they began what they called the Magic Circle, where someone would begin by leading a song, singing a solo, or reciting a poem—sometimes even an original one—and when she finished the person next to her would be responsible for sharing or leading the next one. Around and around the circle they went until someone ran out of something to share. Then, the Magic Circle was broken and it was time for bed. The older kids and counselors who sometimes joined their campfires came with a notebook full of songs and poems. Laura believed with all their material the older campers and counselors probably had Magic Circle all night and well into the morning. But in fifth grade, like she was, mostly they just took turns leading camp songs everyone knew.

She opened the bag and took one more deep inhale of the scent and quickly sealed it up again so as not to waste it. And while she did, she remembered a specific moment in the Magic Circle—not a particularly remarkable one, just a moment when it was her turn. All eyes were on her, waiting expectantly, and she felt the weight of the responsibility. Bedtime hung in the balance. At first she froze, and then *Flicker* popped into her head. "Flicker the light of the campfire . . . ," she began to sing. Relief washed over her when the others joined in and she was no longer singing alone. And more relief filled her still as she realized she had successfully saved them all from bedtime.

Now, as her parents shouted at each other and slammed things in the next room, she quietly sang a line from that song: "Love is for those who find it. . . ." As she did, she thought of her other family—her camp family, the family that was kind and sane and warm and calm. And even though she was only eleven, she knew she had found something her parents had not. They had not known love the way she had known it at camp, and for that she felt sorry for them.

She wedged the plastic bag with the smoky T-shirt back in between her mattresses way, way back and thought to herself, *I will never be like that.* It was more than resolve. It was a fact. She knew another way to be.

LAURA 2012

Laura had noticed that Shannon hadn't returned to the Lodge after she slipped out to go to the bathroom, and now she saw why. Shannon had a little fire going in the fire ring outside their cabin and was reading a book.

As Laura walked up, she asked, "What are you reading?"

Shannon showed Laura the cover. "Rumi. His poems don't always make sense to me, but I like them anyway. There's just something gentle about him."

"You're having a Magic Circle without me?" Laura joked.

"Pull up a stump," Shannon said.

Laura accepted her invitation and then looked up into the forest canopy. "Nice night," she said. "It's getting chilly! The fire feels good."

"There's nothing like a campfire," Shannon replied. And began to sing "Flicker."

Laura continued by singing the next line. "Just give me some friends to sing with, I'll be here all night. . . ."

"I love those sweet songs we'd sing around the campfire—the pretty ones."

"Remember how all our clothes would smell when we left here?" asked Laura. "I used to stick my camp T-shirt in a plastic bag and keep it under my mattress, so I could take it out and smell it when I was missing camp."

Shannon laughed. "That's great."

"I don't know if I ever told you that my dad was abusive. He had a problem with drinking that brought out his mean side."

"I could tell something wasn't right," Shannon said.

"Pretty amazing when I look back that the eight weeks of normal a year that I experienced up here sustained me and kept me sane, because I'm telling you, the other forty-four weeks a year were hell."

Shannon shook her head. "That's amazing."

"Earlier, you were talking about who you would have been were it not for camp. I was thinking about it all day today, about how this place taught me what I needed to know so that I could go on and have a healthy family. I didn't turn into either of my parents. Thank God that because of camp, I had other role models to choose from. I mean what a profound blessing."

"I hear you. I've been thinking about how camp gives only children the really important experience of not being the center of the universe and of belonging to something bigger."

"Thank God for camp," Laura said.

"Thank God for camp," Shannon echoed.

Laura sighed. "It makes me so sad to think of other kids like me not having this escape."

"There's still the YMCA camp across the lake, and there's still Girl Scouts and Boy Scouts."

"True," said Laura. "This isn't the only camp in the whole world. Just the only one I loved."

"Yeah," Shannon agreed. "I love this place, too. I just have to tell myself that it will be okay. Whatever happens, it will just have to be okay. I mean, there's no other choice but to accept what is, right?"

And then they were quiet for a little bit as they stared into the fire, each lost in her own thoughts.

Shannon set her book down on her lap and rubbed her face. "I can't believe that I lost it in school like I did. I wish I could have left with more composure than that."

"We all lose it. We all reach our breaking points."

"Really?" Shannon asked. "It seems like you have it all together."

"The forties are intense."

"You said it."

"It's like it doesn't even matter what you've been doing for twenty years. Whatever it is, you find yourself wondering if you can tolerate it for twenty more."

"For me, that would be a big 'no,'" said Shannon. "For you?"

"I'm thinking about getting a divorce."

"Oh," said Shannon, stunned and speechless. Finally she simply said, "I'm sorry."

"Steve is a good man. It's just . . . you know, we just sent our youngest off to college a few days ago, and now we're both wondering what reason there is to stay. No one has said it out loud yet, but it's coming. I can feel it. He pretends to be asleep when I get in bed at night."

"How do you know?"

"I can tell by his breathing. And I don't blame him. When I get there first, I pretend to be asleep, too. And he waits to come to bed until he thinks I'm asleep. There's something awkward about sharing a bed. Something about it feels like a lie, like we're only pretending to be married. We haven't had sex in years." It felt so good to tell somebody this big secret.

"Oh," Shannon said sympathetically. "That's not good. I always thought that would be the best part of being married—getting lucky on a regular basis."

"It changes when it becomes an obligation," Laura said. "After I'd had Kenan, I was exhausted—way too tired to want to have sex. I confessed this to one of my friends who was also a new mother and she said, 'If you don't, someone else will, and there you'll be, all alone with a baby.' Well, that scared me, so I made myself have sex with Steve even when I was so tired I couldn't keep my eyes open, because that's what wives who wanted to keep their husbands did. During the day I catered to my baby, and during the night I catered to my husband. It seemed there was not a single waking moment I wasn't catering to someone. And as time went on, I grew to hate this drudgery, this chore, this thing I was too tired to do but had to do, too."

"Oh, Laura, that's so sad."

"I know. I remember how it was when we first met . . . and now it's just so wrecked. Decades of damage, you know? I remember when the look in Steve's eyes had changed from a look of pure love to a look where he was simply assessing whether he was making any progress toward pleasing me in bed. And after a few years of that, there was this edge of anger . . . I'm sure from being stuck with a woman that no longer wanted him sexually . . . from no longer being desired. I used to love this man with all my heart, you know? I never wanted him to be trapped in a sexless marriage, and so about a year ago I gave him a good-night kiss that lasted longer than most, and Steve took it for the invitation it was. And I just waited for it to be over. And for the first time, Steve shut his eyes, I'm assuming so he could imagine that he was with anybody but me. He wasn't attempting to connect with me at all. I felt like a big blow-up doll. But I also felt like if that's what he needed after all this time, I owed him that. And then, at some point, he just stopped and said, 'I can't do this. I feel like a rapist.' He got out of bed and watched TV until I fell asleep, and we've been avoiding each other ever since."

"Oh, poor Steve. Poor you. Oh, this is not good. What about counseling?"

"I think if either of us says anything truthful, our marriage will be over in a minute or less."

"Honey, it kind of sounds like it already is and has been for a long time."

"We've got two kids in college. We can't afford to get divorced."

Both women slipped back into the silence of their own thoughts again, hypnotized by the flickering firelight.

After a while, Shannon said, "It's too bad this place is a done deal. Wouldn't it have been fun to run it? Man, I look at Ethel's life and think that's what I wanted. I wanted to work with kids, but like this—like a family, not like a slave master. Campfires inspire kids to love poetry more than tests do. But it's about more than poetry. Poetry is just the vehicle. It's about humanity—it's about being human with one another. Language arts are just the way we express our connection, or what unites us. I feel like school reform is taking out our connection and our unity, and without those things language arts have no meaning. I wonder sometimes if I've wasted my life. Being a camp director would have been so much more meaningful to me. Can you imagine if we had done it together? You could have led the nature walks you loved so much. . . ."

Laura poked at the fire with a stick. "We would have been good at that," she said sadly.

"We would have."

"Spilled milk."

"Yeah, I guess so," Shannon said, her inspired moment deflating back into acceptance of the hopelessness again.

"Maybe tonight we'll have good dreams about what it would have been like if it had worked out that way. Nothing wrong with a good dream," said Laura.

LAURA 1977

The first time she heard it she was seven. She didn't remember what woke her—only lying in her sleeping bag listening to it. Molly, in the bunk above her, was snoring softly like a purring kitten, but even that noise didn't interfere with Laura's ability to hear it. Outside, wind blew in the trees so that they sounded a little like a rushing river, and still Laura could still hear it above that noise, too. Peace. For the first time, she heard peace.

Peace sounded like silence, but less lonely. It sounded like quiet, but better, because she wasn't waiting for the other shoe to drop. Yes, quiet was riddled with dread and anticipation, but peace was clear and warm like a full bath. Quiet was more like a shower where at any moment the hot water could run out, turning the cold water loose like attack dogs.

She drank up the peace with her ears and her heart, unsure of whether this was what heaven felt like or whether this was how people were supposed to feel— whether she was finally experiencing normal.

She rolled over and looked at her counselor, Jannie, sleeping. Jannie was not drunk. She would not be yelling. She had even tucked Laura in, told a story, and sung a lullaby. Maybe Jannie had been able to feel her staring at her, because she opened her eyes and looked at Laura.

"Laura, are you okay?" she whispered.

"Yes," Laura answered.

"Do you have to go to the bathroom?"

"Maybe."

Jannie got up and walked Laura to the bathroom. She wasn't mad. She wasn't even crabby. She even said, "Aren't the stars beautiful tonight?"

Laura studied the small patches of sky not blocked by trees. "Yes," she replied.

And when she was done, Jannie walked her back. As they both crawled back into their warm sleeping bags, Jannie said, "Sleep tight, Laura," gently.

"Thank you," Laura replied.

She shut her eyes so Jannie could go back to sleep, but Laura listened to her new favorite sound a little longer. Peace. Peace was kind. It was a kinder sound than even that of the little frog that had begun to sing outside her window.

wednesday

AMBER 2012

The next morning, Amber's joints felt bruised and swollen from her bike crash. She looked at herself in the mirror after using the bathroom and was horrified to see a bruise on her right cheek under the abrasion.

As she rode her bike to the bus stop, her swollen knee throbbed, and to make matters worse, one of her spokes had broken in the accident, messing up the balance of her tire. Now it rubbed against her brake on each rotation, making her journey even more difficult and slow.

She barely caught the bus.

"What happened to your face?" some guy from the back of the bus shouted up at her.

"Ate it on my bike!" she shouted back, hoping that would end it.

"Gnarly! You look messed up!" he shouted again.

"Yep, I know," Amber replied.

The rest of her day was filled with unwanted attention like that.

Her friends fussed, the lunch lady fussed, and some other kids just pointed and laughed.

"Looking good," Stefani said sarcastically as she

walked past with her entourage. "I like what you did to your face. It's a real improvement." Everyone giggled.

Keep cool, keep cool, keep cool, Amber told herself, and walked on.

But the worst was the way Mr. Morris looked at her when she entered math class. He was going to call CPS. She could see it.

"Bike wreck," she offered, hoping that would end his speculation, but she could see from his face that it didn't. Knowing that she had to stop the chain of events she could see unfolding before her, she showed him her elbow and knee so he could see that she fell and that she wasn't just hit in the face. "I was riding after dark. I got hit by a car."

He studied her closely, as if trying to assess whether or not she was telling the truth, and although she knew she should just relax because she was telling the truth, her heart began to race. She hoped he could not see her panic, but he seemed to. Mr. Morris noticed everything. "Did your mom take you to the doctor to get checked?" he asked.

"It wasn't that bad," she answered, then took her assigned seat and opened her book. She looked at the page but couldn't follow along. Her house of cards was about to come crashing down.

ETHEL 2012

Ethel's bladder woke her around sunrise, and so she rose, put on her jacket, and trekked off toward the bathroom, figuring if she didn't make it, well, she could just pee anywhere. Near the bathroom, she noticed what appeared to be bicycle tracks. She knew none of the three other women had brought a bike. It could have just been a curious mountain biker riding through camp, but nonetheless, after Ethel used the bathroom she followed the tracks.

They led her past three cabins and to the window of the Eagles cabin, the fourth. When she looked in the window, she noticed a little bit of color on the top bunk closest to the window and yes, she noticed that half of the window lock was missing. Although she was uneasy about the possibility of the squatter coming back and cornering her in the cabin, she unlocked the padlock on the door and went inside for a closer look. She stepped on the first rung on the ladder and peered over the bunk. A little stuffed dog had been tucked into a purple sleeping bag, with his head carefully poking out. *Oh no,* Ethel thought. But since she knew camp counselors sometimes brought stuffed animals to camp, she looked for more information.

Bending down to look under the bottom bunk, she found a few bags and pulled the closest one out to see how big this person's clothes were. She held up a T-shirt. Not tiny. Not big. High school? College? She wasn't sure. She put the girl's things neatly back and walked on out. Should she leave the door unlocked? Would the girl even notice? Would it scare the girl if she did?

It wasn't uncommon for former campers to return to Camp Firelight in times of crisis in their lives. She had seen it before. But in the past, she had known all the campers and they welcomed her intervention. In fact, they usually fell into her arms and sobbed. But now it was different. She hadn't been camp director in eleven years. This child wouldn't know her. And this child obviously needed a safe place to be for now.

Ethel left the cabin as she'd found it and walked away. She needed to think about her next move carefully.

ETHEL 1964

As Ethel watched Haddie nail a stand to the bottom of a tree branch in lieu of a Christmas tree, her heart swelled. Haddie knew how Ethel loved trees. Their first Christmas together, Haddie had found a small sapling in an area that was going to need to be thinned, but Ethel had grown so sad watching it slowly dry up and die that from then on they had a Christmas branch instead of a Christmas tree. An extra benefit was that branches tended to be flatter and rested up against the wall instead of taking up the whole corner of their little cabin. They tied red ribbons on the branches and hung the lightweight decorations they had made, which were the key to success when decorating a Christmas branch. Some had been made by blowing eggs and gluing pictures and ribbons onto the shells, while other decorations had been made from starching crocheted stars. When they were finished, Ethel draped a scarf around the bottom as a skirt and then stood back. She wasn't sure anyone but her would appreciate the peculiar beauty of the Christmas branch. Haddie clearly loved her.

On the table sat pinecones, peanut butter, birdseed, and ribbon. Making bird feeder decorations for the tree outside their cabin was step two in their holiday preparations. Christmas music from the radio filled some of the silence as they smeared peanut butter on the pinecones, dipped them in birdseed, and finally wrapped a length of ribbon around the top.

"We got a Christmas card from Little Susan today," Haddie said.

"Oh? *Little* Susan?" Ethel asked, holding her hand out to indicate the height of a small child.

"Yes, Little Susan."

Ethel felt a severe pang in her heart. "She's a cute one."

"Yeah, look," Haddie said, opening the card. "She drew a picture of us."

Ethel smiled and a little laugh escaped as she admired the child's drawing in which both Haddie and she were holding Christmas trees in their hands. She set down the card and then asked, "Do you ever wish we could have kids?" She longed for it so much.

"We have kids. We have about six hundred every summer," replied Haddie.

"You know that's not what I meant."

"I know. It's just . . . Well, we could have kids, but one of us would have to go down to the Timberline Bar and have relations with a lonely logger, and then the rest of the world would see it as one of us being a floozy and having a bastard child. There's no way we'd be able to keep our jobs here if one of us were seen as a floozy with a bastard child. So, I choose just to think about all the children I already have." Haddie picked up the card. "Like Little Susan."

"But Little Susan isn't going to spend Christmas with us."

"No," Haddie said, putting her hand on top of Ethel's. "She's not. Life is full of choices. Choices have pros and cons. Our choices mostly have pros, but this is our con. This is the price of the path we chose."

Ethel looked down. Her eyes filled with tears.

"But the pros are that we have each other, and we live in our own little cabin in this wonderful camp, and each year six hundred kids come to be part of our family for a season."

Ethel still didn't look up. She already knew everything Haddie had just said.

"We could get a puppy," Haddie offered.

A puppy? How could a puppy replace a child? Ethel

wanted to explode but instead stood, kissed the top of Haddie's head, and said, "That's sweet, but no," and then she slipped into the bathroom to quietly cry.

LAURA 1989

Laura hadn't realized that her interest in nature was different from anyone else's until the year Ethel singled her out. It was Laura's second year working at camp as a counselor instead of being a camper or counselor in training.

When Ethel put a hand on Laura's shoulder and asked the other counselor at the other end of the dinner table if she could hold down the fort for a bit, Laura had wondered if she was in trouble, even though she couldn't think of anything she'd done wrong. The kids at their table had not begun to scrape their plates into the old coffee can with a spatula yet, nor had they begun to sing their after-dinner songs.

As Laura followed Ethel out of the Lodge, she noticed that Ethel's posture and expression were disarming, her walk gentle and slow like always, but then, she couldn't imagine Ethel losing her temper even if she was mad.

"I have something very special to show you," Ethel had said, a twinkle in her eye. "But this has to remain a secret because it could cause panic."

Laura was relieved and intrigued. And why her?

Before she could ask, Ethel continued. "In the many years I've been leading kids on nature walks, I've never had one with more genuine interest or better questions than you. You were my little naturalist from day one. That's what I called you."

Laura beamed and followed Ethel out to Moose, noticing the trillium blooms and anemones from early summer were beginning to dry up. As they crossed the wooden
bridge over the little stream, they noticed some skunk
cabbage in bloom, like a calla lily but bumpier. Ethel
noticed a tree frog clinging to the bark of an alder, so well
camouflaged that Laura had no idea how she'd seen it.
Nearby, a stellar jay squawked noisily at them.

And then, between Moose and the beach, Ethel stepped
off the trail, stopped, and rested her hand on the trunk of
an old cedar. Above Ethel's head was a patch where the
weathered gray bark fibers had been scratched off, reveal-
ing the bright orange layer below. At about the height of
Ethel's belly, there was a stain on the tree, as if someone
had poured something on it.

Excitement had filled Ethel's eyes as she had asked,
"Do you know what this is?"

"No," Laura had answered.

Ethel examined the bark and then picked a little bit of
tan fur out of it. She handed it to Laura. "Now do you
know?"

Laura held the fur in the palm of one hand and touched
it with the finger of the other. Was it deer fur? Had the
deer eaten the bark all the way up there? Deer couldn't
reach that high. "No," she answered. "Bears scratch trees,
but their claws go deeper. And this fur is pretty light."

Ethel scoured the ground, looking for a track, but found
none. "Here's your other clue. They generally don't leave
tracks unless they're in mud, sand, or snow. If you did see
one, it would be very large and round, with the print of
each toe about the size of a quarter and no claw mark because their claws retract." Ethel made a circle with her
hands and waited for Laura to think it out.

Bears left large prints, but ones from their back feet
were longer, like a human foot, and their claws did leave

a mark. Laura's eyes widened as she realized what animal it must be. "Cougar?"

Ethel smiled and wiggled her eyebrows up and down. "It's a cougar tree. I've never found one before. They do it to mark their territory. There are scent glands in their paws. And that"—she pointed at the stain—"is where he urinated on it."

Laura walked closer and looked way up at the scratched bark. "Wow," she whispered, feeling very small.

"Yeah, they can be about eight feet long. Add some legs onto that and it's one long stretch."

"Wow," Laura said again.

"I knew you'd like it," said Ethel. "And thanks for letting me pull you away from dinner. I didn't want anyone else to see us staring at it. People get scared, but we're definitely not the preferred food of cougars. And I'm not concerned, because they're always moving through their territory—hundreds of miles. He is long gone by now and may not be back for months or even a year."

Laura touched the tree one more time before they both began walking back to dinner but paused when she heard a woodpecker.

Ethel followed her lead and stopped to listen as well.

"It's over there," Laura said, pointing toward a tree, where a black-and-white bird with a red crest tap-tap-tapped away at the trunk of a tree. "It's a pileated woodpecker."

"Indeed it is. I taught you well. They're very handsome birds, don't you think?" Ethel replied.

"I do," Laura answered, continuing to watch.

Ethel turned to her. "You are a joy, my little naturalist. You fill me with hope."

A dozen words. A dozen words can change a life.

LAURA 2012

Moments of disorientation alarmed Laura. Where was the cougar tree? She supposed it had been over twenty years since she had last seen it, but darn it, she hated moments like these. It was one more way she could not go back in time.

Just when she was about to give up, she saw a patch of bright orange cedar bark not far before her and walked around two other trees to get to it. It had been visited recently. She reached up but still couldn't touch the spot. What a gem. Cougar trees were very, very rare. Mostly, they marked with scratch piles. This was a special tree indeed. Avoiding the stain where the cougar had urinated on it, she put her hand on the tree's bark. The last time she was here, her future had seemed so clear to her. She was going to be a biologist or an ecologist. There had been no question that her future lay in the life sciences.

And then three years into her degree, she found herself pregnant and in love.

Through the years, she hadn't felt that she had missed out by giving up on all that for a family. Until now. Now she wished she could have had it all.

She looked up at the spot the cat had scratched—at what she could not reach, at this spot that had just been uncovered and exposed—and she wondered what to do with her life now. Theoretically, she only had one more year of college to go. Three quarters—that was all. But with two kids already enrolled, it was hardly practical for her to go as well. Plus, she'd forgotten so much content from the prerequisites she took two decades ago, so it wasn't like she could just waltz into a 400-level biology class and pass it now, even if she did live close to a university, which she didn't, and even if she could afford to go, which she couldn't. Besides, what was it she was hoping to do after graduating? Back in the day, she had wanted to work for the U.S. Forest Service, but it and other government agencies like it were all downsizing.

No, it made no practical sense to go back to college. She just had to face that. Everyone had dreams they left behind to pursue new dreams. She wrapped an arm around the back of the tree and rested her forehead on the side, remembering the first time Steve had embraced her. Even though her life was uncomfortable now, she had definitely not made a mistake. Although the chapter of her life when she raised kids was over, she would not have traded it for anything in the world—not even a biology degree. It was a great era. Not an easy era. Not an era that exacted no costs. But it had been truly great.

Maybe there were other ways to satisfy the part of her that had wanted to be a biologist. Maybe she could hike and backpack more. Maybe she could join the Audubon Society and even volunteer to lead walks. Yes, that would be fun. Okay. The Audubon Society. That was a good place to start.

ETHEL 2012

It was eating at her like drips of acid, as it had for years— the hurt she had caused Janet. But now it was intensified by Ruby's presence. Ruby, who had apologized for her wrongs. Was there something healing about an apology? Yes. It didn't undo anything. It didn't change the past. But there was something nice about hearing someone who had hurt you say, "That was wrong and I deeply regret that." The moment of an apology often didn't change a single thing about where a person stood. But it changed the direction she faced, so that when she began to move again she walked in a different direction. She ended up in a different place. And that's what Ethel felt had begun.

Ethel could not go back in time and change anything. But she could acknowledge that what had happened was wrong.

She wasn't sure how to reach Janet, and so Ethel needed to go home to do an Internet search. The winds were up and she knew they would likely pick up even more throughout the day, making the journey back difficult, so she enlisted Laura's help with paddling.

As they left the Lodge, Laura said, "Shannon told me that she saw cougar tracks on the beach. Want to take a detour and see if we can still see them?"

"You bet I do," Ethel said.

So together they walked to the regular waterfront area instead of directly down to Elks Beach. As they passed by Ethel's favorite group of old cedars, she listened the way she used to, but despite the strong wind, they were quiet today. It seemed they had been quiet since Haddie died, and Ethel wasn't sure if it was the grove reacting to Haddie's departure or whether losing Haddie had impaired Ethel's ability to hear them. She suspected the latter. Grief had a way of shutting people down.

But now walking next to Laura looking for beauty and wonder took Ethel way, way back. When it came to nature walks, Laura had been her favorite for many, many years. How she had loved this child. *Child.* It was funny how she could look at a forty-something-year-old woman and still see the child.

As they walked down the steep part of the trail to the beach, Ethel held on to Laura's elbow and it made her painfully aware of how rare any kind of human touch was to her these days.

"Will you look at that," Ethel marveled once they found the tracks. "He was good sized."

"He visited the tree," said Laura.

"I should go out there later." Ethel stood and surveyed her surroundings. "I wonder if he made a kill nearby."

"God, I hope not," Laura replied, looking around nervously.

Cougars buried their kills and returned to the site to feed for the next few days. If there was a kill buried nearby and the women walked too close to it, they would be in danger, but Ethel figured if one hadn't gotten her by now it was unlikely to ever happen. "After all these years, I'd sure like to see him," Ethel said, and began to walk on.

"Shannon saw him cross the road on her way here. She was excited to tell you, but I guess she got distracted and forgot."

"I'm so jealous!" said Ethel.

Ethel always looked for little nature surprises, but she found that in Laura's presence she looked even harder. She so badly wanted to find something wonderful to share. Laura had always received a good find like the present it was. Today Ethel thought it would be fun to find something tiny, but it was October—not a season when she was going to find a tiny flower. It was a season in which she was unlikely to even find a little piece of a mottled eggshell.

After they launched the canoe, they heard it—an osprey. *Cheep-cheep-cheep-cheep-cheep,* it sang out in little staccato notes. The waves on the lake bobbed their boat and tried to turn it sideways, but Ethel put her paddle in the water like a rudder and corrected it, all the while searching for the source of the noise.

"There it is." Laura pointed.

"You know my favorite thing about ospreys?" Ethel asked.

"How they dive?" Laura guessed.

"How they surface." It was true that ospreys could spot a fish in the water from over a hundred feet in the air and once they did they would dive for it and hit the water feet-first, grasping the fish in their talons. They had a longer wingspan to body ratio than any other bird and spread their great wings at the last minute to keep themselves from diving too deep and for pulling themselves back up to the surface. "Whenever I spot them, I feel like the message to me is *resilience*."

Laura said, "For me, it was, *Go after what you want without reservation*. It's been a long time since I've seen an osprey. And it's been a long time since I've gone after what I wanted without reservation."

Ethel considered that for a moment. What did she want with all of her heart—that is, what did she want that she could actually have? After Haddie died, it seemed the will leaked out of Ethel. Now she couldn't imagine wanting anything very much—certainly nothing that was possible to have.

Ethel paused before she asked the question that had been on her mind. "I always thought you would become a biologist or an ecologist or something like that. Isn't that what you were studying in college?"

Laura nodded. "And then right before my senior year, I met Steve while hiking the Wonderland Trail. And I got pregnant."

"Oh," Ethel said without judgment.

"No regrets. I have two great kids."

"Not everyone is that lucky. I would have loved to have had kids." It was true. There had been a time in Ethel's life when the absence of kids had been unbearably painful. "Career fulfillment is great, but it's not the same as family fulfillment. I don't know. We get what we get, and we make the most of it, I guess. At some point, you just make peace with whatever did or didn't happen in your life."

"Ever since we dropped off Alison at the U, I've been feeling a little robbed, like I thought I had paid the price to have them for a lifetime, and now I realize I was only paying rent, and my lease is up. I just keep asking myself, 'Now what?'"

"Isn't that wonderful? I mean, change the tone of your voice just a little—a little more delight, a little less overwhelmed—and you have, 'Now what?' where anything is possible. Anything at all! I don't know if everyone gets moments in their lives when it's as obvious, anyway, that anything, anything, is possible, in the most wonderful way. I'm going to say what I said to you when you were little. Laura, you can do *anything*."

Laura laughed appreciatively as they continued on.

There were four Janet Nelsons in Washington, but only one in Twisp was the right age and so Ethel took a chance by sending a letter to her:

Dear Ms. Nelson,

I'm trying to reach the Janet Nelson who attended or worked at Camp Firelight until 1980. I am spending this week at camp, its final week before closing its doors forever, for its water well has gone dry and the Firelight Girls can't afford any solutions. Janet, if this is you, I want to explain and apologize. Your mom called someone on the board and had Sue Mayer and you blackballed from camp. I stood no chance of changing anything, and I was just trying to keep my job, and so I didn't fight it. I think back on that moment often and wonder what I could have done

differently—what my options were—and after all these
years, it still leaves me feeling as backed into a corner and
powerless as it did then. But Janet, it was wrong. The whole
situation was wrong. You were a truly phenomenal camp
counselor and in no way did you or Sue deserve that treat-
ment. From the bottom of my heart, I am so, so sorry. I want
you to know that. Camp is closing its doors forever in a mat-
ter of days, but should you wish to return, you are incred-
ibly welcome here.

Yours truly,
Ethel

She addressed it, stamped it, and put it in her mailbox
with the flag up. And it felt good. Yes, it felt good to try.
It felt good to be honest.

ETHEL 1955

Ruby. It hadn't really been Ruby's fault, Ethel knew. It
had been a different time. And Ruby wasn't the one who
told her mother about the kiss between Ethel and Haddie.
In fact, Ruby may not have even known. Or perhaps she
had known.

A week after Ruby's disaster wedding, Ethel's mom
beckoned her home for Sunday dinner, but unlike some
of the previous times, she hadn't insisted that she bring
Haddie. And as Ethel walked up the little sidewalk bordered by her mother's rose garden on either side, she knew
deep in her gut that something was wrong. Still, she continued toward the old white house.

Inside, her parents awaited her arrival along with two friends of theirs from church and their nephew. It was an obvious and awkward setup. He stood when Ethel entered the room. He was gawky and lean and looked at the floor. "Ethel, this is Edward," said her mother.

Ethel saw the apology in his eyes when he said hello, an apology she returned with her own eyes.

Dinner was interminable, the air thick with expectation and forced conversation.

Afterward, her mother walked her out to her car. "Well?" she had probed, with excessive hope pouring out of her strained smile.

Ethel had played dumb.

"What did you think of Edward?" her mother asked with dramatic exasperation.

"He seemed nice," Ethel had answered.

"So, should I arrange for you to see each other again?"

"No," said Ethel, watching her mother's expression as she ignited.

"Why? What's wrong with him?" she demanded.

"Nothing."

"Then what is your problem?"

"My problem is that I'm happy doing what I'm doing at camp," Ethel said plainly.

"I've heard about what you're doing at camp," her mother hissed.

Ethel did not know what to say and her mother did not back down from a silence so heavy it pinned Ethel to the ground.

"I don't want to get married," Ethel finally said.

"You are an embarrassment to me—to your father and me." Never in her life had Ethel's mom spoken to her like that.

Shock and devastation sank in along with her mother's

cruel words. Ethel pursed her lips and shook her head. "I'm sorry."

" 'Sorry' doesn't change the fact that you're choosing to be an old spinster in the woods with a bunch of women doing God knows what." Her mother's eyes were hard and sharp like daggers. "Change this course you're on now."

Ethel stared back, scared, and gently shook her head. "No," she whispered.

"Then don't come back," her mother said as she spun round and stormed back to the house.

It felt as if the very ground Ethel had stood on her whole life caved into a giant sinkhole, as if it shattered and crumbled right beneath her feet.

She sat in her car, turned the key, took one last look, and drove away. And she never came back.

Did her mother ever regret that? she wondered. Was there ever a moment when so much time had passed that her mother could not even remember why she had been so mad, but by then she just hadn't known how to bridge their distance?

Ethel didn't know how to bridge the distance either. Thirty-eight years of silence passed, and then one day her cousin had called to tell Ethel that her mother was very sick. The way Ethel's cousin had paused before she had said the word "sick" let Ethel know that this was her last window of opportunity to try to create some healing.

"Do you think I should go to her?" Ethel had asked.

Her cousin paused as she thought. "I don't know. She might just think that you came around after all this time to try to position yourself for her inheritance."

Ethel had not considered that and sure didn't want to be perceived that way. What could she do? After she hung up, she wrote her mom a letter. It took several tries, but finally Ethel felt she had boiled it down to only the most important words.

Dear Mom,

Betsy told me that you're very sick and I realize our time to make peace may run out, so there are some things I want to say. Mostly, I want you to know that I forgive you. I understand that you had only been trying to protect me from an intolerant world, and that you had only wanted me to find the things in life that had given you happiness. In a way, I did. Haddie has been a loyal, loving friend and companion for all these years, and each summer many of the same kids return to camp. They feel like our kids coming home.

The world has changed quite a bit since 1955. It's 1985. I am fifty-one now. Fifty-one. I am very much a grown woman. But still, there is this part of me that wants my mom to say that she regrets discarding me as if I had no value as a daughter or a human being. I still want to hear my mom say that was wrong, and that her judgment about Haddie was wrong, too. Am I the only one who deeply regrets wasting this time together—wasting this lifetime estranged? I can't heal this by myself. If you want me to come to you, I will be there in a heartbeat. I would help you any way I could. But you have to know that I can't change who I am and who I love and I can't heal our wound all by myself.

Your daughter,
Ethel

She had agonized over whether to sign it "Love," but it seemed too much. It was her last opportunity to tell her mom that she loved her and Ethel didn't take it. But did she love her? "Love" just seemed like the wrong word. Ethel forgave her. That was the best she could do.

And then she put the letter in an envelope and walked the three miles down the lake to the store, where she paused in front of the big blue mail collection box. She thought of her cousin's words and hesitated. Would she appear like a gold digger? Her letter wasn't sugary, though. It was honest. It was written with the purest of intentions. She should not fear the truth, she thought as she dropped it in the big blue box.

She never received a reply.

And two months later, her cousin told her that her mother had passed away.

There are things that heal wrong, Ethel thought, *like a bone with a compound fracture or being told not to come back.* There was a small window of time to set them right so that they merely scarred the other person instead of disfiguring them. There were things that caused a rift between two people so wide that it could never be bridged.

SHANNON 1982

The girls from Shannon's cabin trekked up Mt. Dirtyface in the middle of the night to watch the sunrise from the top. One girl, Valerie, was having a really hard time. Laura and their counselor, Janet, stayed back with her, so it seemed like the trip took forever and a day.

Impatient, Shannon ran ahead of the group and reached the top. She stood there on the summit feeling superior and proud and a little . . . well, empty. So, as an act of charity, she hustled back to the group to tell them they were almost there and then hiked to the top again, this time with the group. That second time was more fun because of the collective excitement and collective pride. They sat on boulders together, watching the sun light up the just the very tops of all the peaks below them and witnessing a new day beginning.

Janet pulled a friendship bracelet out of her pocket, the one she had been working on all week. Shannon wanted it badly and hoped that maybe Janet was going to give it to her for being the first to the summit.

"Good mountaineers never go faster than the slowest person in their group and they certainly never leave anyone behind." Janet turned and looked at Laura, who had never left Valerie the whole way up and had encouraged her to keep going. "You are a good mountaineer and a good friend," she said, and tied the bracelet around Laura's wrist.

In that moment, Shannon realized that she had not been a good mountaineer and not been a good friend. She had only been first. It was the first time she realized that there might be more important things than being first or best and that there was virtue in looking out for others.

SHANNON 2012

Since Ethel and Laura had gone canoeing back to Ethel's house, Shannon said, "Ruby, I think we ought to go on an adventure, too. What do you think about walking down the South Shore Trail?"

"I think I would love that," said Ruby.

With that, they set off across the little bridge, across the playfield, and down the trail.

The first part of the trail was usually muddy. In fact, normally hikers put large sticks in the trail to walk on like tightropes or balance beams. But on this day, the mud was dry. Tangled cedar roots stood where mud had washed away, and Shannon held Ruby's hand as they made their way across the treacherous web.

"Isn't it amazing that those trees continue to stand when they have such shallow roots?" Ruby asked.

"It really is," Shannon agreed. And in that moment, she saw herself. These trees had been here for a long time, just like she had been in North Prairie a long time. Despite the length of time they had been there, they had not set down deep roots. It was amazing the trees were still standing and it was amazing she was still standing. She paused and looked back at the roots stretched wide across the surface of the soil. They were exactly what her relationships in North Prairie were like—far-reaching, but superficial.

"What, dear?" Ruby asked. "What are you looking at?"

"Roots," said Shannon. "I was just realizing mine are just like those."

"I don't think mine are particularly deep either," said Ruby.

"I wonder if different types of people are like different types of trees—destined to have one type of root—or if a person can change their root structure."

"I think a person can change their root structure. I wasn't able to change mine, but I think it happens."

"I just wonder about the whole chicken and egg thing. I mean, do I have shallow roots and superficial relationships because I'm independent and self-centered, or am I independent and self-centered because I rarely had the support I needed? You know what I'm saying? Did I create my life or did my life create me?"

Ruby considered that as they continued to walk down the trail. "Probably both. I think in my case, it was both. I can definitely look back and see events that I had no control over and how they changed me, and I can definitely see a couple pivotal moments when I made a choice because of who I am, and those choices shaped my life profoundly."

"Do you think it feeds on itself?" Shannon stood next to Ruby as she stepped up onto the little boardwalk that led through soil that was usually soft and spongy.

"It very well may," replied Ruby.

"I sure hope there are moments in our lives when we have the power to change." Shannon hoped all the way down to her soul that the day she walked out of the school was one of those moments—that it would be enough to create real change in her life, that she wasn't destined to create more or less the same life over and over again in new places.

"I think there are. Every choice that lies before us is an opportunity to change."

"But do you think everyone has choices like that?" Shannon asked, because it sure seemed like a lot of people were cornered in their own lives with few or no choices.

Ruby thought. "Maybe for some of us, it has to start small. Maybe we had to stay near a job because we couldn't afford to leave it. Maybe we had to stay in a certain apartment because we couldn't afford anything else. But maybe there are small choices we can make to create a richer life. Maybe we can smile at strangers. Maybe we can keep our house neat and clean. Maybe we can take a moment to send birthday greetings to our friends. Maybe we can plant a pot of flowers and put it in our window or near our door. Maybe we can go for a walk every day and wave to our neighbors. I don't know, but I like to think we always have the choice to make any situation better or worse."

Little things. Shannon could have invited people over for dinner. She could have traveled more in the summers. She could have given Wade a chance—Wade, who skinned bears in his front yard next to his extensive tire collection. No, she realized, some lives required more than little changes. Some lives needed to be demolished and rebuilt.

Shannon walked behind Ruby and paused as Ruby reached down to pick up a stick that would work as a walking stick. Ruby set the pace, a pace that afforded Shannon the opportunity to notice more beauty.

And it occurred to her that perhaps some ideas she'd had about herself were not completely true. For many years now, she had thought of herself as someone who had become unyielding to anything but her own plan, someone who enjoyed not taking others into consideration, someone who loved to be the captain of her own ship, and it was alarming to consider that those very characteristics likely had created the life she now found unsatisfying. But as she followed Ruby and adapted to her pace and her needs, Shannon realized that she was just as happy. Perhaps she was not the hopeless case she feared she was. Perhaps she had the capacity to create a life she'd find more satisfying after all.

RUBY 1948

The year Ruby was fourteen, her favorite thing about camp was simply that there were no boys there. It was such a relief. As she followed Miss Mildred on a nature hike, that's what kept going through Ruby's mind: *What a relief.*

She had spent the last year enduring a painful crush on Bruce Willaby, a boy in her class who barely noticed her. As a result, Ruby had taken to sleeping in terribly uncomfortable curlers and spending time in the morning fixing her hair. She wanted to wear lipstick like Sandra Ellis, but Ruby's mother said she had to wait until she was sixteen or the boys would think she was cheap. In the mirror each morning, she looked at her face, her face that she used to find beautiful, and thought it was drab and featureless. No wonder Bruce hardly noticed her.

"Can anyone tell me the stages of mitosis? Who studied?" her science teacher had asked in February. Ruby could. She had. But she looked around to see if anyone else was going to raise their hand. She wasn't going to be the only one. And no one else did.

"Ruby Gemill?" He called on her directly.

"Uh-h . . . ," she stammered, unsure of what to do. Then she looked at Bruce Willaby, who hadn't raised his hand, and said, "I'm sorry. I don't know," so Bruce wouldn't feel stupid and he wouldn't think she was too smart for him. Were all the other girls in class doing the same thing? It seemed hard to believe she was the *only* person who had studied.

What a strange feeling, deciding to be less than she was for the comfort of others. It felt a little like wearing shoes that were pretty but too small, only instead of cramming her foot in, she was squeezing her soul.

This was what she thought about as she followed behind Miss Mildred on a nature walk down the South Shore Trail and raised her hand when Miss Mildred pointed to a plant and asked if anyone remembered what it was.

"Trillium," Ruby answered proudly.

"Good memory, Ruby!"

There was something powerful about that moment—that moment she allowed herself to be great again . . . or at least allowed herself to be honest about who she was.

And later, while she washed her hands in the bathroom, she looked up at her image in the mirror and saw her natural beauty once more. Yes, suddenly there was something in her eyes that she recognized—a sparkle, or some confidence. . . . It was hard to name, but it looked like . . . well, it looked like *her*. How wonderful that recognition had felt—like taking her soul out of the too-small shoes and running barefoot in the soft silt. *Ah*.

RUBY 2012

Remembering how here at camp she could be herself, and if that meant being excellent she was free to be excellent, Ruby squatted next to a low cupboard in the arts and crafts area, slid out a box, and, delighted, ran her fingers through countless beads, badges, and a copy of *The Firelight Girls' Achievement Book*. When she was a girl, each little bead had felt like a trophy! She took the box and placed it on the arts and crafts table. "Look at this," she said to Laura.

Laura put a few more things back into the cupboard that she had cleaned out. "Did you find something great?" she asked, making her way over to the box.

"Yes."

"Beads!" Laura exclaimed. "The big vintage ones!" Like Ruby just had, Laura also ran her hands through them. There was something irresistible about a box of beads. "Now that I think about it, it's kind of funny how proud some little beads made me feel."

"Oh, I don't think it's funny," replied Ruby. "I remember looking at all my beads and thinking about how much I had grown. I mean, each one symbolized something new I'd learned or done. To me, it was like the little marks my mom made in the doorjamb of the laundry room when she measured how tall I'd grown. All those beads. All those experiences. All that knowledge. You bet I was proud." Ruby picked up a yellow bead. "How neat is it, really, that we had a symbol like this so we were actually able to see the quantity of new knowledge we acquired in a year? I wish we still had that!"

"Oh, wouldn't that be cool?" Laura held a little red bead. Then, with a self-effacing laugh, she confessed, "I don't think I would have earned very many beads this year. Or even the last five years."

Ruby picked up an orange bead, one that had represented achievements related to home, and handed it to Laura. "Here. This one is for being a mom," and Ruby handed her a red, white, and blue bead that represented citizenship. "This one is for volunteering your time here this weekend."

Laura squeezed them in her hand, smiled, and put them in her pocket. "Thank you."

"Wouldn't it be nice to have a group of friends who would inspire us to get out of our ruts and try new things together?" Ruby asked.

"Firelight Girls for grown women? I love it! What would we be called?"

"Well, hm . . . Old Firelight Girls . . . maybe the Hot Coals," replied Ruby.

Laura started laughing. "I'm trying to imagine how different the last twenty-five years of my life would have been if I'd thought of myself as a Hot Coal, and if I'd earned beads for all the things I did. Maybe I would feel like I had accomplished more than I do right now."

"We'll definitely rewrite the bead book for the Hot Coals," Ruby said. Although they were joking, Ruby found herself wondering if such an organization might actually take off. Was she the only woman of a certain age who still wanted to return to camp, do activities, and sing the songs that she used to sing? Yes, camp for women of a certain age. It would be her fountain of youth. She imagined it, as she remembered all the things she used to love to do. For starters, it had been far, far too many years since she had pulled a prank. Few things made a person feel more alive than running something of someone else's up a flagpole.

Laura joked, "We could get beads for chaperoning our kids' classes on field trips, and baking birthday cupcakes, for cleaning up vomit and going to our first parent-teacher conference . . . for talking to our kids about sex, for dropping them off at college and driving away like we didn't just leave a part of our heart behind. No, wait, we should get a patch for that."

Parenting talk made Ruby a little uncomfortable for reasons that weren't completely clear to her. Maybe it was simply the assumption that she'd had kids. Or maybe it was all of the assumptions about why she hadn't, if she let it be known she hadn't. Maybe it was the sense that others viewed her as lacking some legitimacy as a woman when they found out she wasn't a mother. Or maybe it was simply because it was the territory they didn't have in common.

"I didn't have kids," Ruby said. "But I can think of plenty of other tasks I think I should have gotten a bead for: filing my own taxes, changing my own tire, fixing my own toilet, driving myself to and from the dentist to get a root canal—"

"We should definitely get a bead for any invasive procedure. How about those painful gum cleanings? Mammograms, Pap smears . . ."

"Our first colonoscopy." Ruby laughed.

Laura agreed. "Definitely for our first colonoscopy."

"Just imagine all the beads we'd have by now!" said Ruby. And for the first time, really, she could look back and see her life through other eyes—eyes that were capable of seeing her accomplishments, eyes that could see what she had survived, eyes that saw everything she had done on her own—and she felt proud. Suddenly her life didn't seem so different from going to the archery range where she competed against herself instead of against boys. And for the first time, it occurred to her that perhaps she had created and lived exactly the life she had wanted—at least, in light of Henry's fate. Why had she been so blind to all the wonderful ways life had made her self-sufficient and allowed her to continue to be so? Why had it taken her this long to see her life through the eyes of gratitude instead of victimization? It was so much more pleasant to feel grateful instead of bitter.

"I'm picturing us like those African women with their necks stretched from wearing so many beads," said Laura.

Ruby wanted everyone who hadn't had the revelation she was having to have one as soon as possible. Could an organization like this help other women see their lives in a different light—help them feel proud and, well, simply grateful to be who they were? Ruby wanted to pass the torch to younger women so they didn't waste any more of their life being angry about the hand they'd been dealt the way she had. "The Embers," Ruby said.

"Excuse me?"

"That's what we should be called—the Embers. Remember at the end of the summer how after the fire was completely out, we'd take some embers from the big cer-

emonial campfire ring. . . . Wait, are they technically embers if they've cooled? I mean, we always called them
that, but it seems like embers should be hot. Anyway, we'd
put them in a coffee can, and then stick them under the
Lodge, and then the following year we'd find them and
use them to start the next fire. . . . Did you guys do that?"

Laura nodded.

"Yes, we should be called the Embers, because we
could pass the flame like that. At least we'd like to." Was
this inspired thinking? Was this a vision?

"I love it."

"Well, I just changed my mind again. All you younger
women would be Hot Coals until . . . I don't know, maybe
seventy. And then you'd get to be an Ember. Hot Coals
will be to the Embers what Flickers were to Firelight Girls
or Brownies are to Girl Scouts. You'll wish you were an
Ember. And when you're an Ember, you'll get to wear a
fishing vest like this, so you can carry your wallet and
your tissues and your prescription medications without
hefting around a big old purse that messes up your center
of gravity and your balance. Yes, we will have so much
more fun with both hands free!"

Laura laughed and laughed. "I love it!"

"Well, since getting older is going to happen anyway,
you might as well look forward to it," Ruby replied, turning her attention back to her two remaining cupboards to
sift through.

She mostly looked for anything the next owners would
have no use for—anything related to the Firelight Girls.
She found two boxes—one containing costumes; and the
other, fabric scraps, nothing that had to stay but nothing
that had to go either. Ruby rifled through the costume box,
holding up old wrinkled prom dresses, aprons, wigs, a
dirndl, a tutu, various hats, overalls, flannel shirts, and a
magician's cape. Yes, the next people would probably

enjoy these. She left them as they were, shut the cupboard doors, and then took a seat at the table again. Triumphantly she said, "I did it. I conquered the cupboard."

Laura continued to methodically put bottles of tempura paint back into the last cupboard. "All right! I'm almost done myself!"

"Tomorrow I'm going to attack the closets upstairs in the dorm room. I wonder what treasures I'll find there!"

"I like the way you make us sound like pirates!"

"Arg!"

For a moment they were quiet, and then out of nowhere Laura asked her, "Ruby, you said you never had kids, but were you ever married?"

"No. I never was. Well, wait. That's not completely true. Technically I was married for a night, but I got it annulled."

"Vegas?"

Ruby shook her head. "Wenatchee."

"You just realized you didn't want to be married?"

"He wasn't the one."

"You never met the one?"

"Oh, I met him, but he . . ." She exhaled and swallowed another breath of air. "He went to Korea and didn't return."

"Different guy," Laura clarified.

"Yes, very different guy." Henry and Gil had been totally different. Sweet Henry would have done anything for her. And Gil, well, Gil hadn't even been able to be troubled to attend his own wedding reception. Gil had been cocky and selfish.

"It's nice to be here . . . just us girls. I confess I'm envious of your single life."

"You don't love your husband?"

Laura thought for a moment and then shrugged. "I don't know."

She struck Ruby as so sad.

"Was he your true love?" Ruby asked.

Laura nodded sadly. "He was."

Ruby said, "My true love died in Korea before I was twenty. I never got to marry him or have a life with him. So, it always makes me sad to see people who found it and had it lose it. But hey, at least you had it for a while." A little smile warmed Ruby's face. "I'm envious of that. Some of us never get even that."

"It was really nice while it lasted."

Love, thought Ruby. *It tortures everyone—even those who have it.* Maybe, it occurred to her, everyone felt just as lonely as she did, regardless of their circumstances. Maybe loneliness was just part of the human experience. Maybe there was no way around it. And if that was so, maybe she had been robbed of absolutely nothing and missed out on absolutely nothing. Maybe. Or maybe not. But it was comforting to believe that whatever did or didn't happen didn't matter, because everyone suffered in some way. She felt liberated to let a little more of it go—this anger toward her own life, this anger toward the great injustice of being robbed of Henry.

LAURA 2012

Although Ruby had professed to being more or less blind, she had shot her arrows far more accurately than Laura, who left the archery range somewhere between embarrassed and inspired.

"I still got it," Ruby said.

"You still got it, all right," Laura agreed.

"The difference is, now I need a nap."

Laura laughed.

At the Lodge, Ruby jokingly said good night and went upstairs to sleep, while Laura resolved to clean out the camp craft area. She carried all four large plastic tubs out of the closet, emptied their contents, and began the tedious task of making piles of plates, dishes, little plastic tea-cups, silverware, serving utensils, water bottles, water purifiers, can openers, matches, little containers of salt and pepper, and little bottles of dish soap.

Sorting these things transported her back in time to July of 1990, when her bedroom floor was covered with all the things she had laid out to take with her on the Won-derland Trail, a trail that led all the way around Mt. Rainier. How excited she had been. Anything had seemed possible then. She had felt so capable. What had changed? What had happened? How was it she could sit before these items twenty-two years later and feel . . . sentenced and . . . powerless?

When she was done, she put the items carefully back into the tubs and put the tubs along the back wall in the closet. On one hook hung a dozen cheap compasses, and on other hooks hung red backpacks with external frames that appeared to be in quite a bit of disrepair. Were these the very same ones she had used thirty years ago? It seemed likely. What a shame they hadn't been replaced with something better, because surely the last people to use these had to have been somewhere between inconve-nienced and downright miserable. Buckles were missing; straps were broken. A few backpacks had holes in the nylon that needed to be patched.

For no reason that she could explain, she put one on. She hooked her thumbs into the shoulder straps like she used to and then, feeling silly, took it off and hung it back up. In a cubby sat several tents. It seemed likely that many were missing stakes, poles, or rain flies, so Laura tossed them out of the closet to inspect more closely.

At once, she remembered her first night on the Wonderland Trail when she discovered that she had no tent stakes. Somehow, they had fallen out of her tent bag. If she hadn't forgotten them, she might not be married to Steve today. And although it sounded appealing to be free, she did not regret for even a moment the existence of her children or those two magical weeks with Steve following the day they met.

LAURA 1984

Overnight backpack trips weren't something girls in their early teens uniformly looked forward to. Jen and Teresa in Laura's cabin were having their periods and no one liked to deal with their period while camping. To make matters worse, Heather had just told them that they were five times more likely to be the victim of a bear attack because of it.

"Is that true?" Shannon whispered to Laura, and Laura shrugged.

With that in mind, they all piled out of the camp van, donned their backpacks, and started up the trail to Lake Valhalla with no small amount of trepidation, except for Shannon, who seemed to fear nothing and led the way. Laura followed her. Behind them, Heather had convinced Jennifer and Teresa that if they just sang the whole time they hiked they would scare all the bears away, and so they sang "Little Red Caboose" with great gusto.

Laura had seen a bear once while she played near the

river at her grandpa's house. It wasn't much larger than a dog, and if she stopped to imagine it without fur she realized it really wasn't that big at all. It was nothing like the bear on *Grizzly Adams*. So, while the girls behind her were approaching some level of hysteria, Laura remembered that, and she asked herself if she'd rather run into a bear or into her father when he was drunk. The bear. There was no question. There was a chance she could scare a bear away. There was a chance she could fight a bear off. She could yell at a bear and throw rocks at it— things she could never do to her father. Yes, the playing field was much more level with a bear.

She continued to think about it as they slowly hiked to the top of the ridge and then began the drop into the glacial basin.

Six times. She could tell you that her father had struck her six times. The proof was that there were six birdhouses that hung outside her window, each one an apology. He knew she loved birds. What she remembered most was the initial shock and sting of the first couple of times and then the numbness. The last four times, she had expected it. After all, she had chosen to run between her mother and him after her mother had taken a particularly hard hit. Laura went running into that situation numb with adrenaline, and afterward she lay on top of her mother very still, numbness slowly giving way to throbbing.

Laura crested the ridge and looked at the pristine alpine lake below. It rested against a sharp tooth-like peak whose talus and large boulders spilled into the water's edge. Some were so large that they stuck out of the water like little islands. On the other side, a soft forest bordered the water's edge. It was a place her father would never come and that made it the safest place she could imagine— even with talk of bear. And because of that, the numbness inside of her began to awaken. When the little leaves of huckleberry bushes and the needles of alpine fur brushed against her arm, she didn't tune them out. She felt them, felt their gentleness, felt them tickle. It was almost as if these bushes and trees were new friends reaching out to touch her arm and tell her it was okay—that she was safe now. And she felt love for them and for this wilderness.

When the girls reached the lake, everyone changed into their swimsuits and scrambled out on boulders on the edge of the lake. They hesitated, looking at water that had been snow just seconds ago. It was going to sting their skin and give them headaches. But Laura, fascinated with her renewed senses, dove right in, followed by Shannon. They surfaced together and sang out in shrieks and screams from the cold water. But Laura, in addition to feeling cold, felt alive—more alive than she ever remembered feeling.

She rolled over onto her back and looked at the clear blue sky while her other friends jumped in. Their little cirque seemed like a world unto itself, with nothing but all that was good and pure—water, patches of snow, and friends. It was a completely safe place. She kept expecting the feeling to pass, but it lasted while she lay on a warm boulder and let the radiance of the sun's heat thaw her. It lasted while they pitched tents, made dinner, and sang songs together. It lasted as the talk of girl-eating bears gave way to snoring. It lasted into the night and sank deep into her dreams, so that for once they were good. She even woke up feeling safe and protected in this secret world.

As the other girls rolled up sleeping bags and tents, seemingly both surprised and relieved that they had survived the night without being eaten by wild animals, Laura felt grief. She didn't want to go. She never wanted to leave this sanctuary where she was hidden and protected from everything sick and mean and ugly.

When the time came she put on her backpack and walked out with the rest of her friends, but this time she walked at the end of the line just so she could stay in this little secret world a few more precious seconds. Before she went over the top of the ridge to the other side, she looked back on Lake Valhalla sitting in the cirque like an opal in delicate silver, and there she left a little of her soul behind where it would always be safe.

But then a feeling of empowerment washed over her, unclear at first. It had something to do with how simply loving this wilderness made her different from her parents. And knowing that she was different made her realize she was free to create an entirely different kind of life than they had created. She was not destined to make the same choices as her mother. And something about that made Laura realize that no matter where she was, her soul would always be safe. She would keep it safe. Not locked up by any means. No, she would just put herself in places like this, in places with other people who were gentle enough to love nature the way she did.

SHANNON 2012

"I thought there would be so much to do," said Ethel, joining Shannon where she sat on the end of the dock. "But there's really not. I feel like I'm mostly making busywork for myself, so I don't think about what is actually happening so much."

The cloud that had been blocking the sun blew by so that the glorious autumn light shone down once more. The wind blew whitecaps across the lake, and when they crashed into the dock it bucked wildly. Sometimes water splashed up between the cracks and soaked the fabric of her pants, but Shannon didn't care. She had extra clothes, and out here it seemed she stood a chance of gaining some clarity.

Shannon replied, "I thought it would be nice to come here and say good-bye, and it has been. It really has. I don't mean to sound ungrateful by any means. It's just that being up here with you and Laura again reminded me . . . I don't know . . . It's hard to articulate. It reminded me of what is really being lost here. And I feel it so much more acutely. I thought a week of closure sounded like plenty of time, but now that I'm here, I never want to leave. I certainly don't want to leave knowing I can't come back."

Ethel was quiet for a moment. She looked across the water and down the shore. "When I start to panic about that, I have to remind myself that I can paddle up and sneak into camp almost any time I want. They could never keep me out. But I also have to remember that camp isn't just this place. It's the feelings we have when we're together in this place. It's the friendships we've made. It's the perspectives we now have. It's our confidence and capableness. No one could ever take that away from us."

"Amen," Shannon said sadly. Ethel was right, but still, this place mattered. It did. It was part of all of them, a big reason they became who they became, and Shannon wanted it to become part of more women, too. "I wish Haddie could be here with us."

"Sometimes when I'm wishing she was with me, an animal will come along, and I can't help but wonder if it's her—if she jumped into its body for just a moment so she could have physicality that I could see. On my way down here, a duck landed on the bow of my canoe and looked right at me. Hand to God."

"I almost hit a cougar on my way here," said Shannon. "I'd say just a half mile up the road or so."

"Haddie always said she wanted to come back as a cougar. Maybe it was her and she was just welcoming you home." Ethel smiled. "You know, some Native American tribes say cougars represent leadership," she said. "I know no one believes me about this, but believe me when I tell you that the very first day I showed up at Camp Firelight to move in, I found a great big scratch pile right outside my cabin. It was as if he left me a memo about the decades of leadership ahead of me—only instead of leaving a letter, he left poop. He's a cat. To him, it's the same thing. Cougars don't lie. I wonder what the implications are for you . . . that you're about to run smack-dab into a leadership opportunity, but you can avoid it if you want to?"

"I can't imagine," Shannon said, and then because she found the whole topic of her future overwhelming she changed the subject back. "What animal would you like to be?" she asked Ethel.

"I'd like to be an osprey. Those dives they do just look like so much fun. I'm not sure I'm brave enough to be an osprey, though. I might be a better bear. All those years I worked here, I semihibernated in the winter and each summer I took care of new cubs." She smiled.

When Ethel smiled, a lifetime of joy spread across her face. Shannon had no doubt that this last year had to have been difficult beyond what she was capable of imagining, but as she studied Ethel's beautiful smile lines it was clear the good years outnumbered the bad. Shannon touched her own face and wondered if the same was true for her. What was etched into her face? Worry? Her intense fear of failure and now complete resignation and sense of hopelessness about it? Loneliness? Disappointment? More than ever, Shannon knew that she absolutely had to take the reins and create a more joyful life for herself. There was no more time to waste.

A crow landed on a pillar of the dock a little ways away. "Right now, I kind of think I'd like to be that crow," Shannon told Ethel. "I used to hate crows. They drove me nuts with all the noise they'd make. But now I watch them and appreciate that they're opportunists. They don't force outcomes like the big raptors, you know? Rather than hunt like they do, crows look for the opportunity right in front of them. They'll pillage your garbage can or eat some roadkill, and then with the rest of their day they hang out with their friends. I can respect that."

"They're really quite elegant when you see them with new eyes," said Ethel.

"They really are," Shannon agreed.

"Maybe that's Haddie telling you to look at the opportunity right in front of you," Ethel said. Then she turned to the crow and asked, "Haddie? Is that you?" The crow glanced at them and then looked away without a peep. "It's not like Haddie to be quiet."

Wouldn't it be nice if the crow really was telling her that? If there really was an opportunity? Shannon thought. But it seemed to her that her eyes were open and she did not see any opportunity right in front of her. No, all she saw was that in a couple days they would all leave camp forever and then she would be on her own. Anything would be possible, and while that usually sounded like a wonderful thing, it could be a horrible thing, too. She could have her house repossessed. While she didn't want to keep it, she strongly preferred to lose it by selling it. She could end up living in a tiny dumpy apartment somewhere with mold and cockroaches and neighbors who fought all the time. *Oh God!* she thought, realizing that she could do a lot worse than her life in North Prairie. She could end up homeless and living in a cardboard box.

She could find herself Dumpster diving behind grocery stores for food to eat. What would happen if she got sick?

That was the thing about gambles. They really could go either way. People were not always rewarded for taking risks. In the moment she walked out of her classroom, all she could think about was how it had become intolerable. But maybe she had just come to take the comforts of her life for granted. She had food, shelter, and access to medical care. When she really thought about it, that was huge.

There was no denying that in the same way trees lost branches in the North Prairie windstorms, she had completely lost parts of herself there, too—the parts she had once considered most central to who she was . . . her favorite parts . . . her joy. She had lost her joy. Every day it seemed she wilted a little more, like a houseplant that hadn't seen water in a long, long time.

Leaving was overwhelming and staying was unimaginable.

But maybe joy was too much to wish for. Perhaps the truth was that life had its challenges no matter what a person's circumstances were. Perhaps she just needed to will herself an attitude change and focus on all the things she had to be grateful for: enough food—in fact, plenty of food—a cute little house with a beautiful tree in the front yard; the absence of an overbearing or abusive husband; good insurance; and a retirement account that she could use in twenty-three more years, or maybe more if the retirement age was raised by then. Twenty-three more years of criticism and isolation. Twenty-three more years. She chewed on it, but she could not swallow.

As she waited for clarity that she doubted would come, she continued to watch the crow. It stood very still on top of the pillar, as if it were waiting with her.

SHANNON 1990

Haddie pulled back the string on her bow and released. Her arrow sailed through the air and sank into the center of her target, like all her others. A little smile of satisfaction spread across her face. "Bull's-eye," she said. "But you . . ." She looked over at Shannon's target. "You're off today."

Shannon deflated. She was dropping the ball. It was her last summer working here before she would graduate from college and enter that world of "real life," whatever "real life" meant. So it was her last chance to get her fifteenth rank in archery and shoot a flaming arrow into the lake at the big ceremony at the end of the upcoming week. She had just thirty arrows to get one hundred points from fifty yards. So far, she was blowing it. And here Haddie had been so generous with her time, offering to come here with her after all the kids had left to give her this opportunity.

The feeling in Shannon's chest and her stomach reminded her of the night she broke her ankle in that ballet performance. It was failure. That horrible feeling was failure. So intolerable was it that she wanted to just raise her bow and shoot off her remaining twenty-five arrows and just get it over with . . . move on to something else . . . forget that she was almost great at something. Almost. She had been good. Good. The word sounded a lot like "thud," which was also how it felt as it sank to the bottom of her stomach. Good. To Shannon, "good" felt like a year's supply of macaroni and cheese that a person might win as a consolation prize on a game show. It was just another way of saying "not good enough."

But every time she picked up her bow and aimed, she thought about her goal, and then she thought about life and about how she didn't know what her goals were, really. At the end of next year, she would have an English degree. What good, really, was an English degree? She could teach it. Maybe she could edit for a publisher or write for a magazine. It wasn't too late to change. She could still change the track she was on. But as she mulled over the seeming infinity of other choices, she realized it was poetry that made her heart sing—poetry . . . such an impractical passion. She could hardly blame her father, a very pragmatic medical doctor, for trying to convince her to pursue a career in human resources.

She lifted her bow once more.

"Wait," said Haddie. "You're not present. If you release that arrow, it's going out to another galaxy with all the others. Don't throw more points out the window. Pause. What's on your mind?"

"My future," Shannon said.

Haddie let out a long, slow whistle. "That's a tough one. I wish I could sing 'Que Sera' to you, but the truth is that the choices you make do create your life. Let's just sit for a moment and wait for your mind to run its course. I don't know about yours, but when I'm worried about something I spin out for a while in here"—she pointed to her head—"and then I gently pull out of the slide. But just like when you're driving in snow, you can't overcorrect. You have to hold the wheel still and just wait for the car to correct itself."

Shannon nodded that she understood.

"So let's wait," Haddie said. She sat down on the only lawn chair and rested her bow on her lap.

Shannon followed her lead and made herself comfortable on a log. She thought about holding the steering wheel straight and waiting for her mental tires to grab the road again. She waited and waited, slapped some mosquitoes, and waited some more.

And Haddie, bless her heart, slapped at mosquitoes and waited along with Shannon.

As a half hour passed and then an hour, Shannon felt horribly guilty and embarrassed. She looked over at Haddie, who had new welts on her cheek from where the mosquitoes had gotten her. Surely, there was no way Haddie had imagined Shannon would need to wait so long for clarity.

"It's okay," said Haddie, as if she read her mind. "Sometimes it can take a long time."

And so they sat for another half hour or so, until Shannon decided to become an English teacher, figuring she liked camp because she liked working with young people and teaching would give her freedom in the summer to spend time in nature and pursue other interests. It seemed like such a good idea at the time.

She picked up her remaining twenty-five arrows and shot them one after the other, and one after the other they all pierced the target, most near the center. She knew without counting she had done it—she had earned her hundred points.

"So what's it going to be?" Haddie asked.

"Teaching."

"Good choice."

AMBER 2012

What a long day it had been, thought Amber as she stepped off the bus, walked up the road a bit, found her bike in the woods, and began to ride the three miles back up to camp against a fierce headwind, with her warped tire dragging on the brake. Dang, it was hard, and her knee, wrist, and elbow were all still swollen and bruised from her fall. It was going to be a long ride home.

Every day seemed like such a long day now. Other than finding a bathroom light to do homework by, each day just got harder, it seemed. And as she looked to the future, she honestly couldn't see how she could sustain this. A foster home was such an unknown, and that terrified her. If she couldn't trust her own mother to take care of her, how was she supposed to trust perfect strangers? Why would anyone do that—be a foster parent? What was in it for them? Slave labor? Someone to molest? That had been her mother's experience. No, Amber didn't trust anyone. But it was looking like going into foster care was the only way.

Is there anyone else in this whole world who could take me in? she wondered. Amber's mother had always told her that her father was dead, but she suspected that was untrue. It seemed more likely that there was a man in this world who had no idea she existed. Would things have been better with him in her life, or would they have been worse? In her imagination, she pictured her dad having nice parents she might be able to live with now. She'd so love to have grandparents. Without her mother's cooperation, there was no chance that Amber would ever find them—this family she could have had.

Since her mom had grown up in foster care, that is, until she ran away and had her, Amber had never known her grandparents. She imagined cookies and warmth, wrinkled smiling faces that lit up whenever they saw her. Hugs. She ached for all of it.

No, ever since her mother stopped waitressing at the Diner and started working at the bar when Amber was six all she ever knew was the smell of alcohol and weed lingering in an empty trailer, warm Kraft macaroni and cheese or Chef Boyardee ravioli on a good day and break-fast cereal on most other days for dinner. Instead of bed-time stories, on the rare nights her mother hadn't been working or partying, she had told Amber foster-care stories—stories of cruelty, in which the moral was always the same: Don't tell. Don't tell that Mommy isn't home when you get home. Don't tell that you make your own dinner even though you're only six. Don't tell any-one about the funny cigarettes or all Mommy's visitors. Don't bring friends over. Because even though this isn't perfect, it's better than foster care.

The prospect still terrified Amber, but she had to fin-ish high school and finish with great grades. There was no denying that the scholarship and college plan was a much better plan than anything her mom had ever come up with. God, her mom and her stupid plans for a better life . . .

Oftentimes Amber didn't know where her mother was, but sometimes before a date her mother would tell her who she was going out with and why: *I'm going out with Brad tonight. He has a nice house. Maybe we'll move out of this dump and into it someday. Wouldn't that be nice? I'm going out with Wade tonight. He owns the bar. I think he's going to offer me a job. Wouldn't that be the answer to our prayers? A job! I'm going out with Rod tonight. He has a Corvette. Maybe one day he'll let you come for a ride, too. Wouldn't that be fun? I'm going out with Van tonight. His parents are rich and one day he's going to get a big inheritance. Wouldn't it be nice if I married into that? We would be living the good life then! I'm going out with Mark tonight. He's in the military. If I married him, he'd be gone a lot, so it would still be you and me, but we'd have his paycheck and insurance, so we could go to the doctor when we needed to.* Yes, somewhere along the line, her mother had learned some survival strategies, but even as a little kid Amber always saw that none of these men were going to save them.

Just stay home with me, she had wanted to say to her mom so many times. *You're wasting your time, so just stay home with me.* But she was too afraid to say it. Once, when she was eight, her mother was gone for four days. There had been almost no food left in the house. Amber remembered making rice pilaf and beef gravy and eating that for the last three days while she wondered whether her mother was okay or whether she was coming back at all.

Amber had hated the noises their trailer would make, the refrigerator, the heat, the branches that slapped the roof on windy nights. The windows had no curtains, and outside the night was so very black. Little rituals brought her comfort—cracking the window and yelling, "I know you're out there and I'm calling the police!" before turning out the lights, then getting a running jump at her bed, clearing anything that might reach out from under it to try to grab her.

What a damned hard life it had been. Every day for years she kept hoping it would get easier, but it never did. It just got harder. And there was no mercy in sight. It made her want to pull her bike over, lie down, and just give up.

Maybe it was time to go to the high school counselor and ask for help, to just let Child Protective Services place her in a foster home. The unknown was so scary. She thought of that old expression "the devil you know is better than the devil you don't know" and decided that yes, if it came down to it, it would be safer to just move back in with her mom. Maybe Amber could build some kind of shelter in the woods behind her house for the nights that her mother brought some guy home, so she could slip out and be safe. But then she thought of the way the house smelled. That wasn't good. Her mom and the creepy man had obviously cooked up something in there, and Amber had watched the news enough to know that houses where drugs were manufactured were toxic places, unfit to live in. No, she couldn't go home and she couldn't surrender to the unknown. She was just going to have to figure it out as she went.

When she reached her cabin, she found a surprise—a note on a big paper heart taped to the window:

> *Child,*
> *You are safe here. I will not tell anyone where you are. For many years, I was the camp director here, and it was my experience that when kids found their way here in the off-season, there was a good reason. Please join us for dinner in the Lodge. Surely you are hungry.*
>
> —*Aunt Ethel*
>
> *P.S. I unlocked your door so you don't have to use the window anymore.*

Since she was so hungry, this invitation felt like a miracle, so she opened the door, put her book bag inside, and set off.

RUBY 2012

"Ruby, I'd like to introduce you to my neighbor, Walt. Walt Murdock, Ruby Gemill." Ruby's heart skipped a beat as she took him in. He looked tan, as if he spent a lot of time outdoors, and his distinguished salt-and-pepper hair looked freshly trimmed. He wore a thick wool sweater that zipped up and brought out the green in his eyes.

Walt took her hand. "It's a pleasure to meet you, Ruby. I like your taste in apparel." He pointed toward her fishing vest, and she realized he was wearing one as well.

Maybe it was simply his fishing vest or the fact he was here on Lake Wenatchee—here at camp—but she thought it was something more, something about his gentle demeanor and the kindness in his eyes. He reminded her of Henry.

"Walt's going to join us for dinner tonight," said Ethel.

"I brought perch!" He held up his catch with great pride.

Ethel said, "Walt wants to prepare it in his special way, which he promised would dazzle and amaze us all, so I told him we would give him space and let him work his magic."

"Magic indeed," Walt said with a sparkle in his eye.

As Ruby poured a can of cream of mushroom soup over a panful of Tater Tots to make Tater Tot casserole for dinner, she swore she could feel the electricity coming off Walt, even though he stood three feet away. She blushed, embarrassed about her awareness of him and embarrassed about her silly thoughts. *How desperate and starved for touch must I be to find standing three feet away from a seventy-something-year-old bachelor so exciting.* She stifled a laugh as she thought, *This is the most action I've had in years!*

Next to her, Ethel was making a salad with iceberg lettuce, radishes, and tomatoes. She paused, looking around at Ruby and then Walt, who was breading the fish. "It's always strange for me to see men in camp."

Ruby laughed. "Remember that time that those boys drove into camp? Haddie and I stopped them on the road and told them they had to leave, but they drove on down

toward the Lodge anyway? I cut through camp to inter-
cept them, while Haddie found you so you could get your
car . . . remember that?"

Ethel replied, "Oh yeah! When I drove down, you
and Haddie were hitting their car with brooms! Opal
was there, too, wasn't she? Hahaha! Oh God, that was
funny." Ethel laughed so hard she had to wipe tears from
her eyes.

Walt turned and looked at Ruby. "You beat someone
up with a *broom*?"

"I plead the Fifth," Ruby said coyly.

Ethel replied, "Well, not them—just their car."

"Brooms?" Walt asked. *"Brooms* were your weapon of
choice?"

"It was all we had," Ruby explained.

"So did they leave?" asked Walt.

"We chased them down the whole South Shore Road
in Ethel's car, hitting theirs whenever we could take a
shot," Ethel answered.

"I bet they're still running," Ruby added with pride.

Ethel nodded in agreement. "I bet they are."

"I sure would be!" Walt said, and gave Ruby a wink.
A wink!

Just then, Laura entered the kitchen.

"Laura! My neighbor Walt brought us fish for dinner
tonight. Ruby and I were just telling him about the time
we ran some boys out of camp."

Since Walt's hands were a mess, Laura said hello without shaking hands, and then turned to Ethel and laughed.
"I recall being really little, maybe seven, and some high
school girl's boyfriend and his friend came to camp. . . ."
She turned to Ruby and Walt. "I just remember it was like
a scene from *Godzilla,* you know, where everyone was
screaming, 'Boys in camp!' and running toward the
Lodge, herding all the little girls to safety."

Ethel began laughing even harder. "Oh yes, Kim was a Seattle girl. She was wild."

"Did you all beat them up with brooms, too?" Walt asked Ethel. Then he caught Ruby's eye again and smiled. Was it Ruby's imagination or did his eyes sparkle only for her?

She raised an eyebrow as she looked back at him, and his smile turned just a little deliciously suggestive. *Oh my.*

"Brooms?" Laura asked.

Ethel explained. "In the last story, we chased the boys out with brooms."

"No." Laura laughed. "No brooms. Ethel just called the cops."

"Sheriff Sam showed up and kicked them in the nuts," Ethel said, then covered her mouth as if she had just told a secret.

"Sam kicked them in the nuts? Sam?" Walt asked, surprised and thoroughly entertained.

"Don't underestimate Sam," Ethel said. "He can be a very creative problem solver."

All of a sudden Walt pretended to be concerned. "Boy, I hope he doesn't show up and kick me in the nuts!" That sent everyone into a fit of hysterics.

I hope he doesn't either, Ruby thought with a little smile. This was only beginning to get interesting.

SHANNON 2012

Long after Ethel left, the crow continued to sit on the post as if it were waiting for Shannon to make up her mind. And Shannon continued to sit on the dock, racking her brain for new career ideas. She needed something that didn't involve a lot of bullshit; she had no more tolerance for bullshit.

Reading meters sounded nice. Water or electric. As she thought about it, she realized it had been a long time since anyone had come to read her electric meter. Surely that was done remotely now. But water? Yeah, she could go around reading water meters. *Sure, there would be the occasional biting dog, drug addict, or militia member, but were any of those things really a bigger threat than a class of high school kids?* With that thought, she laughed to herself. *Yes,* she thought. *All of those things were a bigger threat than a class of high school kids.* Maybe reading meters wasn't such a great idea after all.

She heard about people making a lot of money being sales reps for drug companies. Oh, but that sounded like bullshit.

What else, what else, what else?

Maybe real estate. Okay, so the housing market had tanked and people who had been at it for years got squeezed out and had to find another line of work. That was clearly not encouraging, but still, she didn't dismiss it.

Maybe if she sold her house fast enough, she could use the equity to go to trade school and learn to become an auto mechanic. While she never had much patience for broken things—rather, she had a tendency to want to fix things with a hammer once and for all—she could appreciate how there wasn't much bullshit involved with fixing a car. People would come in with broken cars, and she would fix them. It seemed beautifully simple like that. But then it occurred to her that cars had changed a lot in the last twenty or thirty years. They had computerized engines now, and she was willing to bet the technology needed to diagnose problems was far more expensive and complicated than it had been in the past. Maybe mechanics all had to work for dealerships now. She was sure those places had a lot of bullshit trickle down from management. *Okay,* she thought. *Clearly being an auto mechanic was not my calling.*

She thought of the people who worked at Safeway, how they were required to say hello to everyone they made eye contact with and ask them if they were finding everything okay. Bullshit.

Really, working for any corporate entity was going to involve bullshit.

Maybe she was foolish for thinking she could somehow escape it, for thinking that it was going to be better anywhere else. It seemed likely everyone had to deal with bullshit wherever they were. Perhaps she should just suck it up and go back to teaching. While teaching was bursting at the seams with bullshit, there was one facet of it that was real and genuine . . . that meant something. If only she could have that part of it alone. There was no sense in dreaming.

She looked at the crow and jokingly said, "Sorry, Haddie. I'm getting nowhere. I suspect I need to change my attitude instead of my life." She lay back and looked at the sky.

But the isolation. The isolation was too much. Every time she tried to resign herself to returning to her house and returning to her life, she recoiled.

Just then, she heard footsteps on the dock and turned her head to see a young woman walking toward her. Shannon wondered what it was, what combination of subtle clues caused her to look at this young woman and think, *Closed up. This girl is all closed up.* Her hands were stuffed in her pockets, and her shoulders rolled forward a little. There were hints of quiet desperation on her face, small furrows between her brows, lips pursed together. In the ways this girl could have armor she did, and in the ways that she couldn't the whole world could see something was not right. Her medium-length blond hair was unkempt and a little greasy, and Shannon noticed a little hole in her sneaker as she neared. *Hard life* was written all over her.

Shannon sat up and waited for the girl to close the gap. The crow watched her as well.

"Are you Ethel?" the girl asked.

The crow *caa*ed and flew off.

Shannon wanted to jokingly ask whether she looked like an Ethel, but the girl looked so nervous that she simply stood up and replied, "No, I'm Shannon, but I'll help you find her."

The girl attempted to smile with her closed-up face and said, "Thanks," and together they walked back down the dock.

If this girl were in Shannon's class, she'd take her under her wing. She'd take clues the girl gave her about her life and pick out just the right books to make her feel less alone. They'd read them as a class, and as the class developed sympathy for the main character their capacity to be compassionate toward this closed-up girl would grow. The girl would see this and come to trust the group. She'd open up. It happened like that sometimes. That was the part of Shannon's job that was non-bullshit. And that was the part of her job that was becoming derailed by the current tide of education.

As they walked toward the Lodge Shannon tried to make polite conversation, but the young woman was not particularly talkative. It didn't surprise Shannon. Kids like this took a long time to come out of their shell—weeks or months, sometimes even years.

"Hello!" Ethel called out from the cedar grove below the Lodge. "Come look! I want to show you something!"

"That's Ethel," Shannon said. "She always has something neat to show us—something in nature. She notices everything."

Into a branch above Ethel's head a crow flew. Maybe it was the same one or maybe it was a new one; Shannon didn't know. It landed on a branch and called out, *Caa! Caa!* But still Shannon saw no career opportunity in front of her. She only saw the opportunity to see Ethel's latest discovery.

ETHEL 2012

When Ethel saw the girl walk up with Shannon, she met them, took the girls' hands, and said, "I'm so glad you're here."

Confusion swept across the girl's face, and she looked to Shannon for some help interpreting. Shannon just nodded as if to say, *This is who Ethel is and what she does,* and Ethel took that as a compliment.

"What is your name?" Ethel asked the girl.

"Amber," she answered.

"That's a beautiful name."

Ethel looked at the scrapes and bruises on Amber's face, and Amber self-consciously put a hand on her cheek. "I wrecked on my bike."

Maybe she did, Ethel thought, but bruises combined with running away usually meant something other than a bike wreck.

"I was out here thinking about the shallow roots of cedar trees—really studying them. Look how the roots of all these trees have woven themselves together. They hold each other up." Ethel entwined her fingers with those of Amber and Shannon. "Like us."

Just then Ruby yelled out the window. "Hurry up before we resort to cannibalism in here!"

"They're not really cannibals," Ethel assured Amber. "You're just in time for dinner. I'm going to apologize right now for Ruby's cooking. She's been a bachelorette for a long, long time. But Walt is making the main dish—fish—and he's a good cook. Come."

Ethel led the way to the back door of the Lodge, but before she walked in the trees caught her attention. She stopped and looked up at the cedars that she loved so much. Either they were happy about Amber and were making noise for the first time in a good long while or else Ethel was feeling better and could hear them more clearly again. She listened and then smiled. It had been so long. "Can you hear them?" she asked the girls. "They're saying, 'Welcome.' They get really excited when young people come here."

Shannon and Amber paused and listened but didn't appear to hear them. No matter. Perhaps it took practice to hear the language of trees.

The door stuck, so Ethel turned around and kicked it like a mule. Then she put her arm around Amber and announced, "We have a guest!" Amber smiled nervously.

Ruby, Laura, and Walt all said hello and Ruby quickly set another place.

Ethel picked a short grace: "'Neath these tall green trees we stand, asking blessings from thy hand. Thanks we give to thee above, for our health and strength and love. Amen."

As she sang, she glanced over and saw a look of profound gratitude on Amber's face. Yes, Amber was thankful in that way people are when they are very, very hungry and about to eat, Ethel could tell. So, whenever the Tater Tot casserole came to her, Ethel put an extra spoonful on Amber's plate so she wouldn't feel self-conscious about taking too much.

Spending time and sharing space with Ruby had become almost comfortable. Ethel looked around the table at Ruby, Walt, Laura, Shannon, and now Amber and felt warm. She hadn't even realized how much she had missed having a close community like this.

"You're going to like it here," Ethel told Amber, and patted her forearm. "If you need help with homework, Shannon here is an English teacher and Laura knows a lot about science."

"Thanks," Amber said, and looked at Laura. "I do need help with biology."

Laura nodded. "I'd be happy to help you."

Ethel noticed Amber looking at the fish and spooned a little more on her plate. "Excellent job on the dinner, Walt and Ruby. It's delicious!"

Amber held her stomach as she looked at the food Ethel had just put on her plate, and suddenly Ethel was concerned that by encouraging her to eat too much too soon she might have made her sick. "I don't know if I can," Amber said apologetically. "But believe me—nothing has ever tasted so good to me in my life."

"No pressure. Don't make yourself sick."

Relieved, Amber smiled at her. Ethel noticed she made good eye contact. That was a good sign. Yes, it was a good thing this child found her way here. A very good thing indeed.

LAURA 2012

Watching Ethel spoon food onto Amber's plate caused a pang in Laura's heart that she hadn't seen coming. How many times had she done the same thing to her own children's plates? How odd it seemed that she would never do that again. Never. That time in her life had passed, and it was never coming back. Never. No more dressing them up in Halloween costumes and holding their sweet little hands. No more walking them into their new classroom on the first day of the school year. No more of them sitting on her lap at bedtime for a song or a story. All of those things were gone forever. And truthfully, they had been gone for a while, but somehow just having one child in the house was like being thrown scraps. There were rare occasions when Alison said something complimentary to Laura or acknowledged some act of kindness with gratitude. Just one of those moments could sustain Laura for a long time. But now both children were gone, and it was never going to be the same. It was as if a giant steel door like one on a bank safe was shutting—a door to that time in her life, a door to a place she missed but could no longer go—and the permanence of it suddenly overwhelmed her. She tried to take a breath, but the air just wouldn't go in.

"Please excuse me," she said as she pushed back her chair from the table and bolted for the door.

Ethel, Shannon, and Ruby exchanged puzzled looks.

It was Shannon who came looking for Laura a minute later. "Hey, what's going on?"

"I don't know," Laura said honestly, still struggling to take in a satisfying breath. "I think I had a panic attack. It suddenly just hit me that my kids were never going to be little again, and . . . I don't know . . . I just panicked."

"Change is suffering," said Shannon.

"Change *is* suffering," echoed Laura. "And so is not changing. I've got this husband at home I don't even know anymore, but I'm pretty clear he hasn't been in love with me in too many years to count. Shannon, I don't want to go home."

Shannon thought about it for a minute and then said, "Well, you don't have to. At least not tonight. And not tomorrow night."

Shannon's answer wasn't remotely satisfying. "It's just so surreal . . . this thing where you pour everything into your kids, into creating this family and this home—this *life*—and you think at some point that you actually have done it, and then all of a sudden they're gone. They leave you as if you never mattered, as if they never needed you, as if you didn't bring them into this world and feed them and change them and rock them to sleep. There's no commemorative plaque or retirement party. It's just boom! Suddenly I've been fired. That's how it feels. And if I'm not a full-time mother, who the hell am I?"

"Yeah. I get that. I mean, not with being a mother. I have the sense that the magnitude of that is bigger than what I'm going through. But I know. I'm also more or less getting fired from my life as I knew it." Shannon seemed considerably more resigned to it than Laura felt.

Laura paused and then asked, still panic-stricken, "What do we do now?"

Shrugging, Shannon replied, "Well, I think we take these buckets out to the dock and fill them up, and then carry them up the hill to the wheelbarrow so we can wheel them to the bathroom. Ethel says we need more water for flushing. I think that's what we do right now. And the other stuff, well, I think we give ourselves a couple more days to figure it out."

Suddenly Laura exploded into laughter—the kind of laughter that came out when she needed to cry but couldn't. And Shannon joined her because laughter was a considerably more fun way to hit the pressure-release valve in life than crying.

The laughter burst through the barrier that had been keeping Laura from breathing, and now that her body was working again she felt much calmer. "Toilets first, life second," said Laura, beginning to collect herself.

"Or we could have dinner first, deal with toilets second, and deal with life after that," offered Shannon.

"Yes," said Laura. "Dinner, toilets, life. Let's go with that plan."

LAURA 1988

Maybe it was because Laura had been assigned to be the counselor in the Rotary cabin, the cabin with the littlest campers, that Ethel and Haddie had chosen her. Or maybe it was because this cabin was closest to theirs, so they would be able to keep a careful eye on the situation. But Laura liked to think that it was because Ethel liked her best.

Quiet hour was very difficult to keep quiet. Six-year-olds weren't old enough to read to themselves, and their attention span was short. Many needed naps and weren't going to get them unless everyone was quiet, so Laura told stories where the girls were princesses who ventured out into the woods and made friends with animals.

Ethel's footsteps and quiet knock had interrupted her story. One of her campers opened the door and immediately said, "Aw!" which caused everyone to look up. In her arms Ethel held a fawn.

"Her mother was hit on the road this morning. I don't

know what chance she has. She might not make it. But Gayle at the Forest Service has given us permission to try. How would you like to be her foster mother?"

Laura simply nodded, astounded. She accepted the fawn into her arms. The animal was shaking from fear or cold or both, so Laura stroked her soft fur and waited for her body heat to permeate. The girls, of course, named her Bambi.

That summer was a magical blur of a lot of things—bottle-feeding the fawn, the way Laura's campers would squeal every time they discovered more deer droppings in the cabin, the way the fawn would follow them everywhere—even into the shower house. But what Laura remembered most was simply being proud.

By August, the fawn had grown quite a bit. Laura took her to the playfield to graze as she weaned her off the bottle. And one day as they walked down to the hollowed-out tree on Windy Point where they told the campers Winnie the Pooh lived, Bambi wandered off, and though it tore at her heart, Laura let her.

Haddie could tell by the devastated look on Laura's face when she returned and by the absence of the little deer that something had happened, and she simply opened her arms.

"She left," Laura said.

"Congratulations," Haddie replied. "You did it. This is a huge success."

AMBER 2012

"Xylem and phloem," Laura said when Amber opened her biology book to the right page.

"I can't keep them straight," said Amber.

"Okay, 'phloem' starts with the 'f' sound, just like food. Phloem carries water, food, and nutrients. Phloem is soft. Call her 'Flo' for short. She is a waitress. Picture her. She's soft, and she's bringing you food."

Amber laughed.

"'Xylem' is hard. It starts with an *x*. Think of Malcolm X. He was tough. He was hard. He was a preacher, so say it like a preacher. Xylem!"

"Xlylem!" Amber said.

"No, make me feel it. Xylem!"

Amber tried again but started laughing. "Xylem!"

Laura continued. "Xylem is hard and it carries water and minerals. Water pipes are hard. They're made of metal, which is made from minerals."

"I think I got it!" Amber said, amazed.

"Funny voices," Laura said. "They never fail."

Amber laughed again. No one had ever helped her with her homework like this. Was this what other people's parents did? Was this what she had been missing out on?

Laura flipped through Amber's long, dry chapter. "Do you know the trick about reading the first paragraph and the last paragraph of a chapter and then just reading the first sentence of all the paragraphs in-between?"

"No," Amber replied.

"It was the only way I could keep up with all the reading in college. The first paragraph will tell you what's going to be in the chapter—what you should look for. Then I'd read the first sentence of every paragraph. If it was something I didn't understand, I'd read the whole paragraph carefully. But the most important step was reading the last paragraph, which told me what I should have learned. If I didn't learn something, I'd go back until I found it and read about it."

"Brilliant," said Amber.

"Tell you what. Tomorrow after school, we can hike to Hidden Lake from here and look for places where someone sliced a tree that had fallen over the trail, and I can show you where the xylem and phloem generally are."

"I'd like that," said Amber.

Just then, Ethel walked back into the kitchen. "Amber, honey, why don't you move into the loft with Ruby and me? We both snore, but it's warm, and you won't be all alone in a cabin. There's electricity here, too, and you're closer to the kitchen if you get hungry. We'd love to have you with us."

Amber hesitated but then remembered how creepy the dark cabin was when the wind blew the branch against the window and how her stomach hurt when she woke in the middle of the night hungry. "Thanks," she said. "I'd like that."

"Let me get my flashlight, and I'll walk up there with you and help you carry your things."

"Thanks," Amber said, grateful not to have to walk through the camp at night alone.

Ethel went up to the loft and came back down with her flashlight and a stocking cap on her head. Then she took Amber by the elbow and with a big smile said, "Let's go."

Again Amber found herself wondering, *Is this how other people's mothers and grandmothers look at them?* It was powerful. Something about the way Ethel looked at Amber made her feel truly seen. Occasionally a teacher looked at her like that, but most of the time they were busy and distracted. They glanced. Their pace was different. But Ethel took a good long moment to look at Amber as if she was a person of worth. "Generous" was the word that popped into Amber's mind. So much heart poured out of Ethel's eyes that the only word for it was "generous."

"Tell me your story," Ethel said as they walked up the hill. "What brought you here?"

Amber took a big breath and just said it. "On Sunday night, I thought my mom's latest creepy boyfriend was going to molest me and so I ran into the woods and waited for him to leave. It was really scary and really cold and I wondered if I was going to freeze to death before he left. And I just thought, *This can never happen again.* Then when I finally went inside, my mom was vacuuming the same spot over and over. She was on something. So, I took a shower, packed my things, and found this place. I'm sorry I broke the lock on the window."

Ethel waved a hand. "It can be fixed. I'm glad you're okay and that he didn't hurt you." They walked a little farther, and then Ethel asked, "Why did you choose to run away instead of asking your school counselor for help?"

"My only chance of a better life is getting a scholarship, and for that I need straight A's. If they pull me out of my school and put me into another—into new classes—my grades will drop. This is a small community. I don't even know if there are any foster homes here. They might ship me off to Wenatchee or somewhere. And you know, whether it's here or there, who knows whose house they're going to put me in? How do I know they will be good people? I don't know those people. They might be bad people. They might be weird people. How would you like to be plopped into someone's home with no choice about it?"

Ethel listened and nodded, and then she asked, "Is anyone looking for you right now? Your mom? The sheriff?"

"It seems like if they were, they could have found me at school. I seriously doubt my mom would do anything to get the sheriff's attention."

"Who's your mom?"

Amber hesitated. "Why? Are you going to call her?"

"No," Ethel said. "I just need to have all the information. You're a runaway and we're taking you in. That's a risky position for us. I need to assess that risk. If I run into her at the store, I want to know it's her."

"Debbie Hill. She works at the bar."

"I don't know her."

"I don't know why you would. Well, a long time ago she worked at the Diner."

"Hm . . . ," Ethel said, trying to remember but eventually shaking her head. "The Firelight Girls are closing this camp. We've just come out to clean it and say good-bye to it. It's not a place that's easy to get in and out of in the winter. We need to find a longer-term solution for you. What do you say we just take a couple days and think about it?"

Amber shrugged and then said, "Sure." She didn't know what else to do.

"Everything is going to be okay," Ethel reassured her. "You don't have to worry. It's good you're here. You're going to have a great few days with us, and we're going to figure out a plan for you. You're in good hands. I'm an old pro."

Concerned, Amber looked over at her, but seeing Ethel's confidence, she managed a small, hopeful smile.

Ethel looked back at her with those generous eyes, patted her forearm, and said again, "Everything is going to be okay."

AMBER 2001

The smell of vinegar. The way the smooth crayon felt in her hand. The surprisingly bumpy texture of an eggshell. The colors set out before her like a liquid rainbow in steamy little glasses. Trying to balance the heavy egg on the little wire dipper. Amber's first memory was all in fragments.

But what she remembered most was none of those things. No, what she remembered most was the encouraging look in her mother's eyes. "Go ahead, try it!" Amber remembered her mother's hand on her own as they lowered an egg down into a sea of pink.

On the egg, her crayon drawing of her mother's face and hers shone through the dye. As far as Amber was concerned, the egg *was* them. She watched her mother's gentle hand pick it up from where it precariously perched on the wire dipper and gently place it into the security of the container. Relief washed over Amber. They were safe in their little egg house.

She looked up at her mother, who was smiling down at her. How happy they were.

In the beginning, her mother had really tried. Amber couldn't quite wrap her mind around what had made her mother give up—this hard life, this life where she could never get ahead—because even though all of that was discouraging, wasn't Amber worth more than just giving up on?

RUBY 2012

After dinner, Ruby hated to see Walt go. She tried to act casual while she said good-bye, but the little wink he gave her just about made her lose her composure. She was sure she blushed. She knew better than to take it personally. Some men were just charmers and winkers like that.

While Ethel walked Walt back to his boat, Ruby collected herself by going upstairs to assess the raiding potential. It would have to be something pretty harmless. Her reconciliation with Ethel still felt pretty fragile. A simple flagpole raid would do.

As she tiptoed across the little room, Ruby played back her favorite moments from dinner in her mind. She had frequently noticed Walt's gaze out of the corner of her eye. Occasionally she would look up, catch his eye, and give him a little smile. During other moments, she had doubted herself. After all, how long had it been since she'd flirted? However long it had been, it had been at least three times longer since she had actually been courted. Decades. What was this Walt fellow trying to do to her anyway, unnerving her like this, getting her hopes up like this? For a good long while she had avoided eye contact with him, but when at last she could resist no longer she had looked up and seen something new in his expression. Nervousness. And though she had wanted to keep her defenses up, she couldn't help it—she softened. He felt what she felt—the electricity, the hope, and even the terror. He was taking a risk, too. How could she not appreciate that?

Okay, focus, Ruby thought to herself as she unzipped Ethel's large green duffel bag to look for bras and underpants. Ruby couldn't let the attention of a man derail her now. She carefully rifled through the duffel bag, but instead of underwear she found the strange thing that had been sitting on the bathroom windowsill when Ethel had been talking to herself. Ruby took it out and studied it. When she realized it was an urn, she almost dropped it. Haddie. The black yarn, the smile . . . oh, Ethel had been trying to turn these ashes back into Haddie. Ruby shook her head. This was not good—not good at all.

Ruby realized just opening this duffel bag was far more violating than she ever intended, so she zipped it back up without taking anything. No, she absolutely couldn't raid now.

It was hard to let go. She remembered the sound of dirt hitting Opal's coffin. Yes, it was so hideously hard to let go. And yet this thing that Ethel was doing struck Ruby as extremely unhealthy. Could she help? she wondered. How would she even broach the subject? It all seemed so very delicate.

Maybe Ethel needed a ritual to help her let go. Wish boats—the big pieces of bark that they decorated with sticks, moss, pinecones, and a candle and set out on the lake . . . Yes, wish boats might be exactly what Ethel needed. There was something about letting them go at night, candles flickering, watching the light drift away never to return. It really helped a person recognize the beauty of letting go. It was worth a shot, anyway. After all, long ago it had once worked for Ruby.

While she waited for Ethel to return, Ruby wished for the right words to come to her. She prayed for them, in fact, which was uncharacteristic for her. But no words came. And then when Ethel did return Amber was with her, so Ruby said nothing. Nothing but a simple good night.

RUBY 1952

Ruby had stood at the end of the long dock, looking across the water at the small floating dock that was anchored out where kids could swim to it. She was simultaneously admiring her sister's brilliance and fuming at the same time. There was Ruby's bed with her sleeping bag and blanket on top. Under her bed, just as it had been in her cabin, was her canvas duffel bag. As whitecaps hit the floating dock, water ran over the decking and into that duffel bag. All of her things would be soaked. She would not be able to get the bed back by herself, but she could canoe out, get her sleeping bag and duffel bag, and begin to dry out all of her clothes and bedding—she hoped in time to use it, though that was likely overly optimistic.

Usually, there was always someone around to help, but this prank had been pulled during Saturday breakfast, the day all the kids went home. Since everyone was in their cabins packing and soon would be hauling their suitcases up to the top of the hill where the camp bus would pick them up and bring them back to Wenatchee, Ruby was on her own.

The aluminum canoe was large and awkward. Since it was a river canoe, it had no keel. After all, they were often used to canoe the White River, which ended at the west end of the lake, as well as the Upper Wenatchee River, which began at the east end, and in a river a person wanted a boat with a flat bottom. But without a keel it was impossible to paddle in a straight line on the lake in the wind no matter how proficient her J-stroke was. The wind just kept turning her. Finally, she reached the little dock, but with no one to assist her, plus the strong wind, she couldn't get out of the boat. It was hard to even hold on.

"Do you need help?" Ruby looked behind her at a young man rowing a small boat. The summer sun had bleached his short hair and tanned his skin. There was something warm and open about his face, something peaceful about his eyes. She liked him instantly.

"If I get caught with a boy at camp, it will mean certain death!" she called back.

"Okay, then! I won't help!" The cute boy laughed as

he reeled in his fishing line and cast again, clearly entertained by the whole scene.

Suddenly self-conscious, she held on to the dock for dear life with one hand and used her other to snag her duffel bag with her paddle. Since it was saturated, it seemed to weigh at least fifty pounds, and it took all of her strength to slide it into her boat.

Unlike her duffel bag, her sleeping bag was dry, so when she snagged it with her paddle both it and her blanket went sailing in the strong wind and landed in the water.

The boy dropped his pole and raced over to pull them out of the lake just before they sank. She paddled toward him, wary of who might be watching, her canoe going in every direction except the one she wished it to. And then finally, she got close enough that he caught her bow and threw her bedding into the front of her canoe.

"I'm Henry," he said.

"Ruby," she replied. "Thank you very much."

Henry assessed the bed on the dock and asked, "Why do I get the feeling this was an act of revenge?"

"Because it was," Ruby said.

"Was the prank you pulled worth the one you just received?"

"Depends on whether my sleeping bag dries before night or not," she answered.

"So, tell me about this deed that had brought on the revenge," he said with a smile so charming that Ruby found herself suddenly willing to risk being seen with a boy near a bed on the floating dock.

"Well, two days ago, I took all of my sister's things and hid them under her cabin. So yesterday, after she had to borrow a sleeping bag from the nurse's cabin and wear the same underwear for the second day in a row—"

"Clearly she was not happy about that," Henry said.

"Yeah, she was downright mad. Do you know how many kids have peed in those sleeping bags in the nurse's cabin? But it gets worse. I left a note for my sister in her mailbox, directing her to the location of the first clue in a long treasure hunt. I sent her *everywhere*. All in all, no less than three miles. And her final clue was that she had slept on top of her things the night before."

"Oh no!" Henry laughed. "She must have been *really* mad!"

"Well, Opal says she doesn't really get mad—she just gets even."

"So you messed with the dragon," Henry had said.

"Yes, I messed with the dragon," Ruby sighed, "but if I hadn't, I guess I wouldn't be sitting in a boat next to you right now."

Henry flashed her a come-and-get-me grin. "So you're saying going looking for trouble pays off."

Ruby smiled back. "Well, it does look that way, but I'll get back to you with a definitive answer at the end of our date."

"Our date?" he asked.

"I'm free in a couple hours," she said.

"Well then, I guess I should take you out for an ice cream."

"Well then, I guess you should." With that, she turned the canoe around. "Thank you again, Henry, my hero," she said flirtatiously.

thursday

As she always seemed to do, Ethel woke before every-body. During the days it seemed she was distracted enough to be more or less all right, and sometimes at night she was too tired to think, which also helped. But the be-ginning of each day overwhelmed Ethel. She hated wak-ing up without Haddie next to her. Everything just seemed as empty as her bed. Each day, her first thought was, *How am I going to endure another day without Haddie?*

This morning, Ethel could not bear it and caved to the habit that offered her a tiny bit of comfort. She wrapped Haddie's ashes in a towel so no one would think anything other than that she was off to do her morning routine in the bathroom if they saw her carrying it, and with the ashes in her hand she quietly slipped out of the loft, down the stairs, and out the doors.

Frost coated everything. Change was in the air. Ethel did not like it at all. Autumn mirrored every ending in her life, it seemed. The end of Haddie's life. The end of camp. The end of her own life. All of it was beyond un-comfortable.

She made her way to Elks Beach, sat on a log, and

unwrapped Haddie's ashes, but this time she did not talk to them. She only held them in her lap and pondered the various groups who might purchase the camp. It seemed highly likely it would be a church, and when she considered which denominations appeared to own the most camps it seemed highly likely it would be one that was intolerant of gay people. How unthinkable to have her sacred place, her *home,* owned by people who would condemn her. Actually, losing the camp was unthinkable, but losing it to people who thought her sacred love was sinful was just downright hideous. *Could the circumstances be more unkind?* she wondered.

She gripped Haddie's ashes tighter and resolved that no matter what, she would still return here, no matter who officially owned it on paper. Yes, other people might own this place, but this place owned her. She belonged to it. Rain had fallen and filtered through the soil, picking up minerals along the way, seeped all the way to the water table where the old well had pumped it up for her to drink. The minerals from this land were in her bones. The water still resided in her tissues. How could anyone else own that? It would be like someone owning her mother.

Chances were good that the camp wouldn't be inhabited full-time. There would be times when Ethel could still come home for a moment, come home to the place in her bones, to the place where her love still lingered.

ETHEL 2011

Ethel remembered the feeling of Haddie's urn in her hand two days after she died, cold and surprisingly heavy. She had walked out of the funeral home with it into a world where it seemed few had understood that all these years Haddie had been her soul mate, her companion, her beloved, a world that had denied them the comfortable pleasure of walking down the street or sitting in the movies hand in hand, of dancing in each other's arms at wedding receptions, of having their own wedding. Ethel stood on the sidewalk for a moment, holding what remained of her whole world in her two hands, devastated.

Less than a week before, Haddie and she had been stacking wood for the winter, breathing in the crisp fall air, talking about what kind of soup sounded good, how they were going to heat up the fresh-pressed apple cider Haddie had bought at the farmer's market in town, when suddenly Haddie yelped, grabbed her left arm, froze, and fell to the ground.

At first, Ethel dropped to her knees beside her, and Haddie clutched Ethel's hand with her right one and looked deep into Ethel's eyes, pleading. Wanting to save Haddie's life, Ethel had broken free of Haddie's grasp and run to the phone to call for help, but when she returned Haddie was unconscious. Ethel kneeled, put her fingers on Haddie's neck, and leaned over so her cheek was above Haddie's mouth, but she could detect no pulse nor feel any breath. She performed CPR as she had been trained to do throughout her whole camp director career.

In the beginning Ethel was determined, but as the minutes began to pass doubt began to settle in. She pleaded with Haddie to return to her as she placed her hands on the very thing she loved most—on Haddie's heart—and did chest compressions. Ethel willed herself to stay composed enough to continue, to breathe life back into her love with strong, clear breaths, not sobs, but as more and more time passed desperation, horror, and loss began to hit her. The paramedics came, pronounced Haddie dead and took her away.

Now, with the urn in her hands, Ethel didn't know what to do, so she drove home. She tried putting it on the mantel, but it felt wrong. Although it was already dusk, she set out in her kayak with Haddie's ashes and paddled to Elks Beach, intent on releasing them there, but when she got there she just couldn't do it. She just hadn't been ready to let Haddie go. Ethel's mind flashed back to leaving Haddie to die alone while she called an ambulance when she should have stayed beside her friend, when she should have held her hand and said all the right things to make death less scary, when she should have said *thank you* and *I love you* and *I will meet you in heaven before you know it.* She thought of those regrets, of how she wished she would have held on to Haddie tighter, and she could not let go of what remained of her.

With a heavy heart, Ethel had paddled home and put Haddie's ashes on the mantel, right where she knew they did not belong.

AMBER 2012

How nice it was to eat a couple of orange slices and a little oatmeal before she slipped out the door. Amber looked at the food in front of her. It wasn't much—all together, no bigger than her fist. And yet it was huge. Not being scared and hungry was huge.

She could hear Ruby's snoring through the ceiling and wondered how she had slept through that last night. Smiling, she washed her bowl and her spoon and walked her bike up to the bathroom, where she finished getting ready for school.

As she brushed her teeth, she examined her face. It looked better but still not good. The swelling was down, but the bruise on her cheek was a little darker today and her scabs had not changed.

She walked her dilapidated bike all the way to the top of the road and began riding to the bus stop, but she could not stop thinking about the condition of her face and the feeling she had about Mr. Morris reporting her to CPS. Was going to school a mistake? What if she walked into some kind of CPS trap there?

Suddenly Amber didn't know what to do. Truancy wasn't going to get her where she wanted to go, but neither was a foster home. She needed time to think. There had to be a way to avoid losing even more control of her own life and staying on track with her long-term goals. She pulled over to the side of the road and tried to get some clarity, but it never came. Looking at her little alarm clock, she realized that with her warped wheel it was likely too late to get to the bus stop in time now. Should she go back to camp? Would Ethel make her go to school?

She had no reason not to trust Ethel, so she pedaled back to the top of the camp's little road. There she leaned her bike against the gate and sat with her head in her hands. Inside she felt so tired, so tired of how arduous the most basic things had become, so tired of fighting all the opposing forces, so tired of figuring out solutions to situations that quite possibly didn't have solutions. She closed her eyes and let her mind wander back to when life was good, when her mother sat beside her while she took a bath, wrapped her in a towel fresh from the dryer when she stood, and then combed and braided her wet hair.

The wind picked up, blowing a branch off a tree nearby, and startled her out of her memories. As she stood, it hit her hard that there were no magical answers. She was missing school today. It would be hard to make up. And if CPS came looking for her, she could only hide for so long.

RUBY 1952

Ruby had known Ethel and Haddie were waiting just outside the back doors of the Lodge as she played her part in her campers' skit that they were doing in the weekly all-camp variety show. Ruby acted as if she didn't know what was coming, even though she most certainly did. Her ears were alert to the sound of tires on gravel, and her body was ready to run. There was no denying that she had played a lot of pranks in the previous week—as she had every week. And she was about to pay the price—also as she did every week. If her skit finished before she heard her sister Opal's convertible, Ruby might be able to slip out through the front door or the kitchen or at least hide in the closet under the stairs. So far, she had never escaped Ethel and Haddie, but hope sprang eternal, and Ruby hoped that this might be her week to elude them all. Miss Mildred had long ago learned to just schedule Thursday night as Ruby's night off and cover her cabin, because Ruby wasn't going to be there.

Just as they were taking their bows, she thought she heard it. She wasn't sure, due to the applause, and when the back doors burst open, stormed by Ethel and Haddie, Ruby knew she was doomed. Everywhere in front of her, children sat. There was no way to run anywhere quickly. A crowd like that had to be carefully picked through—that is, unless a person was wearing a black Zorro mask, which both Ethel and Haddie were. Then the crowd parted like the Red Sea.

They grabbed Ruby, dragged her out the front door, and threw her into the back of Opal's convertible. Like that they were off to the state park at the end of the road, where they would dump Ruby and leave her, once they dragged her a safe distance from the car so she couldn't chase them down and jump back in. She would then be on her own to walk three miles home in the dark—a penance for putting bunks on the floating dock, running underwear up flagpoles, and hiding prized possessions only to be recovered after a very long treasure hunt.

But that week Henry's uncle Louie, who was the caretaker at the campground, had a surprise for them. Over the years, Louie had taken pity on Ruby during her many abductions and driven her back. Ruby figured he must have gotten tired of dealing with her, because on that particular week he had orchestrated his own masterful prank: the Reverse Kidnap. As Opal, Ethel, and Haddie struggled to get Ruby far enough from the car so that they could take off without her jumping back in, Louie jumped into Opal's car and took off with it.

Opal watched her car disappear down the dead-end road, stunned, and then they just all started walking—that is, until Henry came along in his pickup.

His eyes lit up when he saw her. "Ruby," he said. "We meet again."

This time, she had laughed. "Indeed we do."

"Would you and your friends like a ride?"

She looked over at her three friends nodding.

"Why, thank you, Henry. I know I would." She wanted to make the others just a little nervous that she would abandon them. She should, she thought. They deserved it. But she wanted Henry to think she was nice, so she let it slide and simply said, "That is mighty nice of you to save me for the second time in a week." It had only been five days since he had saved her sleeping bag and blanket from sinking in the lake.

"Well, I am a mighty nice fellow," he said.

Ruby opened the passenger door and slid inside while Opal, Ethel, and Haddie jumped into the back of the old pickup.

"Henry, we must quit meeting like this," Ruby said with a coy smile, running her hand through her coppery hair.

He smiled back, as bright as the sun. "Really?"

Ruby shrugged.

"Because I don't mind too terribly much," he said. Ruby noticed the way his dimples deepened in his otherwise smooth, tan face when he smiled. His light blue eyes waited to see how she would respond. Here was a boy she could be herself with. He seemed to be quite taken with her despite the fact her hair was not styled and she was not wearing lipstick, and despite the fact she hadn't dialed down her personality. Yes, he seemed to like her exactly the way she truly was. Imagine that.

She smiled demurely as he drove on down the road. Ahead his headlights shone on Opal's car, parked in someone's driveway. Henry pulled over and the others jumped out.

"The keys are still in the ignition!" Opal shouted. "Come on, Ruby!"

Ruby opened the door, stepped out, and shut it behind her. She leaned in the open window and said, "Well, Henry, my hero, thank you again." Then she turned and walked to Opal's car, with a little extra wiggle in her walk, just in case he was watching.

RUBY 2012

Henry. What a sweet summer it had been. Lately, as Ruby remembered the independent life she had wanted as a girl and realized that she had actually created that life exactly, the Henry chapter seemed even sweeter. It was no longer made bitter by the sense that she had been robbed—or maybe it would be more honest to say that it seemed less bitter by the diminishing sense that she had been robbed. The shift in her thinking wasn't complete, but it was significantly improving. That's what she could say honestly.

How lovely it had been to walk these old paths and to remember the time in her life when she had been so proud of being independent and capable—when that's all she really ever wanted to be. Funny to think a person could have forgotten something as fundamental as that.

She wanted that for the next generation—for all girls to feel proud of being independent and capable. Maybe girls today already felt that. It was very possible. The culture had changed significantly. But as Ruby tried to remember the last time she saw a young person who wasn't looking at their cell phone or talking into it, she came to the conclusion that today's girls might desperately need the opportunity to turn off their gadgets and explore the peace that nature offered. There was so much power in learning what a person did not need, and camp offered that.

Shannon was brushing her teeth in the bathroom when Ruby arrived. Despite the gallon of water and paper cups that were available in this situation, Ruby, curious, turned the faucet on anyway. There was a slight noise, a little like the ocean, but nothing at all came out—not a single drop.

Pulling a little paper cup off the top of the stack, Shannon poured Ruby some water from the jug.

"Something about a dry well is creepy," Ruby said.

"I know," Shannon agreed, her mouth full of toothpaste suds.

As Ruby squirted toothpaste on her toothbrush she said, "I've been wondering whether camp is really as obsolete as everyone seems to think it is."

"I don't think it's obsolete. I think it's timeless."

"That's what I think, too." Ruby brushed, spit, and rinsed and then said, "I want the next generation to have this place."

Ruby could tell from looking at Shannon that she felt the same way. "I've been wondering how different my life would have been if I had chosen the path Ethel took instead of becoming a teacher . . . how much happier I would have been. And I've been wondering, if I had done that, would camp still be closing? I just don't think that if I had been camp director I would have rolled over and allowed this to happen."

Oh, Ruby realized, *Shannon had grit.* She hadn't noticed that before. Grit could come in handy. Ruby said, "I've been wondering whether the people in charge really exhausted all their options. Do you think they found and applied for every possible grant? Because I am thinking that they did *not* find and apply for *every possible* grant."

Before Ruby's eyes, Shannon's expression slowly changed, transforming from sad and resigned into something more like a question. Yes, Ruby could tell, Shannon was in. She had an ally.

"And I've been thinking," continued Ruby, "of the thousands of campers who have passed through this camp, and of how much this place meant to many of them. Do you think the people in charge contacted every one of them to ask for financial help? Because I am thinking that the people in charge did not contact any of them to ask for financial help."

"But it's too late," Shannon said, shaking her head. They've made their decision."

"Receiving grants might help them reverse it."

Shannon was still unconvinced. "But that can take months."

"I think you, me, and Laura need to join Ethel on that board and take back our camp. I think we should write to the national organization today and tell them what we want to do. Maybe the national office will give us a chance."

Shannon stared at Ruby for a moment. "Oh my God. We could do this. I mean, I don't know if we could really do this. But we could try."

Ruby nodded. "Let's not go down without a fight."

SHANNON 2012

As she cracked and scrambled eggs, Shannon waited with eager anticipation for Ethel to come down. She couldn't wait to tell her about their plan. Was it possible? Was it crazy? Ethel would know. After all, she was an optimistic realist.

Shannon heard footsteps in the loft above her walking toward the door and then descending the stairs. Ethel was coming. Shannon and Ruby looked at each other with something between nervousness and excitement.

"Good morning," Ethel said as she shuffled over to pour herself a cup of coffee. "I didn't hear the bell. Did anyone ring the bell?" Shannon and Ruby shook their heads, so Ethel shuffled out of the kitchen, calling out, "I don't want Laura to sleep through breakfast!"

"Laura's awake. She went for a walk!" Shannon called out.

Shannon heard Ethel wrestle with the sticky back door, ring the giant bell, then wrestle the door shut and shuffle back to the kitchen. The anticipation was killing Shannon. Would Ethel get on board or would she shoot this idea down?

Ruby buttered the toast that popped out of the toaster while Ethel went directly to the cupboards and began to set the table.

"We want to save camp," Shannon blurted out.

Ethel stopped what she was doing and looked up. "I know. We all do. But it's too late."

"What if it's not?" asked Shannon. "What if we write to the national office and run interference—or maybe even call them? What if we wrote a bunch of grants, begged for money from alumni, and raised the money to get this water thing fixed? I mean, that's the biggest obstacle, right? If a new well was put in, the other things would fall into place and work out, right?"

"Well, the Firelight Girls incurred some additional losses last year after they had to send kids home and refund their money. It would take a while to recover those losses and rebuild the camp's reputation, but yes, if it was only that, saving camp would seem possible. But the well . . . that's the part that makes this whole situation hopeless and impossible. It's just so much money and such a gamble."

Shannon didn't know how to argue with that. She could only say, "Ruby and I want to go to the library in town today and look for grants. We want to try. We don't want to go down without one heck of a fight."

Ethel looked at Ruby and said, "This was your idea, wasn't it?"

Ruby nodded hesitantly.

"You knew I'd have a hard time saying no to Shannon."

Ruby waited.

"I just want to be sure that I've got this straight. You think you can succeed where I failed. You think you love this place more than me and will fight harder to preserve it."

Ruby winced, shook her head slowly, and gently said, "I think you and Haddie moved mountains. And now that she's not here, I think you need some backup that you didn't have when this decision was made. I'm on your side, Ethel. I know it sure hasn't looked that way for most of our lives, but in this small way I'd like to try to make that up to you, if you'll let me. This is not a one-woman fight."

Amber and then Laura trickled in just then and took their places at the table, so Ethel started singing "Johnny Appleseed," by far the longest grace in their repertoire, presumably to buy herself some thinking time. Across the table, Amber politely waited for the song to end, but despite her best efforts to hide her impatience, Shannon could still see it and it made her smile.

So," Ethel said as they all sat. "There's a lot going on today and we have a lot to figure out. Amber didn't go to school today because she was afraid CPS would nab her, and Shannon and Ruby want to try to resuscitate camp." Shannon could tell Ethel was still digesting it.

"Really?" Laura asked. "I thought it was a done deal."

"It is," Ethel said.

"But listen to our plan," Shannon said. "First we call or write to the national Firelight Girls office and try to convince them to reject the board's motion and give us a chance. Then we apply for as many grants as we can—"

Ruby continued. "And we contact alumni and beg for money. Basically we try anything and everything to raise all the money that we need. Even though some of the traditional fund-raisers wouldn't raise the amount we needed, they still might be worth doing because they would raise awareness about our need. We could make a quilt and raffle it, have a big garage sale, maybe write a cookbook—"

Shannon finished for her. "We just want the opportunity to try harder to save camp." Ethel winced again and Shannon instantly regretted her word choice, but she went on. "If we can just get the well fixed, I think we can pull it off."

"Yes!" Laura exclaimed. "Yes! Let's do this! What's the worst that could happen? The worst thing that could happen is that the national office would say no and we'd be exactly where we are now. We have nothing to lose."

Shannon could see in Ethel's eyes that she wanted nothing more than to believe it was possible to change this situation, but that she was also afraid to hope for something she wanted so much.

"A new well could cost almost fifty thousand dollars," said Ethel. "I mean, it could cost as little as fifteen thousand, but that's only if they find water on the first try. That's such a big if. So, water could cost thirty thousand or even forty-five. Most grants are for a couple thousand. I can't imagine getting enough grants to pull this off."

"I wonder if we could create some kind of rainwater collection system," Laura said. "There might be more than one way to skin this cat."

Ethel pursed her lips and shook her head slowly. "Even if we fixed the water, it's going to take a lot of time for the camp to earn its reputation back."

Shannon nodded. "Yes, it will. It might take some aggressive marketing to show that it's a new beginning for the camp now that the root of all its problems has been solved. And you're right—it will take some patience and creativity to ride out a couple lean years while our new reputation builds."

Ethel sighed and said, "I know if I walked away from this shred of hope I would always wonder what would have happened if I hadn't stood in the way and I'd never have peace." She looked at Ruby. "You're right. I don't have much fight left in me. You all will have to lead this charge."

Shannon felt determination rising up in her now. She believed in this and wanted to preserve this place where, in Ethel's words, "it was good enough just to be a kid." There was no question that Shannon was willing to fight for it. Believing in something again and feeling like she might have the power to make a difference reminded her of who she truly was and made her feel like herself again.

The group decided that the first step was for Ethel to call the national office. Even though Shannon offered to drive her to her house, Ethel insisted on canoeing, so Shannon offered to help paddle the canoe down the shore to her home.

"Brawn in the front, brains in the back," Ethel said as they approached the boat. Shannon grabbed the handle in the front while Ethel took the one in back, and together they dragged the boat from the shore into the shallow water.

Shannon stabilized the canoe while Ethel stepped in. As they launched it, Ethel said, "Sometimes, Miss Mildred, my camp director, would wake me up and take me out on the lake like this. You know, she was an interesting one. She was camp director for forty-three years. Forty-three. I still wonder about her story before she came here. We knew she was divorced. That was unheard of back in those days. She and her husband lived up in Trinity—you know the mining settlement up north? Rumor was, she left there on a stretcher and never went back. I suspected her husband beat her. That would have been the only legitimate reason for a divorce. I used to think how nice it was that she had found this all-girl place where she could feel completely safe, safe enough to be silly and playful. Oh, she used to get us to prank each other all the time. There was this backpack thing with a hose that was used for fighting wildfires, and she'd fill it up and put in on you and then say, 'You know, Ethel, Ruby over there is looking awfully hot. I'm a little worried she might get heatstroke,' and you had no choice but to run over and spray Ruby." Ethel laughed.

Shannon began paddling and said, "She sounds like fun."

"She was the best," Ethel said. "What you're doing . . . it would make her really happy."

The lakeshore was so quiet. Most of the cabins were deserted until the following summer, and the few year-round residents were still sleeping. Shannon studied their artifacts from sunnier days—their wooden Adirondack lawn chairs, planters that held mostly dead flowers and an occasional one that still held on to a little life, barbeque pits, boats. Place after place, still and lifeless.

Shannon was looking at a red canoe someone had pulled up their steep hill and tied to a tree when she saw him again—the cougar. He looked right at her. She froze and stared back, mesmerized.

Ethel stopped paddling and searched for the cause of Shannon's sudden paralysis. "Oh my," Ethel finally whispered. "He's looking right at you."

The canoe continued to drift forward for a moment, and they all continued to stare. The cougar finally broke his gaze with Shannon, looked at Ethel for a moment, and then walked away from the lake, into the thick, dark forest.

"That was incredible," Ethel said breathlessly. "I've

lived here almost all of my life and have never had an experience like that."

Shannon looked back at her, wide-eyed and speechless.

Ethel continued. "But you've seen him twice in five days. That's weird. That just doesn't happen. I think it was Haddie with a message about leadership for you."

"I can't imagine what it would be," Shannon replied as she began to paddle again.

"Well, teaching involves leadership. Maybe you're going back to that."

"I really don't think I can work in that system anymore."

"Maybe you'll teach abroad and not be in the system. Have you considered that? I think that could potentially be very rewarding." Ethel paused and looked up at the trees along the shore. "I was lucky. Teaching is a hard job."

"Teaching is the fun part. It's all the other stuff that is a waste of my life."

Ethel seemed to consider that. "It's no good to feel like you're wasting your life. It's not like you can run out and get more of it."

"No," Shannon agreed. "I can't." After a few more strokes, she added, "I sure hope I find my place in this world."

"You will," Ethel assured her. "I have no doubt you will."

They paddled on another mile and then docked the canoe at Ethel's place and climbed the steep stairs.

Although Shannon could hardly wait to take a much-needed shower, she paused for a moment while Ethel dialed, held the phone to her ear, waited for someone to answer. Ethel explained the circumstances to the first person, then to the second person, and after that to the third person. Finally, she hung up. "They're going to work on it," she said. "Not a done deal."

"Not a done deal, but not over yet either," said Shannon, feeling more and more hope all the time.

"Why don't you go ahead and take that shower now while I do one more thing," said Ethel. "I was thinking I should draft a letter with my ideas about how Camp Firelight could be managed differently to become a sustainable entity again. I think we have to give the national office reason to believe in us; we have to explain how and why we can create a different outcome."

And when Shannon was finished in the shower, together they read Ethel's letter and added Shannon's ideas for camp programming and for increasing off-season camp rentals to bring in extra income. Ethel sent it off as an e-mail and then printed it off on paper to send as a letter in hopes that would increase the odds of it reaching the right person. Shannon and Ethel both crossed their fingers and exchanged hopeful looks. Ethel affixed a stamp and handed it to Shannon to take to town so it would go out in today's mail instead of tomorrow's.

Suddenly Shannon felt the responsibility of what she had put into motion. Ethel's hopes had been raised. If this plan didn't work, it would crush Ethel all over again, and it would be mostly Shannon's fault. The last thing in the whole world she wanted to do was hurt Ethel. She had to succeed. She just *had* to.

An hour later, at the Leavenworth Public Library, Shannon and Ruby sat side by side at computers. Shannon worked quickly, looking up grants on the American Camping Association's Web site. From time to time, she leaned over to see what Ruby was doing.

Ruby had looked up newspaper stories about camps that had received grants for improvements. On a piece of paper she had written down the amount they were awarded and the business or agency that had awarded it. After that, she had searched for contact information for those agencies. "Brilliant. Excellent job, Ruby," said Shannon.

Ruby looked over at Shannon's notes as well and, pleased, said, "We're off to a great start."

The hours ticked by. As the clock struck 3:00 p.m., which was 5:00 p.m. Central time, Shannon turned to Ruby and said, "What if the national office called back today and said no?"

Ruby shook her head. "We can't think like that. We have to stay positive."

Shannon nodded. Ruby was right.

SHANNON 1980

She remembered the silk ribbons on her toe shoes, winding them around her ankles, first to the front, crossing them, then to the back, crossing them again, and then making a little knot on the inside of her ankle that she hoped would go unnoticed. She stood in the wings of the Seattle Opera House and moved into second position, bending her knees deeply as she moved an arm in a graceful arc to calm herself. For six solid months she had rehearsed every night for three hours to prepare herself for this performance, for this defining moment.

"It's packed tonight!" a stagehand whispered to everyone.

"I'm ready," she had told herself. She was eleven—just eleven—and had only been in toe shoes for one year, but her teacher had told her parents that she'd never had a student so driven and that she thought Shannon had the potential to make it all the way to the New York City Ballet. *The New York City Ballet!*

Her mother had danced as a lead in the Cleveland Ballet for six years before she gave up her career to have Shannon. The New York City Ballet had been her mother's big dream, and when Shannon's teacher used those five illustrious words to describe her potential her mother had lit up, having successfully passed the torch. Her dream would come true after all—only it would be her daughter dancing.

So as Shannon warmed up, she thought about everything she had done to prepare for this moment, of how she'd taken lessons since she was four, of how she'd given up time to play make-believe with her best friend and next-door neighbor, Darcy, so that she could spend time in the dance studio mastering the basics and working on the next steps.

For a moment, it hit her how much she missed Darcy, whom she never even saw anymore. But recognizing what she had sacrificed for this moment only fueled her.

The music started, and on cue Shannon leaped out onto the stage like a loaded spring. She twirled once high on her toes, took two steps, and then *grande jeté,* where she leaped again, kicking both legs high into a perfect split. When she landed, she felt a bone near her ankle in her left foot move but kept dancing through the pain. After all, this was her moment. She wasn't going to ruin the show, and she sure wasn't going to give up the glory she had worked so hard for. Up on the toe of that left foot she went, lifting her right foot high up behind her, holding it, holding it. . . . Her eyes welled up with tears and down she went. What she remembered most was that awkward moment when the music was still going, the stage empty behind her, and she held her ankle as she looked out on the audience, where she spotted her parents.

Her mother's horrified expression seemed angry instead of compassionate. *Get up!* she mouthed emphatically. She had told Shannon many stories of dancing through the pain.

Shannon stood, her head down, tears streaking her cheeks. She listened to the music and remembered her choreography and began to dance again. Graceful arms, graceful arms, plié, fouetté on her right foot, thank God, where her left leg whipped around the back of her right, *fondu* on that right foot with left leg in the air, sous-sou on her toes in a tight fifth position so her legs looked as one. Her foot hurt. But then came the part where she was supposed to do five fouetté rond de jambe en tournant—five spins on her left foot, where she would return to a flat foot on the completion of each spin and rise up on her toe as her right leg whipped around behind her left during each rotation. She thought of those stories where a person lifts a car off someone else to save him, times when someone who should not have had superhero strength did, and prayed for this to be one of those times. Up she went on that left foot, and her right leg whipped. Her left foot felt like it crumbled and she cried out. The right leg that whipped around to propel her spin now only propelled her across the stage on her face. She rolled onto her side, her back to the audience, and she cried. Her teacher came out, picked her up, and carried her backstage.

The music began again and her understudy leaped out and stole all of Shannon's glory.

Determination. It had its limitations. Sometimes determination alone just wasn't enough.

LAURA 2012

Amber and Laura headed off down the South Shore Trail for a mile or so until they reached Glacier View State Park. From there, they cut through the campground to reach the head of the steep trail to Hidden Lake. Laura had come here often as a camper or with campers when she was a counselor.

The sky hung low, occasionally dropping something between mist and drizzle, blocking views, so Laura simply turned her attention toward the small beautiful things that were right in front of her—the elegant lichens, the way the earth sounded like a hollow drum when she walked through a cedar grove, autumn color lacing the edges of leaves. And she looked for good finds to share with Amber—different fungi, birds, and insects.

They did find a fallen tree that had been sliced to clear the trail, and they stopped to look at the rings and the layers of the bark. "There is a lot of xylem in the heart-wood," Laura said, pointing. "The cells that make the in-frastructure that deep in the tree are now dead, just like Malcolm X is dead. But up here, near the cambium, is the phloem. It's alive, just like Flo the waitress is still alive."

Amber laughed and said, "No one's ever helped me with my homework like this before."

Laura didn't know what to say. She quickly considered her options and decided on, "I've enjoyed it. It reminded me of when my kids still lived at home. They're in col-lege now."

Amber and Laura had begun walking again when, from behind her, Amber asked, "Did you have one of those families like on TV?"

"What do you mean?"

"You know, where despite the weekly misunderstanding or conflict, really everyone loves everyone else and their problems are pretty small in the big picture."

"Well, I sure didn't grow up in one of those families. My dad drank and was violent sometimes. But yeah, when it was my turn to have a family, I suppose I did have one of those families like on TV." She turned around and smiled at Amber as if to say, *You could have that one day, too.*

It got Laura thinking about that time before she met Steve, when she could not have imagined ever having a family that was sane and loving. Love terrified her, in fact. At once, she remembered how lucky she had felt when she met Steve so long ago . . . how she just knew she was going to be okay from then on out. Now it left her feeling as if she had wrecked something perfect and priceless, as if she had scribbled on the *Mona Lisa* with a Crayola crayon.

It really wasn't long before they reached their destination. The trek was shorter than Laura remembered it—perhaps because it was the first time she wasn't hiking it as a child or with a child.

How long had it been since Laura had been to Hidden Lake? Years and years. She had brought Steve and the kids up here for a picnic and a swim on a summer day when the kids were still quite little. She had forgotten about that day. Walking a little farther until she reached the spot where she and Steve had sat on the ground next to each other, she remembered how they had leaned back on their hands and watched the kids throw rocks in the lake. Her shoulder had touched his, and at some point she rested her head on it, completely content. *How many people,* she had wondered that day, *had ever felt this level of contentment?*

Such a long time ago. Amazing how things change. She sat on a nearby log even though it was wet and soaked through the back of her pants. Inside her chest, she felt something new—something like longing. She wanted that moment back—that moment with Steve. But it was just a moment, just a memory, from so long ago. It had so little to do with the present day.

"It's pretty here," Amber said.

"In the summer, you can swim. It's warmer than Lake Wenatchee."

"Ice is warmer than Lake Wenatchee."

Laura laughed. "So true." She pointed to some boulders across the lake. "That was always my favorite spot."

As they started back toward camp, two ancient ponderosa pines to their right caught Laura's eye. "Look at that," she said to Amber as she walked over to the one that was closest and put her hand on a huge scar from where a fire had burned all the way through the bark. Despite that wound, the tree appeared to be in great health. "Ponderosa pines sure can endure a lot," Laura marveled.

Amber followed her and put her hand on the tree, too. And Laura didn't have to ask to know what Amber was thinking. She was thinking the same thing as Laura. They *were* ponderosa pines.

LAURA 1990

Laura was lying down on the side of the Wonderland with her feet up when she saw Steve for the first time. Near as she could figure, it was called the Wonderland Trail because a person spent her whole time on it wondering what she had gotten herself into. The trail circumnavigated Mt. Rainier, and that promised spectacular views all the time, right? Well, not really. Her first three days hiking clockwise from Longmire had been spectacularly unremarkable—mostly in the forest.

The biggest challenge was proving to be the intense elevation gains and losses each day as she made her way over the many arms of the great mountain. Five to six miles in a day had sounded so reasonable and had proven to be so brutal. To make matters worse, there were going to be four days on this trip when she had to hike nine or ten miles in a day. How would she ever do it? It was unimaginable. She was in way over her head. Her knees and feet ached like they had never ached before, and she was only three days into a two-week trip.

A man looked at her on the ground and laughed. "Hi," he said knowingly. Around his head he wore a red bandana, which made his green eyes look greener. As he walked by her, she noticed his calves were really large. That's what she remembered thinking.

"Hi," she replied, feeling a little silly.

He had continued on without breaking stride.

Later on, she reached Klapatche Park, her destination for the day. Right in front of her, Aurora Lake glistened in the late-day sun. She could hardly wait to rinse the sweat off herself and soak her inflamed legs in its icy water. She set her pack down, stripped, and wasted no time running in and doing a surface dive. "Woo!" she exclaimed when she surfaced, trying to think of euphemisms for how cold the water was. "Invigorating." "Revitalizing." "Stimulating."

And that's when she noticed the man who had passed her on the trail. He was setting up his tent not terribly far away from her and had surely heard the commotion but was polite enough to pretend he hadn't seen her. She also appreciated that he was polite enough not to look up when she got out of the water, dug a hand towel out of the top of her pack, dried herself off, and dressed again.

Her legs were so achy that she chose not to walk farther than necessary and settled for the next available
campsite, hoping she wasn't committing a breach of eti-
quette by not making an effort to get farther from the
man.

On her first night, she had discovered that her tent
stakes had slipped out of her tent bag at some point. Con-
sequently, she had to be creative about the placement of
her tent and look for things she could tie the peaks of her
pup tent to. If a windy storm set in, her tent was going to
flap everywhere until it was nothing but a wavering sack
of nylon that she was trapped in. Why hadn't she double-
checked her tent? Rookie mistake.

The next morning, as she drank hot tea and ate oatmeal, the man walked by with his backpack on. He
looked at her tent with unmistakable concern.

"I know. My tent stakes didn't make it into my pack."

He winced. "Eesh. Hope for good weather."

She nodded, taking in the kind and intelligent look in
his eye, and then glanced at his broad shoulders as he
walked on.

The next night, they both camped near the South
Mowich River, quite a ways apart but close enough to
be aware of each other. Close enough to wonder about
each other's stories.

That's how it went for a few days as they leapfrogged
and camped near each other.

On day six, he had stopped for water when she caught
up with him. Again they said hello. This time, he asked
her whether she intended to detour to Spray Falls the next
day and they talked about how beautiful they had heard
it was. She said that yes, she intended to go, and he said
that he did, too. And then she and Steve finally introduced
themselves before she walked on.

When she woke the next day to overcast skies, she

hoped it would burn off before she arrived at Spray Park, "the highlight of the whole trip," as another student in the biology department had called it. Laura climbed and climbed up the last part of the trail and walked until the sound of the falls thundered. There she hung her head in disappointment, for she saw nothing but white. Taking a few more steps into the thick fog to see if getting closer would make any difference at all, Laura found it did, but not in the way that she expected.

There was Steve, just off the trail, lying down with his feet up. "Hey there, Laura," he said as if he'd been expecting her. "Come enjoy this spectacular view with me."

Appreciating his humor, she lay down next to him. She had dressed for rain, so the damp ground didn't concern her. "Wow," she said sarcastically. "It's everything I thought it would be."

"Definitely worth the hike," Steve agreed. They were quiet for a moment, and then he said, "It sounds like it's really beautiful, doesn't it?"

Laura smiled. "It sure does."

Silence between them was peaceful—not awkward. Eventually, Steve asked, "How is your tent doing?"

"I've been lucky so far."

"Oh, good."

And again they lay there quietly, just listening to the falls and imagining what they could not see. Then they felt rain on their faces, so they stood and put on their packs.

"Cataract Valley tonight?" he asked.

She nodded.

"You know, I find myself wanting to hike with you, but I came out here to do this trip solo and find some answers, you know?"

She understood and nodded.

"See you there, then?"

"See you there," she replied, and watched him go. He walked a lot faster than she did anyway. She never would have been able to keep up without killing herself trying. So she poked along and watched him disappear.

The cold rain sank deep into her bones and into her core as the day went on. As she grew more tired, she grew colder. Plus, her feet, ankles, and knees ached badly. Again, she began to wonder what she was doing—what she was hoping to find, what she was hoping to prove, and to whom.

She followed the trail higher, across a vast alpine meadow. Were it not for the clouds, she was sure there would have been spectacular views. Then down, down, down she walked into another valley, each step inflaming her knees a little more. She was definitely growing weary of the ups and downs, but especially the downs.

The wind picked up. It was going to be the night she had been afraid of. *In just two more days, I'll be at Sunrise, where I can pull the cord and hitchhike back to my car,* she thought. There was an end in sight.

By the time she reached Cataract Valley, she was in bad spirits. Ahead of her, she could see Steve's tent all taut and ready for anything. Outside he had erected a tarp to cook under. He looked up and waved her over as she walked in.

"I have something for you," he said, and handed her a mug of hot cocoa. She almost cried. There were no words to express how much she needed warmth and chocolate.

Eagerly she began to drink. "Thank you."

"Your tent is going to be a disaster tonight," he said. "Don't even bother setting it up. Just join me."

She didn't want to be an imposition. It wasn't his fault she forgot her stakes. But she imagined trying to sleep with her own tent hitting her in the face all night. Already she was drinking one of his precious cocoas. People didn't bring extra to share when they packed for a solo trip. Everything was rationed.

He noticed her hesitation and assumed she was concerned about her safety. "I promise I won't touch you."

And she laughed. "Thanks. No. That's not what I was thinking about. I was thinking about how I didn't want to impose."

"Well, we're kind of in this together. You can crawl in and sleep the night through or you can spend half the night miserable in your tent and then wake me up when you can't stand it anymore and come on in here. Or you can spend all night in your tent awake and then have an accident on the trail tomorrow because you were sleepy and clumsy, in which case I'd have to carry you out. See, when you look at it like that, coming in now is no imposition at all."

"Well, since you put it like that . . ." She laughed.

She sat on her pack while together they ate their Mountain House meals straight from the bag, rehydrated with water Steve had boiled.

"You're kind," she said.

"I am," he agreed, with a little smile.

"I appreciate it."

"It's nice to be appreciated."

They ate in silence for a moment before she said, "It was a rough day. I lost heart. I lost my will." Her voice broke as she said the last part, and her eyes welled up.

"Tomorrow is going to be an easier day. Only three-point-six miles to Mystic Lake. Is that your next stop, too?"

She nodded.

"There will be lots of time to swim if the weather's nice and just rest and recharge. It will get better."

"Thanks," she said.

When they were done, he put their dinner bags in his

garbage sack and rinsed their forks while she unpacked her bedding.

And then they awkwardly lay in their sleeping bags next to each other until she broke the ice with, "I'm sorry about the way I smell."

"I can't smell you over the smell of me," he replied, and she laughed. The tension was broken.

They talked for hours that evening, and right before she fell asleep he said, "Good night, Laura, and dream of having a burger with me when we get to the lodge at Sunrise." She smiled as if it were a joke, but she really did fantasize about it as she drifted off.

When she woke the next morning, they were spooned next to each other. She stayed very still and listened to his breathing. It wasn't regular like it had been when she woke in the middle of the night and listened to him sleep. He was awake. Maybe he was trying not to wake her. Maybe he was enjoying their closeness. Maybe he was trying to go back to sleep. She didn't know, so she stirred a little, and he rolled over back into his own space. It was more comfortable that way—waking without being too close.

"I had a nice dream. I was having a burger with you at the Sunrise lodge," she said, rolling over to face him.

"I'm going to make that dream come true," he replied, smiling.

The morning was cold and cloudy, but it was nice having a companion while she ate breakfast and packed up her things.

He chose to hike with her that day.

"I thought you were hiking solo to find some answers," she said.

"I found them," he replied, and she wondered if he had indeed found answers or if *she* was the answer.

She walked in front so she could set the pace, because she was slower, and lamented silently that he wasn't where she could see his broad shoulders and big calves. The sound of his feet hitting the trail behind her was still nice.

Shortly after they reached Mystic Lake, the sun burned through the clouds. "Sun!" she cried out happily. As she looked at him, she noticed his lack of jubilation. "Aren't you happy? Look how beautiful that is!" she said, pointing to a snow-covered peak reflecting on the lake.

"Yeah," he said with little enthusiasm. "But without a storm, what need will you have to share my tent?"

She laughed. "Well, on the bright side, I'll be skinny-dipping at some point today. . . ."

He smiled.

"I thought that would cheer you up."

It was such a good day. Of all the days of her life, it might have been her very favorite. They swam in the cool lake and warmed themselves in the sun and swam some more. And for hours after that they talked and ate and laughed.

She shared her chocolate bar with him, and he made blissful little noises as he let it melt in his mouth. "May I kiss you?" he asked after his first little piece of it.

She looked at his mouth and gave him a little nod. His kiss was slow but not deep and it tasted like chocolate. Then he sat back and closed his eyes as a contented smile spread across his bristly face.

That night, she ended up in his tent again despite there being no storm and they kissed for hours before they fell asleep.

He stuck with her for the 8.9 scenic miles to Sunrise and encouraged her with the promise of a burger when she got weary of the giant steps down.

"This is my all-time favorite first date," he said to her as they sat in the lodge with their hot food.

"Mine too," she agreed.

"Let's finish this trip together," he proposed.

And although she wasn't sure whether he was talking about the Wonderland Trail or life, she agreed. "I'd like that."

"Lucky." That was the word for how she felt. So very lucky.

ETHEL 1952

Back in 1952, raids were getting out of control. While one cabin was aiming to put all of the belongings of the other cabin out on the floating dock their canoe capsized and several things sank to the bottom of the lake. Ethel had been livid. How would the girls whose things were lost get through the rest of the summer without clothes and bedding? Was the camp obligated to reimburse the girls for their losses? Lost things were not good for campers and not good for business.

Haddie was less emotional and more pragmatic. First, she offered a dime for every item recovered and a quarter for sleeping bags, which inspired a lot of campers that year to become good divers. By the afternoon, over half of the missing things were recovered and Ethel and Haddie were out about twenty bucks.

They knew part of camp was running wild and occasionally doing something the campers knew was wrong. After all, hadn't Ethel and Haddie enjoyed raiding once? There would be no stopping it, Haddie said, but it could be altered. So she devised a way of counting coup that not only did no harm but also made for a nice surprise. She cut out no fewer than fifty paper hearts and wrote messages on them and then left them all over the "raided" cabin. Sometimes she would tape them to the wall, but tape was hard to come by, so usually she made garlands of them and hung them from the rafters, though she always left a few on bunks and luggage as well. Raiding with love and kindness—that was Haddie for you.

Once, Haddie "raided" Ethel above the kitchen by hanging at least twenty strings of hearts from the edge of the bunk above Ethel's so that she had to crawl through them to get into her bed. How beautiful they had been, all those colors, all those kind words hanging like a beaded doorway that seemed to hide Ethel and protect her from the outside world that didn't understand their love. How safe she had felt in there with Haddie's adoration all around her like chain-mail armor. One read: "You soften me in the very best way." It had been Ethel's favorite because even though all the hearts answered Ethel's question about what Haddie saw in her, this was the one that made the most sense to Ethel and made her feel useful.

When the summer ended, Ethel had carefully taken each string down and stacked the hearts carefully. She wrapped them in tissue paper and put them in her box of favorite things, every bit as precious as gold.

ETHEL 2012

Ethel's mind was pulled in so many directions as she waited for the national office to return her call. Was this last grasp just a cruel joke she was playing on herself?

She looked across the room at a picture of Haddie and knew it didn't matter if it was. It mattered that Ethel tried everything.

She wrote an e-mail to the alumni she still kept in contact with explaining the situation and asking them for help and asked them to please forward this message to other alumni. It felt good to hit the "send" button, like throwing a message in a bottle out into a virtual sea. Suddenly she felt something she hadn't felt in a while—possibilities.

And while all of that was going on, while the place she loved most—her and Haddie's legacy—hung in the balance, there was Amber back at camp who needed Ethel's help. What was she going to do about her?

Waiting was torture. Ethel wasn't sure whether the national office in Kansas City, Missouri, closed at five or five thirty, so she hung on for the last half hour just in case.

Again her thoughts turned back to Amber, so Ethel walked into the guest room and tidied it up just in case.

Pacing the house nervously, she paused in front of each picture of Haddie and talked to her, telling her how she didn't want to let her down and asking for any help she could offer from heaven. Below one picture of Haddie sat Ethel's box of favorite things. She peeked inside. There, wrapped in a small bundle of tissue paper, were the hearts that Haddie had strung for her so long ago. The writing was now quite faded. But on the top was one paper heart that read: "You are a quiet force, but quite a force." Ethel smiled. It did seem like something Haddie might say to her in that moment.

Inspired, she dug through cupboards and drawers until she found a little stash of construction paper and began to cut her own paper hearts.

RUBY 2012

As Ruby sat at the library computer looking for grants, she had a realization and turned to Shannon. "While there are some big jackpots, most of the grants are for dollar amounts that we might be able to raise ourselves. I mean, if we're going to piecemeal this, there are some pieces we could add."

"Like what are you thinking?" Shannon asked.

"I'm thinking about the box of fabric scraps Laura and I found in the arts and crafts area. Not all of them will work, but there were some old prints in there that have a certain special charm. I can make a quilt and auction it off or raffle it off." She paused to picture it. "Maybe a quilt that looks like a forest in a multitude of greens. Yes. It will be magnificent."

"We could all help you. Many hands make light work," said Shannon.

"Great," said Ruby. "My other stroke of genius has to do with s'mores. I think there are other possibilities for this camp treat—possibilities that would take it to the next level. I'm imagining a s'mores cookbook that will be a favorite among families who love to camp."

"Love it," said Shannon. "Imagine how fun the research will be."

"Work, work, work," Ruby said with a big smile. "I know that neither of these ideas will solve the problem by itself, but they might help."

"I think we have to try everything."

"We could have a garage sale and an auction. Maybe we could sponsor a run from Glacier View Campground around the lake to the Cougar Inn."

So, before Ruby and Shannon left Leavenworth they

stopped at the fabric store and the grocery store. They needed to pick up some things for dinner as well as for their projects.

On the drive back to camp, Ruby said, "I want to thank you. Camp Firelight means a lot to me."

"I want to thank *you*," Shannon replied. "It means a lot to me, too. And you're the one that got this ball rolling." She turned and smiled at Ruby. "I keep thinking about how there's some reason each of us came back . . . something that happened to us here that changed us and made us the people we became. What's your reason? What did you love about it?"

"Oh gosh, so many things. At camp, I felt capable, and proud of being capable. It was a different time for women, so it's difficult to explain just how profound that was. But I think what really kept me coming back was my camp friends. I've not had anything like them since. In nearly all my memories, everyone is laughing. I can't say that about any other time or place in my life. How about you?"

"I loved that success meant something different at camp—something significantly more kind and cooperative."

Ruby nodded. "That's true. It does."

For a moment they simply drove in silence, and then Ruby broke it. "Do you know how bad I want to toilet-paper-mummy Ethel to the bed? I think about it every night when she starts to snore. My sister Opal and I once mummied her with three whole rolls. She almost didn't break through it when she woke up the next day. I sure wish I had a picture of that. I'd enlarge it and frame it."

Shannon laughed. "I'll tell you what, Ruby. If the national office has called back and granted us more time, I will, as a form of celebration, toilet-paper-mummy Ethel to the bed with you."

"I can think of no finer way to celebrate," said Ruby.

Back at camp, while Amber finished up dinner preparations, Ruby sneaked out of the kitchen and rifled through the neat and tidy arts and crafts cupboards until she found some construction paper that she had remembered seeing while cleaning with Laura. Since the national office had not called back that day, raiding Ethel with paper hearts seemed appropriately gentle.

But just as Ruby was taking the paper out, Ethel walked in and caught her. "Ruby?" she said questioningly. "What are you doing?"

"Nothing," Ruby replied as innocently as she could muster.

Ethel walked right up to her, stared, and waited a moment for her to break.

Ruby would not.

"Were you going to do this?" Ethel asked, and opened a plastic bag full of hearts, then grinned smugly.

Ruby merely made a big O with her mouth and pointed at Ethel.

"Amber, honey," Ethel said as she poked her head through the door into the kitchen. "Can you hold down the fort for a few minutes? I've got an old-lady situation that I need Ruby's help with real quick. And by 'quick,' I mean quick for old ladies."

"Sure," Amber answered.

Ethel smiled at Ruby in a way that made Ruby feel sixteen again. Eagerly she followed Ethel up the stairs and "raided" Amber's bunk.

AMBER 2012

Amber had just finished grating all the cheese when Ruby returned. Together they assembled English muffin pizzas and made a salad. This simple thing Amber had dreamed of her whole life—making and eating dinner with family. She used to watch commercials and sitcoms around Thanksgiving and ache for it. And now, here at camp, it felt like every meal was Thanksgiving.

She knew it couldn't last, but this moment was so warm and full. It was something. It was a taste of something she had known existed but hadn't tasted before.

Ruby gave Amber the honor of letting her ring the bell, and she loved this duty, too—of calling everyone in. And when they did gather around the table and the women sang grace, Amber folded her hands and let the gratitude in her heart swell until she thought her chest would explode.

Laura, Shannon, and Ruby fussed over how good the food looked and smelled, and Ethel said, "Thank Amber here. She is a great help. You know, if we do manage to save this camp, whoever the new camp director will be should get her to work in the kitchen this summer."

Imagine that—a whole summer of living here and being in the kitchen with other people, ringing the bell to call them in and making the food that kept them coming back. Amber smiled just thinking of it.

Ethel looked up at her both gently and thoughtfully. She seemed to hear Amber's unanswered question, the one she would not dare to ask aloud: *What's going to happen to me?*

And Ethel answered, "I'm working on it."

Amber nodded an unspoken *okay* and *thank you*. It was tough for her to trust anyone completely under any circumstances, but the fact that the others had so much confidence in Ethel carried some weight. Amber also appreciated that Ethel hadn't rashly made promises. No, she'd been deliberate and careful, and that also gave Amber some confidence in her. In the twenty-four hours since they'd met, Amber had been watching Ethel carefully to see if she would tell a lie of any sort. So far, she hadn't. Yes, there was reason to hope that, if nothing else, Ethel would be truthful with her.

Ethel's eye contact was so different from the quick, nervous glances of Amber's mother. Even without speaking, there was so much more conversation.

My mother. Is she concerned that technically I am still missing? Is she worried? Does she miss me?

Does she miss me? What an interesting question for a child to ask. Shouldn't it be a given that any parent would miss her child? But Amber truly didn't know. It was entirely possible that her mother was simply high or simply trying to figure out how to get high again and that was all she was thinking about.

Man, it was exhausting. It really was—wondering what was coming next all the time. Amber felt like a little ship lost at sea just getting pounded by storm after storm. But here in the middle of that stormy sea was a little island where for the moment she was safe. Who knew what was going to happen tomorrow or the day after that? Amber only knew that this moment was good. It was, perhaps, even a little hopeful. She took a bite of her English muffin pizza, fresh from the oven. Heaven.

After dinner, Shannon and Laura said they would clean up, so Amber helped Ruby cut pieces of fabric into little triangles for the forest quilt Ruby wanted to make.

Ethel rummaged through a closet under the stairs

until she found an ancient sewing machine with a pump pedal. Elated, Ruby began to teach Amber how to use the sewing machine.

"Remember, go slow. It's not a hot rod. Don't be a lead foot. And then you push this in to go backward, like this, and that's what keeps it from coming unraveled."

Amber sat down and tried the sewing machine on scraps a few times first, trying to keep the edges of the fabric lined up with the edges of the pressure foot, like Ruby had shown her. Coordinating her hands and foot was harder than she expected, but Ruby was nothing but encouraging. "You're a natural," she said.

It felt good, connecting little pieces of different things into something whole. Amber picked up a dark green calico triangle that would become a tree. Something about the bold color and delicate pattern reminded her of herself, and sewing it into a block and then sewing the block into the forest of trees made her feel like for the first time she was part of something family-like. Ruby hovered nearby, like the grandma Amber had wished for all these years.

Ethel caught Amber yawning and said, "It's somebody's bedtime."

Amber nodded and stood. "Maybe so." She walked up the hill to the bathroom.

As Amber walked back to the Lodge from the bathroom that night, she examined all the happy little painted rocks that lined the pathway outside the bathroom. One had a heart on it and the word "love." It wasn't large—small enough to fit in her pocket, in fact. So she picked it up and held it in her palm. She wanted to take it—something from here—with her. But as she studied it, she knew the girl who had painted it and left it behind here did it because she wanted to leave a part of herself behind and Amber felt she had to respect that kind of wish, so she put the rock back down in its place and returned to the Lodge.

"You were a super helper tonight, kid. Thanks. Sleep tight." And then Ruby gave her a hug. *A hug.* When was the last time anyone had hugged her? She couldn't remember. Tenderness was powerful. It could crack even the thickest, toughest protective layers.

Ethel patted her on the shoulder. "I've seen a lot of kids in my career, and I can read them pretty fast. You're a survivor. You're going to be okay no matter what."

Yes, Amber thought, resigned to her destiny, whatever it was. *A survivor.* She supposed so. How nice it would be to aspire to do so much more than survive, but she could not deny that in this moment surviving was a huge victory.

As she climbed the stairs, she watched the women for a moment as they put away projects and dishes for the night. Her heart ached to stay there with them forever. Who knew where she would be in a couple days? She only knew they were leaving and she could not stay either. How unjust it seemed, to wait so long for this kind of belonging and then only get it for a handful of days.

At the top of the stairs, she turned on the light as she walked through the door and immediately something caught her eye. Above her bunk hung garlands of hearts, each one with a message on it.

She couldn't read the writing from that distance, so she climbed her ladder and read them. "You are resourceful." "You are courageous." "You are clever." "You are independent." "You are still tender." "You are determined." "You are strong." "You are smart." "You are amazingly resilient." "You are a survivor." "You are a good helper." "You can create any kind of life you want to live." Two distinct scripts jumped out at her. It had been a joint effort. Aside from Ruby telling Amber she was a good helper today and an occasional teacher telling her she was smart, no one had ever said these particular things to her before. She touched each heart, as if that would help the messages soak into her.

Wondering what the correct response to this was, she finally crawled down the ladder, walked out the door, and stood on the little balcony outside the room.

Ethel was the first to look up. The warmth in her eyes touched Amber and reminded her of how, so long ago, her own mother's eyes lit up like that when she had looked at her. Wondering how long it would be before anyone would look at her again with warmth like that, she began to feel the inklings of panic. Fortunately, she had learned long ago to wrestle that feeling and win. She knew its heaviness on her chest as if it were pinning her to the wall. She knew its tightness around her throat as if it were strangling her. And she knew that in reality she could move and she could breathe and that it was important to do so. The feeling would pass.

She gave Ethel a little wave, said a simple thank-you, and slipped back into her room before she cried in front of everybody. Just to be safe, she turned off the light before slipping on her too-small pajamas, climbing the little stairs to her top bunk, and slipping into her sleeping bag.

As she stared at the ceiling, all her worries came back. She fully expected Ethel to tell her before the weekend was up that, after much thought, she could not offer Amber help, and there she would be again, all on her own.

And that's when the women began to sing "Goodnight, Irene" together, their voices blending, rich and full. She did not assume the singing was for her benefit. She assumed they were singing just because that's what they seemed to do, but it didn't matter. She let the song cover her like the blanket her mom used to pull up around her chin back when everything was good. When was the last time she had been sung to sleep? When she was four, maybe?

She had only known them two days—just two days, and already they had made her feel more loved than she had ever felt in her life. It was as if she had finally found the place in this world where she *belonged*.

To her surprise, when they finished a couple women called out, "Good night, Amber!" and "Sweet dreams, sweet girl!" Their voices, loud enough to be heard, were still gentle. They *had* been singing to her after all. Amber did not answer but clutched Woof Woof tighter to her aching heart. A couple of tears slipped out of the corners of her eyes, and she wiped them defiantly. *Do not get attached,* she told herself. *Do not.* But she knew it was too late. She already was.

ETHEL 2012

Ethel jumped when Sheriff Sam Riley knocked on the thick door of the Lodge, then opened it and poked his head in. "Hello, everybody," he said in his low voice. "Ethel, always good to see you."

"Sam!" Ethel called out happily. "I'd recognize that giant mustache anywhere! We were just talking about you yesterday in fact—remembering the time you kicked those boys in the nuts when they sneaked into camp."

Sam chuckled. "Now there you go, telling stories again," but everyone could see by his little smirk that he still felt good about what he'd done.

"How are Kathy and Mary?" Ethel asked, and then

turned to her friends. "His daughters were campers here in the seventies, and later went on to work here. I loved those girls!"

"Oh, they're great. Kathy's about to become a grand-parent herself," Sam said.

"How can that be?" Ethel asked.

"Well, you know, her kids were campers here in the late nineties," Sam replied.

"How time flies," Ethel said.

"Say, can I talk to you privately for a moment?" he asked.

"Sure," she said, and followed him outside.

He held up a flier with a picture of Amber on it. "CPS is looking for this girl." Then he held up a paper bag with Amber's name on it. "I found this on the gate, so I thought she might be here." He opened the bag. Inside were bi-cycle lights and a business card. "I called this number, and Mr. Adams said he hit her with his car when she was rid-ing her bicycle in the dark a couple nights ago. He said she refused to go to the hospital, and that she asked him to drop her off here, so he believed she might be living here. The description he gave of her matches the de-scription we've been given." He stopped to study Ethel's reaction.

Ethel wished that she were capable of a poker face. The best she could do was to say nothing yet.

"She was pretty bruised up from being hit by the car, which is what prompted someone from her school to call CPS."

Ethel pursed her lips. "So, if the bruises were from the car and not from an abusive parent, what's the problem?" she asked.

"Well, Child Protective Services went to her house today, smelled meth, and called us. We just took her mother and two others into custody. They were manufacturing. It was obviously a bad situation that girl was living in."

"Poor thing."

"You're holding out on me, Ethel."

"You've known me over forty years, Sam. You know I take good care of kids. If she's here, you know she is safe with me. And you know occasionally there is a foster-care situation that leaves something to be desired."

"There are a lot of nice foster families in this valley," he said. "I know several of them."

"If I meet her, I'll pass that on. But . . . you know, she may have her own reasons for wanting to stay. Maybe the poor kid has just been through enough."

"Don't do this, Ethel. You're putting yourself in a very bad legal position. If you're determined to look after this child, you may want to consider applying to be a foster parent. You have to get a background check—that takes a month—go to the foster-parent classes, and then get a home visit for final approval. All in all, the process takes about three months, which I know is a long time, but it's significantly less time than you'd be in the slammer if you don't cooperate." He put a toothpick in his mouth instead of a cigarette like he used to, thought for a moment, and then spoke again. "If you were a relative, you could bypass all that."

"But I'm n—"

"Don't say it. Amber's mom is in the Chelan County Jail in Wenatchee. You could visit her tomorrow and help her remember how you're related, if you catch my drift."

"Thank you, Sam. I'll do that."

"So the girl is here."

"Yes, Amber is here. She's upstairs, sleeping."

"I'll tell you what. I don't see any point in waking her, the social worker, and her new foster family. I'll pretend like I wasn't here tonight and come back first thing tomorrow morning if you give me your word that you both will cooperate fully."

"You have my word," Ethel said. "Thank you, Sam."

"Good night, Ethel," Sam said as he walked back to the road.

"Good night, Sam," she replied quietly as her heart sank.

RUBY 2012

Ruby sneaked away from the Lodge after Amber went to sleep. Laura was putting away dishes in the kitchen and Shannon and Ethel sat by the fire playing cards and telling stories. Ruby slipped out as if she were going to the bathroom. No one questioned it.

It was dark, but Ruby was prepared with her flashlight in her pocket. Since she didn't want the others to notice the light of her flashlight wandering off in a direction other than the bathroom, she kept it off. Toward Elks she walked with purpose. Oh, how delicious it felt to be naughty.

Once out of sight, she turned her flashlight on, followed the short trail, climbed the stairs, and let herself in. Shannon's bag and Laura's were easy targets. Ruby rifled through them, picking out all the underwear and stringing them to a length of yarn she had cut earlier when she was cleaning the arts and crafts cupboards. Jackpot. It was all too easy.

She put her loot in the front of her coat because she did have to sneak by the Lodge to get to the flagpole, after all. When she reached the end of the little trail, she turned off her flashlight again. Should she walk in front and risk being seen through the window or should she walk around back and risk tripping and falling on all the roots? She opted to walk around the back and use her flashlight to avoid the roots.

The flagpole squeaked as she pulled the line through the pulley to lower the clips, and she feared that anyone who had excused herself to the restroom would hear it and foil her plot. Quickly she clipped the loop of twine in the clasp and raised the collection of underwear up to the stars. *Majestic.* "Good job," she said to herself quietly as she reached over to pat herself on the back.

Although she knew she should return to the Lodge before anyone suspected that she had been up to anything other than her nightly routine in the bathroom, the moon glimmering on the lake was too beautiful to resist, so she carefully picked her way down the steep little trail to the waterfront. It was such a perfect night that she resolved to return and make a campfire and some new-improved s'mores that very night.

She slipped back into the Lodge. Everyone was so engrossed in what they were doing that they barely noticed her. That meant she was free to grab her ingredients and slip out again, which she did.

Down on the waterfront, she took great pride in constructing a log cabin–style campfire, with plenty of bright green Spanish moss in the middle. Back in the day they used to tell campers that it was witches' hair, but that the kids didn't need to worry about the witches because they only ate little kids who ran around barefoot. It had been a clever way to get kids to wear shoes instead of wreck their summer at camp by getting a stick stuck in their foot. Giggling to herself about those old memories, she struck a match and ignited her masterpiece. As fires do, it seemed to hypnotize her as it grew.

Sitting beside it with her back up against a large drift-wood log, she spread the contents of her next generation of s'mores next to her. It was cold and clear, with an expanse of stars the likes of which she hadn't seen in years. She felt inspired.

Throughout her last year at camp, she used to make fires in this very spot almost every night, hoping that maybe Henry would paddle up to the camp and find her after all her campers had fallen asleep. She had fantasized about sitting next to the fire with him and holding his hand. Even then, she knew it was one of those things better left a fantasy. The price of getting caught would have been far too high, which was likely why Henry had been respectful enough to stay at his uncle's place in the state park, as disappointing as it had been.

She looked at the heavens above and remembered the calm and gentleness in Henry's eyes . . . the glint of amusement that lit up frequently in her presence.

But now, all these years later, sitting next to a camp-fire again, she found herself wishing once more that Henry would paddle up the shore and sneak into camp with her . . . that he would hold her hand . . . that he would tell her all the things he wrote to her in his letters and pro-pose the plans he had been making.

A rowboat quietly rounded the corner just offshore. The sound of the paddles dipping in the water got louder and louder. She watched, wide-eyed and confounded. And when she heard a man's voice say, "Ruby?" as the boat continued to approach, she knew she had to be either hal-lucinating or seeing a ghost.

"Henry?" she choked. Tears streamed down her cheeks.

"No. It's Walt."

She collected herself as he pulled up onshore.

"I brought you gals some trout," he said. "It's best when

you bread it and fry it, I think." He stepped out of his boat with a small cooler.

"Oh, that was so kind of you. I'm sure it will be delicious."

"That's a mighty nice fire you have going. There's a chill in the air tonight."

"Come warm yourself, Walt," she said. "You can help me. I'm writing a s'mores cookbook."

He chuckled. "A s'mores cookbook? It's not that difficult."

She rolled her eyes. "I'm thinking of as many different variations as I can."

"Oh, of course," he said, still standing next to his boat. "Wait. I have an idea." He rummaged around in a box under the seat in his boat where he found a couple apples, some tinfoil, and a pocketknife. Then he took a spot on the ground next to Ruby and rested his back against the same log. "What have you got here?"

"Just about every candy bar known to man, a variety of graham crackers and cookies, and a giant bag of marshmallows."

"Do you have caramel squares?" he asked.

"I think so . . . somewhere." She ran her hand through the pile of candy and picked out two and then one more. "Here."

"Remember baked apples?" he asked.

"Of course," she replied, "but this book is about s'mores."

"Imagine, if you will, a s'more inside a baked apple." He cut out the cores of both apples and handed one to her. In his he inserted a caramel square, some graham cracker crumbs, and finally half of a marshmallow. Then he wrapped the whole thing in tinfoil and set it in the fire.

"Genius," Ruby muttered. "I'm going to add some

pecan pieces to mine," she said, assembling her own concoction.

"Brilliant," he said. He watched her quietly for a moment or two and then asked, "So who's Henry? Were you expecting someone else?"

"Just a ghost," she answered.

"I know a few of those myself," he replied.

For a moment, they were quiet.

"I can't see the stars as well as I used to," said Walt. "I mean, I can see they're up there, but I can't identify the constellations anymore. I miss that. I used to tell time by where Orion was in the sky. I couldn't see him from my property, but out on the lake I could see him."

"I miss the texture of my hair before it turned gray. It used to be so silky. Now it feels coarse. It is what it is, and there's no time to waste thinking about it, but if I could have one thing back from my youth, I think I'd pick that."

"I think your hair is very pretty," Walt said.

Ruby blushed. "Thank you," she replied politely.

Again there was a pause, this time more awkward. Walt finally broke the silence. "It smells like autumn," he said, breathing in deeply.

"Indeed it does. The autumns sure seem to come around faster and faster. I don't know where the time goes."

"It's such a nostalgic time of year, isn't it?" Walt poked at the apples with a stick to make sure both sides baked.

"Back to school, apple harvest, Halloween . . . ," Ruby agreed.

"Thanksgivings together as a family . . ."

"Do you have kids, Walt?" Ruby asked.

"Two sons," he replied. "Good men. You?"

"No, I never did."

"Were you married?" he asked.

Ruby thought that question had lost its power, but in Walt's presence she found herself feeling a little deflated. It was an uncomfortable question, because of the unspoken question that followed it: *What's wrong with you?* She took a deep breath and said, "Not really. The one boy I loved died in Korea. I did go through a wedding ceremony after that, but immediately realized I had made a mistake, so I ran away and got it annulled two days later. Ethel helped me."

An amused smile spread across Walt's face, but it wasn't unkind. "How long ago?"

"A million years ago. I was twenty-one."

"Pretty gutsy for a young woman in the fifties." It seemed as if he admired her for it. She did not see that coming. "You must've been a real pistol. Are you still?"

Ruby laughed and dodged the question. She didn't know how to answer it.

"That's okay," he said. "I don't mind a challenge."

Was Walt flirting with her? Walt was flirting with her!

"A real-life runaway bride . . . ," he said as if he were meeting a celebrity.

She knew he was joking and that he meant well, but still she found it uncomfortable, and so she changed the subject. "Have you always had a passion for fishing, Walt?"

"There was a time when I spent considerably more of my days and nights in my house," he said. "My wife of fifty-eight years passed two years ago. I find I do better outdoors now."

"Oh," Ruby said. "I'm sorry for your loss."

He nodded his acknowledgment. "So, now it's just me and the fish. We do all right."

Ruby wasn't sure what to say, and before she could figure it out Walt said, "I'm a lucky man. I really am. I could not have asked for more."

It took grace, thought Ruby, *to be so thankful in the*

face of such loss. This man had grace. And she admired him for it.

With that, he pushed the apples out of the fire with a stick, then carefully and quickly picked at the foil near the top until a little came unwrapped and, holding on to that, lifted them out of the fire, where he set one near Ruby. "They need to cool a bit."

"They smell delicious," she said. "Thank you."

And their baked apples, like Walt's company, were even more divine than Ruby had imagined. Such is the nature of unexpected blessings.

friday

AMBER

Surrender. It was all Amber could do when she saw the sheriff as she descended the stairs. She could not call it a relief, because she was scared of what would come next, but she was aware of the heavy, heavy responsibility lifting off of her shoulders. No longer would she have to try to keep the house of cards from falling. No longer would she have to keep up the charade.

She looked at Ethel and she looked at Ruby, and though it shouldn't have surprised Amber to have been betrayed by them, it did. True, she had only been with them two nights, but she'd thought she'd had a better read on them than this. *Screw it,* she thought. *Bring on the frickin' foster family.* At least with them there would be an agreement. She would get food and a bed, and everyone would understand that for the time being she belonged there. And she could keep her knife under her pillow or mattress just in case someone tried to molest her.

She gave Ethel a look as if to ask, *How could you?*

Ethel, reading Amber's face accurately, answered, "If it had been up to me, you would have stayed with me until you were ready to be out on your own. Sheriff Sam found you all on his own."

As if on cue, he held up the brown paper bag with her name on it. "Mr. Adams left it on the gate." He handed it to her.

Inside she found bike lights. *Darn it*. Mr. Adams had meant well. Who would have thought a well-intended act of generosity would be her undoing?

"Bathroom?" Ruby asked.

Amber nodded, and the sheriff started toward the door as if he intended to escort her.

"Is it okay if I walk her?" Ethel asked. "After all, she's not under arrest."

Sheriff Sam nodded.

"I'll go get breakfast ready," Ruby said, and Ethel thanked her.

Once they were out the door, Ethel put her arm around Amber. "Your mom's been arrested," she said.

Closing her eyes, Amber stopped in her tracks and tried to absorb the news.

"Listen. It will take me months to become an approved foster parent, but if you would prefer to live with me, I'll start the process."

Amber looked at Ethel and nodded.

Ethel handed her a piece of paper. "This is my phone number. If things are not all right with your foster family and your social worker won't help you, call me. I really do think it's going to be fine, though. Sheriff Sam told me about the people you will be living with and he said they are good people. Sheriff Sam is a straight shooter. I trust him on things like this. They live up here on the lake. You won't have to switch schools."

All Amber could do was nod and continue on to the bathroom, Ethel walking beside her.

It was over. The time in her life when she had any control over her destiny was over. She was at the mercy of something much, much bigger now.

She crawled deep inside herself and allowed her body to move forward, to go through the motions of what she now had to do, but she didn't feel it all the way like she would have if she had still resided in the surfaces of her skin. She ate a few eggs and a piece of toast but hardly tasted them, hugged Ethel and Ruby but hardly felt them. Although she did wish that Shannon and Laura were awake so she could say good-bye, she didn't ask anyone to get them. She just packed her things, and walked off beside Sheriff Sam up the hill to the road.

He let her sit in the front of his patrol car, a small act of kindness she appreciated. Turning around, she examined the backseat through the wire mesh, possibly the same backseat her mother had sat in during her arrest. Amber pictured her mother in an orange jumpsuit, sitting in a cell, head in her hands, forlorn and full of regrets, missing Amber. But really, she knew it was more likely her mother was either pacing the floor in a jittery fit of withdrawal or lying down on her side, facing the wall instead of the world, and that she was probably thinking very little about Amber. Mostly her mom would be thinking about the drugs and men she would no longer have access to. With her ability to date completely out the window, she would have no great plan of salvation. No one was going to save her now.

Amber felt conflicted about that. As Sheriff Sam drove down the narrow, windy road, taking her to God only knew where, Amber oscillated between being glad that her mother was miserable, glad that she was being punished for being such a failure as a mother, and feeling huge waves of grief push her over her and pin her down.

From long ago, she remembered the feeling of sand shifting under her feet. Other kids on the beach squealed with delight, but she feared this thing she could not control. She turned to look back at her mother, and that's when a wave hit her little body from behind, knocking her down facefirst. She would never forget the force of it as it pinned her to the sand for that brief moment. In a heartbeat, her mother had been there, grabbing Amber's arm and pulling her up, taking her into her arms and lifting her out of that dangerous chaos, washing the sand off her face, and cooing sympathetic reassurances in her ear. Back when she was a good mom.

Not like now. Not like now when Amber's mom would not be lifting her up by her arm and pulling her out of a foster home. Not like now when Amber's mom just left her in the dangerous chaos of this world to fend for herself as if she didn't care at all. As if Amber weren't worth making the right choices for—even when those choices involved some level of sacrifice or discomfort. Parents were supposed to do that. They were.

"Will I be able to go to school today?" Amber asked. "I missed school yesterday and I don't want to fall further behind."

"I bet that can be arranged. We're meeting your social worker and your new foster family across the lake so you can get settled in first," said Sheriff Sam.

As they passed the bar where her mother had worked, Amber wondered if she should somehow relay the message that her mother would not be in, because surely it would be an inconvenience to them, but then realized with a sudden burst of anger that she didn't care. That bar was the turning point. That bar had taken time and attention Amber had needed for years and years. That bar had opened countless doors to countless wrong paths for her mother. It was the reason they were in the situation they were in today. *Screw them*. If Amber knew she could get away with arson, she'd burn it down, but that was too big of a risk and not worth jeopardizing her future over.

Soon she and Sheriff Sam arrived at her new home, and he left her in the care of the social worker who waited outside. She was middle-aged and overweight and wore eye makeup reminiscent of a peacock feather, but she seemed like a reasonable person. She asked how Amber was and appeared to care about her reply.

And when the social worker introduced Amber to her new foster parents, Amber was pleasantly surprised. Glen and Barbara hardly seemed like the monstrous foster parents Amber's mother had described from her past. Amber followed them into their living room and stood awkwardly, sizing them up while the adults talked. Glen had a mustache and a neat haircut. He wore a polo shirt and baggy jeans Amber suspected he'd had since the late eighties, but when she looked at his face what she saw was effort. This was someone who tried really hard to be a good person. Barbara dyed her hair yellow blond and styled it with hot rollers. Her face was soft and kind, but her smile was a little forced. This was someone who went along with her husband's wishes.

Amber noticed the Christian artifacts on Barbara and Glen's walls just as the social worker said, "Glen is the pastor at the Community Christian Church," and then it made sense. They wanted to parade Amber around their church to show everyone what good people they were. That was fine. If they fed her and gave her a safe, warm place to sleep, they could parade her around. Fair enough. Everyone was motivated by something. Their motives were much better than the motives of her mother's former foster parents. No complaints.

From a bedroom down the hall a baby cried, and Barbara went to him.

"We've also got seven-year-old twins staying with us

right now who are a real handful," said Glen. "Their mom had a drug problem also." It was the first time Amber had heard someone really speak it out loud and she didn't like how it sounded. In fact, it made her bristle. Why? It was the truth, right? Because it made her feel pitiful, which maybe she was, but she'd been suffering that with quiet dignity for years and now her dignity was gone. That's how she felt.

"I'd like to go to school now," Amber said.

"I can take her," said the social worker to Glen. "I'm going back to the office in Wenatchee, so it's on my way."

Barbara came down the hall with a baby in her arms and said, "Let me show you your room. If you have any laundry, just put it in the hamper."

Amber didn't like the idea of some stranger touching her underwear. There was no dignity in that. She could do it herself. Or would Barbara and Glen let her? Did she want to make waves or let a do-gooder handle her dirty underwear? What was the better choice?

Barbara showed her to her new room. It was clean and it didn't smell weird. The walls were light green; and the white curtains, plain and functional. There was even a desk where Amber could do her homework. Plaques with psalms on them hung on the wall. Fine. If converting her to their religion was part of the deal, that was fine. Whatever. She put her bags on the bed. Her clothes were all dirty and smelled bad. She did need clean clothes for school tomorrow, so she reluctantly put them in the hamper. More power and more dignity lost.

As she drove down to town with the social worker, Amber felt generous enough to say, "Thank you for finding me a home where I could stay in my school."

"It's nice when it works out like that," the social worker said before changing the subject. "I'm glad we have this time to talk about some things. Would you like to visit your mother? If so, I'll be the person who schedules it and takes you there."

Amber looked out her passenger side window at the Upper Wenatchee River raging through Tumwater Canyon. It seemed to mirror the tumultuous undercurrent of her life. She watched as the river carried a log through its rapids and smashed it in half against a boulder, and it seemed clear to Amber that when life felt like class five rapids the key to getting through it was avoiding as many obstacles as possible. "No," she said. "I don't want to visit my mother."

SHANNON 2012

When Shannon woke up, Laura was rifling through her things. "Shannon, do you know anything regarding the whereabouts of my underwear?"

"Nope," Shannon said, and then added, "Uh-oh," as the implications hit her. If Laura's underwear was missing and Shannon hadn't taken it, her underwear was likely missing, too. She dug through her backpack. Just as she suspected, her underwear was gone. "Whoever did it got both of us."

"Ethel?" Laura asked.

"Ethel knows us best, but Ruby is not to be underestimated."

"Ruby did disappear for quite a long time last night," Laura said.

Shannon started laughing. "We've been raided by a senior citizen."

Laura looked confused. "I'm not really sure what to do about it."

"I'm thinking we start by looking on the flagpole."

"Yeah, but do we retaliate?"

Shannon laughed as they put their pajama pants back on and walked out of the cabin and down the stairs. "I don't know. A lot of pranks could go terribly wrong. I think we could ethically freeze a pair of her underwear, though."

"It might make her feel included," Laura said as if they would be doing Ruby a big favor by freezing her underwear. "I'll sneak them out while you start breakfast, take them to the lake and get them wet, then leave them in the arts and crafts cupboard until one of us can get them safely in the freezer."

Shannon asked, "Should we leave a note on the freezer maybe at lunch, you know, after they're good and frozen solid, letting Ruby know that she can find them in there?"

Laura replied with mock seriousness, "I think that's just good manners. I mean, we don't want her to think she has dementia when she can't find them."

As Laura and Shannon crossed the little bridge, the flagpole came into view and, sure enough, there was their underwear hanging from the top in a giant wad. "I'm really glad it didn't rain last night," Shannon said.

"Really glad," Laura agreed.

When they walked into the Lodge, they found it empty. It still smelled like breakfast, but instead of food they found a note on the table: "The forces that be caught up with Amber and took her. Ruby drove me to my house to see what, if anything, I can do. Scrambled eggs are in the oven. Hope they're not too dry. Love, Ethel."

"Oh no," Laura said.

"Maybe things will be better for her," replied Shannon hopefully.

"Maybe."

ETHEL 2012

Ethel took out of her pocket the piece of paper that Sheriff Sam had given her, unfolded it, and dialed the number to schedule a visit with Amber's mom. How did this work? What if Amber's mom wouldn't see her?

"What inmate?" the woman on the other end of the phone asked.

"Debbie Hill," Ethel answered.

"Her attorney already has a visit scheduled with her today, ma'am. Inmates are only allowed one visit a day. You'll have to try again tomorrow."

"Can't we just schedule that now?"

"No, ma'am. Appointments must be made the same day as the visit. That is our policy."

"Thank you," Ethel said. There was nothing at all that could be done today. Even though Sheriff Sam had assured her that Amber's foster parents were good people, Ethel worried. She didn't worry about Amber's safety; she worried about her comfort. Changes were tough. Forging new relationships was tough. All of it was tough.

Ruby was studying the old picture on the wall when Ethel hung up—the one Ethel had once smashed.

"Well, there's nothing more that can be done today," Ethel said, disappointed.

"I don't remember this," Ruby said. "I don't remember when this was taken. I love it, though."

"We had just won the canoe scavenger hunt. Remember that? We had to go to the campground and find someone to give us a marshmallow and a fisherman who would give us a lead sinker . . . things like that?"

Ruby laughed. "Oh yes, I do vaguely remember that." She studied the picture a little more. "Look how good we all look in our swimsuits."

Ethel joined her to examine the photo for details that she had perhaps not noticed in a while. "Those were the days," she said.

Ruby paused and then replied thoughtfully, "They were. But so are these. These are the days, too. They're just different."

Unconvinced, Ethel said nothing. It seemed to her these days were a time when a person began to lose everything she loved. Like Haddie. Like camp.

Looking at the picture of Haddie on the dock brought back a memory so intense Ethel feared she would start bawling right there, so she said, "Before we go back, I need to check one thing. Do you want to take a shower? Go ahead and take a shower. Towels are under the sink."

It was just an excuse to hustle out the back door and down the steps to the dock below. Ethel pretended to verify that the kayaks were secured just in case Ruby was watching, but when the odds seemed good that Ruby was in the shower Ethel simply sat on the dock and allowed herself to release some more of the seemingly endless grief.

People said time heals all wounds, but more and more Ethel was realizing that was a lie.

Ethel wrapped her arms around herself and rocked forward and back, looking out at the black lake, so cold and clear and empty on one hand, so full of life and the source of life on the other. So empty and full all at once.

ETHEL 2012

Just two years ago, Haddie had woken Ethel in the middle of the night. "Ethel," she whispered. "Ethel, I just had the loveliest dream about herons. We were paddling a canoe down a river. You were in the back. To our left, a heron took off and flew in front of me. It was the most beautiful dream I've ever had."

"Hm, that's nice," Ethel had murmured, not wanting to come out of her own sleep.

"Ethel, let's go swimming."

"You're crazy. Go back to sleep," she had said. She had come so close to missing out. Thank God Haddie hadn't let her.

"Ethel. This beautiful life is so short. Let's go swimming. Let's look at the moon and stars and feel the water on our skin."

"The *freezing* water," Ethel had corrected. "The *freezing* water on our skin. We won't feel it for long. We'll be numb in three seconds."

"Ethel, come on. Live with me. We're alive now. It is a beautiful moment. Come on, Ethel. Let's live."

And though she asked, "So 'freezing' and 'living' are synonymous?" Ethel reluctantly got out of bed, put on her fuzzy bathrobe, and grabbed a couple towels from the bathroom.

Haddie didn't bother with any of that. "Sometimes," she answered, and walked to the dock naked.

And as Ethel followed her, she admired Haddie's beauty, the moonlight and shadows on her skin, her spirited walk, the same walk that had captivated her so long ago. Haddie, her daring lake nymph.

Thank God, Ethel thought as she remembered back to that night. Thank God she looked up and saw it. Thank God she had the sense to relish it.

Haddie stood on the end of the dock, naked, alive, and brave. She reached above her head, put her hands together, and dove into the deep, dark water.

Ethel was not sure how she mustered the strength to

follow. The frigid lake usually gave her a headache and stung her skin. It had to have been all of thirty-three degrees—barely a liquid at all. But on this night, she simply felt the cold shock tighten her body and then she rolled over onto her back and looked at the stars. "Thank you, Haddie," she had said. "This really is beautiful."

And Haddie, also floating on her back, kicked her way over so that she was beside Ethel and took her hand.

The moment had been transcendent—Haddie's hand in hers, floating under the stars, tiny specks in a world so big. Such tiny, temporary specks.

Although it seemed as if they were suspended there forever, in reality it had been too cold to be still for very long. They let go simultaneously. They were synchronized like that.

"You are good for me, Haddie," Ethel had said, treading water.

"I know," Haddie had replied, reaching out to put a hand on Ethel's cheek. Haddie kissed her in the water like she had when they were young.

It was a kiss Ethel would remember more vividly than most—Haddie's cold, wet lips, the heat of her breath on Ethel's face, the beautiful drops of water in her eyelashes.

They had climbed the little ladder on the side of the dock, and Ethel had handed Haddie a towel. Instead of drying off, Haddie had spread it out on the dock and lain down as if she were sunbathing.

"Lay with me, my love," Haddie said.

And thank God Ethel did. Thank God she touched Haddie and kissed her.

How symbolic it seemed that the two of them, each so cold on her own, had been able to warm each other.

LAURA 2012

Ruby and Ethel stopped on the road to ask Shannon and Laura if they wanted a ride to Ethel's house, where Shannon intended to write grants. Laura politely declined. She needed these two miles to figure some things out, and Shannon was a willing sounding board.

"I took a shower!" Ruby gloated.

"Feel free to take showers at my house where there's water," Ethel said.

"She means *please* take showers!" Ruby shouted, holding her nose, making Shannon and Laura laugh.

After Ruby and Ethel drove off toward camp, Laura said, "I know it's just on a road, but it's nice . . . you know, walking together again."

"Yeah," Shannon agreed. "Remember that time we all went to Valhalla and all the girls were freaking out about being eaten by bears while they had their periods?"

"Poor things," Laura said with a sympathetic smile.

"Nothing like periods to traumatize young women," Shannon stated.

"That's a fact," Laura agreed. "But you know, I wasn't scared at all on that trip."

"No? I wasn't scared exactly, but I was a little nervous that they might attract a bear. I sure wasn't going to show it, though. I figured you just weren't showing it either."

"No, that wasn't it. Compared to my dad, a bear was not a big problem."

"Oh."

Laura wanted to get off the topic of her dad, so she quickly said, "Remember how we all tried making tinfoil stew for dinner that night and everything was burned on the outside and raw on the inside? Those were gross. I think we all survived on biscuits on a stick alone."

"Biscuits on a stick. I had forgotten about those. Better living through processed foods. Was there nothing we couldn't do with Bisquick?"

"How did we eat that crap?" Laura asked.

"Truly, I don't know. I've not eaten it since," Shannon replied.

They walked along in silence for a while. And then Laura said, "I realized this week that somewhere along the way I lost the part of myself that I liked best when I stopped making time to go on hikes—especially with my husband."

"I get it. I've felt more like myself in the last twenty-four hours than I have in what seems like forever," said Shannon.

The South Shore Road was narrow, windy, and wooded, without much traffic, but when they heard the occasional car or pickup come barreling down the road they trotted over to the inside of the turn where it was safer and got off the road when they could.

Drizzle fell softly, and Shannon lifted her face to let it fall on her skin. "This rain feels like gentle kisses," she said.

Laura lifted her face and felt it, too. It reminded her of lying near Spray Falls with Steve so long ago, and she smiled. "It does." After a moment of quiet, Laura asked, "So, you said you never got married, but did you ever come close?"

Shannon shrugged. "Living in a small town is akin to living in a convent."

At first Laura laughed, and then she said, "I'm sorry. That's not really funny."

Shannon smiled and shrugged. "There's no question

that it's time to change my life. I was eating a bowl of Grape-Nuts the morning before I melted down in class, thinking about how many tens of thousands of times I've eaten at that table alone. I did some math. Over a hundred thousand times I think. I didn't used to think about it too much, but lately, I don't know, I've just found eating alone almost unbearable. I eat cereal in the morning and canned soup in the evening so I can just mindlessly pour it in a dish and eat up quickly and be done with it. Sometimes lately, I just haven't eaten at all because I just can't stand it anymore. It's been really nice to eat with everyone this week."

"Oh," Laura said sympathetically. It wasn't really something she could relate to. She had been cooking for other people for so long that the idea of eating breakfast cereal and canned soup day after day sounded rather indulgent. "Maybe you should work in a restaurant," she said.

Shannon shrugged. "Maybe so."

"Any new ideas for your future?"

"I don't know. I've been thinking about some of those European movies like *Babette's Feast* and *Antonia's Line* where they all eat at a big table together and the meal goes on for hours. I've been thinking maybe Europe. I don't know what it's like to teach English there, but maybe it's not as restrictive as teaching English here."

"European men with sexy accents . . . ," Laura suggested playfully.

Shannon shrugged and grimaced. "That's the tough part. European men are into fashion and the end result is that my brain registers all of them as gay. Seriously, how can any woman look at a man in a T-shirt with capped sleeves and think desirous thoughts? No, I'm just not attracted to European men. Except cops in uniform. Oh, the cops in Athens . . . I want a Cops of Athens calendar."

They laughed.

"I hope whatever you wish for finds you," Laura said. "I mean, in a good way—not because you're getting arrested in Athens. . . ."

"Thanks. Yeah, I'm too pretty for the pokey."

"Clearly." There was something Laura wanted to say, but despite her attempts, she felt like it just wasn't coming out. She tried once more. "The plan was to leave tomorrow and I'm not ready. I mean, I love Steve, but I keep thinking about how lonely I feel with him. I'm so much lonelier with him than I am by myself."

"Oh no. That's not good." Then, slowly and quietly, she said, "Oh my God, Laura, what if *no one* is happy? What if *everyone* is lonely—no matter what we choose? What if we're all doomed to several more decades of this?"

Laura thought about it for a few minutes and then said, "I don't think it has to be like that. I think it's like that for a lot of people, but I don't think it *has* to be like that."

"So you think it can be different?"

"I don't know. Maybe my marriage and my life doesn't *have* to be like this. I mean, it just can't be like this. I'm at my breaking point."

"I hope your husband and you rediscover each other and begin a really happy new era," Shannon said. "I mean, I remember when you wrote to me after you met him, and in the beginning, you were happy. That's got to mean something."

Laura nodded. "Yeah," she said sadly.

They reached Ethel's little cabin, found the key under the mat, and let themselves in. Shannon turned on the computer.

"Is there anything I can do to help?" Laura asked.

"If there was another computer, there would be," Shannon replied. She paused and thought and then shrugged apologetically. "I'm sorry, Laura. I don't know what you could do."

"Well, if there's only one computer, there's only one computer. I think I'll take that shower."

There's nothing like a shower after days of not taking one, Laura thought, her mind drifting back to the first shower she took after hiking the Wonderland Trail with Steve. That one she'd had mixed feelings about. Steve's smell and his kisses had still lingered on her skin. She'd hated washing them off. But today she felt no such conflict. It was just pure bliss.

Afterward, she awkwardly said, "Well, you're sure there's nothing I can do to be helpful?"

Shannon replied, "I'm so sorry, but there's really not."

"Okay then, I guess I'll go on back . . . maybe walk the South Shore Trail again."

"I wish I could go with you," Shannon said.

"You will, one of these days. Thanks for what you're doing to try to save camp. God, wouldn't be wonderful if it worked out?"

"It feels like too much to hope for, but I feel like I have to try anyway."

"Well, thank you," Laura said. "See you back at camp later."

As she began walking back, feelings of uselessness flooded her. It was so similar to what she felt at home now that the kids were gone. "Well, what am I going to do about this?" she asked herself. The answer wasn't clear.

She thought about Steve and about how all he ever wanted from her was her love and a family. He never asked her for more. And she wondered if he still felt that way and, if he didn't, what use she could possibly be to him.

LAURA 1990

"I'm scared that if I go back to Seattle, the spell will be broken," she had confessed to Steve on their last day on the Wonderland Trail. "I look at my parents and I know most people never find this."

"This?" he asked.

"You know, this thing that's happening between us."

"Love?" He said it.

Wow, he said it. "Yes. Love."

"Well, then move to Leavenworth and be with me." She knew he worked in the family business—a lumber store that had been passed down for two generations and would one day be his.

At first, she smiled. In that moment, she felt as if she would follow him anywhere. She had never known anything like it and knew it didn't come twice in a lifetime.

And then she choked. What if he let her down? What if he let her go? She would need a backup plan. It just wasn't wise to be at the mercy of another for basic survival needs. Only one more year, she thought. It seemed like such a small price to pay for so many more choices and a small price to pay for independence. That's what she had thought, and the panic had shown on her face.

Steve's smile fell, and he shook his head. "I'm sorry. Forget it. That wasn't a fair thing to ask of you." He turned away and started walking on down the trail again.

Laura hadn't known what to say. She caught up with him and put a hand on his arm so that he stopped and turned around, and when he did she simply put her arms around him—as much as she could with his backpack on—and rested her cheek on the scratchy wool shirt he was wearing. Three tears slipped out. Until now, the only time she ever cried was when she left camp for the summer. For most of her life when she wasn't at camp, she had simply felt numb. As the severing pierced her deeply and tore her apart, she had watched the tears bead up on Steve's shirt.

Steve had taken a deep breath and wrapped his arms around her head.

"I don't know what else to do," she said.

"I know," he replied.

It took a moment for her to summon the courage to say it. "I've never felt like this before."

"I know." He understood. He felt the same. The sadness in his voice was like lead.

A few hours later, they were back at her car in Longmire saying good-bye. She could hardly breathe. "We'll visit each other," she said, trying to convince herself that it was okay, that it wasn't really good-bye. "We'll . . . do other backpack trips like this."

"Right," he said, not sarcastic, but not as if he believed her either. He simply said it because it was the right thing to say.

"We'll figure it out. It's just a year."

Steve looked at the ground and then up at the sky, blinking back the tears he did not want her to see. "My dad always said that when I met my future wife, I would just know. I never knew what he was talking about until now. And I sure never thought it would hurt this much."

Future wife? She nodded. "I know. I just can't imagine not being with you."

"You don't have to. Just . . . remember that."

He kissed her one last time, but she started crying in the middle of it, which wrecked it. She rested her forehead on his chest for just a moment and whispered, "Good-bye for now." Then, without looking at him, she turned away, got into her car, turned the ignition, and backed out. Before she put it in first gear, she looked up at him. His hand was on his heart as if it was breaking, and he raised the other one in a weak good-bye wave. She put her hand on her heart, too, cried harder, and drove away.

And then, three weeks later, just four days before classes were starting, she was leaving Planned Parenthood with life-changing news. She was pregnant. *Pregnant.*

She drove directly over Stevens Pass to Leavenworth, figuring she could find him at the lumber store if she got there before five or six. What was she going to say? She hadn't chosen a life with him when she'd had the chance. She had chosen other dreams instead. And now, well, what did she expect after she sort of rejected him? Did she expect him to suddenly make her world okay? It seemed more than a little audacious to even hope for that. These weren't the circumstances under which she wanted to start a family. This wasn't how she wanted to get married. She was sure they weren't the circumstances Steve dreamed of either.

But when she walked into the lumber store, he lit up and jogged over to her. "You're here!" he said joyfully.

Her terror must have shown, because Steve looked confused. "What's wrong?"

"Can we go outside?" she asked, and took his hand. "Sure."

And there on the sidewalk in front of the store, she took a deep breath and just said it. "I'm pregnant."

To her shock, Steve smiled. "Oh," he exhaled. "What a relief. I thought you were breaking up with me."

That sent Laura into escalating laughter.

Steve joined in, still holding her hand. "You know, I know this wasn't your plan, but I'm kind of glad. I mean, if this means that you're going to move here and marry me and be a family."

No, becoming a mother at twenty-one hadn't been her plan and neither was getting married because she was pregnant. But then again, hiking the Wonderland Trail with Steve hadn't been her plan either, and it had not only turned out to be even more wonderful than her original plan of hiking it alone; it had also turned out to be the best week of her life. And somehow, she suspected life would be no different. She hugged him tight for the longest time and then whispered, "Thank you."

"Hey," he said so she'd look up at him, and when she did he kissed her. "Everything's going to be okay."

And she believed him.

She once had heard Haddie say that every path had a price and every path had a payoff. Laura left a part of herself behind that day, the part of her that dreamed of being a field biologist in wild places all over the globe, dreamed of saving animals and changing the world. But she married a man she loved and had two beautiful children. Neither path had more value or virtue. Life was life, however one lived it. And Steve had been right. Everything had been more or less okay. Yes, "okay" was the perfect word for what it had been.

RUBY 1952

On a Saturday at the end of summer, after the campers had gone, Henry met Ruby at the rockslides with a picnic. Together they climbed over the larger boulders and jumped from rock to rock on the smaller ones. She noticed his tan legs and the way his muscular shoulders stretched his T-shirt. And when she got tired of climbing, he'd flash her that sweet smile and she knew she had no choice but to go on. She was so smitten.

About halfway up, Henry found a large rock that satisfied him. It was flat and had room for two and a view of the lake. As she sat next to him, she noticed his handsome profile, the dimples when he smiled, how much the sun had bleached his hair. Noticing the warm way he smelled after he broke a light sweat, she had a strong impulse to lean right into him. She looked out at the beautiful view of the lake and the mountains behind it. It was the perfect place for a romantic kiss, but Henry seemed a little distracted, a little distant. She couldn't put her finger on it. When he looked at her with those beautiful blue eyes, she knew it was something else—not her. She could tell that much.

They ate turkey sandwiches and carrot sticks, and then Henry broke the news to Ruby about his deployment to Korea, completely blindsiding her. As she looked at the broken pieces of rock all around her she understood what must have happened to the mountain. It must have had its heart broken. In the seconds that followed his announcement, she felt the same crumbling inside of her.

"Will you take care of this while I'm gone? My grandpa gave it to me." He took off his prized fishing vest and handed it to her. "I'll be back for this. As long as you have it, you know I'll be back."

She held it in her shaking hands and tried to think of a response that would hide the level of her despair. She wanted to scream, *No!* and turn and run. Or she wanted to throw herself into his arms and beg him not to let go, not to leave her. But neither of those responses was appropriate, and so she put on a fake smile and joked, "Oh, so it's the vest you're coming back for and not me."

"Oh, I'm coming back for you, Ruby Gemill. I'm just giving you my prized possession so you know there is no question."

She held it up and looked back and forth between the vest and Henry. It was as if when he slipped out of it he had begun slipping away, in the same way people who die just slip right out of their skin and leave it behind. It was all ending. Sadness filled her chest with broken boulders and stung her eyes. She couldn't hide it all.

"I'll be back, Ruby," he whispered, putting a hand behind her head and kissing her. He pulled back to look at her and, seeing how sad she still was, kissed her with even more intensity. "I'll be back," he said again. And at the time, she believed him.

But he didn't come back.

She had received three letters from him—the first two of which she had read so many times that the creases where the paper had been folded threatened to fall apart. She had memorized them.

Dear Ruby,

Boot camp is rough. We run, do push-ups, and clean things with toothbrushes. That pretty much sums it up. But our country is worth it to me. We cannot let the Communists take over the world. There are causes bigger than ourselves. It's an honor to sacrifice two years of my life for this one. I endure it all by thinking about you, by thinking about how I'm doing this for our children, so that they may grow up in the land of opportunity instead of a world that offers them only the limitations of Communism. I can't wait to be with you again. I hope you will wait for me.

Fondly,
Henry

Dear Ruby,

Korea is much like Washington State as far as the weather goes. It's cold and damp. The Koreans eat this stuff called kimchi. It's spicy fermented cabbage. At first I didn't like it, but now we all find it keeps us warm.

War is different from what I expected. There is a lot of waiting. It gives me time to really contemplate the fact that I have committed to being here for the next two years. I have only been here a week. Two years seems unfathomable to me. It gives me time to think of all the ways you could move on and forget all about me. I pray that you don't. I pray that I haven't ruined my chances of spending this life with you.

I often return to Lake Wenatchee in my mind, and remember the sun in your hair, the way your eyes matched the forest, how beautiful you are. Most of all, I remember laughing together, wondering what antics you would be up to next in your perpetual quest for well-intentioned mischief (if there really is such a thing). You are a joy, Ruby. I carry you in my heart and it strengthens me.

Please wait for me, Ruby. I cannot imagine any other man appreciating you the way I would. It would be tragic if you spent your life with anything less.

Yours truly,
Henry

The third envelope had come in his handwriting, which made its contents an especially cruel shock:

Dear Ruby,

If you receive this letter, it means I am not coming home. I am leaving it with my uncle to send to you just in case I don't make it back.

Ruby, truly I cannot imagine not coming back to you. I think about you all the time. I think about all of your dif-

ferent smiles—the one that's pure and joyful, the one that has blatant hints of mischief, the hopeful one you give me right before I kiss your beautiful lips. I think about the sunlight on your hair, the way all that copper sparkles, how I long to touch it. And how I long to touch you.

I often worry that another fellow will swoop you off your feet and be the lucky one to spend his life entertained by your humor and charm. You absolutely have charmed me, Ruby, and I want to be the man you spend your life with. I'm enraptured by everything about you. I love you, Ruby. Plain and simple as that. Not returning to you is unthinkable to me because I have plans for us— big plans. And the first thing on that list is taking you in my arms again and kissing you, and then taking you to city hall and making you my wife so that I don't have to wait one more day to be with you and begin our new life together.

So, Ruby, if you are receiving this, I want to apologize from the bottom of my heart. I want you to know this was not my plan, not at all. My plan was to be there with you and for you, for us to raise a family together, and to spend every day loving you with all my heart. But Ruby, if you receive this, I also want you to know that I died for something I believed in. I died for freedom.

With love,
Henry

Ruby read it and in her head believed it but in her heart could not. Logically, she knew it was true. She knew soldiers died. She knew he would not be coming home to her. She knew he would not be taking her in his arms and kissing her like in the photos she had seen in the news. But in her heart, she could not picture it. She could not conceive that someone so young and full of vitality could be anything but alive. It was unreal. She spent the next two years in a state of confusion and grief.

Henry had been the only boy she'd ever met for whom she didn't feel she had to diminish herself to make comfortable. He had been the only one who had ever seemed completely smitten by her natural beauty. He had been her only true love, and only after Ruby settled for something so much less did it seem acutely clear and real—this loss of him and of the future that should have been theirs.

RUBY 1953

Ice edged the lakeshore, so Ethel and Ruby carried the aluminum canoe out to the dock and launched from there, bypassing the crust. Ethel had called Miss Mildred and told her about the final letter Ruby had received from Henry, and Miss Mildred, feeling sympathy for Ruby's loss, had suggested this idea to Ethel, for she knew how sometimes a friend and a canoe could really help a girl find peace.

Ethel was the only woman Ruby knew who was quiet like this, quiet in a comfortable way. Not very many people could even tolerate it, but Ethel seemed to know what a gift it was and that there were times when the very best thing in the world a friend could do to help another was simply let them be silent together—just show up and be there, just paddle in the back of the canoe.

The lake seemed so different than it had in summer when leaves were lush and the laughter of children floated on the water. It looked different without Henry in his little rowboat floating on it. Now everything looked dead. It was hard to believe another summer would ever return—that's how hopelessly dead Ruby's world appeared.

At the same time, there was a persistent part of Ruby that simply would not believe the news. Instead of using this outing to say good-bye in her heart to Henry, as Ethel had suggested, she spent the day pretending Henry was in the back of the canoe instead of Ethel until it seemed so real that her voice shocked Ruby when she finally spoke.

"Do you hear that?"

Ruby paused and listened. The honking was coming from the head of the lake.

"Trumpeter swans! Let's go find them!" Ethel said excitedly, turning the canoe around.

Ruby didn't have it in her to paddle hard, so it was Ethel's enthusiasm alone that propelled them up the lake. As they passed by camp, Ethel looked at the sky and said, "We shouldn't go that far. It's going to be dark soon." But then she paused and said, "Let's do it anyway!"

It didn't really matter to Ruby. Her imaginary date with Henry was over now that Ethel had begun to talk a little more.

After they rounded Windy Point, they saw them—huge white swans, honking intermittently at one another. How picturesque it all was—the sky beginning to turn pink, mountains white with snow, the water reflecting the pink sky, and the white birds in the foreground. Everything was pink and white, pink and white, like a valentine. Ruby wondered if the scene was a postcard from heaven sent by Henry, for its beauty was not something she ever could have imagined.

Ethel wanted to see how close she could get and slowly, gently, approached the swans. Suddenly the birds launched and flew right over them. Their huge white wings reminiscent of angels filled the sky for one long, magical moment.

Ethel gasped. "That was amazing."

Ruby watched the magnificent white birds grow smaller and smaller in the darkening sky. "Everything flies away," she said sadly.

ETHEL 2012

Ethel sat on the end of the long dock alone. She had spent the day wishing so badly that Haddie had been there. This was the very spot where so many years ago they had lain in the sun after a swim, shivering, waiting for the sun to warm them again, when Haddie had turned her head to look at Ethel and said, "You're lovely."

"What?" Ethel had asked.

"You're beautiful."

Ethel had never really thought about herself that way. That night, though, as she stood in front of the mirror brushing her teeth she tried to see herself through Haddie's eyes, and for a moment Ethel thought she saw it—her own beauty.

They had such different kinds of beauty. Haddie was like a dark, smooth river cobble—polished and bold—whereas Ethel was more like a feather found on the ground, something that blends in at first, something with rough edges, but when a person stopped to really examine it she could appreciate its softness, its complexity. Maybe. Maybe that's what Haddie saw.

Ethel heard footsteps and turned to see who it was. Ruby made her way down and sat quietly next to Ethel, in the spot where Haddie once lay. "You know what I remember most about Haddie?" she said as if she knew exactly what Ethel was thinking. "How she sang. She had a Broadway voice. You could always hear her above all the others."

"She did," Ethel agreed.

"There was a week one summer when I was too sick to go serenading with all of you after the ceremonial fire, so I was in my bunk when you all serenaded my cabin. I could pick out Haddie's voice and I remember thinking it was silky. That was the word that came to my mind. Remember how when she led the livelier songs at meals or campfires how much joy would just pour out of her? You couldn't help but want to join in."

Ethel laughed. "I was just thinking about how beautiful she was."

"She was beautiful. I always thought she looked like Elizabeth Taylor."

Ethel smiled. "Yeah. I always wondered what exactly she saw in me."

"She had the strength, but you had the warmth, and I think she needed warmth," Ruby said. "Think about her family. Not exactly warm."

It was true. Her father had been a preacher and found sin in everything she did—and that was without Haddie even ever telling him about being gay. Her mother had died when she was young, and Haddie's two brothers were much older than she was. One became a professor; and the other, a preacher like their father. Haddie exchanged Christmas cards with them, and that was about it. Ruby was right. Haddie had needed warmth.

"I didn't have a service for her," Ethel said quietly. "I just felt like the truth was sacred, and I didn't want anyone showing up and judging her or our life together. I just didn't need anyone to make it hurt worse."

"We could have one," Ruby offered. "We could have one right now. We could make wish boats and paddle out in the lake and set them afloat."

"Wish boats," Ethel said. Oh, she loved that idea.

"Haddie was the queen of wish boats."

"She really was. She'd like that." Ethel thought for a moment. "I need to let her ashes go. I wanted to do that here this weekend. I know this is where she'd want her remains to be. And while I hope camp will be saved, and while I think it will, it's still not a done deal. This might be my last chance."

"You can always sneak back in. You don't have to release her ashes until you're really ready."

"Tonight feels like the night," Ethel said bravely. "It's not good to be as attached to them as I am. Haddie wouldn't like that."

"How do you want to do this? Do you want me with you?"

"You know, I think I want to go to a few places alone, and then a little later when we launch our wish boats I'll dump the rest of her ashes in the water then. But let's collect things for wish boats first."

"Okay," Ruby said supportively.

Wow, she was going to do it. She was going to let Haddie's ashes go. She really was. Ethel was proud of herself, proud that she was strong enough to do what she should have done a year ago before it became this hard.

"Remember that time you took me out in the canoe after I got the bad news about Henry?" Ruby asked as they wandered up to the woodpile below the Lodge and looked for large pieces of bark, which often fell off when people chopped firewood.

"Yes," replied Ethel.

"That meant a lot to me. I don't know if I ever told you that."

"I knew."

Together they each collected several large pieces of bark, pinecones, moss, and little sticks. Ruby ducked into the arts and crafts area and returned with a dozen tea lights and a book of matches. Gratitude filled Ethel's heart. For so long, she felt like she had been carrying the weight of this loss all alone. Now here was Ruby, who understood something about what was lost, and here they were together back at camp, in the place where it all began.

They wandered down to the beach and put all of their things in the middle of Ethel's canoe. "How about I meet you back here in forty-five minutes?" Ethel asked.

Ruby looked at her watch. "That would be fine."

So Ethel slipped past the group in the Lodge, retrieved Haddie's ashes from her bag, and slipped back out. For a moment, she considered inviting the others to Haddie's service, but somehow it felt right to Ethel to keep it small, to keep it to just Ruby, who had known Haddie during that time in their lives, that time that had no name that did it justice, that time of unlimited potential, that time that had something to do with glory.

The first place she went, of course, was Elks Beach. She opened the urn and sprinkled some ashes there, where Haddie had come out of the water in the lightning storm, and there, where they had slept together, and where they had showered in the rain. She left a little of Haddie outside of the shower house, outside of the Firelight House, the house they had shared, outside of the Lodge, and just off the dock where their picture had been taken.

At times Ethel cried as she returned her dearest friend to the very earth that had nourished her, shaped her, and sustained her . . . to the very earth Haddie had loved so much. But at the same time, Ethel felt something like release, like she was finally setting Haddie's spirit free, like she was finally giving Haddie her blessings to go live in heaven.

Ruby showed up just a little early, which was perfect.

By now, it was beginning to get dark. Silently she and Ethel got in the canoe and paddled out a ways. There, by the light of Ethel's headlamp, they assembled pinecones, moss, and little sticks onto the pieces of bark, sometimes like a floral arrangement, and sometimes in ways that were supposed to look like something, for instance a tipi or a log cabin. Finally, they added a candle to each one. One by one, they lit the candles and set them gently in the water to float away.

Ruby began singing "Barges," and Ethel joined along. It was the perfect way to honor Haddie, and Ethel was so grateful that Ruby had known so. Tears streamed down Ethel's face.

As they drifted just offshore, Ethel looked at camp in a new way, as a place that now held her heart in not just a spiritual way but in a very physical way. She dipped the urn in the cold water and washed the rest of Haddie's remains out of the vessel and into the collective soul of the lake.

As they slowly began to paddle back, Haddie's ashes floating behind them, Ruby said, "Haddie had something inside her we all wished we had—verve. She had verve. And gumption." Then she laughed. "Remember when Haddie made a hula skirt out of skunk cabbage?"

Ethel smiled. "She claimed it would keep mosquitoes away."

"Did it?"

"No, she got devoured by them."

They laughed a little more.

"She raided my cabin once, you know—Haddie-style. I still remember what the heart she placed on my bunk said."

"What did it say?" asked Ethel.

"It said: 'You make everything more fun.' I still wonder if it was coincidence, or if she picked it just for me."

Ethel said, "Knowing her, she picked it just for you."

Ruby smiled. "That's nice. I like to think so."

"Well, it *is* true," Ethel said. "You do make everything more fun."

"Why, thank you." After a quiet moment, Ruby said, "I remember once after the kids left on a Saturday, we were taking showers before going to town. You were there, remember? We got out of the shower, and while you and I were wrapped in towels, Haddie was naked as a jaybird. She stood in front of us and pointed to her chest like this and said, 'Look. Look how much larger this breast is than this one. I don't care. I still think my body is beautiful.' I still remember that. In that moment, she taught me something about how to love myself."

Ethel smiled.

They docked the canoe and carefully got out, but instead of leaving, Ethel tied the boat up and they stood on the dock, watching the wish boats floating on the lake.

"I fell in love with Haddie the summer that I was in Elks and she was next door. It began to rain, and she went outside in her bathing suit and began to shower in it. Even though I was still shy then, I went out in my bathing suit and joined her. That's the effect she had on me. She made me brave. And she made my world okay. And I just miss her so much."

Ruby put her arm around Ethel.

"After she died, I didn't know what to do. I didn't know who I could count on to see the beauty of the love we shared . . . the beauty of all that she was."

"I see it," Ruby assured her.

"Thank you deeply for that." Ethel began to cry. "There is a huge hole in my heart," she said plainly, and looked in Ruby's eyes to see if she could find any answers.

Ruby just nodded sympathetically. There were no answers. There was just time and nature, and friendship.

Ethel rested her head on Ruby's shoulder and watched the wish boats drift away just as Haddie had.

"Good-bye, Haddie," Ruby whispered. "We miss you."

AMBER 2012

Glen had not been kidding when he said the twins were a handful. "A nightmare" was more like it. One screamed because the lights in the kitchen were too bright. The other screamed because the first one was hurting his ears. That, of course, set off the baby.

Amber knew the polite thing to do was stay in the kitchen and endure it, but she couldn't take it any longer, so she told Barbara and Glen that she needed to do her homework, which she did, and slinked off to her room, sat at her desk, and took out her books.

How could anyone hear herself think in this madness? She sat for a half hour and did nothing but rub her temples. By the time Glen came in to check on her and ask her to help set the table for dinner, she was close to tears.

"I know this is probably a pretty big change," he said apologetically.

"I've pretty much lived alone for the last nine years," she explained. "My mom worked a night shift."

"Oh, so this is a *very* big change."

"Yes."

"I think God sent me those twins to keep me humble and keep me from getting lazy about prayer. Lord knows, they really test my limits. Maybe God sent you here so that they could turn you into a praying person as well." He laughed.

Although she feared the twins might turn her into a crazy person instead of a praying person, she didn't say so. She simply smiled politely and stood to go help.

In the kitchen, one of the twins had begun to cry on the floor because he saw his initial on the other twin's sock and was upset about his brother wearing his sock. The second twin took off his shoe and waved his stinky foot in the first twin's face, making him cry even harder. Amber looked at them both with extreme irritation as she made her way to the silverware drawer, and that made the second one cry.

"She's looking at me!" he cried. "She's looking at me! Tell her not to look at me!"

Barbara walked away from the stove, the crying baby still in her arms, and put her arm around the boy with the other boy's sock. "She's just curious about who her new brother is," she explained. "Aren't you curious about your new sister?"

Amber hoped the look on her face didn't show her true feelings. These boys would never be her brothers. Fortunately, they felt the same way.

"She's not my sister!" the one standing shouted while he took off his other shoe and threw it at Amber's head. She ducked just in time, and the other, thinking that was funny, threw his shoes at her head, too. This earned them both a blessed seven-minute time-out in their bedroom. From the kitchen Amber, Barbara, and Glen all could hear shoes and toys hit the wall until Glen finally had enough and walked back to put a stop to it.

While he did that, Barbara explained, "Their mom had been addicted to drugs when she was pregnant, so they have sensory issues. They're very easily overstimulated, and then they just melt down. They can't help it. It's a physical thing."

It was at that point Amber realized she must be in hell.

She was pretty clear that she'd rather live in a cardboard box than live with these little brats one more day, but she knew she couldn't run away without causing more problems once she was eventually caught. Somehow, she would have to endure them. Or drown them. No, endure them. She would have to find a way to endure them.

ETHEL 2012

Ethel finished up her nightly routine in the bathroom and then turned around before she walked out to take it all in one last time—how this place looked and smelled and felt. Reality sank into her chest like a lead apron at the dentist's office, and she realized she was foolish to have jumped on board with Ruby and Shannon's surge of blind hope. There really was no hope. People didn't just give away tens of thousands of dollars—especially not to something that was perhaps antiquated in today's society. Ethel shut the door behind her.

It was time to get back to the business of saying good-bye, so she walked into the cold, damp shower house next door to the bathroom. Why she had bothered to unlock it she didn't know. After all, nothing had happened when she had turned the faucet handles. But it was a special place to her, so she sat on a bench and breathed in deeply the smells of earthy dampness and Pine-Sol.

Then, just as she stood to leave, a tree frog croaked long and low as if it was in slow motion. Ethel turned and took a few more steps down the aisle in the middle of the room past two shower stalls and peeked in the third one on the left, where she thought the noise was coming from.

Stepping inside, she examined the log wall behind the showerhead, and there it was. Was it a coincidence?

Ethel reached out to gently touch the frog's tiny back with the tip of her finger. It didn't jump but just sat and watched her until at last she turned to leave the same stall where Haddie had once washed her hair. Just as Ethel walked out, the frog croaked again. "Good night, Haddie," Ethel replied.

Walking back to the Lodge, she put her hand over her heart, as if she could hold the pieces of it together. Her hands felt so empty without so much as even an urn to hold.

Grief had a way of ambushing her in moments she least expected it, leveling her with an intensity she thought had passed. Sometimes a year seemed like enough time to have done some healing. Sometimes a year seemed like nothing. At the moment, it felt like nothing—her loss felt every bit as acute as it had been last fall. Maybe the sounds and smells of fall were intensifying her grief.

She couldn't go back into the Lodge like this, so she walked a little farther, down to the concrete porch of the the Firelight House, the house she and Haddie had lived in when they ran the camp. There Ethel sat and cried. She had learned she could either cry when it came up or be a loaded spring waiting to go off at a less convenient and more public moment. *When would all the tears be gone?* she wondered, but at the same time she knew. They never would be.

But here was the difference between last year and this year: Last year she could not imagine that she would ever be okay again, and this year, even though she was still in a great deal of pain, she knew that somehow she would. In fact, more and more she had moments in each day when she already was.

ETHEL 1953

On a Saturday night between sessions, Ethel and Haddie had been camping under the stars on Elks Beach. Ethel's head itched and was keeping her awake. Maybe she'd had a mosquito bite on her scalp, or maybe it was her new shampoo.

Haddie watched her misery and said, "I want to wash your hair for you, with my shampoo, in case you're allergic to yours." Ethel had been nice and cozy in her sleeping bag and unenthusiastic about the prospect of leaning over a cold bathroom sink for a hair wash and then going to bed with a wet head, but Haddie said, "Trust me. You'll love it." And well, Ethel couldn't say no to that.

The rest of the camp was dark and asleep. Who knew what time it was? All Ethel knew was that it felt deliciously naughty to be sneaking through camp at night with Haddie, who took her hand and led her up the hill to the bathroom and the shower house.

To her surprise, Haddie led Ethel not into the bathroom for a beauty salon–style hair washing over the sink but into the shower house, and there she undressed her as well as herself, never breaking her mesmerizing eye contact. She carried her shampoo to the third shower stall on the left, turned the water on, waited for it to heat up, and then waved shy Ethel over.

Ethel walked to her and followed Haddie's cues to stand in the stream and wet her hair. After that, she stepped to the side to share the hot water so that both of them could stay warm. She turned around so her back was to Haddie, and Haddie squirted some shampoo in her hand, rubbed it over Ethel's hair, worked it in with her fingers, and finally scrubbed vigorously. Then, touching Ethel's shoulders, Haddie turned Ethel around to face her and scrubbed along Ethel's hairline near her face. Ethel closed her eyes when she felt the shampoo dribble down her forehead. Haddie's hands slowed, and when she reached behind Ethel's head to scrub the back of her hair again Ethel felt Haddie's naked body press against hers.

Haddie guided her back under the spray to rinse and still, in what had become an embrace, ran her fingers through Ethel's hair to help with the rinsing. Wiping the soap off her forehead, Ethel opened her eyes slowly, just in time to see Haddie's lips meet hers, but just as Haddie kissed her a tree frog croaked from where it sat on a log behind Ethel, causing Ethel to jump. Together she and Haddie laughed until Haddie silenced her with another kiss and another and let her hand slide down to Ethel's hip. All the while, the frog continued to sing.

RUBY 2012

The cold drizzle bit the front of her legs through her jeans, and suddenly she realized how silly it was that she was out there pining for Henry or Walt or both. Was she even really longing for them or was she simply longing for an experience she'd never had? *Ah,* she thought, shaking her head, *longing and pining are a waste of precious life.* Back at the Lodge, an old friend and two new ones awaited. Ruby didn't have to long or pine for any of those three. They were right there just waiting.

She paused for moment before she left just to feel the cold lake air on her face and to listen to the night sounds. More and more, she was aware of certain moments not coming around again, and she knew this was one of them.

Although it was cold and she was filled with longing and pining, it was admittedly a good moment. Perhaps simply because all of these feelings were what it meant to be alive, or perhaps simply because she was in her favorite place and that was enough.

Breathing in deeply, she turned and walked toward the steep little trail that led away from the beach. She had greater awareness of her feet on the pebbles, the way they slid and sank with each awkward step, and awareness of a breeze in the treetops. At times, it seemed the wind was calling her name.

But then in a moment of stillness, she heard her name being called and it was not the wind at all. She turned and looked out on the lake and there was Walt, paddling furiously toward her. "Ruby! Wait!"

As he neared, he shouted, "Thank you for not throwing mud balls like you did back in the early fifties!"

She laughed as she met him on the shore. "Walt! My goodness! What are you doing paddling in this cold rain?"

He laughed. "I came to see if you'd like to join me for a milk shake at the Diner tomorrow evening. Whatever your favorite flavor is, they have it!"

"You paddled down here in the rain to ask me out for a milk shake?" she asked.

"Yes, I did." He looked so handsome sitting there in his boat. What strong shoulders, arms, and chest he must have. She couldn't help herself and wondered how they might feel.

"Well then, how could I say no?"

"How's seven thirty? I'll meet you at the Lodge."

"I'll look forward to it," she said, sure that the smile on her face was beyond pleasant and now in the realm of ridiculous.

Walt began to paddle backward, back out into the

water. "Good night, Ruby," he said, low and sweet, like warm milk before bed.

"Good night," she replied before turning and starting up the steep path with new vigor. He had paddled all the way here in the rain just to ask her out for a milk shake! And she was going to see him tomorrow! At the top, once she was sure she was out of view, she began to sing, "Da-da-da-da-da-DA! Da-da-da-da-da-DA!" as if she were in a conga line, taking three steps and then kicking to the side. Joy.

saturday

Hard living was written all over the face Ethel saw through the Plexiglas window in the Chelan County Jail visitation booth. Debbie Hill's eyes were hard and cold, her cheeks sunken, her lips shriveled. She looked old beyond her years.

"What do you want?" she asked Ethel, with a twist of anger but mostly suspicion.

It should not have thrown Ethel, for she had dealt with many angry kids in her day, but in this particular case there was so much at stake. Would she be able to get through? "I'm s-s-orry," she stammered as she recovered. "Of course. My name is Ethel Gossman. I was the camp director at Camp Firelight for many years and was back there this week preparing it for sale. Your daughter, Amber, showed up there and eventually found her way to me. We—the other women who were there helping there and I—fed her and helped her with her homework. . . . Ruby taught her to sew. . . ."

Ethel kept waiting for something in Debbie's eyes to soften, for there to be something there that Ethel could connect with, but instead all she saw was cold and hard with moments of agitation, but she pressed on anyway.

"Amber was happy with us. And then, after you were arrested, the authorities came and took her to a foster home."

Those were the two words that made Debbie wince. It was subtle, but Ethel saw it.

"The sheriff assured me that her foster family is very nice. But Amber wants to be with me."

"So, you want to take my daughter now?" Debbie's tone was defensive. This conversation, it seemed, was about to go very wrong.

Ethel shook her head and looked down. She was starting to lose hope and give up. "No," she said. "I just wanted to offer her refuge. I just wanted to make her life easier and more stable. She's a very intelligent young woman, and I don't want to see her aspirations derailed by instability."

At this, the corners of Debbie's lips turned slightly up. "She is pretty smart, isn't she?"

Suddenly Ethel could see what Debbie needed—some affirmation that her life wasn't a total waste. "You brought a lovely spirit into the world."

"She's the only thing I ever did right. I mean, choosing to have her when everyone told me I shouldn't. I've done a lot of things wrong since then. I bet she hates me."

Slowly, Ethel shook her head. "I think this situation makes her sad, but I don't think she hates you."

"I could be here a long time," said Debbie. "I don't know how you make that up to a kid."

"Well, maybe you start by helping her live where she wants to live in the meantime."

At first, Debbie said nothing. She looked to the side and down to try to hide the tears that were brimming. And then, quite suddenly, she turned back to face Ethel. "How?" she asked, her voice breaking.

"It would take me about three months to go through the process of becoming an approved foster parent, and even then, we would be at the mercy of the system. CPS could decide to take her out of my house at any time. But if I was a relative, they would send Amber to me immediately, and leave her there. So, you see, I could be your aunt. Aunt Ethel. Ethel Gossman, who lives on the South Shore Road."

Debbie's eyes fell again. "I can't believe how bad I've screwed up." For a moment, she looked completely lost. Then she looked up into Ethel's eyes and asked, "You would take good care of her?"

"I would take excellent care of her."

"Would you . . . come here sometimes and . . ."—Debbie choked as she fought back tears—". . . tell me how she's doing?"

"Yes," Ethel said.

"Okay," Debbie replied, her overwhelming sadness obvious. "Thank you for coming to visit me today, Aunt Ethel." She turned and walked away without looking Ethel in the eyes again.

ETHEL 2012

Ethel decided to drive all the way back to camp rather than park at her house and take the canoe the rest of the way. Even though she preferred the quality of journey her canoe gave her, these days it seemed like there was lots of going back and forth and as long as she didn't have heavy or large and awkward things to transport it was easier to drive.

Pulling into the camp parking lot, she noticed a very large red pickup truck next to Ruby's giant land yacht, Laura's Suburban, and Shannon's 4Runner. Who could it belong to?

As Ethel trekked downhill, she didn't get very far before she saw two women pacing back and forth near the bathroom. One was tall and slender, with glasses, and her shoulder-length hair had a little salt in it. The shorter one was sturdier, with a stylish short haircut and a smile that lit up the forest. The taller one walked in a way that could only be described as bouncy, whereas the shorter one had a more level and determined walk, like a tractor. By her walk alone Ethel could tell she was a force. Not recognizing them right away, Ethel walked up to greet them, hoping her memory would not fail her.

"Ethel?" the tall one called out. Who used to have a bouncy walk like that? Ethel recalled noticing someone's bouncy walk in the past.

"It's me!" Ethel called back. "Who's that? I've got old-lady eyes now!" It wasn't a complete lie that her eyes weren't what they used to be, but for the most part it was a convenient card to play in order to spare others' feelings.

"Janet. Janet Nelson, and Sue."

"Sue Mayer," the other woman added.

Yes, now that they were getting close, Ethel was able recognize them. Their faces were still so sweet and just looking at them broke her heart wide open so that she burst into tears as she opened her arms. "You're back. I'm so glad you're back."

They both walked up and hugged her, although Ethel could tell it was more a courtesy hug than something that mirrored what she was feeling. They were friendly but guarded, and she understood. Friendliness was more than generous.

"Your letter meant a lot to me," Janet said. "All this time I didn't know what had happened. I thought I had done something wrong. I mean, at some point I wondered—"

Ethel put her hand on her heart because it ached so much and she said, "If I could change just one thing about my life—just one thing—Janet and Sue, it would be that. I should have at the very least told you what had happened."

"Janet's mom put you in a tight spot," Sue said understandingly. "I mean, you and Haddie were together, right?"

Ethel nodded.

Sue said, "You really had no choice."

Ethel shrugged and shook her head.

Janet took her hand and said, "It's okay."

"What a tough world we've endured," said Ethel.

Janet and Sue agreed.

"It's getting better, though." Ethel tried to turn the conversation in more positive direction.

"Much better," said Sue, and then she said, "Ethel, we've got some good news for you."

Janet couldn't wait and spilled the beans. "We're digging a well for you."

"What?" Ethel asked.

Sue explained. "My dad and brother have a drilling business. I was telling my dad about your letter, and he wants to help. His equipment uses lots of fuel, and I don't know how long it might take him to drill—it could take as little as a couple hours, or it could take days if he has to go through rock. If it takes days, it would be nice if we could do some fund-raising to compensate him for fuel and for the cost of the pipe, but either way, we're going to make it happen."

"Oh my God! I can't believe this is happening! All of

it. Having you two back here means the world to me, and a new well? Okay, I'm not exactly sure how this works. The board of the North Central Washington Firelight Girls voted to dissolve. I called the national office yesterday and asked that it be reversed. Do you remember little Shannon—competitive kid with the cast?"

Janet laughed. "Of course! The ballerina. Yes, she was in my cabin! She's here?"

"Well, she's at my house working on grants," replied Ethel. "She started writing grants yesterday. She wanted to try saving the camp. I didn't see how she could, but I didn't stop her either. And now, with your gift, any grants she might get would likely be enough to dig out of the mess the camp is in. The well was the insurmountable part. I can't believe your family is doing this for us. Wow. I just can't believe it. Okay, but still, I wouldn't want to tell you to proceed and then find out that it really was too late. Let me talk to the national office on Monday and see if they see this as the game changer it is. I'm really hopeful they will, though. I mean, how could they not?"

"Well, we sure hope so," said Janet.

And suddenly a huge wave of emotion washed over Ethel and she started to cry again. "That was the worst part about losing this place," she said. "It was where I met Haddie and fell in love. It's where we lived our life together. I'm just . . . I'm just so relieved. And it means even more to me coming from you two. What big hearts you have. Thank you for your forgiveness and thank you for your generosity."

Sue put her arm around Ethel. "I have a good feeling that everything is going to work out just fine."

"Are you staying tonight or at least for dinner?"

"We'd love to stay the night," Janet said.

"Elks is taken, but you can have any other cabin that you like," Ethel told them.

"Koalas," they said simultaneously.

The Kiwanis had built it years ago, but all the other fraternal lodges that had built a cabin here at camp had animal names and Miss Mildred had liked having cabins named after animals. Somehow she charmed the Kiwanis into letting her call their cabin Koalas instead. Miss Mildred could charm anyone into anything.

"It's yours," Ethel replied.

Janet said, "Before we go settle in, let me tell you the rest of what you need to know about the drilling process. Sue's going to dowse and select a site for the new well—somewhere her dad can get his equipment to. We'll go forward with doing that this weekend. Then, after the national office of the Firelight Girls gives their blessing, you'll need to apply for a permit from the Department of Ecology. That will take about a month. After you have your permit, we'll drill—hopefully before the snow flies. And finally, when that's all done, we'll need to find someone with an excavator who will dig a trench and lay pipe from the new well to the old main line and fit the new pipe to that."

"We'll put our feelers out and see if we can find more volunteer labor for the trenching," Sue said.

"I want you to know that this feels like a miracle to me," said Ethel.

Janet replied, "It feels like a miracle to us, too, Ethel."

SHANNON 2012

Shannon heard tires skidding to a stop, and then Ethel raced in and breathlessly said, "You will never guess what just happened." She went on to tell Shannon the story about Janet and Sue, about forgiveness and the well that would in all likelihood be enough to save the camp. If only it weren't a Saturday. If only they didn't have to wait to know for sure.

"Unbelievable," Shannon replied as she tried to absorb it. This huge obstacle that may have taken twenty-five or even more grants to surpass was suddenly removed. It left Shannon a little disoriented, as if the boulder she had been trying to push suddenly gave way on its own and began to roll downhill.

"And that's not all," Ethel continued. "I visited Amber's mother this morning and it went well. I don't know how fast the outcome will be, but she has agreed that I can be her aunt, so that CPS will return Amber to me."

"Holy moley! Wow! You wake up to one set of reality and then in a matter of hours it has all changed this profoundly? Amazing. Really, it's amazing."

"I'm going to hang out here in hopes I hear something about Amber." Then Ethel noticed the five sealed, addressed, and stamped envelopes in front of Shannon, all ready to send off. "Way to go," Ethel said, and gave Shannon a thumbs-up. "With the well and some grants, the camp should be out of the hole and back in business in no time." Shannon wasn't sure why pleasing Ethel felt better than pleasing just about anyone else in the world, but it did.

"I wanted to send the national office an e-mail, as well as leave a message on their answering machine, so that they have this information first thing Monday morning. Hey, why don't you come back to camp now? There will be time for more grant writing later, but right now everyone is there together, and I think we all should just enjoy that. Moments of togetherness are rare." And then, with a sudden burst of vision, Ethel exclaimed, "I know! I will plan an all-camp event! Ooo! I'm already getting ideas!"

Shannon laughed. "Wouldn't miss it," she said.

Ethel seemed truly happy for the first time all week—happy in that way where every cell hums, where not a single one holds back. Shannon noticed that. Ethel had a passion for camp that Shannon did not have for school, and Ethel had a passion for planning all-camp activities that Shannon no longer had for lesson planning. Ethel's professional life had been so much more aligned with her soul than Shannon's professional life had been with hers. How good it would feel to be that integrated. She envied Ethel and wondered who the lucky person would be who would get to be the next camp director. Probably someone who had majored in outdoor recreation. Shannon kicked herself again for choosing education instead of something fun.

But maybe life would still work out for her. Maybe Laura was right. Shannon could work in a restaurant. There she would bring lonely people into the fold and feed them. She would eat with others—even if it was in the kitchen standing up while working. There had to be something more aligned with her soul than what she had been doing.

As Shannon walked back to camp, it struck her funny that keeping this camp open mattered this much to her when she'd never spend another summer here, but it did. Just something about knowing it was there made Shannon feel like there was refuge if she ever needed it. It was a touchstone.

And now she was going to get to see her favorite counselor of all time. So much excitement filled her that she took off running and as she passed the gate she began to call, "Janet! Janet! Janet!"

Not too far from the bathhouse, she finally heard Janet answer, so Shannon cut right through the thick woods in that direction. There she was, and her friend Sue, who had been a counselor in a neighboring cabin. Sue was holding a dainty metal instrument that looked a little like a wishbone. Shannon didn't remember her really well but enough so that she looked familiar. Running toward them, Shannon screamed with delight and hugged Janet and then Sue.

"Shannon? Is that you?" Janet asked.

"It's me! It's so good to see you again!"

"Oh, it's good to see you, too!" Janet said. Sue simply smiled.

"And this huge thing that you're doing . . ." Shannon shook her head. "I don't know how to begin to thank you."

"We love this place, too," Sue said.

Shannon inhaled deeply and smiled as she exhaled. Then she said, "Okay, well, in your honor, we'll be having tinfoil dinners and biscuits on a stick at the beach tonight!"

"Oh no!" Janet said. "That was awful!" Janet turned to Sue and explained. "We had some disastrous tinfoil dinners at Valhalla one time."

"Burnt and raw all at once?" Sue asked.

"Burnt and raw all at once," Shannon confirmed.

"Mm! Can't wait!" Sue laughed.

Shannon continued. "Oh, and Ethel is having visions of an all-camp activity!"

Janet rubbed her palms together in anticipation.

"What will it be? What will it be?" said Sue.

"I don't know," Shannon said, "but you know it will be good! Okay, well, I'll leave you to your work, but I just had to come and say hi. God, it's good to see you."

Janet gave her another hug. "It's great to see you, too, Shannon."

AMBER 2012

Barbara, bless her heart, had spent the morning trying to bathe the horrible brats while Glen rocked the crying baby and put the finishing touches on his sermon for tomorrow.

Amber could hear the bath drama through the wall. One of the boys threw a bar of soap at the other, and the other threw a bottle of shampoo at the first. The screaming began and continued.

Then the phone rang. She heard Glen talking to someone but couldn't make out the words. Shortly after, there was a soft knock at her bedroom door and then Glen stuck his head in and said, "It seems DSHS has located a great-aunt of yours. Ethel. Someone will be by shortly to take you to her house. I'm so sorry that you're leaving us so soon, Amber. I know God has great things in store for you."

"Thank you," she said, trying to conceal the full extent of her joy. Aunt Ethel? Amber wasn't sure how Ethel had pulled that off, but she was so thankful. "And God bless you for taking me in." She figured that since Barbara and Glen had agreed to take her in even with the nightmare twins, the least she could do was speak their language.

It pleased him. "Do you need help packing?" he asked.

"Nope," she said. "I don't have much."

And when finally there was a knock at the door and Sheriff Sam stepped in, she could not have been happier if she had won the lottery. In a way she had. Sheriff Sam was a man of few words, but he did give her a wink when no one else was looking as if to let her know that he had been in on the plan. *Thank you,* she mouthed to him emphatically, and he cracked a smile.

Barbara came out, drenched, to give her a hug good-bye while the twins yelled things like, "Good-bye, poop-face!" from the hallway, and just as soon as she could politely leave Amber was out of there and into the front seat of the sheriff's car.

Ethel waited for her on her back porch and smothered her in a big hug as Sheriff Sam drove away.

"*Aunt* Ethel?" Amber asked.

"I visited your mother this morning and she remembered that I'm her aunt."

Stunned, Amber said, "I can't believe you did that. I can't believe she did that either."

"Even though she's a broken person, she actually loves you very much. You're the one thing she did in her life that's she proud of. Just know that."

"Love isn't something you say—it's something you do, right? And she hasn't done it in nine years," said Amber.

"Honey, if you can, forgive her for being broken, and see that when she allowed me to be your guardian, it was a huge act of love."

Amber just nodded. She would try. For Ethel.

"Now, let's go back to camp. I have some fun planned!" And with that, they left most of Amber's things inside the house and then walked back down to the canoe to paddle back to the first and only place Amber had ever belonged.

ETHEL 2012

On the dock, each team sat with their feet in their canoe: Laura and Shannon, Janet and Sue, and, in Ethel's boat, Amber and Ruby. Ethel stood and announced, "In the immortal words of Ruby, this event is going to be the Hot Coals against the Embers, except we get Amber on our team. And I'm sorry to inform you, Hot Coals, that the Embers are probably going to win. This is a performance scavenger hunt. It's like performance art, only it's a scavenger hunt. On this paper, you will see a list of things you can do and their point value. All events must be recorded. For some things, a simple photo will do. For other things, video footage is needed. Laura, Sue, do your cameras take video footage?"

"Yes," both Laura and Sue replied in unison.

Ethel continued. "It is one thirty now. When I hand you the list, the race is on, and each team has until four o'clock to earn as many points as possible and return here." She sat on the dock, put her feet in the back of their canoe, and shouted, "Ready? Go!"

With that, the women gingerly slid off the dock and into their boats and set off.

In the middle of the boat, Amber rode garbage. She had no canoe experience, but Ethel figured that if Ruby tired Amber could take over for her. In the meantime, Ethel urged Amber to read the list aloud.

"You have got to be kidding!" Amber shouted as she listed the items.

"I assure you that I am not!" replied Ethel, satisfied that she had created an entertaining list.

Ruby turned around and weighed in. "If we moon the YMCA camp, it's three easy points. Let's start there! After that, I think we should go to the state park and see—wait! There's a fisherman over there! Go over there and let's see if he has any beer! Come on, Ethel! Paddle harder!"

It warmed Ethel's heart, hearing Ruby holler like that again. It took her right back to the old days.

As they neared the boat, Ethel realized it was Walt, and his two sons.

"Walt!" Ethel exclaimed "Steve and Randy!"

"Ethel! Ruby! Amber!" Walt exclaimed. "What a surprise! Ruby, these are my sons, Steve and Randy—"

But Ruby cut him off. "Walt, I'm sorry. We have no time for pleasantries. We are on a scavenger hunt and time is of the essence."

Walt laughed. "Of course."

Ruby continued. "I'm hoping you can help us with two things. First, have you had any luck today? Because we need a picture of one of us kissing a fish."

"Steve?" Walt prompted, and with that Steve opened an ice chest and pulled out a trout.

Ruby looked behind her. "Any takers? No? Okay, I'll take this one for the team. Camera ready?"

Amber snapped a photo with Ethel's digital camera as Ruby kissed the fish.

Walt sighed and joked, "I've never wanted to be a trout so badly in all my life."

Ruby laughed and said, "Walt, are you getting fresh with me?"

But before he could answer, Ethel said, "Steve, hand me your beer."

Steve looked surprised but did, and Amber documented Ethel drinking some of it and then handing it back.

"I had no idea you ladies were so wild," Walt said.

"Don't you forget it, Walt," Ruby replied coyly. Ruby. After all these years, she still had it.

"Okay, ladies! That's two points for us! Onward!" Ethel shouted.

"Sorry, Walt! You'll have to continue to flirt with me later!" Ruby called out as they paddled off.

"Seven-thirty!" he answered.

"Seven-thirty?" Ethel asked as they voyaged on. "Do you have a date with Walt?"

Amber appeared every bit as interested in the answer as Ethel was.

Ruby simply turned around and made her eyebrows wiggle up and down.

The wind was at their backs and pushed them on toward the YMCA camp. "Get up nice and close so we can get the sign behind us," Ethel said.

The canoe tipped this way and that as Ethel and Amber traded places so that both Ruby and Ethel could be in the picture. Then Ruby and Ethel waddled around trying to find a stable way to finish the task. "I think we should try it kneeling," Ruby said.

"You're the expert," Ethel replied.

"Expert?" Amber exclaimed.

"Expert," Ethel confirmed.

"I'll have you know I have never mooned this camp before," Ruby said.

"Ruby, I'm sorry, but your memory has failed you. You mooned this camp on several occasions," said Ethel.

"What?" Ruby exclaimed incredulously, unzipping her pants and pulling them down.

"Yes," Ethel said, doing the same. "This is not your first time."

"You're thinking of someone else," Ruby insisted.

Amber asked, "Can you prove it with a picture?"

"Oh, heck no," Ethel said. "Cameras were expensive. That was why we all were able to be so wild. No one could ever prove we did anything wrong."

"I think you guys are going to have to squat. That's not good enough!" Amber called out. "If you do it right, the photo won't be obscene. I'll just see a crescent of skin above your faces."

"Amber," Ethel said. "If we go in the drink, you better help us get out, because we won't be able to kick with our pants around our legs like this."

Amber laughed hysterically as the two old women repositioned themselves, nearly tipping the canoe. "Yes, that's it! That's the money shot!" Amber called out.

Ethel and Ruby began to laugh so hard that Ruby said, "I may have just wet my pants."

"You're not wearing pants," Ethel reminded her.

"Thank God! Okay, that was a three pointer. We're up to five. Hurry! Pants up, Ethel! We've only got an hour and a half left! What's next, Amber?"

As Ethel and Amber precariously traded places once more, Amber answered. "We've got a choice—to the state park to do a synchronized swimming act on the beach for any campers that might be there and maybe make a s'more with a stranger or to the Forest Service station and try to kiss someone in uniform."

From the front of the boat Ruby shouted, "Call it, Ethel!"

"It's October! No one is camping! Let's go to the Forest Service beach! We can kiss someone there and then do our synchronized swimming routine on the beach there! Let's go!"

Ethel was in heaven. Five and a half decades fell away, and here they were again, like something that had been peeled to reveal just its truest essence.

Ruby turned around and with a big smile said, "Of all the days I've had in the last fifty years, this one is my favorite!" To Amber, she said, "Remember that. Remember this when you're knee-deep in troubles—that you could be seventy-eight and still have your best day. Remember that if you hang around, days will come that surpass your greatest hopes."

"I will," replied Amber.

And while Ethel could not say it was her best day in fifty years, she could say it was a pretty incredible one. Had Haddie and Opal been with them, it very well may have been Ethel's best day, but camp was going to get a new well and Amber was hers until she was ready to strike out on her own. Those were two huge miracles. It was, without question, Ethel's best day since she lost Haddie. She could say that much. For much of the year she had thought she'd never laugh again, and now her sides hurt from laughing so much. For the first time in a long time, she felt genuinely hopeful about the good things the rest of her life held. Yes, it absolutely was her best day since her loss.

LAURA 2012

Janet and Sue had Laura and Shannon laughing from the moment Ethel, Amber, and Ruby set off in the other direction.

"We're going to let them win, right?" asked Laura.

"Oh yeah," answered Janet. "But we have to make it look like we tried." Janet and Sue had begun paddling, but they weren't synchronized and often paddled on the same side, causing them to zigzag at best. "Like right now Sue and I are pretending we forgot how to canoe. It will lower the expectations so we can go on a leisurely paddle to Glacier View and just enjoy ourselves. But you guys should go faster until you get around that little point so it looks like you're trying. You could wait for us there if you want."

"Genius," Shannon uttered as if in awe. "After all these

years, you're still imparting outdoor wisdom." And with that, they took off, paddling furiously.

Once or twice Laura looked back at Ethel, and noticed that sure enough Ethel appeared to be watching them, which made Laura grateful for Janet's advice.

After they were all around the point and out of Ethel's line of vision, they relaxed and caught up on one another's lives. At first, Laura gave them the edited version of hers, but that felt wrong to her—like lying—so she finished her story with, "And now I'm trying to figure out whether my marriage is over."

"Oh, sweetie," Janet said sympathetically.

But Sue, in her matter-of-fact style, said, "Janet and I joke that it feels like we've been married three times— just all to the same woman."

"What do you mean by that?" asked Shannon. "Do you mean that there have been three distinct eras in your lives together or that there were two times when you were certain it was over?"

Sue answered. "Both. And I have to clarify that the first time it felt like it was over and we resurrected it, but the second time it really was over and we had to choose it again and create it again. We had to give ourselves permission to let it completely go so that we had the freedom to rediscover each other and fall in love all over."

"You make it sound so simple, Sue," said Janet. She turned to Laura. "It wasn't simple at all. It was hard. I mean . . ." She turned back to Sue and asked, "Is it okay for me to tell the story?"

Sue seemed uncomfortable but answered, "Yeah."

"Sue had been working a lot—a lot of long hours, a lot of weekends, and even when she was home she brought work home with her. And on one hand, I knew she was doing it for us. And on the other hand, months went by and I felt like we hadn't had any meaningful connection.

We were simply roommates. I felt abandoned. And I felt like I didn't know her anymore. I even left for a while. I went to visit my grandma and my great-aunts out in Montana, so I was able to make it look like I hadn't left Sue but was just visiting family, but really, I had to get out of there. I was dying inside."

"But I knew," Sue said. "I knew. I thought I'd lost her forever and it broke my heart, but I felt powerless to do anything about it. I couldn't just drop work and it felt like it was too late anyway, so I had no choice but to let go."

"When I finally came home, I intended to tell her that I was leaving, but she had left a journal on our bed for me." Janet rested her paddle in her lap and wiped the tears out of her eyes. "I'm sorry. This part makes me emotional. It was a gratitude journal all about me."

Sue explained. "I figured if she was leaving, I wanted to say thank you for all the things I was so grateful for. I didn't want her to look back and feel like she had wasted her time with me. I wanted her to know what she had meant to me."

"So there I was reading this journal and crying my eyes out when Sue got home, and well, here we are today."

"But I don't think it would have worked if I had tried to get her to stay," said Sue. "I think I had to let her go so that she could see my love instead of my desperation."

Janet looked Laura in the eye and said, "We don't mean to make this sound simple in any way. It wasn't simple. The cost of her letting go so I could see her love was that I had to forgive her for letting go. I had to face my fears about this thing I thought was so indestructible actually being very, very fragile. And I had to be willing to look in the mirror and see that I had let go, too. So, anyway, I know that you and your husband aren't Sue and me. The point in telling the story was simply to tell you that it is possible to rediscover each other, forgive each other, and fall in love all over again. And since we're always growing and evolving, when you fall in love again it can feel like falling in love with someone new. It can be better than it's ever been."

"I think what I realized," said Sue, "was that a lot of us in long-term relationships counted on our history to be our foundation, and it can't be. The present has to be the foundation. It's like . . . pretend history is chocolate sauce and the present is the ice cream. You can't replace ice cream with chocolate sauce. You can only drizzle the history on the present to make it a little sweeter."

That made Janet explode with laughter. "Sue, you're so funny. I love you." The tenderness in Janet's voice touched Laura, and she tried to remember the last time she and Steve had talked to each other like that.

"I love you, too," said Sue.

By then, they had reached the shores of Glacier View Campground.

"I smell smoke . . . ," Shannon said optimistically.

"Well, time to get down to business," Janet said, looking at the scavenger hunt list. "Come on. Let's go roast marshmallows with strangers and serenade them with a camp song. Then one of you can go into the outhouse and shout, 'It smells so good in here! I love how it smells in here!' over and over for one whole minute. Got it!"

"What?" Sue asked, laughing. "Oh my God."

Laura looked at Shannon, who stood right next to her. "You're good with skipping that one, right?"

Shannon replied, "Oh, absolutely." She pointed to another item on the list. "I'm willing to kiss a fish, though."

"The outhouse is worth two points . . . ," said Janet, trying to entice somebody.

"No," they all said in unison.

But Janet would not give up. "Think how happy it would make Ethel, though."

"Ethel . . . or you?" Sue asked.

"Both," Janet said with her very best charming smile.

"Okay, I'll do it," Sue said begrudgingly.

And as they all stood outside the outhouse—that is, un-til they fell on the ground laughing—while Sue shouted praises for the outhouse's odor for one whole minute, Laura thought, *That's love.* Yes, if Sue could spend a whole minute inside a Forest Service outhouse, clearly not holding her breath for much of that time but, in fact, breathing in deeply through her mouth where she could taste the air, just to make Janet laugh, surely Laura could step out of her comfort zone for Steve, too.

Or maybe it was time to say good-bye like Sue had, to speak the truth and let the chips fall where they may.

AMBER 2012

"Turns out, mushrooms, olive oil, and pre-cooked shrimp are the secret to a decent tinfoil dinner," Ethel said. "One night, Haddie and I were determined to finally get it right, so we tried all the things kids hate." They had no shrimp but had used small pieces of the trout Walt had given Ruby instead, and to Amber it was delicious with the po-tatoes, carrots, onion, and mushrooms. Each had prepared her own meal in a piece of tinfoil and set it in the fireplace near the edges of the embers.

As they ate, Amber laughed harder than she'd ever laughed in her life as the three teams shared their photos and video footage with everyone else and Ethel marked a large chart with points once each scavenger hunt submission was approved by the group. Never had Amber felt so included. How strange it seemed to think that just this morning she had woken up in a foster home. It felt like she had been here much longer than that.

Even though she had only known Ethel and Ruby for a few days, already they had become the two closest things to grandmothers Amber had ever known. Of course, she knew it wasn't the same as if they actually were her grandmothers. Other than the scavenger hunt today, they had no mutual history, and without that, well, there were limits to how family-like they could be. Shared history took time.

Near the fire, Janet and Sue played their guitars while Ethel, Ruby, Shannon, and Laura sang song after beautiful song with them. Here were women who were strong and healthy and clear. Here were women who cared about something other than just themselves—this camp, each other . . . even her.

Sometimes when the women were singing, everyone but one or two people would forget the words and that one person or those two people would carry the song for a moment until the others nodded as if to say, *That's right. I remember now,* and joined back in. Hundreds of words— thousands, more likely—each something they learned together or from one another . . . each word was the common history that Amber wished she'd had with someone. When she tried to think of anyone she'd had common history with, something more meaningful than being in the same class or saying hi in the halls, she had her early history with her mom and then she had nothing—just a whole lot of years of being all alone in that trailer trying to solve problems she didn't have the resources or skills to solve, problems little girls shouldn't have to solve.

But tonight Amber sat near the fire among women with

whom she did not share history, who sang songs so softly she wanted to crawl up on them, rest her weary head, and sleep. At first, it seemed the songs were like a bed at a mattress store that she could only view through a showroom window. She could only look and want. And then Ethel disappeared and came back with an old binder full of lyrics handwritten, faded but still legible. This was where it began—scavenger hunts, learning the words, creating the history. It had to start somewhere.

RUBY 2012

As Ruby dolled herself up for her big date, Ethel kept bringing her wrinkled and tattered old prom dresses from the dress-up box, suggesting she wear them instead. At some point, Ethel's legs got tired, so she started sending Amber up the stairs with new ensembles to consider. Each one made Ruby laugh harder—especially when Ethel began to accessorize with things like hard hats and lumberjack suspenders. They were in tears and Ruby feared her eyes would be red and swollen by the time Walt arrived.

It didn't help that when that moment came Ethel asked Walt what his intentions were and told him to have Ruby back by nine thirty. From upstairs where she had overheard, Ruby began to peal with laughter once more. She descended the stairs as quickly as she could to save him from this torment.

"Please accept my apology for Ethel's behavior," Ruby said, trying to compose herself again.

Walt, entertained by it all, said, "No apology necessary. She made me feel young again," and then once they had stepped out the door together he said, "You look very pretty tonight, Ruby."

"I laughed so hard for so long today that I can no longer feel or control my face," she confessed, with a little more laughter.

"That's wonderful," he replied.

As they walked up to the road and then drove to the Diner, they shared about how their day had been—her day on the scavenger hunt and his day fishing with his boys— and it struck Ruby how natural it all felt.

When they reached the Diner, Walt came around to her side of the truck and opened the door for her. How funny, it seemed to Ruby, to be treated like a lady when she was dressed in her dirty camp clothes and hadn't properly bathed.

She ordered a strawberry milk shake while he went with a butterscotch one, and something about that surprised her. She had him pegged as a vanilla purist kind of guy—someone who kept it simple—but she was wrong.

He was full of surprises. He had been raised on a ranch in southern Arizona and used to work cattle, but he grew up to become a dentist. Ten days a year for twenty years, he had traveled to various countries in Africa to provide dental services to people who desperately needed them— mostly extractions. He loved wine and had a few of his own barrels in his garage, which he hoped would turn out to be more than swill.

She felt so boring in comparison. But she did have one good story. In 1978 she told her boss that she had chicken pox so that she and Opal could spontaneously drive to Graceland in Opal's convertible (which by then had 195,000 miles on it) for Elvis's birthday. It was the first one after he died. Since it was early January, they had encountered many storms, several of which Ruby was pretty sure they would not survive. On the way home, the transmission went out and had to be replaced, and Opal's husband had been livid about that. But Ruby had no regrets. They had gotten to see a bit of history. That was as interesting as she got. She had spent the rest of her life as a secretary in an insurance agency, and there wasn't much to say about that.

But Walt seemed captivated nonetheless, and on the way home he said, "Ruby, I'm having so much fun getting to know you. I wondered if you might like to join me for Sunday dinner at my house tomorrow."

"I leave tomorrow," she nearly whispered.

"No," he said, disappointed.

"I'm afraid so."

"This is the last time I'll see you?"

"I don't know. I just know everyone is leaving to-morrow."

He looked at her and smiled, as if to tell her it was okay, but his eyes were sad. "Back to Spokane," he said.

"Back to Spokane," she echoed.

They were quiet for a few moments as Walt turned up the South Shore Road. The windy road gave him an excuse to drive slowly. They conversed about light things— the weather, the winter ahead, the holidays—and before she knew it they were back. He took her hand as he walked her down the hill and outside the Lodge said good night and that it had been a pleasure to have met. He hugged her and then walked away. She paused before going inside and watched him walk up the hill until he disappeared . . . the first shot at love she'd had in decades, gone. With a heavy heart, she went inside, finding herself wondering again why some people had been given the gift of love while others like her were given only crumbs.

RUBY 2012

Ping. Ping. Ping. What was that? Was it a leaky faucet? *Ping.* No. It was coming from the wrong direction. In fact, it was coming from the window. Was it a nocturnal woodpecker? Was there such a thing? These were the things Ruby thought as she came out of sleep and into consciousness. *Ping.*

She got up and looked out the window. Someone blinked a flashlight at her and then shone it on himself. Walt. She smiled. Imagine, Walt throwing stones at her window as if they were sixteen. She waved and then put sweatpants on under her nightgown and threw on her coat.

Quietly she crept out of the room and down the stairs, heaved open the large, heavy door, and shut it behind her as quietly as she could. Ruby patted her hair self-consciously. Why had she not thought to check her hair?

Outside, Walt waited with a big smile on his face. "I'm sorry. I'm not ready to say good-bye."

She smiled. "I confess, I wasn't either."

"Come with me," he said.

"Where are we going?" she asked, following him toward the beach.

"I'm going to take you to my favorite place," he said.

His favorite place, as it turned out, was his boat, in the middle of the lake.

The moon was waning but still large enough to cast light on them. It glistened on the small waves. Ruby looked up at it and listened to the rhythm of the oars in the water. Peace filled her like the stars filled the Milky Way.

Behind his seat, Walt kept blankets in a large plastic tote. Carefully, he spread them over the bottom of the boat and inched his way off his seat and onto them, cross-legged, facing Ruby. She followed his example and did the same. Then he reached into another box that was stashed under his seat and poured each of them a big ceramic mug of cocoa from his thermos. Gentle waves rocked the boat, making it a little tricky to pour and drink.

"This is nice," she said as she took a sip. "I like your favorite place."

"This *is* nice," he agreed. "I like your company."

Looking into Walt's eyes, she saw sadness.

"This doesn't happen every day," he said.

What didn't? She wasn't sure what he meant, so she erred on the side of caution. "That's true," she said. "This is the first time a gentleman caller has thrown pebbles at my window and then rowed me out into the middle of the lake, where he poured me some fine cocoa."

"That's not what I was talking about," Walt replied.

"Oh," Ruby said. Seriousness hung in the air.

After an awkward pause, he said, "Well, at least it doesn't for me. Maybe it does for you."

"No," she said slowly and carefully. "It definitely doesn't for me." She dared to look up into his eyes. They were kind but unsatisfied. He wanted a solution she couldn't offer. It *was* sad. Walt was so kind and so handsome.

He finished his cocoa, shifted, and lay down with his knees up and his head pointed toward her. "Stargaze with me," he said.

Ruby set her empty mug down and lay down the same way. They repositioned themselves so that he was on the right side of the boat and she on the left, with their heads near each other's feet. Above her it seemed there was so little dark space between the stars. A comet streaked across the sky.

She was quite aware of the heat radiating off Walt but was still surprised when she first felt his fingertips touch hers. He reached a little farther and took her hand. His was calloused from his oars, but the warmth of it felt good on this chilly night. With her thumb she stroked the skin on the back of his hand.

"Stay," he said. "Stay here at the lake with me. I have a guest room with a lock on the door. You don't have to worry about any funny business. Just stay and let's continue to get to know one another."

Ruby quietly considered that.

"I think there's something between you and me that is a gift. There's already precious little time left for us to explore it and enjoy it. So, please forgive me for being so forward, and please consider being bold."

She squeezed his hand and then sat up so she could look at his face. He sat up as well and met her gaze. She searched his eyes for some kind of answer, but instead of speaking he answered her by leaning in for a short but soft kiss.

"Please stay," he said again.

She paused and then answered. "Okay."

LAURA 2012

Laura woke from a nightmare where she had been at a graveyard, standing next to the hole over which men positioned Steve's casket. As they began to lower it, Laura desperately tried to push it back away from the hole. Inside, she knew Steve was still alive. Pure panic coursed through her veins, even after she woke up. How desperately she wanted to put her arms around him and rest her head on his chest and hear his heart.

She knew there was only enough reception at the end of the dock to send or receive a text. She'd have to drive to Leavenworth, a half hour away, to get enough reception for a call. By then she'd practically be home, and she didn't want to go home yet. She wanted Steve to come there. No, there was no reception on the dock, but out on the lake she stood a chance.

She got out of her cozy sleeping bag, put on warm clothes, and woke up Shannon.

"Shannon," she whispered. When Shannon opened her eyes, Laura said, "I'm going to go call Steve. I'm going to be out for a good long while, and I didn't want you to worry."

"Come on, Laura. This is cuckoo middle-of-the-night thinking. Whatever you have to say to Steve can wait until tomorrow."

"I just finally got the clarity I've been waiting for. The moment is now. Now is the moment when I can say it. Now is the moment when he will hear it. I'm going to go out on the lake to get reception. I just didn't want you to worry."

Shannon started laughing. "You woke me up in the middle of the night to tell me you're going to wander around camp by yourself when I've seen a cougar twice this week and then you're going out on the lake by yourself and I'm not supposed to worry?"

"See? Look. This is what it's like to have a teenager. Now you can see that you didn't miss a thing!"

"Carry a big stick," Shannon said.

"Better yet, I'll sing 'Little Red Caboose' over and over."

Shannon groaned, and with that Laura ran to the beach by the light of her headlamp, dodging roots and twigs, her feet pounding on the rich earth.

The canoes they had used that afternoon rested on the

beach, so she pushed one into the water, got in, and took off, paddling furious J-strokes toward the center of the lake. Since the lake was huge—about six miles long and one mile wide—this was no small feat.

A light breeze blew strands of hair that had escaped her ponytail into her face. Clouds blew by slowly overhead, occasionally hiding the waning moon. Although it was a relatively peaceful night, she attacked the water with determination.

There was a distinct moment that she felt it in her chest, like cathedral doors opening, the light inside shining out, love and spirit, her truest self no longer concealed by all the warped stories she had told herself about obligation. Her truest self that simply loved Steve was at last released.

She checked her phone to see if she had any reception bars. There was one more than there had been on the end of the dock but not enough to make a call. She paddled on until at last there were enough, and then bravely she dialed.

As it rang and rang, her heart raced. What if he didn't pick up? What if he would never know the truth of this moment as she could only share it now? What if this moment passed and lost its momentum? She prayed for him to wake up and pick up the phone.

"Hello?" he finally answered in his groggiest voice.

"Steve," she said, starting to cry as relief washed over her.

"Laura? Are you okay? Where are you?"

"I'm okay. I finally am. I'm in a canoe in the middle of Lake Wenatchee where there's cell reception. Steve . . ." She started to cry again. "I don't know where to start." The breeze pushed her boat gently, causing her to drift to the east as they spoke. "I love you. I love you so deeply. And I want you to come out here with me and make love to me under the trees, under the sky like when we first met. I want to make love to you all night." She was sure the whole lake could hear her shouting into the phone because of how sound travels over water, but she didn't care.

Steve was silent.

"Are you there?" she asked.

"I thought you were going to tell me that you were in the hospital, or that someone died, or that you were leaving me."

"I'm sorry for scaring you. I just . . . I just feel like I woke up after sleepwalking for fifteen years and I miss you so much, and I . . ." She broke down again. "I just want to be with you so badly tonight . . . outside, in the mountains . . . away from everything that distracted me for so long. Please come," she pleaded.

"I'm on my way," he said simply.

"Meet me on the dock."

"Okay," he said. "I'm coming."

She hadn't realized how long it had taken to paddle out until she paddled back—over a half hour. As she neared camp, she saw him there on the dock, his arms full of blankets and sleeping bags. He was watching her.

"It's so good to see you," she said, paddling next to the dock into the shore.

After he helped pull her boat in, he took her hand and helped her out, and then he held her close. He kissed her and guided her down to the blankets he had set down, putting his hand behind the back of her head to lay it down gently. In his eyes she could see he forgave her and saw her for who she was in this moment, not who she had been last year, or last month, or last week, or even yesterday. He accepted this new beginning with grace and love. What a miracle, it seemed to Laura—that he could let go of all of that pain and join her in creating this new beginning.

Laura, so overcome by his grace and her awakening, kissed him alternately tenderly and passionately. She looked into his eyes with apology and gratitude and deep, deep love. Gently, she unzipped, unbuttoned, and pulled his clothes off him, and slowly, he did the same. She touched expanses of his body, noticing the ways in which it still felt familiar and the ways in which it had changed since she had last visited, an odd mix of a reunion and a reacquaintance. And he touched hers, lightly at first, like a guest on his very best behavior, like he had on the Wonderland Trail so long ago.

"I'm so sorry," she whispered.

"Welcome home," he whispered back.

Home was togetherness. How it touched her to be welcomed back into the fold like that. Her face contorted as she fought back tears and lost.

He put his hand behind her head again and pulled her face close to his. "Welcome home," he whispered once more, his lips almost touching hers. And then he kissed her with profound sweetness.

When he stopped, she asked him, "How are you doing this? How are you able to forgive me for fifteen years of neglect?"

"Oh, Laura, don't you know? I love you. You're all I ever wanted. And I'm just so glad to have you back."

For a moment, she could not get past her sense of not deserving this man, but he kissed her jaw, her neck, her shoulders and breasts, so she decided to stop worrying about it and just be thankful. Instead, she let herself be very present in her body, let herself feel all of the pleasure of his touches and kisses, let her body take its time to feel need until at last she could stand the space between them no longer. Kissing him hungrily, she wrapped her legs around his, and he, understanding what she wanted, looked deep into her eyes as he closed that space between them and moved with her to the rhythm of the waves lapping the shore.

Afterward, she melted and lay languidly on top of him. Lightly he stroked her back with just his fingertips. "Laura?" he said, and when she pulled back to look at him he touched her face and kissed her once more. "I just wanted to see your face."

She slid off him and lay on her side so that they could drink each other up like new lovers do, and he reached up and smoothed back her hair a few times before he entwined his fingers in hers. He searched her eyes and, happy with the answer he found, relaxed and looked at the sky above.

She watched him carefully and saw it all—every thought, every nuance. She still knew him well enough to decipher his unspoken language. He still loved her. Completely.

sunday

AMBER 2012

Long before the sun rose, Ruby's snoring became so loud it woke Amber up. Truly, Amber could not figure out how one small old lady could make so much noise. Amber leaned over the side of her bunk to see if Ruby was sleeping on her side or her back.

That's when Amber heard Ethel giggling. "I think Ruby swallowed a tractor!" she whispered. Then she got out of her bed and gestured for Amber to come down. Ethel reached into her big green duffel bag and brought out a roll of toilet paper. "Come on. Help me mummy Ruby."

"What?" Amber whispered.

"Can you fit back there behind the bed?"

Amber nodded.

"Just take the roll when I hand it to you and roll it back to me under the bed."

Amber's eyes widened.

"I promise I won't rat you out. I'll tell her Shannon helped me."

Out of respect for her elder, Amber gingerly slipped back into the little space between the bed and the wall. If

Ruby woke up, this would be mighty hard to explain, however, her deafening snores continued steadily, so Amber took the roll when Ethel handed it to her and rolled it back to Ethel under the bed over and over and over until Ruby was completely wrapped. Part of Amber had a hard time not laughing, while the other part of her found it completely wrong to mummy a little old lady.

Afterward, Amber slipped back out of that space undetected. She breathed a sigh of relief.

Ethel sniffed the air. "Do you smell that?"

Amber sniffed but didn't smell anything. She shook her head.

Ethel sniffed again. "It's the smell of a kitchen raid. Want a snack?" She made her way out the door and Amber followed.

"We should make something loud like popcorn just to wake her up," said Ethel. It was kind of comical when Ethel tried to be sinister, because Amber could tell she wasn't capable of any kind of cruelty.

In the end, Amber had some cornflakes and Ethel ate some leftover lasagna.

"What do you think? Is there anyone else we should mummify?" Ethel asked her. "It's our last chance."

Amber smiled and shook her head emphatically no.

"Ah, you're no fun. But don't worry. I'll bring you to the dark side yet."

That made Amber laugh. Ethel? The dark side? If only Ethel knew what the dark side really was. Amber had been living in the dark side for almost ten years. She knew dark. Ethel was anything but.

"We could hide all Ruby's underwear and send her on a scavenger hunt looking for them," said Ethel.

Amber laughed and shook her head.

"Yeah, you're probably right. She'd probably trip while looking for them and break a hip and it would be all our fault. Good call. Well, thanks for indulging me in a little bit of mischief." Ethel inhaled deeply with a smug smile on her face. "Sometimes there's nothing like a little harmless mischief to make a person feel alive."

Amber carefully watched the events of the morning unfold, wondering if this was going to be the last time she saw the rest of the women.

Shannon was scrambling eggs when Amber returned to the kitchen hours later. "Hey, champ," she said.

"Hey," Amber answered.

"You know, I'm so glad the universe conspired to keep you with us," said Shannon.

Keep you with us, she had said. *Keep you with us.* That was a good sign.

"Me, too," said Amber.

Janet and Sue came in next, groaning for coffee.

"Seriously. Is a breakfast bell at eight o'clock really necessary on a Sunday?" asked Janet. "I mean, it's a Sunday."

Shannon laughed. "Remember how you used to yodel in the morning when we didn't wake up after the first bell? Karma's a bitch, isn't it?"

"You loved my yodeling and you know it," Janet said.

Sue kept her eyes on her mug of coffee, waiting for it to begin working.

Ethel and Ruby strolled in next. Ethel made her rounds, hugging everyone, while Ruby announced, "Someone mummied me last night. And also, I'm going to move in with Walt."

"What?" Ethel said, spinning around.

"He offered me his guest room so we can continue to spend time together and get to know one another. I think we'll end up having a torrid affair."

"What?" Ethel said again.

"I think he's the cat's meow," Ruby said plainly. "I figure, what's there to return to in Spokane, really? Nothing. I figure I'll keep my apartment for a month and that way if it doesn't work out I'll just go home. But I have a feeling I'll like it here." She looked at Amber. "You'll like having Aunt Ruby for a neighbor, won't you?"

Amber's face broke into a big smile as she nodded.

"We'll finish our quilt," said Ruby.

Our quilt. Our. Amber marveled at the power one word had to pull her into the group. "I'd like that very much," she said, and as she looked at Ruby she could see that Ruby would like that very much, too. *Aunt Ruby.*

Laura walked through the door, holding a man's hand. "Everyone, this is my husband, Steve." She made introductions, and he shook hands. Laura actually looked happy, Amber noticed. She also noticed that there were sticks in Laura's hair, and while that mean girl Stephani would have something to say about that, Amber took it as a good sign and was simply happy for her.

They all stood at their places at the table, ready to eat, and Ethel began, "Dona nobis pacem, pacem . . . ," and two by two, the other women joined in. Amber couldn't tell if it was a round or if they were all singing different parts, but of all the beautiful songs she'd heard them sing in the last three days, this one was by far her favorite.

And as they sat at the table, the smells of eggs and bacon, French toast and syrup, all blended together like something out of a very good dream. If the feeling that everything was going to be okay had a smell, it would smell like that—full and warm, sweet with the low tones of sustenance.

"I know we all came under the pretense of cleaning camp for a prospective sale," said Ethel. "But it's hard to clean with no running water. And I'm still hoping that there will be no sale. Let's just do our dishes, sweep, and call it good."

"It feels strange to leave without closure," said Shannon.

Everyone was quiet for a moment until Ruby looked around and said, "I don't know. I got closure. It just wasn't the kind I expected when I arrived." She and Ethel exchanged looks.

"Me, too," said Ethel.

Laura, Janet, and Sue all nodded agreement. Amber joined them. Yes, she came looking for shelter for the winter, and apparently she'd found it—even though it wasn't what she expected.

"I'm the only one that didn't get closure?" Shannon asked.

The others shrugged as if to answer, *Yes.*

"Maybe that's because you still have business here to finish," said Ethel.

"Should I stay?" asked Shannon.

Ethel shook her head. "No. You've got things to deal with at home. No matter what the national office decides, nothing is likely to happen all that quickly. You'll probably want to suspend your search for grants until we get a green light, just so you don't waste any more of your time in the event things don't go our way. I just don't think there's anything left to do right now except wait, and you don't have to be here to do that."

Shannon nodded. "It's funny. I know I have to go back and disassemble my life as I've known it. I know I can't hide here forever. But it just feels so wrong to leave."

Leaving felt wrong to Amber, too, although she was looking forward to being able to go to the bathroom at night without having to walk fifty yards through the woods first.

"I used to feel sick on the last day of camp," said Laura.

"Every year it physically made me sick to leave." Then she looked at Steve. "This is the first time I feel okay about it."

Steve looked at Laura with a deep tenderness that Amber had sure never seen in the eyes of any of her mom's boyfriends. If Laura could come from a messed-up home like Amber's and marry a man who looked at her like that and have a family, it seemed entirely possible to Amber that one day she might, too. And they would all make and eat dinner together every night. She wouldn't have to shout out the window or get a running start at the bed to clear the monsters under it, because a husband like that would keep all the monsters at bay. She wanted that life—all the comfort, all the togetherness, all the things she never had. If it happened to Laura, it could happen to Amber, too.

SHANNON 2012

After Laura and Steve, Janet and Sue, and Ruby had all left, Shannon knew it was her turn. She had stalled as long as she could, sweeping cabins and the bathroom. She hated good-byes and tried to do them quickly. "See you soon. Let me know how it goes and what I can do," Shannon said as she hugged Ethel good-bye.

"I will," Ethel told her.

Shannon hugged Amber next. "I don't know what to say, Amber. It's been a pleasure. I'm sure our paths will cross again."

"Bye," said Amber, as if it was final, which maybe it was.

As Shannon walked out of the Lodge, she passed the

old cedars, the ones Ethel had once told her talked. She rested her hand on the trunk of one and tried listening with her heart, but all she heard was her own fear that this would be the last time she was here. There was reason to hope that wouldn't be the case, but it wasn't known.

A crow flew into the tree, perched on a low branch, and looked directly at her, just as it had before.

"Is that you, Haddie? If so, good-bye, Haddie," Shannon said sadly, and walked away, up the hill, past the bathroom, to the parking lot.

It had always been hard to say good-bye to this place even when she knew she was coming back the next year, but this time was worse because of the uncertainty. It might be her last time here. It might. She remembered what Ethel had said about sneaking back in even if it did sell and smiled. Property ownership really was a funny concept when she thought about it. Part of her simply belonged here, and that truth was bigger than any paper deeding ownership.

It helped that the drive home was extremely scenic, through forests, by the raging Wenatchee River, past the charming Bavarian-themed town of Leavenworth. As she drove on, she willfully replaced the dread she felt in her heart about returning to North Prairie with excitement for her future by picturing at least a hundred things she might do now that she had set herself free. Just beyond Leavenworth to the east, apple orchards lined Highway 2. Their autumn colors looked brighter than they had a week ago, and Shannon wondered whether that was due to changes in their leaves or changes in her perspective. Everything looked brighter.

On some trees where the leaves had begun to fall away apples still hung like prized rubies, and something about that resonated with Shannon—something about the parts worth keeping being revealed when the temporary things blew away. The things she was going home to deal with were like autumn leaves she was going to rake up—her house, her job, her solitary life. They would all blow away. What would remain like the apples Shannon wasn't sure, but she looked forward to finding out.

ETHEL 2012

"Well, kid, it's you and me," Ethel said, after they had said their final good-byes to everyone else and walked down to the waterfront with their things.

Amber looked at her and smiled. "Thank you."

She was a quiet one, that Amber. Ethel wondered whether that would change as Amber became more comfortable or whether she would always be a quiet one.

Small swells rolled across the lake diagonally, pushed by the wind, but Ethel wasn't concerned. The waves were still much smaller than they often were. The dock sheltered her and Amber while they got into the boat with their things and pushed off.

"Keep paddling on that side at about a four on a scale of one to ten as far as strength goes. Save your strength. There will come a time when I'll ask for something more," Ethel said. Canoeing was such an interesting dance of partnership, Ethel mused, so many little things to work out and refine.

It was tricky paddling close to shore without setting them up to be hit in the side by swells when paddling out around little points. It was an awkward balance of going forward and turning perpendicular to the wave at the last minute so it didn't roll them or swamp them. With their things in the boat, it rode lower, so there was a smaller margin of error. Ethel had hoped for a smoother and gentler beginning with Amber, but life, it seemed, had something more interesting in mind. At least the wind was at their back.

A person could learn a lot about what kind of partner another person would be by paddling a canoe with her, and here was what Ethel learned about Amber: Amber listened and trusted her even though she was a little afraid. She didn't panic or lose her head. *Yes,* Ethel thought, *Amber and I will do just fine.*

When they got home, they unpacked in somewhat awkward quiet, sporadically broken up by Ethel's attempts to make conversation. Yes, beginnings were awkward. It took a while to settle into peaceful silence.

But as Ethel walked by the guest room that was now Amber's and looked at Amber's things—her backpack on the floor, her textbooks on the desk, and the little stuffed dog sitting on her bed—she realized how much she had missed having a family, even though in her adult life it always had only been a family of two. And it struck her as funny or ironic, or maybe simply beautiful, that while she had gone to camp to say good-bye to the place where her last family had begun—that is, her union with Haddie—she had inherited a brand-new family. A new chapter was before her now. A full and happy chapter—at least for the next two and a half years, maybe more.

monday

Amber marveled about how almost everything on the surface looked the same. She went to the same classes. The girls near her locker still acted like friends even though they had no idea what big chunks of her life entailed. She still knew she'd have to get perfect grades in order to get the opportunities she needed to get out of poverty and live a better life.

And Stephani still made rude remarks and Amber still wanted to punch her right in her big obnoxious face but she still chose to refrain.

But here was what was different: Amber belonged somewhere. She wasn't alone. She had two grandmas now and maybe a couple of aunts. She had breakfast and lunch, and tonight she would have dinner. Not only would she have dinner, but she also would help make it and then she would eat it with her new grandma, even if that grandma's official title was great-aunt. No longer would Amber have to be distracted by issues of survival. Instead, she could concentrate on her classes. It felt as though a huge and heavy burden had been lifted. Something inside her felt solid, peaceful, and complete for the first time in a very long time.

When she walked into Mr. Morris's room, she smiled at him in a way that she hoped let him see that she was okay now. He studied her for a moment and then smiled back. Yes, he seemed to understand.

A week. What was a week? A week was nothing. It was a blink. And yet somehow it was enough to change her life completely around. Tonight when she and Ethel said grace over dinner, Amber was going to give thanks for a week.

ETHEL 2012

The phone rang. Ethel froze for a minute, staring at the phone as if it might bite. Then, she took a big breath and walked across the room toward it, and picked it up. "Hello, Ethel Gossman speaking."

"Hello, Ethel, this is Mary Stevenson, vice president of the National Association of Firelight Girls calling from the national office in Kansas City. We received your messages and have given careful consideration to the circumstances there."

Ethel held her breath.

"We respect our local boards, and make it our policy not to undermine their authority."

Ethel shook her head slowly. *How could they take this stance? Stupid, stupid, stupid,* she thought. "I see," she said. It was over. She had tried. She had gone to the top. There was no other recourse after this.

"Wait," Mary said. "I'm not done. While it is not our policy to undermine local boards, it's our primary mission to serve as many girls and young women as possible, and your commitment to the girls and young women in your region is an inspiration. We are all in your corner here at the national office and want to support you in any way we can."

Ethel wiped grateful tears from her eyes. "Thank you, thank you, thank you," she said emphatically.

"No, Ethel. Thank *you*," said Mary. "We've been discussing the best way and the easiest way for you all to go forward, and we think it would be to make you the temporary executive director of the North Central Washington Council of Firelight Girls. We know you're retired, but if you'd be willing to come out of retirement until your local council is back on its feet we believe that would be the shortest and most effective path to success. You have a track record. You've managed camp successfully in the past. By accepting the title of temporary executive director, you have the ability to manage funds, hire staff, and recruit new board members. Do you need time to think about it?"

"No," Ethel said. "I accept."

"Well, we at the national office thank you, Ethel. In the last two years, regional councils have closed eleven of our camps. Yours is the only one to be pulled from the ashes. We are so grateful for you and your team of alumni."

"I can't wait to notify them of your decision. Again, thank you."

"Call us if we can help you further, Ethel. We'll do everything we can."

After Ethel hung up the phone, she looked for a piece of paper and a calligraphy pen. In her fanciest script she wrote:

Dearest Ms. Shannon Meyers and Ms. Laura Hart,

Your company is requested for a luncheon tomorrow at noon to be served at the Lodge of Camp Firelight. Attire is formal, but will be provided. There is an urgent matter to discuss. Please RSVP.

With love,
Ms. Ethel Gossman

And since there was no time to waste, she scanned it on her printer and sent it off as an e-mail document to both of them.

Would Shannon check her e-mail? She was likely packing. What if she had already packed her computer? But within five minutes Shannon had replied: "I will be there."

The morning became early afternoon, and the early afternoon became mid-afternoon. Ethel whipped up some chocolate-chip cookies to welcome Amber home from school, waiting impatiently until she could pull them from the oven, break one in half, and conduct a quality standard test. That's what Haddie had always called it when they ceremoniously broke the first cookie in half and tasted it. Each time, Haddie had proclaimed this to be their best batch ever. And on this day, when Ethel sampled the first cookie, she said aloud, "Haddie, I do believe this is my best batch ever."

Amber knocked on the door when she arrived, prompting Ethel to laugh and holler, "You live here, Amber! You don't have to knock! Come in!"

Awkwardly, Amber did.

Ethel asked her how her day was, and Amber replied, "It was the best day I've had in a long time."

"Really? What happened?" asked Ethel.

With a smile, Amber said, "Nothing in particular," as if that were the best thing in the whole world, as if an ordinary day had been her greatest wish.

"Well, that's wonderful," Ethel replied, because she knew. After all her grief, she knew what a blessing an ordinary day could be.

"Smells wonderful," Amber said with a hopeful smile.

"They're for you," Ethel replied, pointing toward the cookie sheet on the stove. "Knock yourself out."

Amber took two, then pointed to her bedroom door. "I'm going to get my homework done."

Ethel nodded approvingly.

Mid-afternoon had turned to late afternoon and Laura had not answered her e-mail, so Ethel picked up the phone and called. Laura answered on the fourth ring, and Ethel extended the invitation.

"Oh, Ethel, I'm sorry. I have two appointments tomorrow. I can't make it. Is camp saved? Is that what this celebration lunch is all about?" Laura asked excitedly.

"It might be," Ethel said in a tone of voice that gave it all away. "But there's more I want to talk to you and Shannon about. We need to make some decisions about leadership."

Laura was quiet for a moment. "What do you mean?"

"Well, let me ask you this," Ethel said. "Would you be interested in co-leading camp?"

Again, Laura was quiet, and Ethel waited as patiently as she could.

"As much as I love camp . . . I don't feel I can make that commitment right now."

"Oh," said Ethel, disappointed.

"It's just . . . I neglected my husband for years, and now that the kids are gone, there's this opportunity to reconstruct our relationship while we rekindle our love. And you know, I think after being a mom all these years, I'm ready to shift my focus from kids to . . . I don't know . . . something else. But I would love to come up once a week during the summer and lead nature walks. I would enjoy that very much."

Ethel smiled. "I can think of no better person for that job," she said.

So it would be Shannon alone. *Yes,* Ethel thought. *She will do fine.*

ETHEL 1954

In typical Miss Mildred style, a formal invitation arrived in the mail. On the off-white envelope, Ethel's name had been written in calligraphy. A wax stamp with the letter *M* sealed the back.

March 21, 1954

Miss Ethel Gossman,
  You are cordially invited to a formal lunch at Camp Firelight on April 2, 1956, at noon. Formal attire (to be worn over your regular clothes), and snowshoes will be waiting for you in the parking lot. RSVP, please.

Miss Mildred Ford

Ethel dropped her father off at the apple warehouse where he worked that morning so she could borrow his car and then headed up to Lake Wenatchee, where she drove the icy curves of the South Shore Road with great trepidation. Sure enough, near the entrance of the camp two snowshoes were stuck in the ground, and a long red ball gown—a castoff from a Shakespeare production—hung from a clothes hanger on a branch of a tree. The gown was barely large enough to slide over her coat, but it eventually did. As she put on one snowshoe, she noticed a tiara sticking out the webbing in the other and put it on over her stocking cap, fastened the other snowshoe to her other boot, and started off.

As she walked down the hill into camp, she heard the dinner bell ring, and so she went to the Lodge instead of Miss Mildred's house. The door was unlocked. Ethel stepped in and unfastened her snowshoes.

Hearing the commotion, Miss Mildred stepped into the doorway of the kitchen in another Shakespearian gown—a violet one, which dragged on the floor because Miss Mildred was rather short. On top of her wild gray curls sat a tiara. She clapped her hands and began to sing. "I welcome you to Camp Firelight, mighty glad you're here. I'll send the air reverberating with a mighty cheer! I'll sing you in; I'll sing you out! To you I'll give a mighty shout! Hail, hail, the gang's all here! Welcome to Camp Firelight!"

Miss Mildred was always smiling and her smile was contagious. It was impossible not to smile in her presence, so as Ethel clapped along with the song a big smile spread across her face as well.

"Oops!" Miss Mildred exclaimed, and went running back into the kitchen to check the toasted cheese sandwiches on the griddle. "Whew! I thought I'd burned them!" With that, she flipped them onto two tin plates, spooned a serving of layered Jell-O salad with canned pineapple chunks and mandarin slices, and handed one plate to Ethel. Together they walked back into the main room of the Lodge, where Miss Mildred had set a table near the crackling fire.

They sang "Back of the Bread" for grace because it was the fastest one and Miss Mildred said she had important things to talk about.

With great anticipation of both the food and conversation, Ethel sat and waited for a cue that it was okay to eat. To her relief, Miss Mildred picked up her sandwich and took a bite. When she was done chewing, she said, "You're probably wondering why I asked you here today."

Ethel waited for her to say more.

"You have been going to this camp since you were six. Over the years I've noticed you have a way of making everyone feel included. Your leadership is quiet and subtle yet steadfast, and that's important, because camp is about letting everyone discover their own leadership abilities. You offer campers that and still keep them safe. In addition to all of that, there is so much joy inside of you, and it's infectious.

"This year is going to be my last year and then I'm going to retire, as unthinkable as that is. I want you to be my assistant camp director this year, so I can train you to take my place when the time comes. I won't have the power to hire you, but I can make a strong recommendation to the board, and I believe they will listen to me."

Ethel gaped for a moment and then tears of joy escaped her eyes. "This has always been my dream," she said.

"So you'll do it?"

"Absolutely!" Ethel stood and walked over to the other side of the table and hugged Miss Mildred.

"You just made my heart glad, my dear Ethel," sighed Miss Mildred. "I knew I could pass the torch to you and you wouldn't drop it."

Miss Mildred imparted as much wisdom as she could in the remainder of their lunch, and then they did the dishes and put away their costumes. Finally, they snowshoed back up to the parking lot together, where Miss

Mildred took Ethel's snowshoes and waved her off. And as Ethel put the car in gear before pulling out of the parking lot, she looked back at Miss Mildred waving ... looked at herself in the future, and she felt truly happy.

Then ever so carefully, she put her foot on the gas pedal and drove back to the present. She couldn't wait to tell Haddie that it was coming true—their dream, their vision for the future. It was all coming true.

tuesday

Something red caught her eye as Shannon pulled into the parking lot. Someone's old prom dress, hanging on a tree branch. On it was pinned a note that said her name. Shannon stepped out of her car and put on the tattered old taffeta dress. It was wrinkled from being stuffed in a box for who knew how many years, and dirt stained the very bottom. *Lovely,* thought Shannon as she slipped it on over her head.

Ethel must have heard Shannon's car, because Shannon heard the bell ringing. Quickly she walked down the hill to the Lodge, where Ethel awaited her, wearing a silver lamé dress.

"Lady Shannon," Ethel greeted, in a fake English accent.

"Lady Ethel," Shannon replied.

"Look. I sort of look like an Airstream trailer in this dress."

"I sort of look like a girl from the eighties that got drunk for the first time at prom and spent the last hour puking on the side of the road in this dress," said Shannon.

"Oh dear. I smell our lunch. It might be burning," and with that Ethel scurried off to the kitchen.

Shannon followed her and found that Ethel had set a table for two with a bouquet of autumn leaves in the center.

"I'm afraid Lady Laura will not be joining us today," Ethel told Shannon, assuming her fake English accent once more.

"Oh?"

"She is otherwise engaged." Ethel winked.

"Oh, that's good!"

After Ethel put a bowl of tomato soup and a plate of rather dark toasted cheese sandwiches on the table, she took Shannon's hands and sang "Back of the Bread."

"So, I'm sure you're wondering about my big news and the plan of action I'm going to propose," continued Ethel. "Camp has been saved."

"Ya-hoo!" Shannon shouted with glee. "We did it!"

"And the national office has appointed me temporary executive director, which means I have the power to hire. Shannon, I would like to offer you the job of camp director."

That stopped Shannon in her tracks. She stared at Ethel to see if she really meant it, even though of course she meant it—Ethel wouldn't say something like that as a cruel joke. And then as it all began to sink in, Shannon's hand went to her mouth and she cried. She would live in this beautiful place and have a camp family the way Ethel had. In the summers, Shannon would eat at long picnic tables filled with people, sort of like those European movies she loved. There would be joy and kids, and she wouldn't have to judge them. Her only job would be to encourage them. She could teach them to love poetry by firelight. It felt as if Shannon's very soul had been saved. "Thank you," she said. "Thank you."

"No, Shannon. Thank *you*. I know you'll protect the legacy and longevity of this place. You'll make things happen here. You're a dynamo. You always were. You have no idea what comfort it brings me to know it's in good hands."

Shannon hugged Ethel, and then, after they ate their lunch, Ethel took her out onto the back deck.

"I want you to listen to the trees," said Ethel. "If you're going to be camp director, you really should refine the art of listening to the trees."

Shannon listened to the wind blowing through the branches of the old cedars just to make Ethel happy, but somehow Ethel knew she had it wrong.

"No," Ethel said. "Listen with your heart, not your ears. Feel their joy. They are so happy you're here. These trees have watched over you from the time you were a girl. They remember you. Yes, they are so glad it's you. They know you're going to do a great job. Listen to them. They get really chatty each June right before the kids come. I swear I used to hear them whisper excitedly to each other, 'The children are coming! The children are coming!' I think they like all the songs."

Shannon looked up high into their branches. It was quite a thought—these trees witnessing her history like that. She tried to open her heart so she could hear, and if she could hear anything it was simply a sigh of relief. Maybe it was from the trees, but most likely it was her own.

Just then a crow landed on a low branch just like it had before, looked right at her, and cawed.

"Hi, Haddie!" Ethel said. "Did you hear the wonderful news?"

The bird cawed again.

"Haddie says congratulations."

Shannon just smiled. Whether it really was Haddie or not who knew? It made Ethel happy to think so, and maybe she was right, so just in case Shannon said, "Thank you, Haddie," to the bird right before it took off.

next summer

The trees woke Ethel up. From all the way to her cabin, she could hear them. *The children are coming! Today the children are coming!* Those generous and jubilant trees. Ethel looked at her clock. *Oh, trees,* she thought. *It's going to be a few hours yet.* But she could understand how time would be different to old trees.

As much as her soul wanted to go back to camp to visit Shannon and bask in the excitement of the first day, Ethel remembered all the responsibilities that day entailed. There were so many things to think of and so many people to greet. No, it was best to stand back and let Shannon do her job rather than distract her on this day.

But maybe it wouldn't hurt to kayak down and bask in the excitement from the lake.

Even though the night before had been Amber's night off between staff training week and the start of camp, she had chosen to spend it there helping Shannon and the cook with whatever they needed. Amber had just come by Ethel's house to tell her the plan and do a load of laundry. She hadn't even stayed for dinner. Ethel missed her terri-

bly but hid it. After all, independence was success. Ethel
had to keep reminding herself that.

She packed a lunch and slid into her kayak. The wind
had not yet reached its afternoon highs but was blowing
enough to fill the lake with small waves. On and on she
paddled through the bumpy water toward camp and its
happy trees.

Passing Elks Beach, she felt calm, secure that her sacred place would be there for her whenever she wanted to
come back and visit, and paddled on just a little farther.

The children are coming! The children are coming!
called the trees like children on Christmas morning shouting that Santa had come. She hadn't heard joy this loud
since she'd lost Haddie, and it seemed a good sign that her
capacity to hear joy had returned.

At the edge of the swimming area, she held on to the
rope that marked its boundary and she watched the parents get out of cars with kids, some excited and some
scared, and walk to the greeting area that Shannon had set
up. Through the crowd, Ethel could see her, smiling, shaking hands with parents and kids, checking them in, and
sending them off with counselors and other staff. She was
wearing Haddie's old hat, red canvas with a brim, which
Ethel had given her the night before staff training week
began. Just seeing that hat made Ethel's eyes water.
Haddie would have wanted Shannon to have it. The hat, it
seemed, was back where it belonged.

Nearby stood Amber, ready to escort the next child to
her cabin. Shannon rested her hand on Amber's shoulder.
All of it was so profoundly beautiful to Ethel that it moved
her to tears.

Next to her kayak, an otter surfaced and dove back
down. Haddie always said otters were about the happiest
animals she could think of.

And that was when Ruby and Walt paddled up in their rowboat right next to Ethel's kayak and Ruby found words for what Ethel was feeling. "The torch has been successfully passed," Ruby said as she reached out and took Ethel's hand just like she had when they were only six and Ethel had been homesick.

"We did it," Ethel said simply.

"We did it," Ruby echoed, Walt smiling behind her.

ACKNOWLEDGMENTS

This book was inspired by, but not based on, a group of women who called themselves FOZ, Friends of Zanika, who really saved Camp Zanika when it was going under. One summer, when many of us returned and volunteered to keep the camp's doors open, I worked with several FOZ members and enjoyed hearing their stories and what it was about camp that pulled them back all those years later. They've been having annual reunions since the early 1970s and invited me to their last few. Just witnessing the depths of their friendships and listening to them sing the sweet old songs together moved me to tears. So, first and foremost, I want to thank them for their friendship and inspiration, and for sharing their stories and reflections with me. And I want to thank them for being powerhouses that really made a difference: Sammy, Lou, Luv, Jan, Casey, Karen, Kate, Kris, Mary, Sandy, Sandy, Jeannie, Ann, Kim, Kathy, Ina, Becky, and especially Rodie.

Thank you to Sue Hart, Lisa Stevenson, and Gail Bennett, for sharing camp stories. Thank you to Sue Hart and Minda Rose, for telling Wonderland Trail stories. Thank you to Chris "Croc" Stevenson for archery information. Thank you to Branden LeBlanc, for CPS information. A big thank-you to Lance Ballew at Tumwater Drilling, for information about wells on Lake Wenatchee.

There were some story lines I didn't go with, but researched. Thank you Sherry Krebs, for loaning me your old copies of *Book of the Camp Fire Girls,* and to Connie Coutellier at the Camp Fire national office, for giving me permission to use excerpts from those books. Thank you James Begley, Derek Salmond, and Nathan Fairchild, for cougar information. Thank you Joe Fountain, Vince Sianati, and Mike "Mad Dog" Magnotti, for law enforcement information. Thank you Tom Gambill, for information about working in Alaskan fish factories. Thank you Andy Bower, for information on Forest Service science jobs. Thank you Esther Woodward, for information on Forest Service contracts. Maybe some of that information will find its way into future stories.

Thank you to my parents, for raising me to believe I could do anything, for their ongoing moral support, and for taking me in when I had to evacuate my home due to a wildfire and needed a place to be and finish this manuscript.

And of course, thank you to my fairy godmother agents, Christina Hogrebe and Meg Ruley at the Jane Rotrosen Agency, and to my editor, Jen Enderlin, at St. Martin's Press, for their tireless dedication to helping me make this book the best it could be and for believing in me. Thank you to the whole team at St. Martin's Press, but especially Katie Bassell and Sarah Goldstein, for all they've done for me. Thank you, thank you, thank you.

Turn the page for an excerpt from

The Road to Enchantment

by Kaya McLaren

Coming in trade paperback
from St. Martin's Griffin

1

Maybe it was the fact my feet hadn't touched real dirt in so long that I suddenly became aware of them when they did. Sure, they had been in sand not that long ago, but sand lets all things pass through it—water, crabs, and people. Clay doesn't. Clay holds what lands on it. This thought terrified me. I never did like this place and I sure didn't want to get stuck here.

Glittery glass shards from broken bottles littered the side of the remote dirt road. I stood outside the gate and looked over into my mom's world, into my past. Some things were exactly the same. For example, the old 1953 pink Cadillac still poked out of an arroyo in the bull's pasture like a fossilized dinosaur unearthed by the elements. And by "pasture" I did simply mean a large fenced-in area full of sage and not much else.

Señor Clackers, my mom's Toro Bravo Spanish fighting bull, had been her answer to a security system, a way to keep the drunks and thieves out, and he had just noticed me, so I knew I had only seconds to make my move. He was roughly fifteen hundred pounds of pure muscle that rippled under his shiny black fur when he moved, but at the moment he stood still, his head held high, sniffing the air, his regal horns reaching clear up to the sky. My mom had installed a system of gates so that the bull blocked a narrow section of the driveway when she wanted protection, but kept the bull out of the driveway when she wanted to welcome a visitor or go in or out herself. I quickly crawled over one metal gate and pushed another gate shut, blocking the bull from the drive-way and allowing me to walk through safely. Curious, he trotted over to me, his massive testicles swinging back and forth as he did, the characteristic for which Mom had named him. Bull testicles were something I hadn't seen in my twenty-one years of city life and now struck me as somewhat obscene even though rationally I knew that was ridiculous. I took a step back, lacking complete confidence in my mom's aging fencing. Señor Clackers' long horns hooked forward as he snorted through the fence.

Mom's two dogs, Mr. Lickers and Slobber Dog, no-ticed us and began to bark and run toward me jubilantly, as if they had mistaken me for my mom, and I wondered what similarity they saw that caused them confusion— our frame? Our posture? Our walk? As they neared, they balked, as if they realized I was not my mom after all. The dogs and I had met twice before, but still, I spoke to them calmly, wondering how protective of my mom's estate they would be.

"Estate" was actually a word far too fancy for what lay before me.

I bent down to see which dog was male and which one wasn't, so I could remember which was Mr. Lickers and which was Slobber Dog. They were siblings and looked remarkably alike, built much like blue heelers, with four colors of fur all mixed in together, white paws, white stars on their chests, and white stripes down their noses. I let them smell my hand and then pet each one before I continued my slow walk up the driveway.

I didn't know how I was going to find homes for all of my mom's animals. In addition to the bull and the dogs, there were the horses, the donkey, the llama, and the guinea fowl. The livestock would be a pain to sell, but the dogs . . . No one around here needed two more dogs. I looked down at their sad faces and wondered whether the Vigils farther up the road would take them back.

I scanned the nearly three hundred acres, wondering where exactly Mom had fallen off her horse and why. Maybe a rattlesnake had spooked it. Maybe coyotes or a cougar. Maybe it had been stung by a wasp or a bee. I would never know.

As I continued to walk toward the house I had once shared with my mom, the guinea fowl ran to get out of the way, eventually flying up to low branches on a nearby juniper. Their black feathers with little white polka dots littered the gravel. I picked one up and admired its elegance. Was I really going to catch all of these birds? No. Maybe I could advertise that I would give them away to anyone who would come out and catch them.

Since I had been here last, Mom had built a structure into the side of a hill on the other side of the barn. She had told me about it, but I had never seen it. The front was stucco with wooden timbers that poked out above the windows, and a hand-painted sign above the door that read, "The De Vine Winery." Behind it, the five acres of grapes Mom and I had planted had filled out, now striping the nearby hillsides with bold green lines where only small green circles had dotted the landscape not that long ago.

A white vinyl couch sat facing the large arroyo where coyotes used to hide, and next to the couch, sun shone through the green glass of an empty wine bottle.

And to my left was the house and garage, something between artistic and ramshackle that a friend of my mother's old friend had built out of straw bales, stucco, and salvaged materials. It looked boxy, even with solar panels sitting on the flat roof. The walls were fat with deep windowsills that I had loved to sit in, soaking up sunshine while I did my homework on cold winter days. Over the door was a stained-glass window he had salvaged from a church that had burned down, a window depicting the Nativity. It had been damaged so he'd had to cut off Joseph and the wise men, leaving Mary and her baby alone with the livestock and the Angel of the Lord. He had built a large frame around it before he had set it into the wall. Turquoise paint peeled from the wooden door and window frames. Near the door grew oregano, black-eyed Susans, and hollyhocks, an odd combination of survivors.

In every direction it seemed there was a doorway I was afraid to walk through, not wanting to see the archaeology of my mother's last day—the rag she'd used to disinfect the bags of the goats she had milked that morning, the rake she had used to pick stalls, the pans and buckets that were undoubtedly still in the drying rack, the clothes she hadn't laundered, her hair in the shower drain.

At once, a momentary wave of fever and weakness washed over me as my stomach turned. I dropped down on all fours and abruptly threw up. I had been doing this for the last two days and chalked it up to grief.

I sat back on my knees, looked up at the front door of the home where my mother's absence felt so wrong, where it was finally real in a way it hadn't been until that very moment. Then overcome by weakness, I lay down on the gravel, rolled over, and looked up at the sky above.

It was clear and blue with only one cloud in it—a large bear that floated in the southeast over the Vigil place. A bear. My old best friend, Darrel. The sky seemed to be telling me he was coming, and so I shut my eyes and waited.

2

I was thirteen the first and only day I had ever seen a cloud shaped like a cougar in the sky, an animal that sneaks up on you from behind and attacks before you ever see it coming. I had seen it as I rode my bicycle home from the old brick junior high school through the maze of old neighborhoods and into progressively newer ones.

Only after I had turned a corner did I notice the very large plume of black smoke coming from the vicinity of my house. As I neared, I could see my mother in the driveway, sitting in a lawn chair roasting something over a flaming mattress. Neighbors peeked out of their suburban ranch homes to monitor the situation, and in the distance I heard a siren.

My mom had an extra lawn chair and marshmallow stick waiting for me when I pulled up on my bike. On the chair sat a bag of Peeps, those marshmallow chicks Mom put in my Easter basket every year even though for years now I had been way too old to be playing along with the Easter Bunny. Mom had speared one of the Peeps and something about it was a disturbing and grotesque sight roasting over the mattress fire.

"Hi, baby," Mom said as she pulled the bright yellow marshmallow off her stick, and washed it down with a swig of cheap Chardonnay. Then she put a hot dog on her stick and offered one to me.

I shook my head as I assessed the situation. To be honest, I wasn't sure whether Mom had finally slipped right over the edge. I decided to begin gently. "I'm sorry you had such a bad day," I said calmly.

"Your father has a new girlfriend. Surprise," she replied.

Seven words seem far too few to completely turn a person's life upside down, and yet they did. "What?" I asked, stunned. "Is he leaving us?"

"Yeah, he's leaving us, baby."

While I didn't want to inflame an already critical situation, I was furious and couldn't stop myself from saying, "You should have been nicer to him."

"Did you ever see me be mean or disrespectful to him? No. So don't be mad at me. He's the one who left. And I'm the one who wouldn't leave you for all the tea in China."

Unsure of what to do or say next, I scanned the neighbors' windows to see who was watching as I listened to the sirens of the fire truck get louder and louder, and waited for the inevitable scene. Just then, Ms. Nunnalee, my social studies teacher, drove up to her house across the street. On a normal day, she stopped at her house quickly to let her dog out before going back to school to coach whatever sport the girls were playing that quarter, but on this day she looked at my mom with wide eyes and kept driving. God. How horrifying.

Even though I was sure the engine was racing through town, everything seemed as if it was in slow motion. After what seemed like an eternity of embarrassment, the fire engine finally arrived. My mom's wiener was only half roasted.

"Hi, Monica," the oldest of the four men said delicately, while the others went to hook a hose to the nearest hydrant.

"Hi, Dave," Mom replied. "Hot dog?"

"Um . . . Actually I just ate. Perhaps another time," said Dave diplomatically. "Um, Monica . . . You know we have to put this out, right?"

"Yeah, I know." With that, she picked up her lawn chair and walked into the garage, resigned.

"Sorry about my mom. Apparently my dad has a new girlfriend," I explained to them, as if that would make everything okay. Still stunned, I picked up my lawn chair too and followed Mom into the garage, where she then shut the automatic garage door behind us.

She began to riffle through an old box on the shelf, and near the top, found what she had been looking for: an old poster of Sam Elliott. She grabbed the hammer and some nails, along with her bottle of Chardonnay, and walked purposely to her room where she tacked Sam on the wall behind where my parents' bed had been. She took a long swig, then lay down in the pile of blankets and rolled herself up. "God, I smell him everywhere," she muttered to herself. "This whole damn house stinks of him." She fell asleep or passed out next. I wasn't sure which.

The next morning was foggy. Foggy in spring? Fog was typically an autumn phenomenon in western Washington, so this struck me as a very bad thing. And I knew what it meant—it meant that I could not see what was coming at all. But this much I knew about fog—it was never a good sign. No, fog never foretold good things, like surprise birthday parties. Fog was always creepy.

But after enduring a whole day of school being the target of all the day's—and probably the week's gossip—I wished the fog hadn't burned off so I could just disappear right into it. I hopped on my bike after the final bell and got out of there just as fast as I could, angry about the damage my crazy mother had done to my social life.

When I returned home, my mom was standing outside of the house next to a green pickup truck, all loaded high with boxes, wearing the overalls she always wore when she was doing a big job, and a red bandana tied around her head to keep her hair out of her face.

"Hi, baby. Get in," she said, like nothing was unusual or downright wrong. She took my bike and loaded it into the pile in the back of the green Ford pickup, and then with a rope, tied it to the heaping mound of our other selected belongings. "I traded in our station wagon today."

I took a deep breath and looked up at the truck. I had not seen this coming—no, not at all, but I figured we were simply moving across town to a different house—one that didn't smell like my dad.

Above the pickup floated two clouds shaped like geese. *Geese fly south.* For better or worse, I accepted moving was my destiny, opened the door, and stepped into the truck.

When Mom first pulled away, I simply felt numb. I didn't panic too much right away, figuring that my parents likely needed to sell the house and each get smaller, less expensive places. But then Mom turned right instead of left, and we began to drive in the wrong direction.

"May I ask where we're going?" I asked.

"New Mexico," Mom answered.

Shocked, I had to verify that I had indeed heard correctly. "New Mexico?"

"A friend of an old friend of mine bought some cheap land there long ago, and built a small house on it that's off the grid. Do you know what that means? It means no power lines or phone lines go to it. It has solar power. How about that? We're going to be completely self-reliant.

Anyway, now that guy is on to other things so he offered to sell it to me for a song and carry the contract, which is great because I would never qualify for a loan."

"New Mexico?"

"It's beautiful. I've seen pictures. Georgia O'Keeffe country."

"Am I going to see Dad again?"

"Of course. He'll fly out and visit you. Or maybe he'll send you plane tickets so you can fly back and visit him."

"So, wait. I'm going from seeing Dad every day to seeing him what—once or twice a year?"

"We both are," Mom answered plainly.

"And there's no phone so I can't even talk to him?"

"Nope. Sorry. Maybe he'll send you a phone card so you can call him from a pay phone sometimes. Write him a letter and suggest that."

Panic rose up in my chest through my throat, but I tempered it in my mouth because I always got further with Mom when I used a calm, big-girl voice. "I can't believe you're taking me this far from him."

"I can't believe he didn't value his family enough to keep it in his pants," she retorted.

I buried my face in my hands. This couldn't really be happening. It made no sense—except that when I looked at my mother, it kind of did. She would not be an easy person to live with. After all, she didn't seem to care very much about what other people wanted and she definitely drank too much. "You drove him away. You're the reason he left me."

My mother turned and looked at me, at first angry, and then she softened a little bit—enough to go back to looking at the road anyway. She didn't reply. We drove in silence, with the exception of Mom occasionally asking me whether I needed her to pull over at a rest stop or whether I was hungry. I would answer with a nod or by shaking my head.

As each hour passed, I felt the growing distance acutely. My sense of severing overwhelmed me. Sometimes tears would escape as I looked out the passenger-side window. After I wiped them away, my mother would look over as if to say, "Stop it," and it fueled my silence.

The green forests and pastures along the I-5 corridor in Washington led south to Oregon. And the cliffs of the Columbia River Gorge gave way to open desert and golden wheat country. We passed the Blue Mountains and the Wallowas of northeast Oregon, drove over the Snake River and into farmlands of Idaho. Each change in topography was one more world apart I was from my home, my dad, and my friends.

Somewhere around midnight, we pulled into a Motel 6 in Boise, brushed our teeth, and fell asleep in silence.

And the next day, no apologies or comfort were offered either. Farmland turned to ranchland. Little junipers sprang up in the high country between Idaho and Utah. Then, on our left, the Wasatch Mountains towered above the Great Salt Lake on our right.

As the afternoon crept on, we crossed the mountains and entered a land completely alien to me. Eastern Utah stretched out before us, so vast I could see all the way across it to Colorado. The mesas with their flat tops rose over carved canyons, and the whole country seemed painted in shades of tan, pink, gray, and orange. It appeared as if almost nothing lived there. *Such lonely country,* I thought. As we drove south to Moab, the rocks and cliffs actually glowed like amber coals.

New Mexico wasn't what I expected—at least the part we were in, the north. It didn't look barren like eastern Utah. Hills and mesas in sandy tans poked out from behind forests of small junipers and pines. And the largest elk I'd ever seen fed on grass in the lowlands.

We entered the Cestero Apache Reservation, but for miles and miles and miles, there was no one.

It was twilight when we dropped into Sweetwater, and in the dark, it looked like a quaint mountain village tucked in against the mesas and mountains. Upon closer inspection, I noticed bars on the windows of businesses, and buildings in disrepair. We passed through as quickly as we had driven in—so quickly that if we had blinked twice we would have missed it, and just a mile beyond Sweetwater, we left the reservation and entered Coalton, which looked even poorer.

After a few more miles, my mother turned south into Monero Canyon, our new home. The dirt road was badly rutted, and a flooding creek threatened to wash out the little wooden bridge that my mother fearlessly drove over. Farther and farther we drove into the dark canyon, until finally our headlights shone on a little house on the left. I could not believe how far out in the middle of nowhere we were.

Mom pulled in, parked, and pulled a flashlight out of her purse. I followed her as she walked up to the little house, pondering the irony of feeling both so hidden and so exposed all at once. Anything could happen to us here. Anyone could drive up to our house, and we would be defenseless. Being off the grid meant we could not call the police—if there were any police out here. The windows had been boarded up, making it seem even less friendly, and there were actual bullet holes in the door— bullet holes! I pointed to them and, alarmed, asked, "You're kidding me, right? We're going to live in a place with bullet holes in the door?"

"Now that we're here, no one will shoot. Someone was just shooting at a vacant house. That's all."

" 'That's all'? Does Dad know you're endangering me like this?"

"Stop being dramatic."

Incredulous, I simply shook my head.

"It's been a long day. Help me unpack until we find the boxes with our blankets and sheets, and let's get some sleep. Tomorrow everything will look better."

Only the next day, it didn't look better at all. It looked like a dump. I wasn't sure who to be angrier at—my mother or simply at life in general. I looked to the sky for clues that somehow it would all be okay, but saw nothing but blue. The sky was only smiling—not talking at all.